RELEASED FROM CIRCULATION

OCT 0 2 2024

CENTRAL
GROSSE POINTE PUBLIC LIBRARY
GROSSE POINTE, MI 48236

One Big Happy Family

Also by Susan Mallery

For the Love of Summer
The Summer Book Club
The Happiness Plan
The Sister Effect
The Boardwalk Bookshop
The Summer Getaway
The Stepsisters
The Vineyard at Painted Moon
The Friendship List
The Summer of Sunshine & Margot
California Girls
When We Found Home
Secrets of the Tulip Sisters
Daughters of the Bride

Wishing Tree

Home Sweet Christmas
The Christmas Wedding Guest

Mischief Bay

Sisters Like Us
A Million Little Things
The Friends We Keep
The Girls of Mischief Bay

Blackberry Island

Sisters by Choice
Evening Stars
Three Sisters
Barefoot Season

...and the beloved Fool's Gold and Happily Inc romances.

For a complete list of titles available from Susan Mallery, please visit susanmallery.com.

One Big Happy Family

SUSAN MALLERY

CANARY STREET PRESS

CANARY
STREET
PRESS™

Recycling programs
for this product may
not exist in your area.

ISBN-13: 978-1-335-00840-4

One Big Happy Family

Copyright © 2024 by Susan Mallery, Inc.

All rights reserved. No part of this book may be used or reproduced in any manner whatsoever without written permission.

Without limiting the author's and publisher's exclusive rights, any unauthorized use of this publication to train generative artificial intelligence (AI) technologies is expressly prohibited.

This is a work of fiction. Names, characters, places and incidents are either the product of the author's imagination or are used fictitiously. Any resemblance to actual persons, living or dead, businesses, companies, events or locales is entirely coincidental.

For questions and comments about the quality of this book, please contact us at CustomerService@Harlequin.com.

TM is a trademark of Harlequin Enterprises ULC.

Canary Street Press
22 Adelaide St. West, 41st Floor
Toronto, Ontario M5H 4E3, Canada
CanaryStPress.com

Printed in U.S.A.

For Kathy—you and those you love
are the absolute definition of "one big happy family!"

So this is for you, Ed and James. Kay, Bob, Patty, Steve and George.
And, of course, in loving memory of your beloved father.

May your holidays always be warm and loving.
Merry Christmas to you and yours.

1

"But you're a woman."

"Does that matter?"

"I don't know. Do you know how to tow cars?"

Julie Parker did her best not to roll her eyes. At her age, it was a much less charming look. But still.

"Your car is fine," she said, trying for patience, but failing to hit the mark and landing on snark instead. "You ran out of gas on the 405 freeway. If we should be questioning someone's ability to exist in the world, we should probably start with you."

"Hey!" The young twentysomething finally looked up from her phone and frowned. "You have attitude."

"I do, and a busy schedule. Do you want help or not? It's twenty bucks for the gas and seventy-five for the service visit."

"Ninety-five dollars for a few gallons of gas? That's robbery."

"It's also the price you were quoted when you called the company."

Cars and trucks sped by on the busy freeway. It was a cold, rainy December afternoon, and Julie had a date with her very handsome boyfriend in a few hours. The last thing she wanted to do was waste time arguing with someone younger than either of her adult children.

The young woman shook her head. "I'm not paying that."

"Fine by me."

Julie started back to her tow truck, gas can in hand. The woman hurried after her.

"Wait. I'll do it. So ninety-five dollars?"

"Yes. Tax is included in the price." She fished her credit card reader from her overalls. "You pay, I pour."

The woman gave her the stink eye, then reluctantly pushed a credit card into the machine. Less than five minutes later, Julie had her money, and the unhappy motorist had enough gas to get her on her way.

"Is this your car?" Julie asked, telling herself to walk away but unable to do so.

"It's my boyfriend's. He said I could drive it."

Julie pointed to the instrument panel. "You probably always know how much gas is in your own car. It's something we keep track of without thinking. But when you get into someone else's car, check the gauge. When the weather's like this, you can wait a long time for a tow truck, and the side of the freeway is a dangerous place."

"Oh." The other woman looked at the rushing traffic, then slid into the driver's seat. "Thanks. I'll keep that in mind."

"Have a nice day," Julie called as the twentysomething pulled away, sending gravel up in a spray.

She made her way to her truck, telling herself she'd gotten her good deed for the day out of the way early, so that was something. Thirty minutes after that, she pulled into the tow yard, driving under the big Parker Towing sign her grandfather had installed nearly fifty years ago. She parked the small tow truck she'd used for the call, then ran through the pelting rain to the safety of the main office, where Mariah Carey's version of "Santa Baby" played over the speakers. She hung the keys on the pegboard in the locking cabinet and put the credit card reader on the docking station where it would automatically download and tally the transaction.

Huxley, the office manager slash driver whisperer slash mother hen, looked at her over his reading glasses.

"Why do you do that? Why do you take a call like that? I go to lunch, and when I come back, you've taken one of the trucks and gone out to face God knows what in this kind of weather. I don't like to worry. When I worry, I get hives, and then I have to go see the doctor and that costs our insurance company money. Do you want the premiums to go up? I don't think so. But you do this. Every six months or so you think it's twenty-five years ago and you're still driving a damned tow truck. You're the boss. You've been the boss for a long time. It'd be really nice if you remembered it."

"I was delivering gas, not doing a repo. I was fine. Besides, it's fun to take one of the trucks out every now and then. I want to keep my hand in. The men need to respect me, and for that I need to prove my skills."

"A chicken could drag gas out to some fool who forgot to fill up his car. What skills are you going on about?"

She laughed. "I had a good time. I'm allowed. Leave me alone."

"I can feel those hives popping out all over my body," he said as she started for her office. "And Axel's waiting to talk to you. He has today's list."

Julie's good mood instantly faded. She walked purposefully toward her office, not breaking stride as she crossed the threshold and headed for her desk. She ignored the tall, fit man standing by the window, a folder in his hands. As she took her seat, she allowed her gaze to linger on the baseball bat leaning casually against the corner.

From the time she was eight until she was thirteen, her father had insisted on weekly batting practice at the cages up by the park. After all those sessions, she had a hell of a swing, and she wasn't afraid to connect with a ball or anything else that needed hitting.

Not that she went around beating people with a baseball bat, but it had been a deterrence on more than one call, and keeping it nearby in certain situations gave her a sense of security. The world was a better place, at least from her perspective, when she knew she could handle whatever came at her. She never asked for help—instead, she took care of the problem herself.

She drew in a breath, then raised her head and looked at the man watching her. "Axel."

He moved toward her desk and set down the folder. "I have five for tonight."

"Five's a lot."

She glanced at the papers. Sure enough, there were five cars the bank wanted back. They were all high-end, late models with appropriately high repo fees.

After taking 25 percent off the top to cover expenses, including the lookout car, the company and repo guy split the fee fifty-fifty. It was dangerous work for not much reward and a part of the business she'd never understood. But repo guys lived on adrenaline, and she supposed someone had to go out and take back that which had not been paid for.

She closed the folder and pushed it toward him. "Try not to get shot."

Axel flashed her a smile. "Me getting shot would solve a lot of your problems."

"Why would you say that? You're my repo guy. I have no interest in finding another one."

"You're still mad at me. Any chance you could see your way past that?"

Mad didn't come close to describing what she was feeling, she thought grimly, taking in his handsome face and dark eyes. He was the kind of man women noticed. A little dangerous, a little sexy, a lot of trouble.

"How long did you go out with my daughter?"

His smile faded and he took a step back. "About two years."

"How many times did she foolishly let you back in her life so you could break her heart yet again?"

His eyes became unreadable. "Three."

"My count is four, but I'm not sure that matters. I'll see my way past what you did to her when I'm good and ready. I'm thinking about thirty years, give or take."

He hung his head. "I'm sorry."

"Don't," she snapped. "Don't apologize to me. I only hate you by association. And if you really care about her, then stop screwing with her life. Leave her alone."

"I'm trying."

"Try harder."

"The heart wants what the heart wants."

"I'm pretty sure your heart isn't the body part creating all the trouble."

He looked at her. "You want me to quit?"

Some days she did, mostly when she was holding Dana as her daughter cried because Axel had once again dumped her. Because he'd been right—when it came to him, Dana's heart did want what it wanted and, unfortunately, that was him. But on the rest of the days, she liked having Axel around. He was dependable, he understood the business and he had a habit of taking new hires under his wing, so to speak, and teaching them the tricks of the trade.

"You're good at what you do," Julie said reluctantly, staring out the window. "Stay away from her and we'll be fine."

"You're a good mom."

Words that should have pleased her but instead sent a quiver of guilt trickling through her. While she usually fell firmly in the "good mother" category, lately she'd been keeping secrets. Well, one secret. One big, tall, boyfriend-size secret.

At some point she was going to have to come clean about him, just not today, she thought. It was three weeks until Christmas. Her kids had plans that didn't include her, Heath—the boyfriend, though she didn't say that word aloud—didn't have *his* kids for the holidays, so the two of them were going to hole up at her place and enjoy a little one-on-one time with nowhere else to be. She honestly couldn't wait.

She carefully put the happy image out of her head, then returned her attention to Axel.

"Go get the cars," she told him. "The weather's going to get worse. Remember that and don't try any fancy moves. Those big trucks you're driving belong to me."

The smile returned. "Yes, ma'am."

He took the paperwork and left. When Julie was sure he was out of earshot, she murmured, "And don't get dead." Because while she was pissed as hell at Axel, she wasn't heartless. Besides, except for when he crapped on her daughter, he was a good guy and secretly she liked him. Well, at least when it came to Parker Towing.

As for Dana and her devotion to the man, well, her daughter was an adult. At some point she was going to have to figure out how to move on. Because that was how life worked. You tried something, and if it didn't go well, you moved on. Julie's father had taught her that, along with how to swing a bat, and she'd learned both lessons very, very well.

"They're a little thick and chewy for a cookie," Peggy murmured doubtfully.

"It's a brownie," Fred told her. "Not a cookie. A brownie."

"I don't care if it's popcorn—it's too chewy." Peggy looked up at Blair. "Are there nuts? You know I can't have nuts."

"No nuts," Blair said cheerfully. "Just organic ingredients and a lot less sugar."

"That's why it's so chewy." Peggy shook her head. "I hate to be blunt, dear, but it's a no from me."

"I like it." Fred swiped another brownie from the holiday-patterned plate. "You put in prunes, didn't you? It's your tell. You know what they say about prunes and old people is a myth."

"It's not a myth." Cordella smiled at Blair. "I love prunes."

"The first cookies weren't chewy at all," Peggy murmured. "I liked those better."

"Now, those were cookies." Fred grinned at Blair. "I like them both."

"Thanks for the feedback." Blair rose from the table and collected the sheets the residents had filled out. "I'm determined to get in a better selection of low-sugar desserts. We can't keep relying on fruit, gelatin and whatever we can buy from our supplier. Would anyone be interested in a cooking class? Maybe we could all bake a couple of days a week."

Fred stared at her blankly. "I don't know how to bake."

"You could learn."

He shook his head. "Sorry, Blair. My wife baked for me for fifty-two years. I'm too old to learn something that complicated now. Besides, my dance card's pretty full these days. But you ask the ladies if they're interested."

With that, he rose, picked up his cane and scurried as quickly as his bad leg would let him. Blair grinned.

"So that was a no?"

"I bake," Cordella offered. "Although my days are pretty full, too." She patted Blair's hand. "I'm afraid you're on your own, my dear. But the cookies were delicious. You should talk to the kitchen staff about adding those to the menu. They'll be a hit."

Cordella smiled, then rose and waited while Peggy carefully backed her motorized scooter out of the room. Just before they left, Peggy paused.

"If I don't see you before the holiday, Merry Christmas, my dear. We all love that you try."

Blair waved at her, then began to clean up the plates and napkins from the dessert sampling. Today's tasting was her third with the new batch of cookies and brownies, and at each of her get-togethers the comments had been the same. Everyone loved the cookies, but the brownies were less popular. Still, a 50 percent success rate was great considering she was doing her best to develop healthy, tasty desserts for her residents.

She dropped off the last of the samples in the staff break room, then started toward her office. Through the big windows in the hallway she could see it was still raining. It was barely three and already getting dark, typical of Seattle in December. She had two more weekly menus she wanted to review before her four o'clock meeting with the head chef. As the gerontologist nutritionist for the retirement community, what everyone did or didn't eat was her responsibility. While the holiday menus had already been approved, she wanted to go over snack options for the various parties the residents would be attending.

She'd almost reached her office when one of the receptionists texted on her cell phone.

There's a really handsome guy with a tow truck out front. Any interest or should I let the single ladies know he's up for grabs?

Blair grinned as she texted back a quick, **No way. Nick's mine and you know it.**

She was still smiling as she entered the large, open foyer of the main building. Her husband was leaning against the reception desk, talking to one of the volunteers.

As always, the sight of him made her heart beat just a little bit faster. Nick was tall and strong, with an easy smile and an even more easygoing personality. That was one of the things that had first drawn her to him—he was rarely rattled. While she lived by schedules, regimens and precision, he rolled with the punches. She admired that about him and wished her various gastrointestinal ailments allowed her to do the same.

"In my next life," she murmured. In her next life she would be normal and be able to eat whatever she wanted without worrying about how her system would react. In her next life she wouldn't know the location of every "safe" bathroom between work and home or home and the grocery store. Her activities wouldn't be defined by whether or not she was going to have a "good" day or if she would be suffering. There would be no pills taken at precise times in an effort to keep things calm "down there."

As she approached, he chuckled at something the volunteer said. As always, he wore jeans and steel-toed boots. A waterproof vest was zipped up over a warm plaid shirt. Nick didn't believe in wearing jackets—they got in the way of his work. Nor did he seem to react to the damp cold that came along with the Seattle winter.

He looked up and saw her. Instantly his expression softened and his eyes filled with affection.

"Hey, you."

She hurried toward him. He pulled her close and hugged her, but gave her only the lightest of kisses. They were at her work, after all.

"What brings you to our neighborhood?" she asked, leading him to one of the conversation areas by the window. At this time of day, there weren't many residents around, so it was easy to find a quiet space. They sat on one of the sofas and faced each other.

"I had a lockout and car to tow to the dealership not too far from here. When I was done with those, I thought I'd swing by and say hi."

"Hi."

He chuckled. "Hi, back." His gaze lingered on her face. "You look especially beautiful today."

"I feel good."

"I like hearing that."

She knew he meant the words—not just because if her tummy was calm it was a whole lot easier to have sex, but because he genuinely worried about her. While he didn't keep the detailed log she did, noting what she'd eaten and when she had her attacks, he could always sense when she started to feel bad. More than once, he'd been the one to quietly tell her where the closest restroom was before she'd had more than her first twinge indicating trouble.

He leaned forward and took one of her hands in his. "I'm sorry."

"Don't." She squeezed his fingers. "Nick, it's totally fine. I love you. We'll go to Hawaii in March, like you said."

"I'm messing up everything."

"You're not."

"We had a plan." His dark gaze locked with hers. "I want to go away with you, but…"

She took his other hand and squeezed them both. "Nicholas James Parker, you stop right now. It's been a stressful year. We had our wedding planned, then two weeks before, you lost your father. No one expected that. We were all devastated. He's your *dad*. You don't get over that in a few months."

They'd postponed the wedding until May, but hadn't been able to get away on their honeymoon because of her work. They'd agreed they would spend Christmas in Hawaii—just the two of them. After a big family Thanksgiving, they'd thought they would be fine going away. Only Nick was having second thoughts.

"I still miss him," he said quietly.

"Of course you do. I lost my dad four years ago and I think of him all the time. This is big. The spirit takes a long time to heal, and the emptiness never fully goes away."

She swallowed against the protest she secretly wanted to voice.

She loved Nick and would do what was best for him, but spending Christmas here? Ugh—it was going to be a nightmare.

"We had an old plan and now we have a new one," she said cheerfully. "You're going to talk to Dana tonight, and if she agrees, we'll talk to your mom at dinner tomorrow and let her know we've changed our mind. We all want one big happy family Christmas up at the cabin. I'll see if Uncle Paul wants to join us, because more is better. We'll do the whole thing—the trees, the time in the snow, all the traditions. We'll talk about your dad and when you were little and it will be sad and wonderful and you'll feel so much better when we come home."

"What about your mom?"

And there was the real reason Blair had been so happy they'd planned to go away. She released his hands and looked away. "I don't want to talk about her."

"She's a problem."

"She's always a problem."

"We could not tell her," he began, his tone tentative.

She sucked in a breath. "I wish, but that's not an option. She's here. I have to deal."

Blair's mother, Gwen, had recently made the stunning decision to move from Boise, where she'd always lived, to the Seattle area. She'd sold her house, packed up her belongings and had basically shown up with little warning. She was renting a little condo until she figured out where she wanted to live permanently. After years of being a comfortable five hundred miles away, she was now annoyingly close.

"Thanksgiving was easy," Blair admitted. "She flew back to Boise to spend the holiday with her friends. But she'll be here for Christmas. It was one thing to leave her while we went on our belated honeymoon. It's another to abandon her while we head off to the mountains with family. She's going to have to come with us."

"You should talk to *my* mom."

"And say what? I love your mom and she loves me. No way I'm going to admit that I have issues with my own mother. She'll think I'm heartless or a freak."

Worse, *issues* didn't come close to describing the problem. Blair and her mother hadn't been close for decades. She had no idea what Gwen thought of her, but there were days when Blair knew her greatest shame was that she actively disliked and resented her own mother.

"I wish she'd stayed in Boise," Blair grumbled. "It was so much easier when we spoke every five or six months and we never saw each other. She doesn't know anyone here. She's having to start over with friends and doctors and everything else. She should have stayed where she knows people."

"She knows you."

"Ha ha. The less time I spend with her, the happier I am. She's going to ruin Christmas."

"She's not."

"You wait. Two days in, you'll be apologizing for being wrong."

Still, there was no getting out of it. That was the real rub. She could complain and wish things were different, but she didn't have it in her to simply leave her mother alone over Christmas, no matter how much she didn't want to even be in the same room as her.

"At least Uncle Paul will be there," Nick offered. "Everybody likes him." He frowned. "Until the wedding, I hadn't seen him and your mom together. They really don't get along."

"It's more of a cool acceptance. He was my dad's brother, not hers. I think he was fine with her until…you know. When everything changed."

But he'd always been supportive of Blair, and when she'd needed a place to go, he'd opened his home to her. She'd stayed with him through high school and then while getting her degree at the University of Washington. They'd been there for each other when she'd lost her father and he'd lost his only brother. He'd been the one to walk her down the aisle when she'd married Nick. *They* were family. Not her and her mother.

"We need to make it clear to Julie what she's getting into," she said. "I bring baggage and only half of it is fun."

"You know Mom lives to fix things. She'll take charge and everyone will end up doing exactly what she says." He grinned. "She can be determined. Maybe by the end of the holidays, she'll figure out how to get you and your mom to be friends."

"Unlikely." A word so much nicer than what Blair really wanted to say, which was "I don't want to be friends with my mom. I want her to go live somewhere else so I never have to see her or deal with her again."

And that made her a horrible person, but she was willing to live with the guilt. She worked on her karma in other areas of her life. She was a good friend and generous to charities, and she was an excellent listener. She just really, really didn't like her mother.

She looked at her watch. "I need to get to a meeting and you have tow truck duties. You're dropping by Dana's before you come home?"

"Yeah, I'll swing by her place when I finish my shift."

They both stood. He touched her cheek. "We'll figure this out."

"We will and we'll get through it." She looked into his eyes. "You need the family time, Nick. It's important. This is the first Christmas without your dad. We'll honor that. Everything else can wait."

"Why are you so good to me?"

"Because you're actually the best man ever and I'm the lucky woman you married."

He smiled. "We'll argue about who's luckier later. Love you."

"Love you, too. Be safe."

"Always."

He walked toward the main exit. Blair allowed herself a second to watch him go. As always, a tiny knot of worry took up residence in her chest. Being a tow truck driver could be dangerous work. Some inattentive motorist could easily sideswipe him while he was working on a disabled car on one of the freeways. A drunk or drugged-out driver could pull a gun on him, which had happened and was the reason he kept a 9 mm semiautomatic gun locked in the glove box of his truck.

He was out in the elements, dealing with all kinds of people, going to dangerous neighborhoods at night. She'd never liked what he did, but given that it was a family business, she'd never expected him to find something else. Julie planned on her only son taking over Parker Towing, and it was always where Nick had seen himself. He wasn't enthused about running things, but it had been his life plan.

Until recently, she thought as she hurried back to her office. Nick hadn't made up his mind completely, but she knew he was leaning toward accepting Uncle Paul's generous offer. And if that happened, Nick's future would look very different. She could let go of the worry, and he could be excited about his job again.

The only problem was going to be telling Julie that there wasn't going to be a third generation at Parker Towing, and neither of them wanted to be the one to break his mother's heart. Or very possibly piss her off.

2

Dana Parker hadn't realized it was possible for her hands to cramp from curling ribbon, but it was. The stacks of donated *unwrapped* presents had been transformed into stacks of wrapped presents, each with a color-coded and numbered tag. G7-10 meant the gift was appropriate for a girl between seven and ten. When the wrapped gifts were distributed to the various local charities, the coded tags would be replaced by personalized ones.

In the interest of speed and efficiency, the volunteers had broken up into groups that either wrapped or added curly ribbon and the tags. Dana had joined the latter, something she now regretted. Paper cuts seemed easier to deal with than finger cramps.

"But it's for a good cause," she reminded herself. Because it was the season and she was all about good causes and helping others and staying busy, which was why she'd spent the previous weekend packing backpacks for schoolchildren who wouldn't get meals from school during the holidays and was this afternoon maiming herself in the name of curly ribbon.

Her phone buzzed in her jeans pocket. She pulled it out and glanced at the text from her mother.

I have lamps. They're fabulous. When will you be home?

Lamps? Her first instinct was to ask why, but her mom had better taste than her, so the lamps were likely to be perfect for her recently redone bedroom.

I finish here in about ten minutes, then I'm going home.

Good. I'll leave them by the front door. They're wrapped in plastic. They'll be fine. Love you.

Dana sent back heart emojis, then refocused on ribbon curling. She finished the last gift three minutes before four, then looked at the impressive pile of presents they'd all finished. They'd done good work here, and she was happy to have helped. It had been worth taking the time off work.

"We're going to make a lot of kids happy this Christmas," the woman at the next table said with a smile. "All this in three hours. Now I have to go home and wrap my own presents." She opened and closed her hands. "Okay, maybe not today."

"I'm with you on that," Dana said, her tone light.

She rose, collected her bag and went to sign out before heading to her car, careful to avoid the other volunteers. She didn't want to get into a conversation about families and holidays and gifts. No matter how she talked about her life, she sounded pathetic. If this were a century ago, she would be referred to as a spinster. A lonely, single, manless woman desperately in love with someone who kept walking away. She was a fool. Worse, she was a fool who was incapable of learning a lesson.

She drove through the rain, trying to ignore the burning in her eyes. She was done crying over Axel. She had a plan.

Maybe not a great one, but a plan nonetheless. Forward movement and all that.

She'd already painted her bedroom and replaced the furniture. No more sleeping in a bed he'd been in. Starting Saturday, she was off until after the first of the year. Come January 2, she would not only be dealing with the thrill of tax season, she would be enjoying the first day of her new life. Between now and then, she was going to get over Axel, completely organize her closets, sign up for a new dating app, start taking yoga and learn to crochet. Ambitious, yes? But doable. Because she was done living her tragic little half life, watching other people get what they wanted. She was done waiting for a man who'd claimed to love her, yet continually walked away, breaking her heart over and over again. She wanted to be happy.

To that end, she'd planned nearly every moment of her time off. She was on the wait list for a yoga retreat. She'd created a schedule for cleaning her entire condo and Marie Kondo–ing her closets. She'd found an online beginning crochet class that would, for a mere twenty-seven dollars, teach her everything she wanted to know about the craft. She had movies picked out on Netflix, a list of take-out places she was going to try and several thoughts on what she would take to her mom's for their low-key Christmas dinner. With Nick and Blair on their honeymoon, it would just be the two of them, with the possible addition of Huxley, from her mom's work. She was thinking of some kind of cranberry apple salad.

As she turned the corner onto her street, she saw her neighbors had put artificial cardinals on the evergreen in their front yard. The birds always made her think of her dad because he'd always talked about how his grandmother had loved cardinals. The birds had appeared a couple of days ago, and every time she saw them, she felt a little twist in her heart.

The feelings made sense, she thought as she pulled into her

condo garage. This was the first Christmas without him. Everything was going to be different.

She went in through the garage, then back out by the front porch, where a plastic-wrapped box was waiting, safely tucked out of the rain. Once she had it on her kitchen counter, she cut it open, then stared at two perfectly elegant, mid-century modern lamps. The glaze on the base had an ombré effect, starting a couple of shades darker than the pale gray wall color she'd chosen for her bedroom and morphing to a beautiful deep purple that pulled bits of color from her bedspread. The lampshades were a neutral white that went with the trim and baseboards.

She was about to pick up her phone and call her mom to thank her and gush about how great the lamps were when she heard someone knock on her front door. She found her brother standing in the rain.

"Hi," she said, stepping back to let him in. "Did I know you were coming by?"

"No. I should have texted, but I took a chance. You got a sec?"

She had all the seconds, and the minutes, too. "Of course."

They went into the family room. Rather than taking a seat, Nick walked to the window and stared out into the darkness.

Dana took in his stiff shoulders and the set of his head. Trouble, she thought. There was definitely a problem.

"What?" she asked. "Just blurt it out so we can start finding a solution."

He turned back to her and grinned. "You sound like Mom."

"Some days that would bug me, but today I don't mind you saying it." After all, her mother had her life together. She always had.

Julie was one of those people who took charge. She never had to ask for help because there was never a problem she couldn't solve on her own. Take over her father's towing business at age twenty-four? No big deal. Deal with two little kids at the same time? Take them to work with you and turn your office into a preschool fantasy. Get divorced and have to start dating? Dive headfirst into the single scene, fight off the scores of men interested, and in your free time, buy the perfect little house and fix it up so it looks like something out of a magazine.

"I need to be more like her," she murmured. Julie would never allow herself to fall into the "pathetic" category of womanhood.

She shook off that thought and pointed at her brother. "Talk."

He crossed to the sofa but didn't sit down. "I miss Dad."

Dana thought of the cardinals and her own feelings. "Me, too. It's been nearly a year since we lost him, but this is our first Christmas. Thanksgiving wasn't so bad. He was never into the holiday, and after the divorce, he preferred to spend it by himself. But Christmas was always a big deal."

Even after he and her mom had split up, her dad had joined them up at the cabin, more years than not. Dana didn't know if it had just happened, or if her parents had arranged it, but even if one of them had been seeing someone, the current love interest was never invited. The cabin was just for family.

"I've been talking to Blair," Nick continued, holding her gaze. "I don't want to go to Hawaii over Christmas. It doesn't feel right. We need a family Christmas at the cabin to celebrate Dad's memory."

"But you were going on your honeymoon."

"I know. Blair's being great about it. We'll go in March." His mouth turned down. "I know you have plans and stuff, but could you change them?"

Dana thought of the "fifteen ways to a better life" regimen she would be starting, of the online crochet class and going through each of her closets as she desperately searched for some way to forget Axel. Being with her family would be so much better than being by herself.

"I'm in."

"You sure?" he asked.

"Absolutely. Let's do it. You're right—this is a tough Christmas. We should spend it together. I know Mom hasn't rented out the cabin—she never would for the holidays. We just have to tell her there's been a change." She looked at him. "It's a lot more work for her."

"We can help. Oh, it won't just be me and Blair. Her uncle and mom will be coming, too."

"I like Paul," Dana said, not sure what she thought about Blair's mother. She'd only met the woman at the rehearsal dinner and then at the wedding and reception. Gwen had mostly kept to herself. She'd seemed a little standoffish, but maybe that was because she didn't know many people at the celebration. "I'm sure Gwen will be fine. There's plenty of room at the cabin."

Nick surprised her by stepping close and hugging her. "Thanks, sis. I mean it. I need this."

"I do, too. It's a good idea. Are you going to tell Mom? Do you want me to?"

"We're all having dinner with her tomorrow. Let's do it then. We can work out the logistics and come up with a plan." He grinned. "You know in our family, we always have to have a plan."

"Absolutely!"

When her brother had left, Dana carried the new lamps into the bedroom and plugged them in. They added a warm glow to the newly redecorated space.

As she looked at the simple dresser, the lamps and the fluffy throw rug at the foot of her bed, she knew there wasn't anything left of Axel in this room. Not anymore. Slowly she was exorcising him out of her life. The next step—by far the hardest—was to do the same with her heart.

Maybe time at the cabin, with the people she loved, would show her the way. All she needed was not to care about him anymore. Once she had moved on, she would be free of him and ready to be happy again. It was past time for her to reclaim herself and find a fresh beginning.

★ ★ ★

"I like the gray tone of that one," Julie said, snuggled up on the sofa, her head on Heath's shoulder, his arm around her. She held his iPad as he flipped to the picture of the next floor.

"Lighter gray or darker gray?" he asked.

"My heart says the darker floors look great, but my sensible head says a lighter floor doesn't show every little thing. You have two kids and Rufus."

"Yes, Rufus. He who sheds by the pound. The lighter color it is."

He put the iPad on the coffee table, then turned his attention to her. "Dinner or sex?" His yummy mouth curved into a smile. "I'm not saying you have to choose. Obviously we'll have both. I'm questioning the order of the evening."

"Dinner," she said firmly. "Because we just had sex twenty minutes ago."

In fact, the second she'd walked in his front door, he'd grabbed her and pulled her close. His welcoming kiss had ignited into something very quick but intensely satisfying, right over there on the entry table. Luckily, Heath had sturdy furniture, a plus considering they'd made love on most of it.

He was a very generous lover with an unexpectedly high sex drive. Twice a day was almost their norm. Three times wasn't unheard-of. She supposed it was because things were still relatively new between them. Or maybe it was the fact that with their busy schedules, they couldn't see each other as often as they would like. She refused to consider the possibility that it maybe could almost be because Heath was twelve full years younger than her.

"Dinner it is," he murmured, shifting her until she was lying back on the sofa. One large, warm hand slid under her sweater and found her left breast while his lips nibbled along her neck.

She shifted from hungry for takeout to hungry for him in an eighth of a second and began unbuttoning his shirt. Once they were naked, he brought her to orgasm with an efficiency that made her want to send a very expensive gift to whomever had taught him the, um, ins and outs of female anatomy. She came a second time with him inside of her, then lay there boneless and trying to catch her breath.

"You're an amazing lover," he said, returning from the bathroom where she assumed he'd disposed of the condom and cleaned up. "I can't get enough of you."

She smiled. "I like that you can't get enough of me. But now you have to give me food."

While she dressed, he placed the take-out order. The logistics taken care of, they settled back on the sofa.

"I think I'm ready for the work on the house to be done," he said. "Paint on the walls, then refinishing the floors." He glanced at her. "You sure you're okay with me moving in for two weeks?"

"I am," she said quickly, thinking he didn't need to know she was the tiniest bit nervous. They'd never spent so much time together. What if they got on each other's nerves? But the thought of Heath in her bed every night for two weeks was far more powerful than her fear of finding him annoying.

"Are you going to be all right?" she asked, lightly touching his hand. "You'll be missing your kids."

"Yeah, that part sucks." He glanced at her as if concerned she would take the comment wrong. "What I mean by that is..."

"I already know." She gave him a sympathetic smile. "It's your kids and it's Christmas. They're only ten and eight. Having every other holiday with them is the worst. You worry about what you're going to miss and the memories you're not going to make."

"Thanks for understanding."

"Of course."

It wasn't anything she'd had to deal with. When she and Eldon had split up, their two had been pretty much grown. Plus, the divorce had been friendly enough that Eldon had spent every Christmas after the divorce up at the cabin. But it wasn't like that for Heath. His kids were younger and he treasured time with them.

"While we're on the topic of the holiday, what are your expectations?"

He raised his eyebrows. "Now, there's a question."

She laughed. "I'm not talking about sex. I mean, what do you want for the Christmas season in general and the day in particular? A big tree? A traditional dinner? Something quieter?"

His gaze locked with hers. "Julie, whatever works for you works for me. With the kids, I want to go all out, but I'm not looking to make you do extra work just for me. What would you do if I wasn't here?"

"Nothing," she blurted, then shrugged. "Sorry, but it's true. We had a big family Thanksgiving, and while I loved it, cooking for two days isn't my idea of fun. I'm happy to just let the whole season go by uncelebrated."

"Then let's do that."

She drew in a breath. "I don't mean to sound like Scrooge or anything, but going to the cabin is so much work. It's days of decorating, then getting food in and cooking for everyone. Dana helps and now there's Blair, but I'm the one in charge, so it's—"

He silenced her with a quick kiss. "Stop. I get it and I'm not asking to go to the cabin. We were planning to stay here. I'm good with that. Quiet is fine."

"You sure?"

"You're the one I want to be with. The rest of it doesn't matter."

Relief made her relax. "Thanks. We'll still have a small Christmas dinner. Just you, me, Huxley and Dana."

As she spoke, she tried to keep her tone light because it was no big deal and just one meal and...

Heath surprised her by laughing. "If you could see your face."

"What?"

"You still haven't told her." The laughter deepened. "Oh, Julie, this isn't like you. You always have a plan. What's going to happen? Dana shows up expecting you and Huxley and we pretend I'm not at the table?"

While part of her appreciated he wasn't the kind of man to be offended by the fact that she hadn't told her kids about him, the rest of her was trapped in the reality of what he was saying. It was past time to tell her children about the man she was seeing. Although in truth, Nick wouldn't care. She was much more concerned about Dana. She and her daughter were tight—they did things together, they talked about their lives. But somehow Julie had never found a way to explain Heath.

"If you weren't so young," she grumbled. "And good-looking."

"You want me to be old and ugly?"

"No, but you know, older and maybe only a little ugly." She sighed. "I'm being silly. Dana won't be upset." At least that was her hope. It was just...she was fifty-four and Heath was only forty-two. Most of the time she didn't care, but every now and then she found that particular truth a little cringeworthy. People judged, and while she didn't care what "people" thought of her, she very much cared about her daughter's opinion.

"I'll tell her," she said. "I'm having dinner with Dana, Nick and Blair tomorrow. I'll say something."

"I've heard that before." His tone was teasing, his expression good-natured.

She looked at him. "Why aren't you mad I haven't said anything about you?"

He lightly stroked her cheek. "My kids don't know, either."

"That's different. They're young."

He gave her a slow, sexy smile. "You watch me."

"What?"

"When you think I don't know, you watch me. There's a look

in your eyes. I can't explain it but I like it. So I don't care who you tell or don't tell. I know how you feel about me."

Wait, what? He knew how she *felt* about him? He couldn't—*she* wasn't sure. They'd only been dating three months, and with him having his kids every other weekend and them both being busy with their respective companies and everything else, they simply didn't spend that much time together. Whatever feelings she had—and she wasn't saying she had any—were completely undefined.

"I'm glad you're not mad," she said, with a casualness she sure didn't feel.

"Not my style."

"I do like your style."

"I like yours, too."

"So Christmas. Low-key and easy," she said. "And I'll tell my kids about us tomorrow night. After they've both had a drink."

"They'll be fine," he said. "I'm not a big deal." He grinned at her. "Except for the young-and-handsome part. You're right—that's going to be a problem."

She laughed, as he expected, but couldn't help thinking that there was a very good chance Heath was actually telling the truth.

"We should talk about Christmas," Julie said, taking the visitor's chair by Huxley's big desk. She smiled brightly. "We're not going to the cabin. I know we usually do, but with Nick and Blair finally taking their honeymoon, it's just the three of us and it's so much work, so we're not going."

She fought against a wave of guilt, telling herself she wasn't obligated to go to the cabin and what she did with her holidays was her business, but still, the guilt remained.

"Are you upset?" she asked in an uncharacteristically small voice.

Huxley stared at her as if she'd sprouted a few feathers. "Did you hit your head? Why are you asking me that? You invite me to Christmas every year, and I go because it's always nice and I don't have any family of my own. You do understand it's about spending time with people I like, because God knows there aren't many of those left in this world, so why would you think I give a rat's titty where we're going to be?"

"Because Christmas is always at the cabin."

"I'm there for the company and the food." He flashed her a smile. "You do make a fine meal."

"Rat's titty?"

"I stand by what I said. You're a good woman, Julie, and I appreciate how you look out for me."

She smiled back at him. "You're welcome." She looked around at the office, taking pride in the business she'd grown. "You think Nick is ever going to make a decision about joining me?"

"He will. The boy needs time."

"I didn't need time." She'd always known she wanted to run Parker Towing. The difference was, after all these years, she figured Nick would be taking on more responsibility by now.

"I'm tired of doing everything," she said. "I'd like a business partner."

"You mean you'd like Nick or are you open to someone else?"

"What? Not someone else. I meant my son. He needs to stop just driving trucks, like an employee."

She was ready for him to start learning the front-office job so he could eventually take over from her. Only he kept putting her off.

She looked at Huxley. "You want to buy me out?"

He laughed long and loud. "If I had me a few million squirreled away, the last thing I would do is buy into this business. Instead, I would take my old bones somewhere tropical." He gave her a little wink. "But I'd come back for Christmas because you do make a fine meal."

3

Dana arrived at the restaurant where she was meeting Nick, Blair and her mom. The mid-December Seattle weather was typical—forty-two degrees and raining. As it was nearly six, it was, of course, two hours past sunset. Ah, the thrill of a Pacific Northwest winter. But today the grimness didn't bother her as much as usual. She was feeling pretty good about things. She'd spent two hours helping a single mother of two set up her online accounting program for the ice cream shop she was opening. She'd spent her lunch hour at a beginner's yoga class, and her new plans for the holidays included being around people she loved rather than stewing by herself.

She stepped inside and immediately spotted Blair and Nick, already seated at a table.

"I'm with them," she told the host, then crossed the crowded restaurant to join her brother and sister-in-law.

Blair saw her and waved, then rose to give her a hug. "It's been raining all day."

"You sound surprised."

"What happened to our warmer and dryer than usual winter?"

Dana shrugged out of her water-resistant coat and hung it on a nearby coatrack. "Were we supposed to have a warmer and dryer winter?"

"No," Nick said with a chuckle. "We never are, but Blair is an eternal optimist."

"Sometimes wishing does make it so." Blair smiled. "At least I tell myself that."

Blair was a pretty brunette with delicate features. She was all of five-three, and next to her sometimes Dana felt like a chunky giant. She'd inherited both of her parents' height and was nearly five-nine in bare feet. But while her mom was tall with a lean, athletic build, Dana...was not. It wasn't just the bigger bone structure she'd gotten from her dad, but her habit of eating her feelings that had her carrying an extra forty pounds. On her good days she told herself that once she got her emotional life together, she would lose the weight and be happy. On her bad days, she wondered how much more she weighed than her brother, who was nearly six-two and muscled.

She'd been a skinny kid, but at college had packed on the freshman ten every year for four years and had spent her life since trying to get rid of them.

"We should figure out what we're going to say," Nick said, drawing her back to the table. "To Mom."

Dana frowned. "Other than some version of 'we want Christmas at the cabin'?"

"I thought we'd ease into it."

Dana laughed. "Yeah, Nick. Great idea, because you're so good at subtle."

She had more teasing in her, but just then Blair looked toward the front of the restaurant.

"Julie's here."

Dana immediately felt guilty, which was ridiculous. She hadn't done anything wrong. The holidays were supposed to be about family, after all, and—

"Hi, everyone," Julie said cheerfully, as she approached. "I'm just going to say it. I have a very good-looking family."

"You mean me, right?" Nick asked, coming to his feet and hugging her. "Hey, Mom."

"Hey, yourself."

The rest of them stood and hugged her. Julie hung her coat, then took the last seat at the table. But the second she sat down, her smile faded.

"What?" she asked, her voice sharp. "There's something, I can tell." She swung her attention to Blair. "Are you feeling all right? Is it your tummy?"

"I'm fine." Blair looked at Nick. "It's been a good couple of days."

Julie didn't look convinced. "It's something. Just say it."

Nick caught Dana's eye and waved slightly, as if wanting her to speak. Dana shook her head. No way—this wasn't her party.

Nick gave her an eye roll before turning to their mom.

"Everyone is fine," he began.

"I don't believe you."

"If you'd let me talk."

Julie crossed her arms over her chest—a sure sign she was annoyed. "I'm listening."

Dana groaned. "You're doing this all wrong," she told her brother. "What happened to easing into it? Now she's pissed."

"I'm not pissed," Julie said, still sounding slightly annoyed. "I'm letting Nick talk."

"See." Dana poked him in the arm. "You're an oaf."

"Hey!"

Dana ignored him and smiled at their mom. "Everyone is fine. It's not about us. It's about the season."

Slowly Julie's arms relaxed. "What does that mean?"

"It's our first Christmas without Dad," Dana told her. "We miss him."

Julie's expression softened as she reached out a hand to both her children. "Of course you do. I'm sorry. I should have thought of that. It's been nearly a year since you lost him, but it was late January. So this is the last of the holidays to get through."

"I thought it would be okay," Nick told her. "You're right. It's been a year, but it's Christmas. You know he always loved this time of year."

"I do. He enjoyed every part of the season. Up at the cabin, he was always into the decorating, and when you kids were young, he would start planning what presents we'd get as early as September."

"He's been on my mind a lot. Dana's, too. Even you have to be thinking about him, Mom."

Dana wanted to kick her brother under the table. Their mom wasn't missing their dad. The divorce had been more than ten years ago and the marriage had been on the rocks for years before that. But Dana knew their mom would never correct Nick's assumption. Julie was tough, she was fair, she was capable of doing anything, but she was also a total sucker when it came to her children.

"Family matters even more this time of year," Julie said diplomatically. "I understand that. Nick, are you worried that you and Blair are disrespecting your father by taking your honeymoon? You're not. He wouldn't want you to give that up. He would want you to be happy."

"I know." Nick and Blair exchanged another look—one that spoke of silent communication and connection. "So here's the thing. We do want to go to Hawaii, just not right now."

Julie looked confused. "I don't understand."

Nick looked at Dana, silently asking for help. Dana groaned. "Seriously? I have to be the one to say it?"

Nick shrugged.

Dana leaned toward their mom. "We want to spend Christmas at the cabin. All of us. We need the family time, Mom. To reconnect and remember. We want to honor Dad with that."

Julie's eyes widened slightly as she drew back in her chair. The movements were subtle, but Dana caught them.

"You don't want to," she said.

"What?" Her mother instantly smiled broadly. "No, of course I want to. That sounds...well, it sounds like a lovely family Christmas."

Dana heard the words but knew something was off. The tone maybe? "Are you okay?"

"Me? I'm fine. Why wouldn't I be? I just wasn't expecting, you know, a big family get-together. I haven't done any of the prep work. It's so much to get ready, but yes, let's do that."

Blair, sitting across from Julie, drew in a breath. "We'll help," she said quickly. "All of us. I know this is sudden and not what you had planned for the holidays. You probably weren't even going to decorate your place."

"I wasn't going to," Julie murmured. "I never do. We're always up at the cabin. But it's fine."

"Did you have plans, Mom?" Nick asked.

"Me? Not really. I mean, I wasn't going anywhere, if that's what you're asking."

Dana studied her as she spoke. There was something for sure. "Mom, you sure you're all right?"

Julie patted her hand. "Never better." She looked around. "Where is our server? I could use a drink."

"We'll be on our best behavior," Nick promised. "Dana and I."

"I'm always on my best behavior," Dana told him. "You're the problem."

"Am not."

"Are too."

Blair waved her hands in front of them. "Hey, is this an example of good behavior? You're not very convincing."

Their server appeared and told them about the specials. Julie rushed her along, then asked for a glass of red wine, and whatever they were pouring was fine with her. Dana asked for the same and Nick ordered a beer. Blair got herbal iced tea, as per usual.

When the server had left, Blair looked at her mother-in-law. "So it's not just going to be the four of us."

Julie smiled. "You're right. Huxley will come up on the twenty-first."

"I meant..." Blair cleared her throat. "There's my uncle Paul."

Julie's smile softened. "We love Uncle Paul."

"And my mother."

The words hung there. Dana had the thought there should be "and here comes the villain" music playing.

"She moved here," Nick added. "I told you about that, Mom."

"Yes, that's right. From Boise. Has she found a place yet?"

"Not a permanent one. She's in a rental and we're looking for something for her to buy." Blair dropped her gaze to the table. "It was different when it was us going on our honeymoon. I was comfortable leaving her by herself, but if we're in town then—"

"Of course she'll join us," Julie said firmly. "It's Christmas. I look forward to getting to know her better."

"Don't," Nick muttered.

Blair nudged him with her shoulder. "We've talked about this. Only I can say bad stuff about my mom. You have to remain neutral because I don't want to have to defend her."

"Sorry."

"Let's do a head count," Dana said, wanting to change the subject. "Us four, plus Paul and Gwen and Huxley. That's seven."

The server walked over with their drinks. Julie gulped half of hers, then asked the server to give them a few more minutes. When she'd left, Julie glanced around the table, her gaze lingering on Dana.

"It's not seven—it's eight."

Dana looked at Nick, who shrugged as if he didn't get it, either. "Who's the eighth person?"

"Heath."

"Who's Heath?" Nick asked.

Julie drew in a deep breath. "He's the man I've been seeing."

Dana stared at her mother, trying to make sense of her words. She understood them individually, but collectively...what was she talking about?

"Wait. You're dating someone?" Dana couldn't believe it. "You can't be. You would have told me."

She paused, fighting hurt and confusion and a strange and unexpected sense of betrayal. "You never said anything about him and now you want to spend Christmas with him? You've never brought a guy to Christmas. Is it serious? You are in love with someone and I don't even know you're dating?"

The tightness in her chest was as big as the surprise. She and her mom talked all the time. They hung out, they shared their lives. Julie always told her when there was someone new in her life.

"We're not in love," Julie said firmly. "We've been seeing each other for a few months—"

"Months? You've been dating for months?" Dana tried to make sense of it while ignoring the hurt in her heart. "Is he the reason you didn't want to go to the theater that time? And why you canceled on dinner a few weeks ago? I thought you were busy at work, but it's been him all along?"

Julie's guilty expression spoke for her. "I didn't know what to say." She looked at Dana. "I was going to tell you before Christmas dinner."

"Because he was going to be there?" A stupid question, she realized. If her mom was going to bring him to the cabin, of course he would have been at the dinner. "Who is he? How did you meet? And why didn't you tell me?"

"Dana."

Nick's voice was quiet, but it cut through her confusion enough to make her realize she'd gotten a little loud and a little shrill. Only she couldn't help it. She was confused and surprised. Nearly as bad was her knee-jerk response of wanting to tell Axel what was happening and have him promise she would be all right.

"I'm sorry," her mother told her. "I understand you're upset and you have every reason to be. I should have said something sooner."

Yes, she should have, Dana thought, not sure which was more startling—that her mom had kept the secret or that the guy was important enough to bring to Christmas.

"We should change the subject," Dana whispered. "Talk about something else."

Silence descended. After a few seconds, Blair said, "The salmon looks good. I think I'm in the mood for fish."

"Me, too." Nick shifted in his seat. "Or what about the pork chop? It comes with grits."

"I'm not much for grits. I'm getting the salmon."

Dana tried to read the menu to offer her own thoughts, but it was difficult to focus through the shock and pain.

How could her mom have kept the guy a secret for so long, and why? That wasn't how they were in their family. They'd always been close, sharing important events. They'd all known within two dates that Nick felt he'd met "the one" and was crazy about Blair. Her mom had been the person she'd turned to every time Axel dumped her. Yet for some reason, Julie had kept Heath from everyone, and Dana was determined to find out why.

"So, Christmas," Blair said, passing her uncle baseball caps from the open box on the counter. The custom-ordered hats were all branded with the Nothing After '72 logo. "There's been a change in plans."

She explained how Nick was missing his dad and wanted to be up at the family cabin for the holiday. "We'd like you to come along."

Her uncle, a cheerful, kind man in his late fifties, raised his eyebrows. "You're putting off your honeymoon for the second time, Blair. Should I worry?"

She smiled at him. "No, you shouldn't. We didn't go after the wedding because I couldn't get away from work. So that doesn't count." Her smile faded. "Paul, Nick really needs to be at the cabin. He's missing his dad and needs to say goodbye with Dana. It's a whole thing."

"I get that." His voice was sad. "I remember when we lost your dad. Given he was five hundred miles away, I never got to see him as much as I would have liked, but he left a big hole in my life. One I haven't figured out how to fill. I'm delighted to spend the holidays with you. You know that. I just want to make sure you're going to be happy. Nick's a great guy, and you deserve that in your life."

"We're fine," Blair told him, making an X over her heart. "I promise. I want to do this for him. We'll go to Hawaii in March and have a great time."

The honeymoon was less of an issue for her. She knew they'd get there, and Nick needed to finish healing.

"Then I'm in," her uncle said. "Last year was fun. There's plenty of room and a lot to do." He grinned. "Plus, your mother-in-law is a great cook."

"Julie does know how to pull together a meal." Even more important to Blair, Julie was great about taking her dietary restrictions into account. "But there's one problem." She paused as she handed over the last of the hats. "Well, two."

Her uncle took the box from her and cut the tape on the bottom to flatten it out. He put it on top of the others they'd already emptied, then met her gaze.

"I can guess the first one."

"You can't mention the business." She waved her hand to encompass the store. "Julie doesn't know you and Nick have been talking."

He shook his head. "It's never a good idea to keep secrets.

People find out eventually, and if you don't control the telling, there can be unintended consequences."

"I know, but until Nick makes up his mind, there's nothing to say."

Paul's store—Nothing After '72—sold replacement parts for old muscle cars. There were four lifts out back customers could rent to work on their vehicles and a covered picnic area where enthusiasts could gather over coffee and talk torque and restoration or whatever it was car guys talked about.

Blair had never been interested in learning more, but Nick had been intrigued by Paul's place from the second he'd heard about it. In the last year, Nick and her uncle had had several intense conversations, the upshot of which had been Paul offering to sell to Nick, while carrying the financing himself. Paul would stay on for a year, to teach Nick all he knew, then retire down in Key West, where several of his friends had bought condos in the same complex.

Nick was torn—he wanted the business, although he worried about his lack of retail experience. Complicating the situation was Julie's expectation that Nick would take over Parker Towing one day. Blair tried to stay out of it as much as she could, but she knew her husband was clear on her preference, but that she would support him, whatever he decided. She was totally on board with him buying Paul's business. Towing could be dangerous with long, unpredictable hours, and she desperately wanted him to have a more "normal" job. Unfortunately, the price of that might be breaking Julie's heart, and neither of them wanted that.

"I won't say a word," Paul promised. "But the sooner Nick tells his mom what he's considering, the easier he'll sleep at night."

"He knows. He wants to wait. Right now he's focused on dealing with losing his dad. After that, he'll come clean."

At least that was what he'd promised, although he'd said he would tell her in early November, then right after Thanksgiving, so Blair wasn't sure what was going to happen.

"You said there were two things." Paul looked at her. "What's the second one?"

Blair held in a groan. "My mom. I can't not invite her to the cabin with us."

"Ah, Christmas with Gwen. Won't that be fun."

His tone was neutral, but Blair knew her uncle well enough to understand what he was thinking.

"I'm sorry," she told him. "I don't want her along, either. If I could figure out a way to get her to spend the week back in Boise with her friends, I would do it. I would drive her there myself."

Because having her mother along would ruin everything, she thought, knowing if she spoke those words she would sound like a pouty toddler.

"She's just so difficult," she continued, unable to stop herself. "Life was easier when we never saw each other and only spoke once or twice a year, but ever since she moved here, she's everywhere. She calls, she wants to know all the details of my life. She's being intrusive. Why did she have to leave Boise? She was happy there. She should have stayed."

Her uncle gave her a sympathetic smile. "She misses your dad."

"It's been four years. We're all dealing." Blair still thought of him often, but lately without the sharp pain of loss. "She had a whole life back home."

"Now she wants one here. With you."

"I don't want her in my life." Blair consciously lowered the pitch of her voice. "It's too late. She had her chance. From the time I was four until I left when I was fifteen, she was gone. Living in the house, but absent emotionally. She was like a ghost, there but not there. All that time she could have reached out, she could have been my mother, but she didn't bother. She let Dad handle everything."

She blinked away familiar tears, telling herself her mother didn't deserve them. "When I moved in with you, she wasn't the one to call and check on me. She didn't visit. That was all Dad. So fifteen years after that, she wants to be my mom? I don't think so."

"She loves you."

Blair glared at him. "Why do you take her side? It's not as if you like having her around."

"I'll admit Gwen can be difficult, but she loved your dad with all her heart. She made him happy and that's what matters to me."

He was right. Her mother had loved her father and he'd loved her. Everyone had seen how they adored each other. In a way, their devotion had made her mother's indifference even more painful. Blair could see she was capable of love—she just chose not to love her daughter.

"She doesn't care about me," Blair said firmly. "I don't know why she's moved to Seattle and insists on torturing me, but it sure isn't because of love."

Frustration made her pace the length of the front counter. "I don't want to have to spend Christmas with her at the cabin. I don't. But I can't bring myself to say she's not invited. I'm spineless."

"No, you're a good person who won't let her mother spend Christmas alone."

"Ugh. I know I'm repeating myself, but you wait. She's going to make the whole time awful for all of us."

"Not if we don't let her."

A nice sentiment, Blair thought grimly. But one that was unlikely to be true.

"Tell me what's wrong," Heath said, his tone completely reasonable and calm.

Julie faked a smile. "How do you know there's something wrong?"

"It's been fifteen minutes of 'hi, how are you' and we're still not naked."

Julie picked at the sleeve of her sweater. "We don't always have sex that fast."

Heath studied her. "Okay, that was supposed to be a joke. There *is* something. Julie, what's going on?"

They sat at her kitchen island. Copies of cookie recipes were scattered on the quartz surface, along with a list for menu ideas. Eight people were a lot to feed and planning was required. There was the whole block cookie exchange she thought she'd gotten out of, so she would be baking cookies and probably some pies. She had to get organized. But first she had to come clean to Heath.

She looked at him, at his dark eyes and too-long, dark hair that he was forever promising to get cut. He had broad shoulders and the kind of muscles that said he didn't just own the roofing company—he was plenty capable of getting up there and doing the work himself.

"It's my kids," she said, forcing herself to meet his steady gaze. "They want to have Christmas at the cabin."

She waited but he didn't say anything, nor did his expression change.

"They lost their dad in late January, so although it's been a while, this is the first Christmas without him. Eldon loved Christmas and would come up to the cabin, even after the divorce. It's a big deal for them and I couldn't tell them no."

He smiled at her. "Why would you? They're your children and you love them."

She dismissed that comment with a wave. "I understand what they're going through, but did it have to be this? I wanted those two weeks with you. I wanted us to spend time together and not have to always be running off to deal with work or a family thing."

She'd wanted to get to know him better, to have long days

in bed and evenings talking in front of the fire. She wanted to build memories and be a normal couple.

"Now it's going to be a bunch of people, which I normally like, but not this one time. Is that so awful?"

"It's not."

She sighed. "Plus, I told them about you, and Nick and Blair are fine, but Dana was upset." She dropped her gaze to the counter. "She's ghosting me. I get it. I never said anything and that hurts her, so I have to make this right."

"Hey." He touched her chin to make her look at him. "It's okay. I'm sorry you're having to deal with so much, but we'll be fine. There will be another two weeks when we can be together. Your kids need you and time with their family. That comes first. I'll figure something out. You don't have to worry about me."

She stared at him. "What are you talking about?"

"For Christmas."

He wasn't making any sense. "But you'll be at the cabin."

His expression turned quizzical. "You still want me to come?"

"Of course. Why wouldn't I? It won't be the same because of the crowd, but…" She pressed her lips together, suddenly unsure. "Do you want to come to the cabin?" Maybe he wasn't interested in family time with her kids. Maybe he would rather be somewhere else.

His pleased smile reassured her. "I want to come with you, if you're comfortable with that."

"Heath, I wasn't just going to leave you alone for Christmas." She knew that without *his* kids, he didn't have any family in the area. "I wouldn't do that to anyone. Plus—" She ducked her head. "I'd miss you."

"I'd miss you, too. So speaking of sex, what are the sleeping arrangements going to be?"

She laughed, the last of her tension fading. She looked at him and raised her eyebrows. "Why do you ask?"

"You know why."

"We have our own room with an attached bathroom."

He took one of her hands in his and laced their fingers together. "So nights together for sure."

"Yes, nights," she murmured, her voice a little breathless at the thought. "The days will be busy. We'll have to get a tree for the family room. Dana and Nick will argue about it until I want to crack their heads together." She motioned to the recipes and lists scattered on the island. "There's baking and meals to prepare. We go skiing and ride inner tubes down the mountain. When the kids were little, we used to wait for a new snowfall, then go make snow angels, but they don't do that anymore."

He squeezed her fingers. "You have a lot of good memories of the cabin."

"I do."

"You sure you want me to come?"

She met his dark gaze, thinking he was such a good guy. If only he was maybe six or seven years older. "I want you there, Heath. We'll make it a good Christmas. Blair is bringing her mom and her uncle. Huxley will come up. It'll be a fun group." She paused. "Well, I'm not sure about Blair's mom, but we'll make it work."

"Tell me about Eldon."

The question surprised her. "What do you want to know?"

"You said Christmas was his thing."

"Yes, it was always a big deal for him. He wanted all of it—the tree, the traditional dinner, lots of presents. My dad bought the cabin when I was maybe ten. It was brand-new. The guy who built it ended up moving back East and wanted to unload it quickly, and my dad had the cash. The first time Eldon saw it, he adored it. We spent every Christmas there."

Heath watched her as she spoke. She had no idea what he was thinking, but he seemed more interested than concerned by what she was saying.

"How did you meet Eldon?" he asked.

She couldn't help laughing. "I got a call for a guy with a flat tire at the Microsoft campus in Redmond."

He grinned. "Back when you were a sexy tow truck driver?"

"You're saying I'm not sexy now?" she asked, her voice teasing.

"You are the sexiest, and I think I've proved I genuinely believe that."

"You have." She leaned in and kissed him, then continued her story. "So I take the call and there's this guy. He's cute and flustered and obviously one of the computer geeks who made Microsoft what it is today. I changed his tire and we got to talking. I could tell he liked me but didn't know how to ask me out, so I asked him."

"I like when you take charge."

"I appreciate that you're not threatened."

"I'm not."

Because Heath was comfortable in his own skin. He didn't have to worry about not being strong enough or confident enough. With Eldon, things had been different.

"We dated, we fell in love. After Eldon proposed, my dad took me aside and told me while Eldon was a great guy, he wasn't for me." She still remembered how shocked she'd been. Her dad had always supported her.

"He said we were too different and over time we would grow apart."

"You didn't listen."

"No. I thought Eldon was the one. We got married and had the kids. A few years in, I realized my dad was right—we weren't well suited. We both tried to make it work, but in the end, there was nothing to save, so we divorced."

She looked at him. "It was very quiet, very low-key. The kids weren't even surprised. That first Christmas after, I invited Eldon to the cabin and he came."

"Very civilized."

"We did okay. My only regret is we didn't divorce a few years sooner."

"I don't regret my divorce, either. I wasn't as in love with Tiffany as I thought." He shrugged. "I knew she wanted a family, and looking back, I wonder if that was part of the appeal for me. I was ready to have kids and there she was, offering to be a mom."

"But you do wish you had more time with your children."

"I do. I wanted joint custody, but that freaked out Tiffany. She says they're too young to go back and forth. We're going to talk about it in a year or so."

"You're a good dad. I look forward to meeting them."

They'd agreed to wait a bit until introducing her to them, which was fine with her. Meeting Heath's kids would take things to a level she wasn't comfortable with. Not yet.

He stood and pulled her into his arms. "How about meeting them after Christmas? We're sure to know each other a lot better then."

She smiled up at him. "You're on," she said, right before he kissed her.

4

"The greenbelt is pretty," Blair said, telling herself not to clench her teeth. She didn't want to have to start wearing a mouth guard. Unfortunately, spending any time with her mother made her insane, and then she got tense and the teeth grinding followed.

"It's a lot of trees," Gwen said, staring out the main bedroom window. "Maybe too many."

"How can there be too many trees?"

Her voice came out sharper than she intended, causing her mother to flinch, which made Blair feel like a monster. They were three hours into condo shopping, which was two hours and forty-five minutes too long. Patience, she told herself. Patience.

"Trees are a Northwest thing," she said, her tone lighter. "This is considered a premium view."

Her mother circled the large bedroom. "The rest of the condo is all right, I suppose."

"Mom, do you know what you're looking for? You said the first one we looked at was too big and the second was too small.

This one has too many trees. Maybe you should stay in your rental until you feel more settled."

"I'll know it when I see it. We need to keep looking."

Oh, could they, Blair thought sarcastically, but carefully kept her mean-spirited comment to herself. What was it about her mother that brought out the worst in her? Some of it was resentment, she thought grimly. She'd given up her Saturday afternoon to go look at open houses with her mom, and she had a thousand things she would rather be doing.

Blair glanced at her phone, where she'd stored the list of condos they would be viewing. "Okay, we have two more. We'd better hurry if we're going to get to them both before they close."

They walked back to her small SUV. Once they were in the vehicle and Blair had plugged the next address into her GPS system, she backed out of the visitor space and tried to think of something neutral to talk about.

"I think you're going to like spending the holidays at the cabin."

"Up in the mountains? I don't think so."

Blair held in a groan. "It'll be great. A real family Christmas."

"It's too many people, if you ask me. I don't know why we can't stay in Seattle and have something small at your place. Then it would just be the three of us. Four, I suppose, with Paul."

Blair glanced at her. "Mom, it can't be just the four of us. We'll be with Julie and Dana."

Her mother looked out the window without speaking, her disapproval plain.

"Nick needs to spend the holidays with his family."

"And the boyfriend."

Blair ignored the scandalized tone. "I'll admit, I'm excited to meet Heath. I've never met one of Julie's guys before. Knowing her, I'm sure he's great."

"I can't believe she dates, and at her age."

"Why shouldn't she? She's been divorced for ages. Julie deserves someone in her life."

"You *would* take her side."

Blair tightened her grip on the steering wheel. "Mom, there's no sides. Why do you care if Julie is going out with someone?"

"I don't care." Her mother sniffed. "I have no idea why we're talking about this."

"Me, either. Oh, we've figured out the dates. We're going up on the seventeenth and coming back on the twenty-seventh."

Her mother stared at her in horror. "That long? You expect me to spend the holidays with *those people* for ten days?"

Blair told herself to breathe. She just had to get through this conversation and two open houses. Then she could drop off her mother and not think about her for several days.

"I'm not sure what you mean by quote-unquote *those people*. If you mean Nick's mother and sister, then yes, I do expect you to spend the holidays with them."

She pulled into the visitor parking lot for the next condo on their list, stopped the engine and faced her mother.

"I don't understand what's happening here. Your attitude puzzles me. I'm married, Mom. Nick and I are together and we both have families. He lost his dad less than a year ago and this is the first Christmas without Eldon. He's missing him and is really sad. Dana's the same way. They want a traditional Christmas to help with the healing. I don't think it's too much to ask that we help them through this difficult time."

Her mother pressed her lips together and looked out the side window, without speaking. Blair wanted to throw something.

"Mom, I don't understand what you want. You didn't tell me you were moving to Seattle. You just showed up and announced you'd rented a place. Then you want me to help you find something to buy, but you hate everything we see. You're not happy, you won't tell me what's wrong, and now you're picking apart the holiday plans."

"Plans that don't include me."

"What are you talking about? You're coming with us."

Her mother swung to face her. "You never asked me what I wanted to do. Maybe I don't want to go to the cabin."

If only, she thought longingly. "You are very welcome to come, but if you'd rather not, then you can stay home."

"By myself," Gwen said bitterly. "You'd like that."

A horrifying thought occurred to her. "I'm not staying here with you."

"Yes, you've made that clear."

"As I just said, Nick and I are married. News flash, Mom, but this is our first Christmas as a married couple. I'm not staying in the city with you while he goes away with his family." She tried to drop the energy level. "Is that what you thought would happen? That I'd abandon Nick for Christmas?"

"He would hardly be abandoned. He has his family."

Jeez, that *was* what her mother had expected, or at least wanted. "I'm his family."

"Now. You weren't before. You barely knew his father. What do you care if he's not there at Christmas?"

Blair couldn't help wishing Julie was with them. Nick's mom always knew the right thing to say, even if her delivery was a little blunt from time to time. She would be able to handle Gwen, change out a transmission and bake up some brownies without breaking a sweat.

"I'm not leaving Nick for Christmas."

"So you've said."

"We're going to the cabin on the seventeenth. If you'd like to come later, I'll arrange to pick you up closer to Christmas."

She mentally crossed her fingers, hoping her mother would say she wasn't coming at all. Only if that happened, she would feel guilty and end up begging the other woman to join them. Honest to God, when it came to Gwen, there was never a win.

"I wouldn't want to put you out," her mother said with a

sigh. "I'll do whatever you tell me to. What I want doesn't really matter."

"Do you have to be the martyr?"

"I don't know what you're talking about."

Blair unclenched her teeth. "Do you want to go see this condo or are we done for the day?"

"I think we're done."

"Fine by me."

As she drove her mother back to her rental, Blair once again asked the Universe why oh why couldn't her mother have stayed in Boise. Why did she have to move here and ruin everything?

"You lied to me."

The flat statement had Julie wincing. "Really? A lie? That seems harsh and a little dramatic."

Her daughter stared at her, unblinking. "Mom, you lied. You've been seeing someone for over three months. It's serious enough that you want to spend Christmas with him, and you never told me."

Tears filled Dana's eyes. "I never thought you'd do that. What other secrets are you keeping?"

"None! I swear."

Julie glanced at the sandwich she'd ordered—it was her favorite. Ham and cheese with tomato, lettuce and avocado from the great deli just down the street from the tow yard. She always ate too much and rued the calories, so she rarely indulged. She'd been so looking forward to having one today while she and Dana hashed out what had happened. But suddenly she didn't feel like eating.

She pushed away her plate. "Dana, please don't make this more than it is. You're right—I didn't tell you about Heath and I should have. It just kind of crept up on me."

Her daughter didn't look convinced as she picked at her salad. "What crept up on you? You didn't notice you were dating?"

"Not exactly." She hadn't noticed he was flirting with her. Okay, she'd noticed, but had thought she was misreading the signals. "I should have said something. You're right to be upset with me about that, but seriously, Dana. Ghosting me?"

Her daughter shifted in her seat. "I wasn't."

"What would you call ignoring my texts and calls?"

"I was busy."

Julie stared at her daughter without speaking. Dana shifted again.

"Fine," she said with a sigh. "I was ghosting you, but you really hurt my feelings."

"I know and I feel awful about that. I'm sorry. I should have told you about Heath. I just didn't know how."

"What does that even mean?" Dana's eyes widened. "Mom, is there something about him I should know?"

Now it was Julie's turn to be uncomfortable. "No, of course not. He's very nice, perfectly respectable. He owns a roofing company. That's how we met. The guy who does estimates called out sick, so Heath was taking his appointments. He came to the house and looked things over."

"Are we still talking about the roof?"

Julie felt herself flush. "Yes, the roof. He gave me an estimate and we started talking."

"And he asked you out?"

"No, that was later," Julie hedged. "He came by the tow yard a few times to give me updates. That's where he asked me out."

She'd been shocked and hadn't known what to say. A first for her when it came to men.

Dana's expression turned quizzical. "You're not making any sense. What aren't you telling me?" The color drained from her face. "Oh, no! He's married!"

She practically shrieked the words, causing other patrons to turn and look at them. Julie did her best not to shrink in her seat.

"What? No! Don't say that. He's not married."

"Then what?"

Julie ducked her head. "He's younger."

"That's it?" Dana almost sounded disappointed. "He's younger? That's the big secret?"

Julie looked at her. "Twelve years younger."

"He's forty-two?"

Julie briefly closed her eyes. "Yes."

"You go, Mom."

She stared at her daughter. "You don't care?"

"I'm impressed. You've always been so in control when it comes to guys. You tell them exactly what you expect, and if they're not interested or willing, you dump them. You never get your heart broken. You have fun and move on. Dating a younger guy is just an extension of that. Why did you think I'd be upset?"

"I didn't, exactly. I just feel a little weird about the age difference."

"Mom, you don't look your age at all."

"Thank you, but sometimes I feel it. Heath's kids are so young. Ten and eight. I haven't met them yet, and believe me, I'm willing to wait on that for a long time. I'm afraid people will think they're my grandkids, which makes Heath what? My son?" She shuddered. "His age complicates things."

"Only in your mind."

"I wish that were true." Julie leaned toward her. "I'm sorry I didn't say anything. When Heath first asked me out, I figured nothing was going to happen, so I didn't bother mentioning him. Then we kept going out and it became a thing and I didn't know what to say. I was wrong. I should have told you."

"It's okay." Dana looked at her. "I get it. You were embarrassed, but you shouldn't have been. I wouldn't judge you."

Julie smiled at that, thinking they all judged each other. Maybe not harshly, but it happened. She judged Dana for being such a pushover when it came to Axel. The man broke her heart on a regular basis. At some point, Dana was going to have to learn to say no and mean it.

"So he's nice?" Dana asked.

"He is. I think you and Nick will like him. He works hard, loves his kids. He's busy, like me, so we don't get a lot of time together. He has his kids every other weekend. This year it's his ex's turn to have them for the holidays." Her tone turned wistful. "He's getting his house painted and floors refinished, so he was going to move in for a couple of weeks." They were going to have all that glorious time together—just the two of them.

Dana groaned. "Then Nick and I messed up your plans."

"We'll still be together, just up at the cabin." Which wasn't the same, but she didn't want Dana feeling bad. "It'll be a big family Christmas and that'll be great."

"It's just we need this," Dana said. "Nick and I."

"You do. Don't worry about me." She picked up her sandwich. "Enough about my personal life. What's going on with you? Anything interesting?"

Dana sighed. "Mom, I'm the actual definition of *not interesting*. You should know that by now."

Julie figured she'd worked things out with half her children, now it was time to conquer the other half. She waited while Huxley checked out the men's room at the tow yard. When he walked out, his expression amused, and said, "All clear. Nick's the only one in there," she thanked him, went into the five-stall bathroom and locked the door behind her.

"Hello, Nick," she said calmly.

Her son, in one of the stalls, no doubt reading something about sports on his phone while he did his business, yelped. "Dammit, Mom. I'm in the bathroom."

"I'm clear on that."

"Doing bathroom things."

She held in a smile. "I assumed that. I doubted you were masturbating or shooting up drugs."

He groaned. "Can I please get some privacy?"

"No, you can't. I've sent you three emails to schedule a conversation and you haven't answered me." She paused. "Both my children ghosting me in the same week. I've failed as a parent."

"No one is ghosting you. I talk to you every day. It's only the emails I'm not dealing with."

"We're dealing with them now."

She folded her arms over her chest, prepared to wait him out. It only took a few seconds for Nick to sigh in defeat.

"Fine. I'll talk to you as soon as I'm done here."

"You promise?"

"Yes."

"On Blair's beating heart?"

Another sigh. "Yes."

"I'll be in my office."

Seven minutes later he made good on his word and took a seat across from hers. His slumped shoulders told her he wasn't looking forward to what she was going to say.

"Why won't you commit to the business?" she asked bluntly. "We've talked about this all your life. You were going to start out as a driver, then slowly take over. You've been working here for ten years. It's time to start learning how to run things, but every time I try to talk to you about it, you slink away."

"I don't slink," he said, avoiding her gaze. "I move quickly in the opposite direction."

"I don't understand. This was always our dream. What we were going to do together. You and me running Parker Towing. Don't you want that anymore?"

He looked at her, then away. "Mom, it's not an easy thing to decide. I've never done anything but this. Maybe I'd like a different job."

She did her best not to shriek. "This isn't a job," she said as calmly as she could. "It's an inheritance, Nick."

She looked at him, not sure what he was trying to tell her. He was a great guy with a big heart, but he'd never been ambitious. Not like her. She'd wanted to know everything about the company from the time she was five. She found it all fascinating.

"I know it's a great opportunity," he said. "You've done well, and I get after all this time, you want to start sharing the load."

Which sounded right, but she couldn't help thinking there was something he wasn't telling her.

"What does Blair want?" she asked.

"We're still talking about things." He sat up and faced her. "Mom, it's nearly Christmas and I'm thinking about Dad a lot and Blair's dealing with her mom. Can we table this conversation until after the first of the year? I promise I'll be straight with you and we can figure out a plan."

She would rather they talked now, but understood she couldn't push him. Not on this. "All right. We'll talk the first week in January. But it has to be then. No more avoiding me."

"Deal."

Julie looked up from her computer, surprised to see Heath walking into her office. Sometimes, if he was in the area, he dropped by, but he usually texted first. Even more concerning was the look on his face—two parts guilt, one part apprehension.

"What?" she said by way of greeting. "Something's wrong or something happened." She stood and circled the desk. "Just blurt it out."

She told herself she could handle whatever it was. She was tough, she'd been through some things in her life. When there was a crisis, she got calm and took charge. Any freak-out happened later, when the problem was solved.

He hesitated.

She poked him in the chest. "Talk. I mean it."

"Tiffany's boyfriend invited her to the Bahamas for Christmas and she wants to go."

Julie was good at not assuming the worst. She'd refused to consider that Heath had decided to break up with her or that someone she cared about was in the hospital. But she sure hadn't been expecting an update about his ex-wife's travel plans.

"Why would that be a problem?" she asked, even as the answer became painfully obvious.

"No, I get it." She took a step back. "She wants to go away, so asked if you'd take the kids and Rufus." She nodded slowly. "You want to spend the holidays with them, so you're all in."

He studied her as she spoke. "It's a complication."

And two more bodies, she thought, not to mention a dog, although he would be easy. She loved dogs and had always had one. But when Brownie had passed away a few years ago, she hadn't had the heart to start over with a puppy again.

"We'll get a couple of hotel rooms," he said. "The Residence Inn is pet friendly. I'm going to call them and see if they have any availability."

"What are you talking about?"

"Me and my kids." He moved closer and rested his hands on her shoulders. "Julie, come on. It was enough of a stretch when it was just me, but now it's two kids and a shedding dog. I want to spend the time with you, but it's my kids at Christmas. I need you to get that. This isn't about you or us."

She stared into his dark eyes. He was telling the truth about all of it, she thought. And as a mom, she totally got the whole kids-holiday connection.

"You're not going to a hotel," she told him. "What kind of Christmas would that be? You'll bring the kids up to the cabin. Rufus, too."

The place was made for kids, she thought, swallowing hard at the thought of explaining Heath's kids to her own. Plus judgy Gwen.

His gaze turned warm. "You're a hell of a woman."

"So I've been told."

"We're not coming to the cabin."

"Why not?"

"It's too much. You haven't met my kids, and there's not enough room. But I like that you offered."

She put her hands on her hips. "Listen very carefully, because I'm about two seconds from getting annoyed with you, and let us all remember the last time you tried to tell me what was best for me."

His lips twitched as if he were trying not to smile. "It didn't go well."

"It didn't go well," she repeated sternly. "You are *not* spending Christmas in a hotel. The cabin is plenty big. There's a room downstairs with double bunk beds. The kids can each have a top bunk and Rufus can sleep on one of the bottom ones. There's plenty to do, both inside and out. Maybe being around them will show Nick and Blair how great it is to have children, because I'm ready for Blair to be pregnant."

"They've only been married six months."

"I know, but tick, tick, tick. Anyway, everyone will have a good time. As for me not having met them, well, we need to make that happen." She sucked up any concern and plowed ahead. "I should meet Tiffany, as well. So let's set that up. When's the last day of school?"

"The seventeenth."

"So next week. That's a Tuesday, right?"

He nodded.

"You and I will still go up the weekend before and start decorating. You'll head home Monday morning and come back with the kids Wednesday morning. We'll all stay until the twenty-seventh. I'll make a list of what they should bring."

She had more to say but Heath pulled her close and held her so tight, she could barely breathe.

"You're incredible," he murmured. "You don't have to do this."

"I know, but I want to." She was a little apprehensive, but she would just keep moving forward and eventually everything would be fine.

He stepped back and looked at her. "You sure? It's a lot of people."

"I can handle a crowd." She would pull together menus and a shopping list. "Okay, head count. You, me, Dana, Nick, Blair, Paul and Gwen. Plus Madeline and Wyatt, and Huxley for Christmas. That's ten."

"And Rufus."

"Yes, Rufus. Thankfully, he doesn't need a seat at the table."

Heath repeated the head count. "You sure there's room? For all of us?"

"Yes. There's four bedrooms on the second floor and two downstairs. In a pinch the living room and family room on the main floor have very comfortable sofas."

He stared at her. "Your cabin has six bedrooms?"

She walked to her desk and picked up her phone to check her calendar. "Uh-huh. You need to get in touch with Tiffany and get our little meet and greet scheduled. We leave for the cabin in four days, so there isn't much time."

"Six bedrooms?"

She looked up at him. "Why does that surprise you?"

"How big is this cabin?"

"Big, but that's not the point. The kids are going to need winter coats, boots, gloves and hats. Do they snowboard or ski?"

"No. Madeline can ice-skate a little."

"Maybe Nick can teach them." She put down her phone. "I haven't looked at the weather. There had better be snow. We need a white Christmas."

He stared at her. "Just like that? I tell you I have my kids and you start making menus?"

"I haven't started making menus yet, but I will. We need to bring up as much food as we can. The local shopping is good but not great."

He pulled her close and kissed her. "Thank you."

"Of course." She was nervous about meeting them, not to mention Tiffany, but knew she would muscle through. "It's your kids at Christmas. We're going to have a great time."

"We're getting further and further from the low-key, intimate vacation we had planned."

"Yes, we are, but maybe this is better. We'll be making memories."

"I want to make memories with you."

He kissed her again, lingering this time. Her hormones, usually quiet, but always on alert around him, started to stir. She pulled back and pushed him toward the door.

"I'm running a business here, mister. None of that sexy stuff during work hours." Her voice softened. "We'll work on the details tonight."

He grinned. "I like working on your details."

She laughed. "You know what I meant."

"And you know what I meant."

She did. The man was the best kind of trouble. She would think about that and not the horror of sitting across from what she assumed was his younger wife and his still-young children. As long as no one said the *g*—as in *grandmother*—word, she would be fine.

5

Dana limped into her condo from the garage. She was sore, she was hungry and she was crabby. Not a great combination. Most people waited until after the first of the year to begin their "new me" program, but she'd wanted to get a head start. She was doing a beginner yoga class at the Y two nights a week and had promised herself to only eat low carb until she left for the cabin. She still hadn't fit any kind of aerobic exercise into her routine. She wasn't one to get up at five to go walk on the treadmill for an hour. Instead, she'd been strolling around her office building at lunch, which was, unfortunately, making her coworkers nervous.

Still, progress was being made, she thought virtuously. This was day six without wine, so yay her. Tonight, after she changed into her jammies, she would enjoy a delicious dinner of stir-fry shrimp with vegetables, served over seasoned cauliflower rice.

Okay, maybe not delicious, she amended as she dropped her bag on the table by the garage door and started flipping on lights. But healthy and that was good. She was leaving for the cabin in less than a week, when all bets were off, food-wise, but if she could lose a couple of pounds between now and then, that would be great.

She hung up her work clothes, then pulled a long sweatshirt over her yoga pants and tank top. She was starving but didn't think there was enough shrimp and vegetables in the world to satisfy her. What she really wanted was good Chinese food—like that place by her condo that delivered. Their Honey Crispy Shrimp, maybe some Kung Pao Chicken and a carton filled with fried rice. Oh, and ribs. She wanted those spicy ribs with the sauce that dripped down her chin. She wasn't usually a beer drinker, but with Chinese, yes please.

Her stomach growled and her mouth watered.

"Not tonight," she told herself firmly. She was sticking to her diet until the seventeenth. Low carb and healthy. That was her. She walked back to the kitchen just as someone rang her bell.

A quick glance at the wall clock told her it was nearly seven thirty. She wasn't expecting anyone to drop by, unless one of her neighbors was bringing a package that had been delivered to the wrong address. This time of year, that happened a lot.

She opened the door, prepared to smile at someone she recognized but couldn't name, only to see Axel standing on her front porch.

"Hello, Dana."

He had one of those low, sexy voices that always sounded like he should have made a career on radio as a DJ. Despite the fact that it was forty-two and raining, he wore only a black leather jacket over jeans and a T-shirt. Axel had never believed in wearing a winter coat or something to repel the rain. He wasn't a rule follower, in or out of bed, and when the man smiled at her, she melted.

Fortunately, his expression was serious, which allowed her to stay in control and add a little indignation to her tone as she asked, her voice laced with acid, "What are you doing here?"

"I want to see you. I miss you."

He missed her? He *missed* her?

"You don't get to miss me," she said, careful to keep the volume down. Her neighbor's front door wasn't all that far from hers. "You don't get to have anything to do with me. No. Just no. You are not waltzing back into my life for a few weeks, telling me this time is different and that you get how important I am. I'm done with you, Axel. Done. You're bad for me, and I'm not willing to play your game anymore. You always stay just long enough to get me to believe in you. Then you walk away, taking my heart with you."

She glared at him. "Not again. Do you hear me? No more."

His dark eyes were unreadable and nothing about his posture changed. For all she knew, he wasn't even listening—except she knew he was. She knew he was hearing every word. The question was, this time would he listen? Or maybe the real issue was, did she want him to? Because even as she got all high-and-mighty in her righteous anger, she wanted him to do what he'd always done, which was ignore her. She wanted him to pull her close and kiss her in that way of his—like he couldn't get enough of her and them. He'd always kissed like he meant it.

Axel pulling her close was always the best part of her day, and every fiber of her being wanted him to touch her in that way of his. When she was with him, she was fully alive. Loving him was one thing she did incredibly well.

But he didn't make a move toward her. Instead, he nodded slowly. "You're right. That's what I do, but not for the reason you think."

"You still walk away," she told him. "I don't know why. Sometimes I think it's because of how your dad turned his back on you and your mom, but at this point, the reason why doesn't matter."

She felt herself weaken. Longing grew until she wanted to say the pain that would follow didn't matter. Just a couple of nights with him. He was like the pre-diet binge. *Tomorrow I'll be good.*

Just let me have this today. Only Axel wasn't just an extra bag of chips. While he was with her, she felt as if she could conquer the world. But when he left, she was shattered. She honestly didn't know how many more times she could put the pieces of her heart back together.

She wanted what other people took for granted—a life partner, kids, a cute little house with a yard. Maybe a couple of cats. But she couldn't have that while she was still missing Axel.

Gathering the little strength she had left, she forced herself to speak the truth.

"I can't do this anymore. If you ever loved me, like you claimed, leave me be. Please."

Something flashed in his eyes. She wanted to say it was pain, but that was probably wishful thinking on her part.

"I won't bother you again," he told her. "Merry Christmas, Dana."

He turned and walked away. She watched him go, holding on to the doorframe to keep from following him. She knew if she asked, he would turn back to her, that he would follow her inside and make all her dreams come true. At least for a night or two, or maybe even through the holidays. But eventually, he would leave, because that was what Axel did best.

She shut her door and locked it, then brushed away tears. No, she told herself. No crying. He wasn't worth it. Of that she was sure. Only the tears kept coming and the emptiness inside of her had nothing to do with the fact that she hadn't had dinner. It was instead the place in her heart that only Axel could fill.

Julie had always been an extrovert. Back in school, she'd been the one to welcome the new kid to class and sit with them at lunch. She gave people the benefit of the doubt, liked having a crowd around and easily took control of almost any situation. When her kids had been growing up, theirs had been the house where all the friends hung out. She was the fun mom and rarely worried about not fitting in. Which made her flash of nerves both unexpected and uncomfortable.

Telling herself it was nothing, that she would be fine, didn't seem to be helping.

"You're fidgeting," Heath said from the driver's seat. "There's no reason to worry. You'll like Tiffany."

She didn't like that he could read her that easily. "I'm not worried."

He smiled without looking at her. "If you say so."

It was just… "She's younger than you, right?"

"Yes."

Yes? He didn't want to elaborate? "Like by how much?"

"You'll be fine," he told her. "Tiffany's a nonissue, and the kids are going to love you."

Right, the children. They were the main reason she and Heath were heading over to his ex's house.

"You told them about spending Christmas up at the cabin. Were they excited?"

Heath glanced at her. "They're a little concerned about being in a strange place and not knowing anyone."

"That makes sense. Plus, they don't know me. You want to make sure they each bring something from home, like a stuffed animal or a special blanket."

She had more to say on the subject but just then Heath turned into the driveway of a traditional two-story house. The neighborhood was relatively new in a planned community. The houses were all variations on a theme—probably around twenty-eight hundred square feet with a fenced-in backyard.

She opened her door and stepped out into the light, misty rain. Heath joined her and took her hand.

"You'll do fine."

"They're going to think I'm your mother."

He laughed at that. "Sorry, not even close."

The front door opened before he got there and an eight-year-old boy raced toward them, a large, long-haired dog at his heels.

"Dad! Dad!"

Heath crouched and grabbed his son, then swung him in the air. "Hey, Wyatt."

Julie had a brief impression of reddish-brown hair and big eyes. A slightly older girl stood in the doorway, glancing between her and Heath.

He rested Wyatt on one hip before hugging his daughter and petting the dog. Then he smiled at Julie.

"These are my kids. Madeline, Wyatt, this is my girlfriend, Julie."

Girlfriend? He'd never actually called her that before, and she'd only ever said the *b* word in her head, never aloud. They weren't in high school.

"And this is Rufus."

"Hi," she said cheerfully, telling herself to deal with the problem at hand. There would be plenty of time to freak later if she felt the need. "I'm happy to finally meet you."

She offered Rufus her hand to sniff. He gave her a quick once-over, then offered a lick of greeting.

Madeline, pretty and slight, studied her. "You're dating my dad."

"I am."

"I didn't know."

"Because you didn't need to." Heath ushered everyone into the house. "Madeline likes to get in people's business."

Julie grinned at her. "I can respect that."

Wyatt ran to the stairs. "Mom!" he shouted. "They're here."

The house was messy but welcoming, done in warm colors. Backpacks sat open on the entry table, and there were dinner dishes on the island. Julie fought against an instinctive need to start straightening.

"I'm coming," a woman called as she started down the stairs. She stepped into the entryway.

Julie told herself not to react, but it was difficult not to gawk at the attractive redhead smiling at her.

Tiffany was young—really young. Like Dana young. Julie told herself not to do the math in her head, but it was hard not to think that Heath's ex-wife was about twenty years younger than she was. Her skin had that *I'm barely thirty* glow. She was fit, with giant boobs and a perky smile.

"Finally," she said, holding out her hand. "I'm Tiffany."

"Julie."

She pulled her kids close and hugged them. "You sure about taking on these two for the holidays? They can be a handful."

"Mom!" Madeline stepped away. "We're not a handful."

Everyone went into the family room and found seats on the large sectional. Heath stayed close, which Julie appreciated. Rufus settled on his dog bed and started chewing on a toy.

"The kids will be fine," Heath told his ex-wife. "Julie says the cabin has a lot for them to do."

"It does." Julie smiled at the children. "We have fun traditions, including going into the forest and picking out a giant tree."

"Are there bears?" Madeline asked, looking more apprehensive than intrigued.

"They hibernate in the winter."

"What if we get snowed in?" Wyatt grinned at the prospect. "We could starve to death."

"Unlikely. I keep a plow attachment in the garage. It hooks up to my SUV, so I can take care of any snow we get."

Wyatt's eyes widened. "You drive a snowplow?"

"Yes."

"Can I do that?"

She laughed. "No, but you can come with me."

"He'd love that." Tiffany looked at Julie. "Heath said you have a couple of kids of your own."

Julie did her best not to flinch. "They're a little older." A lot older. She smiled brightly. "You're going to the Bahamas. That will be fun."

"I'm really excited. Ryan got us a room on the beach."

Ryan?

"The boyfriend," Heath explained.

Madeline and Wyatt exchanged an uneasy glance. Julie guessed they weren't thrilled about the change in plans.

"Do you like decorating Christmas trees?" she asked them.

Wyatt nodded vigorously. "We do."

"Good, because we have to decorate that giant tree I mentioned. We also bake cookies and have s'mores. I checked the weather and there's plenty of snow on the mountain, so we can go sledding or ride inner tubes. There's a bedroom with two sets of bunk beds, so you can each be on top and Rufus can sleep on a bottom bunk."

"I've never slept in a bunk bed," Madeline admitted. "That could be fun." She looked at Heath. "You'll be there the whole time?"

"Yes, with you and Wyatt and Rufus."

The kids exchanged another look.

"I guess it will be okay," Madeline conceded, not sounding too enthused.

"I know staying at the cabin isn't what you expected, but I think you'll have a good time," Julie told them.

"You're going up on the seventeenth?" Tiffany asked.

"Julie and I are going the weekend before to start decorating, but I'll come back and get the kids."

"That's perfect. Ryan and I leave two days later." Tiffany beamed at everyone. "So it's settled."

They all talked for a few more minutes. Then Heath and Julie left. When they were back in his SUV, she waited until they were on the road to say, "The kids are a little nervous about the holidays."

"They don't know anyone. They'll get comfortable quickly."

Julie hoped that was true. "I wish we had kids their age in the area, but all the neighbors are my age or older, so their children are grown and any grandkids are babies."

"You worry too much. Everyone is going to help them fit in and have fun, so they'll spend the holiday being spoiled."

She smiled. "That's probably true." She paused. "Tiffany seems nice."

"She's enthused about her trip."

"I got that. So she's what? Thirty? Thirty-one?"

"Thirty-two." He glanced at her. "You're obsessed with age."

"Not usually." Thirty-two? So younger than Nick but older than Dana? Ugh. "She must have been what? Twenty when you got married."

"Just about." He glanced at her before turning his attention back to the road. "She wasn't ready to be married. She wanted to be a mom, but the whole husband-wife thing was too much for her. She was never happy."

"She's ten years younger, I'm older than you. What do you have against women your own age?"

"Obsessed," he said lightly.

"You're not answering the question."

"I like who I like." He shrugged. "I love my kids, but marrying Tiffany was a mistake. I was coming off a bad breakup and wondering if I would ever have the family I wanted. I met her and she was so enthused about being a mom and falling in love. She was an easy choice but not the right one for me."

"Still, you have Madeline and Wyatt."

"I'm grateful for them every day." He stopped at a red light and turned to her. "You okay with all this? The kids and I can still go to a hotel."

"Not happening. We're all going to the cabin and we'll have a great time. Even Rufus."

She meant that. She didn't have a problem with Heath's children coming along. It was more the visual proof of the fact that they were at different stages of their lives. She wanted that not to matter, but she knew in her gut that it did.

"You're the most annoying person on the planet," Huxley said, his eyes narrowed. "You do this every year. How long have I worked for you?"

"You were here before I took over the business."

"You're right. I was, which means I probably know how to do my job." His tone was pointed. "This is not the first time you'll be gone for a few days and it's not the last. The company has yet to fall apart without you here to guide it, so stop micromanaging me or I swear, I'm going to quit."

She grinned. "You threaten that a lot."

"Only when I'm dealing with you."

Nick walked into the office. "Hey."

"Hey, yourself," Julie called.

"Run," Huxley told him. "Run now. Save yourself."

Nick laughed. "Mom, stop torturing Huxley. He's a good guy." He walked to the old-fashioned time clock and picked up his card. After punching out, he moved next to her.

"Blair wants to know what we should bring to the cabin. I've told her you don't trust anyone enough to give them a list, but she's determined to contribute."

"I'll keep her plenty busy when you get there," Julie told him. "We'll have baking and decorating. Plus the cookies for the exchange. Although her main job will be to keep you and Dana from fighting."

"We don't fight."

"You argue like two old hens."

"Hens argue?"

Huxley pointed to his computer. "Unlike you people, I still have work to do. Leave me be."

They walked into her office. Julie closed the door and faced her son.

"There are a few things she can bring for me," she said. "I'll email her a list tonight."

"That will make her happy. Thanks."

He was about to leave, but she called him back.

"Nick, I've given you plenty of time to think about your future. I need you to make a decision about coming on board with me."

He looked at her. "I promised we'd talk after the first and I meant it."

She wanted to believe him, she thought. She mostly did.

"Then that's what we'll do, but I have to tell you, I don't understand you. This is what you've always wanted. Are you changing your mind?"

"No, of course not." He looked away. "What I meant is… Sometimes I think about…" He shook his head. "No. We're doing this after the holidays. Not before."

She didn't like the sound of that. "What aren't you telling me?"

"Nothing," he said, without meeting her gaze. "It's all good."

Was it? She couldn't tell. Her guess was he was keeping something from her—she just didn't know what. But he was right—they shouldn't get into it now.

"You should go home to Blair," she said. "We'll talk after the first."

"For sure." He made a beeline for the door. "Have a good night."

She was about to say she would when Axel stepped into the office. Her smile instantly faded.

He handed her a folder. "Three new ones."

"It's been a busy month."

"People have other things to spend their money on."

She scanned the repo list and handed it back to him. "What are you doing for the holidays?"

"I'll be working."

"If you weren't such an asshole, you could be with my daughter and the rest of us up at the cabin."

She spoke impulsively, then had to deal with the fact that she'd just crossed the line, but before she could apologize, he spoke.

"You're right. It's all on me."

"I don't want to be right. I want—" Her wants didn't matter, she reminded herself. And this wasn't her business. Still, Dana was her daughter.

"I hate that you hurt her, and don't you say 'me, too.' You're the one doing it."

"I am. Like you said, I'm an asshole." He waved the folder. "I'll get on these."

With that, he left. Julie watched him go and, once again, when he was out of earshot, murmured, "Don't get dead."

6

Heath stared at the house, his mouth hanging open. "You said it was a cabin."

"It is."

"That is not a cabin. How big is it?"

Julie walked to the back of her SUV and popped it open. "I'm not sure. Six thousand square feet maybe."

"That's no one's definition of a cabin."

Julie looked at the house, trying to see it as Heath would. It *was* big—two stories on this side, three from the back, where it sloped down the hill. The four-car garage was around the side, and a big wraparound porch circled the place. Tall trees separated the large lot from her neighbors. About two feet of snow covered the ground.

"So it's a large cabin," she said with a grin. "Isn't that better than a small one?"

"Size matters."

They gathered as much as they could carry and started for the front door. Both his truck and her SUV were jam-packed with suitcases, presents and food. Lots of food. Starting the seventeenth, there would be nine people to feed, ten when Huxley arrived. Three meals a day plus Christmas Eve and Christmas Day. She'd worked out tentative menus and planned as much as she could. There was a local grocery store for the fresh stuff and they'd probably eat out a few lunches, but still, supplies were needed.

They went inside. Julie led the way to the large open kitchen, calling out rooms as she went.

"Formal living room on your left. We don't use that much. Dining room. The table pulls out long enough to seat sixteen. Butler's pantry. The family room is past the kitchen. There's a big alcove we use for board games and puzzles, a bathroom, and a craft room beyond that."

They unloaded both cars, stacking suitcases by the stairs leading to the second floor. Julie had him store the bags of presents in the closet off the game alcove.

They put away the groceries first. Julie showed him the pantry, empty except for a few staples. She filled the refrigerator and freezer, keeping the twenty-pound turkey and fifteen-pound ham off to the side.

She unrolled the large paper calendar she'd brought and hung it on the wall in the kitchen. She'd already marked out the various dates.

"Today is Saturday," she said.

"I knew that."

She smiled at him. "I have a point here."

"I'm listening."

She touched the calendar. "You drive back on Monday to get the kids. You'll come back here Wednesday morning. Dana, Nick, Blair, Gwen and Paul arrive Tuesday afternoon. I'll have my kids and Blair help me with whatever decorating isn't finished. Once you and your kids get here, we'll go buy a big fresh tree for the family room. It sits in the garage overnight and we'll decorate Thursday."

"Why does it sit in the garage?"

She looked at him. "Because we'll be cutting it down from the forest and things will be in it. Better to let them crawl out in the garage than in the family room."

He grinned. "Good point."

"I'll start baking Thursday. We'll figure out what everyone wants to do once they're here. Oh, we go to evening services on Christmas Eve. I hope that's good with you."

"We wouldn't miss them."

She looked at him. "This is going to be okay, right?"

"It's going to be perfect. We're together, Julie. Everything else will take care of itself."

His words gave her a little flutter in her belly.

"Grab the turkey," she said, taking the ham and leading the way downstairs.

There was an extra freezer in the garage. They stored the meat there, and then she showed him the second family room with a large wood-burning stove and a giant TV.

"If there's an argument about what to watch, the group splits up," she told him. "But mostly we end up watching the same thing upstairs." She pointed to the hallway. "The kids will be in here."

The big open room had a large window with a view down the mountain. Two sets of bunk beds were pushed up against the walls. A mural of the forest, complete with cartoon animals and smiling sun, covered one wall. A long dresser had plenty of storage, and there was an attached bathroom with two sinks and a tub/shower combo.

"The cleaners came through last week," Julie said, peeling back one of the comforters. "They put fresh linens on all the beds." She pulled open one of the dresser drawers and removed a walkie-talkie. "Short range, so it only works in the house, but they should help the kids feel connected to you. The other one is upstairs in the master."

Heath looked stunned. "You thought of everything."

She smiled. "The house has evolved over time. After my dad bought the place, he started renting it out when we weren't using it and he paid attention to guest feedback."

She led the way to the second bedroom on that floor. It was L-shaped with two queen-size beds and an attached three-quarter bath.

"I figured Paul would stay down here. Huxley will join him when he arrives."

"That works."

"And now for the part that will really get your heart pounding. Once we clear this out, we can store the Christmas presents inside. Away from prying eyes."

She pulled a key out of her jeans pocket and unlocked a closet door. After opening it, she turned on the light and stepped back so he could see inside.

"The Christmas decorations."

Heath glanced in the closet. "How much is— Holy crap." He disappeared inside.

She followed, walking between built-in shelves stacked with labeled bins. The storage area went back about twenty feet before making a turn to the right. There were five or six artificial trees, dozens of wreaths, strings of lights, miles of garland, two separate Christmas villages and enough faux candles to light Milwaukee.

Heath reached the end and turned to face her. "These are all Christmas decorations?"

"Yes."

"And you expect us to get them all in place in two days?"

"That's not going to happen, but we'll do the best we can."

"You said something about decorating, but I thought you meant a fake tree and some holiday towels."

She laughed. "Now you know why I was so pleased about a quiet Christmas at my place." She looked around at all the bins.

"Although now that we're here, I'll admit I'm kind of excited to spend the holidays here. We'll have a good time."

He moved toward her and put his hands on her hips. "You're always a good time."

"So are you."

He kissed her with a thoroughness that left her breathless. When he finally drew back, she found it a little difficult to speak.

"So, um, let me show you the rest of the house. We'll unpack, then start decorating."

He raised one eyebrow. "Is that really what you want to do?"

She pretended to consider the question. "Maybe it would be better to make love, unpack, *then* start decorating."

"I agree."

They walked to the stairs.

"Do me a favor," she said. "Stay here until I reach the second floor. I'll call down when I'm there. I want you to talk to me in a normal voice."

He frowned. "I don't get it."

She grinned. "Oh, you will."

She took the stairs to the main floor, grabbed a couple of suitcases and made her way to the second floor. After setting down the suitcases, she leaned over the railing.

"I'm here. Say something."

She spoke in a quiet tone, knowing her voice would carry.

"There's no way you're going to be able to hear me."

"I can hear everything."

There was a moment of silence when she figured he was staring up at her, not sure how that was possible.

"Tiffany got implants."

Julie felt her eyes widen. "They're implants? Really? I thought they were just hers. I had no idea. So do they feel different? They must. Why didn't you tell me this before?"

Heath appeared at the base of the stairs. He picked up the remaining suitcases and carried them up to the second floor.

"I'm not discussing my ex-wife's breasts with you."

"You started it." She grinned. "Implants, huh?"

"Yes. What's with the sound carrying down two floors?"

"I have no idea. I assume it's just a quirk of the house, but consider yourself warned. If you're not in a room that has a closed door, assume everyone can hear everything. There's zero privacy in the house."

As they walked toward the master, Julie pointed out the other bedrooms.

"Hall bath," she said, nodding toward an open door. "There are two bedrooms across from it for Dana and Gwen."

"Gwen's Blair's mother?"

"That's her."

At the next bedroom, she paused. "Nick and Blair. There's an en suite bathroom. And this is us."

Double doors stood open at the end of the hallway. To the left was a sitting area with a gas fireplace. To the right was the king-size bed. Two of the walls were windows with views of the mountains, the trees and the fresh snow.

"There's a private balcony," she said, putting down her suitcases and pointing to the French doors. "It's a little cold this time of year, but nice to use in the summer."

She walked over to the doors and pulled back the draperies. The familiar view awaited, as always, making her smile.

She hadn't been at the cabin since late summer—just before the leaves had started to turn. Back then the view had been all green with the grass and leaves on the trees. Now only the trees with needles had any color—dark green against the white snow and gray sky. The sloping lawn was covered with snow, as were the roofs of the neighbors they could see on one side.

Heath came up behind her and wrapped his arms around her waist, pulling her close. "Beautiful," he murmured.

"It is. This is a good house with happy memories."

She led the way into the bathroom. A huge claw-foot tub

sat in the center of the room. There were double sinks and a shower for two, along with a separate toilet room and a huge walk-in closet.

Heath grinned at her. "Cabin, huh? We need to define our terms better."

"It's what we've always called it." She stepped into his embrace. "I want this to be a happy Christmas for you and your kids."

"Me, too."

She had more to say—things like how *her* kids would revert back to bickering with each other and how she was nervous about having Gwen around—but Heath started kissing her and she decided all that could wait.

Blair kept a hand pressed against her lower belly, silently repeating calming phrases to herself in an attempt to ease the pain and pressure. They were only a few minutes from the cabin, and she had to hang on until then. They'd already had to stop twice so she could race into a bathroom and have massive diarrhea. Honestly, she didn't know how there was anything left in her intestines to poop out, but the signals from her body told her otherwise.

"I'm freezing back here," her mother said sharply. "Is it really necessary to have the window open?"

"Sorry," Blair said, not sure what would happen without the cooling air blowing on her face. Still, her mother had a point. It was twenty-five degrees outside, and even with the truck's heater going full blast, they were all dealing with the cold.

She sucked in a deep breath, told herself that she would be fine and reluctantly closed the window.

"You don't have to do that," Nick said quietly, his tone concerned.

"It's not that much farther," she said, grateful for his ever-present support.

With a limited diet and medication, she was usually able to keep her IBS under control, but any high-stress event was often enough to push her over the edge. Spending ten days in the same house as her mother was the definition of a triggering event, and she'd been having issues for the past couple of days.

She'd skipped breakfast in an effort to keep her stomach quiet, but not eating was a hit-or-miss strategy and one that hadn't worked today.

Nick exited the highway and started up the well-plowed feeder road. Five minutes later they were heading toward the upscale neighborhood of Alpental. Her stomach gurgled ominously.

"Two minutes," he told her.

She nodded, telling herself to stay calm and relaxed. She consciously slowed her breathing. Two minutes. She could make it.

She focused on how beautiful the houses looked with a fresh dusting of snow. She had the brief thought that the cabin's driveway might be a problem, then smiled. If there had been snow, Julie would have hooked up the plow and cleared it that morning. The woman could do anything.

Seconds later, Nick turned into the long driveway with snow neatly piled on the sides. He parked next to his mom's truck, leaving plenty of room for Dana, who was right behind them. Blair immediately scrambled out of the truck and breathed in the cold air. Her stomach started to settle.

Julie walked out of the house, waving. "I've been watching for you," she called out. "How was the drive?"

"Easy," Nick said, opening the door for Gwen, who got out slowly.

Dana and Paul got out of her SUV. They were laughing and talking and obviously had had a more pleasant drive. Dana glanced over at Blair.

"You okay?"

Blair breathed in a couple of times and nodded. "Things are calming down."

Julie joined them and everyone (except Gwen) helped collect luggage and bags of presents. As they climbed the stairs to the porch, Blair felt herself starting to relax. Last year she'd had such a good time with Nick and his family. Hopefully this year would be as fun. She ignored the voice in her head that whispered that wasn't possible with her mother tagging along. She wasn't going to assume the worst, she told herself. Besides, there were plenty of people around to act as a buffer.

Once they were inside, Julie hugged everyone, hesitating only a second before reaching out to Gwen. Her mother stiffened before accepting the hug with obvious reluctance, holding her body away from the other woman's.

"You've been working hard," Paul said, taking in the garland on the railing and the Christmas village set up in the family room.

"There's a lot more to do," Julie said cheerfully. "Let's get you all settled. Then we can meet in the kitchen and have lunch while we discuss the plan for the next few days. I also have some tentative menus worked out." She touched Blair's arm. "I think I got all the food right, but you can tell me if I messed up."

"I'm sure you did fine. You're always so careful. Besides, I can usually find something to eat."

Her mother watched the exchange, frowning as if she disapproved of Julie's effort to accommodate Blair's food restrictions.

Whatever, Blair thought. Julie was a sweetie who took care of her family. There was nothing wrong with that.

Julie smiled at Paul. "I put you downstairs again."

"Excellent." He winked at her. "That big TV in the second family room is perfect for those nights I can't sleep."

"Again?" Gwen glanced between them. "You've been here before?"

Blair turned to her mother. "Uncle Paul spent Christmas with us last year."

Her mother's expression tightened as her gaze turned accusing. "You had your uncle out here for Christmas, but not me?"

Blair's stomach immediately flopped over. "You were staying in Boise with your friends. I mentioned coming to the cabin, but you said you already had plans."

"I didn't think you were having a big family gathering and excluding me."

The hurt in her tone instantly made Blair feel guilty, even as she told herself she hadn't done anything wrong.

"You're here this year," Julie said brightly. "We're going to have a great time." She paused. "And before we scatter to get settled, I have an announcement."

Blair looked at Dana, who shrugged as if she had no idea what it was.

"I was going to say something before," Julie continued. "I probably should have, but we've all been busy and I…"

Dana gasped. "You and Heath eloped!"

"What? No. God no. I'm not getting married again. Besides, we've only been dating for three months. We're not married or getting married."

"Well, you can't be pregnant," Gwen said. "You're too old."

"Mom!"

Julie looked at Gwen. "Thanks for sharing that."

Gwen flushed. "I didn't mean it how it came out."

Blair glared at her mother. How could she be so rude?

Julie brushed off the comment. "No problem. Heath's kids are going to spend Christmas with us. His ex was supposed to have them but she's going away, so he gets them and they're coming here."

Blair looked at Nick, who grinned at his mom. "That's great, Mom. How old are they?"

Julie cleared her throat. "Um, well, eight and ten."

Dana's lips twitched. Blair felt herself starting to smile. Paul grinned.

"That's a good age for Christmas," he said. "They'll be in the room with the bunk beds?"

"That's the plan. Oh, and they're bringing their dog, Rufus."

"A dog?" Gwen sounded horrified. "He'll be indoors?"

Julie frowned at the question. "Of course. Dogs are family."

"Eight and ten?" Dana repeated, her voice teasing. "Oh, Mom. How old is Heath again? Thirty?"

Julie rolled her eyes. "Very funny. You know very well he's in his forties."

"You're dating a younger man?" Gwen asked, sounding scandalized. "How much younger?"

"Mom, that's not our business."

"If he's going to be living here, I would think it was."

"It doesn't matter."

Her mother turned away. "Of course you'd take her side."

"What does that even mean?"

"He's forty-two," Julie said. "So yes, twelve years younger. Now, if we've talked about this enough, can we please let it go?"

Nick put his arm around his mother. "I'm with Paul. Kids make Christmas better. I'm glad he's bringing them. And Rufus will be fun. It'll be like when we were their age."

"That would be good." Julie briefly leaned into him. "All right, everyone. Rooms."

"I know the way to mine."

Paul collected his luggage and headed downstairs. Everyone else trooped upstairs. Blair noticed that, once again, they all carried bags except her mother. Blair didn't get it. So far her mother seemed to disapprove of everything—Julie most of all. So why had she insisted on joining them for the holiday? Why hadn't she flown back to Boise to be with her friends in familiar territory?

There weren't any answers, nor were there likely to be, she

thought grimly. There was just her mother and the long ten days between now and when they could drop her off at her condo.

When they reached the top of the stairs, Julie started pointing. "Dana, I put you in the end bedroom." Her tone was faintly apologetic.

Blair understood. The room was small and tucked under the eaves, so it had a sloping ceiling. Dana smiled.

"Don't worry about it, Mom. I'm happy to be here. I don't mind where I sleep." She carried her luggage into her room. Seconds later, her bag thumped to the floor, and Dana burst into tears. "I can't believe what you did."

Blair looked at Nick, who shrugged. Together they walked into the bedroom, and she immediately saw what had caused Dana's emotional reaction.

The long dresser was covered with a Whoville village, based on the Dr. Seuss book *How the Grinch Stole Christmas!* The Grinch was in his sleigh, with Max beside him. The Whos formed a circle around a Christmas tree. Little houses glinted with light from the flameless candles. On the usually bare walls were poster-size blowups of photographs of Dana with her father, first when she was a baby and one when she was eight or nine and a third at her college graduation.

Dana threw herself at her mom and hung on tight. "You did all this for *me!*"

"You and your dad love that silly Grinch. I thought, given why you wanted to come, you'd like the memories." Julie drew back and cupped her face. "Too much?"

"It's perfect. Thank you."

Blair glanced at Nick. "I can't wait to see what surprise she has for you."

Nick swallowed hard. "Whatever it is, I'm not gonna cry."

She squeezed his hand, knowing he might tear up a little later, when it was just them. Getting through his first Christmas without his father was going to be tough.

"Gwen next," Julie said. "You're in here. The bathroom's nice and close."

Gwen blinked. "The bathroom isn't in the bedroom?"

"No, it's not an en suite," Julie said brightly. "And you'll be sharing with Dana."

"What?" Gwen pressed her thin lips together. "Perhaps I'd be better off at a hotel."

Blair gave in to the anger bubbling up inside of her. "Maybe you would, Mom. Should I start looking online to see if there are any rooms available?"

Her mother's expression shuttered, but not before Blair saw a flash of hurt. She immediately felt small and awful, which didn't make sense. Her mom was the bitch here, not her.

"I'm a good bathroom roommate," Dana said quickly. "In and out in a flash. Actually, I can use the three-quarter bath on the main floor."

Gwen turned away. "Don't be silly. Of course we can share."

Julie carried Gwen's bag into her room. Blair went with them, prepared to come between her mother-in-law and any snippy comments Gwen might want to make.

The bedroom was a good size, with a big window and a view of the mountains. There was an electric faux fireplace in the corner. A small Christmas tree sat on a small table, and there was a wreath on the opposite wall, along with several flameless candles.

Julie put the suitcase on the bed, then picked up a remote. "This works the fireplace. It's not just decorative—it puts out a lot of heat. Just in case you get cold."

Gwen drew in a breath. "I'm sure I'll be very comfortable. Thank you. Now, if you'll excuse me."

Julie offered a tight smile and backed out of the room. "Of course. You need to get settled."

She led the way to Nick and Blair's room. It was a second, smaller master, with an attached three-quarter bath. Blair appreciated the close proximity to a bathroom, just in case she had a bad night. But what she was most interested in seeing was how Julie had decorated it for the holiday.

"Oh, Mom."

She followed Nick into the room and immediately smiled.

Julie had gone with a *Toy Story* theme, but all the toys had been decorated for the holiday. Woody's vest was a red-and-green plaid, and his cowboy hat had been replaced with a Santa one. Buzz sported a cape of garland. In fact, all the toys from the movie had been Christmas-ified.

The pictures on the wall were just as special as Dana's had been. There was a four-or five-year-old Nick walking with his dad on the beach at sunset. Another one with Nick's dad handing him the keys to his first car. The last picture showed Eldon standing between Blair and Nick at their engagement party.

Nick set down his suitcase and crossed to Julie, then pulled her close in a silent hug. They hung on to each other for a long time. When he stepped back he said, "You're the best, Mom. Thank you."

"Merry Christmas, firstborn."

He gave a strangled laugh. "Merry Christmas, Mom."

7

Dana unpacked quickly. Her clothes fit easily in the dresser and large closet, but she hesitated when it came to her cosmetic case. Normally she would simply put it on the bathroom counter, but given that she was sharing with Gwen, she felt that wasn't a smart move. Better to keep it in her room and drag it with her when she needed it, she thought. A pain, but probably safer when it came to family relations.

She had no idea what was up with Blair's mom. According to her sister-in-law, Gwen had practically demanded to be included in the holiday festivities, but since arriving, she'd been nothing but disapproving and unhappy. It seemed like she didn't want to be here at all. So why had she come?

Dana didn't have an answer to that, nor was she likely to get one. Families could be difficult. Her friends often complained about theirs. She supposed she was lucky. Her mom was great, she and Nick got along, and she adored Blair. She walked over to the poster of her and Dad, when she'd been a baby. His expression of love and wonder brought tears to her eyes.

"Oh, Dad. Why'd you have to go so soon?"

One Big Happy Family

She pressed her hand against the picture. Thank goodness she and Nick had realized this was where they had to spend Christmas. Yes, thinking about her father not being here would be painful, but remembering him, missing him, *loving* him would honor his memory.

She tucked her cell phone in her jeans pocket and went downstairs. As she suspected, her mother was already in the kitchen, collecting ingredients for lunch. The large panini press sat out on the counter.

"We're starting with easy food," her mom said with a smile. "Grilled cheese sandwiches and tomato soup."

"Sounds good." She looked at the decorations tucked in corners and on the buffet in the eat-in kitchen. "You and Heath were busy, Mom. I can't believe how much you got done."

"We worked hard over the weekend, and I had all day yesterday to finish up. There are still a few things to put out, so I was hoping you and I could do that this afternoon."

"Of course." She studied her mother, taking in the faint shadows under her eyes. "You okay? You seem tired."

"I'm fine."

Dana wasn't sure. "Are you worried about Heath's kids coming here for Christmas?"

"A little," Julie admitted. "I don't know them at all. Heath and I hadn't gotten around to meeting each other's family because we haven't been together that long and didn't see any reason to rush things. Then Tiffany got invited to the Bahamas for Christmas. She wanted to go and of course Heath wanted the time with his children."

"Tiffany?" Dana asked, her voice teasing. "Tiffany?"

"It's a good name."

"It's the perfect ex-wife name. Do we hate her?"

"No. I barely met the woman but she seems fine. It's not a competition." Julie leaned against the counter and sighed.

"Okay, I'll admit she's young. I mean, seriously young. That was depressing."

"Mom, Heath's with *you*."

Julie waved that comment away. "I'm not worried about him wanting to get back together with her. It's just…she's really young."

"You seem hung up on age, which isn't like you." Dana thought about her mother's dating life since the divorce. "You've never been so worried about a guy before. Heath must be special."

"I wouldn't say that." Her mother paused, then shook her head. "That came out wrong. He's great and I like him a lot. That's not the problem. It's just we were going along at a certain pace and suddenly everything is different. We're spending Christmas together with all of our kids, and I wasn't expecting that."

"Are you worried about them being comfortable with everyone?"

"A little. They don't know us and the house is unfamiliar. I want them to be comfortable and have a good holiday." She looked at Dana. "Maybe it's the realness of the situation. I knew about Madeline and Wyatt, but only in theory. Now they're a thing, and they're going to be part of our traditions. It's Christmas." She paused. "This sounds ridiculous, but I want them to like me."

Her mother's unexpected vulnerability surprised her. "They're going to love you."

"Maybe."

"They are."

Dana was sure—nearly everyone adored her mom. When she'd been young, hers had been the house all her friends had come to. There was always plenty to eat, lots of things to do, and while Julie kept track of what was going on, she'd never been intrusive. She was the mom her friends went to when they couldn't talk to their own mothers.

"I'll keep an eye on them," Dana said. "Make sure they're comfortable. At least then I'll have someone to hang out with."

She instantly wished she'd phrased that just a little differently.

"What's going on?" her mother asked, looking at her intently.

"Nothing. I'm fine."

Julie stared, obviously prepared to wait forever.

Dana sighed. "I'm trying to figure things out. Everyone has a better life than me."

"If you don't like what's happening in your life, then change it. You have the power."

Typical Julie advice, Dana thought with a touch of frustration. "That's easy for you to say, but I'm not like you. I don't instinctively take charge. My first reaction is to step back and assess the situation. You're the one who plows ahead and gets it done."

"Sometimes you need to have a little faith in yourself." Her mother's tone softened. "Or is Axel the real problem?"

Dana told herself not to flinch. Hearing his name was no big deal. "We're done. It's over."

"You're still in love with him."

Aware of how sound traveled in the public rooms, Dana glared at her mother. "Don't say that out loud."

"You want me to write it on a note?"

"You know what I mean. And I'm not still in love with him."

Her mother raised her eyebrows but didn't speak. Dana groaned.

"I'm less in love with him than I was," she amended.

"Love is or it isn't. There's no 'little bit.'" Julie shook her head. "When I get back to the tow yard, I'm going to fire him."

"What? You can't do that. No. You're not going to fire Axel on my behalf. I don't want that."

"We have to get him out of your life."

"No, Mom. No! Don't fix this. You're right—it's on me and I have the power. I need to use it."

Her mother didn't look convinced. "Axel is your greatest weakness. I don't like seeing you unhappy."

"I'm dealing. Please. Promise you won't fire him."

Julie hesitated. "Wouldn't it be easier if he was gone?"

"I won't be responsible for him losing his job. That's not who I am. And you firing a guy because he broke your daughter's heart isn't you, either. It's not right. We'd both feel awful. I want your word."

"Fine," her mother grumbled. "I won't fire him, but I'll give him the stink eye when I see him."

"I'm fine with that."

Paul walked into the kitchen, rubbing his hands. "Tell me lunch is soon, because I'm hungry."

Dana laughed. "We got coffee and doughnuts on the way. How can you be hungry?" They'd stopped for them when Nick had needed to pull off the highway so Blair could use a restroom.

Paul grinned. "I'm a good eater."

He was also tall and thin, Dana thought, trying not to be bitter about her extra weight. She'd managed to lose three pounds with her soul-crushing low-carb and healthy regimen. Unfortunately, given how great the meals always were at the cabin at Christmas, she would put them back on and a couple more.

She started down the path of beating herself up for not being stronger, then mentally put on the brakes. No, just no. It was Christmas. She wasn't going to worry about anything but being with her family and remembering her dad. That was the entire point of coming up here.

"We'll get started just as soon as everyone else joins us," her mom said.

"After lunch I want to make my rum cake," Paul said. "I brought all the dry ingredients. I'll need eggs and butter from your stash."

"I can do that." Julie laughed. "I remember your rum cake from last year. It's a whole thing, but it's worth the work."

Dana agreed. Once the cake was made, it was stored in an airtight container. Paul doused it in rum a couple of times a day until Christmas. When it was served, it had a nearly lethal dose of rum in every piece, but it was about the best thing she'd ever tasted.

Paul walked to the sink, where he started to wash his hands. "In the meantime, I'll set the table."

Dana helped him. They'd just finished when Nick, Blair and Gwen joined them.

"Let's deal with logistics before we have lunch," Julie said with an easy smile.

Blair grinned at Dana. "The rule portion of the afternoon."

"It wouldn't be my mom's house if there weren't rules."

"Rules are our friend," Julie told them. "Okay, there's a running grocery list in the pantry. If you use the last of something, put it on the shopping list. If you can't find something you want or need, ask me and I'll tell you if we have it or not. There's a menu list through the twenty-seventh on the wall in the pantry. Look it over, people, and give me feedback. This is the time to make changes. Having said that, I'll point out all the proteins are in the freezer, so let's try to stick with those if we can."

"You buy snack stuff?" Nick asked.

His mother nodded. "Tons of it, along with supplies for cocktails. Dana was in charge of the wine."

"We unloaded three cases from my car."

Julie looked at Blair. "I need your input most of all. I did my best to get it right, but I might have missed on a few side dishes."

"I'll be fine," Blair told her. "I can work around whatever you have planned."

"Still, take a look."

"I will."

Julie seemed to steel herself as she offered Gwen a smile. "I'd like your input, as well. I'm familiar with everyone else's tastes. I wouldn't want to serve something you wouldn't like."

Gwen's face puckered. "Thank you," she murmured, somehow managing to make her tone sullen.

Julie glanced at all of them. "Every night at dinner you'll tell me if you want the breakfast I'm fixing. You're welcome to eat on your own, but I need to know in advance. Mealtimes are set by the group. We'll prep and clean up on a rotating schedule. Everyone participates in chores. Any questions?"

Dana wondered if Gwen was going to protest being expected to help, but Blair's mom stayed silent.

"Good. Now, house rules. No loud music or TV. Keep the volume at a reasonable level." Julie stared at Nick as she spoke.

"What?" he asked with a grin. "I barely watch TV."

"You crank up the volume when you watch sports, and some of us don't like that."

"I have no idea what you're talking about," he murmured.

Julie ignored him. "We're living in tight quarters. Let's be pleasant and give each other the benefit of the doubt." She pointed at Dana and Nick. "I'm talking to you two."

Dana took a step back. "What do you mean?"

"You and your brother bicker."

"We don't." The response was automatic even as Dana thought maybe her mother was right.

"You do. It's like you're both five again and arguing about the other getting better presents."

"Nick always got better presents."

Blair laughed. "This is going to be fun. Last year Nick was on his best behavior. This year I'll get to see the real him. I can't wait to see if it's as bad as Dana claims."

Nick put his arm around her. "Last year I was trying to win you. But I'm not the one who starts trouble. That's all Dana."

"Everyone knows that's not true," Dana grumbled good-naturedly. "You're the spoiled big brother. I'm perfect."

Nick snorted.

Julie rolled her eyes. "Thank you for illustrating my point. Blair, I'm putting you in charge of keeping them in line."

"Me?" Blair's voice was a yelp. "I don't want that responsibility."

"Too late." Julie smiled at Gwen. "You were a schoolteacher. I know it's not the same as having two kids, but you must know what I mean. Sibling rivalry. It's a whole thing."

They all turned to Gwen, waiting for her reaction. Dana thought she might be snippy, but never expected Blair's mother to burst into tears.

"How could you?" Gwen demanded before running from the room.

Dana watched her go, unsure of what had just happened. Her mom took a step, as if to follow Gwen, then stopped.

"I don't understand," Julie said, her expression troubled. "What did I say?"

"Nothing." Paul sounded frustrated. "That woman has always been difficult. You didn't say anything wrong. There's no way you would have known. This isn't on you."

Blair nodded. "He's right. I don't know why she came. She's not happy being here. Please don't let her destroy the holiday."

"But why did she cry?" Julie asked. "How did I upset her?"

Blair looked at her uncle, then back at Julie. She hesitated only a second. "It was the two-kid thing."

"Because you're an only child?"

"No. I had a baby brother. I was four at the time, so I don't remember much. He died of SIDS three weeks after he was born. She couldn't deal with the loss and got caught up in a depression spiral that went on for years. That's the only thing I can think of that would upset her."

Her voice sounded bitter. "Or maybe this is just who she is now. I don't know her well enough to say."

Nick pulled her closer. "That's not on you. She's the mom.

It's her responsibility to reach out. The fact that she didn't is her loss."

Dana tried to take it all in. "Your mom lost a baby?" What a terrible thing for any parent to deal with. Her mom looked equally shocked.

Blair sighed. "She did. Everyone said it was a bad time. I don't remember much."

There was something in her tone that made Dana wonder if she remembered more than she was letting on. Dana knew that Blair and her mother weren't tight, but not the details. Nick had mentioned that Gwen had been emotionally absent during most of Blair's childhood. A bullying incident during Blair's sophomore year of high school had left Blair shattered and terrified to go back to classes, so her father had sent her to live with his brother. According to Blair, Paul had been exactly who she needed. But where had Gwen been when all that had happened?

"What a painful time for everyone," Julie said. "Losing a child. I can't imagine."

"I apologize for my sister-in-law," Paul said. "Gwen used to be fun. All that changed when she lost her son. It was tragic and life-changing. I get that, but somehow she never got over the loss. I thought eventually she'd recover, but she never did."

"I'm sorry I upset her," Julie murmured.

"Don't be." Blair's tone was firm. "You had no way of knowing. None of this was on you."

"My mother makes me crazy," Blair said after lunch when she and Nick were alone in their room. "Why does she have to be so difficult? Why does she have to be here?"

Instead of answering her unanswerable questions, Nick bent down and began nibbling on her neck. Instantly flashes of desire ignited.

"I was having a rant here," she murmured, melting against him. "Isn't this more fun?"

"Much." She turned to face him and wrapped her arms around his neck. "So what were your plans for the afternoon?"

He smiled. "I thought I'd tempt you into our bed. After that, I'm open to whatever interests you."

She kissed him. "You interest me."

They moved toward the bed, alternating between kissing and taking off articles of clothing. When they were naked, they slipped between the sheets. Nick took his time arousing her. Once she was breathless and close to her release, he shifted so he was lying on his back.

She raised her eyebrows and smiled. "So you want me on top."

"It's my favorite."

Hers, too, she thought, straddling him. She'd reached between them to guide him inside when the bedroom door opened and Gwen walked in.

"Blair, do you have a minute? I thought—"

Blair shrieked and reached for the sheets. "Get out. Get out!"

The door slammed shut. She collapsed onto the mattress and buried her face into the pillow. Horror and embarrassment burned on her cheeks.

"Tell me that didn't happen."

Nick stroked her back. "We should have locked the door."

She raised her head and stared at him. "She should have knocked. I can't believe she just walked into our bedroom. Why does she have to be here? She's ruining everything."

"You okay?"

"No." She looked at him. "She broke the mood."

"We'll try again tonight."

"Thank you for not being mad."

"I love you." He kissed her. "It's okay."

"It's not, but I appreciate the lie."

After getting dressed, Blair went in search of her mother. She found Gwen in the downstairs family room, a magazine on her lap.

"You don't knock?" she asked, her voice thick with annoyance.

"I didn't realize what you were doing." Her mother looked at her, obviously more put out than chagrined. "It's the middle of the afternoon, at someone else's house. What were you thinking?"

"That I love my husband. I don't have to justify any part of our relationship to you." She had a lot more to say but knew she would end up making comments she would regret. "I don't know why you wanted to come with us," she said instead. "You disapprove of everything, you're obviously unhappy. What's the point of it?"

"We're family. We should spend the holidays together."

Seriously? "Since when? You never showed up for them when I was little, and I haven't seen you at Christmas since Dad died."

Gwen flushed. "I was there when you were little."

"If you're saying you were in the room, then sure. If you're trying to say you participated, you didn't."

Her mother had been an emotional ghost. There but not there. She'd gone through the motions of handing out presents, opening hers and thanking the giver, but her expression had been blank, her voice monotone. Most Christmases she'd retreated to her bedroom by three, leaving Blair, Paul and her father to have dinner without her.

"I was dealing with a lot of pain," Gwen said.

Blair wanted to point out that she'd been a little girl dealing with the loss of both her baby brother and her mother but knew there was no point. Gwen would never see anyone's side but her own.

"We have ten days here, Mom. You might want to think about making an effort."

With that, she walked up the stairs, wishing her mother had stayed in Boise. Preferably for the rest of her life.

Even though there were only six people for dinner, Julie pulled out both electronic pressure cookers to make carnitas.

They would have the meat tonight, along with roasted vegetables and scalloped potatoes, then use the leftovers for enchiladas later in the week.

She was using her favorite recipe—omitting the onions in deference to Blair. Her daughter-in-law could handle the rest of the ingredients, but onions were always iffy for her stomach.

She'd just finished up browning the large chunks of pork shoulder when Gwen walked into the kitchen.

The two women stared at each other. The last time Julie had seen Blair's mother, she'd run out of the kitchen in tears. The last time she'd *heard* her had been while she and Blair were having what sounded like a heated discussion. Not wanting to know the topic, Julie had retreated to her room until they'd finished.

"You're starting dinner early," Gwen said, motioning to the pressure cookers.

"The carnitas take about an hour plus the time for a natural release."

"I've never been a fan of Mexican food."

Julie had no idea what to say to that. "As I said earlier, you might want to look at the menus. I have enchiladas and tacos planned."

Gwen waved away the comment. "It's fine. I'll eat what everyone else does."

While complaining, Julie thought grimly. Blair was right—her mother was a nightmare. That thought was followed by instant guilt as she remembered Gwen's loss. Which meant she should be more understanding.

She put the last of the browned meat into the second pressure cooker, added broth, spices and the peppers, then closed it before setting the timer. Once that was done, she had no choice but to face Blair's mother.

Gwen was around her age, she thought. They'd both raised children, held down jobs, been married. Surely they had to have something in common.

"I'm sorry I upset you earlier," Julie said, telling herself to be the bigger person. "I'm not sure what happened, but I obviously said the wrong thing."

"It's not you." Gwen pulled up a stool at the island. "I've been on edge lately. The move has been difficult. I can't find a condo I like and I miss my friends. But that's not the problem. Can I be blunt?"

Oh, if only she wouldn't, Julie thought, even as she smiled and said, "Of course."

"My daughter hates me."

Julie leaned against the counter. She hadn't been expecting that. "No one hates you," she said automatically. Yes, Blair resented her mother and wished she'd stayed in Boise, but that wasn't the same as hating her.

"We've never been very close," Gwen admitted. "I suppose a lot of that is on me. But it was just the way of things."

"You live five hundred miles away. That makes it tough to maintain a relationship." Plus, according to Blair, Gwen had never been very interested in her daughter's life.

"I doubt it is because of proximity." Gwen shook her head. "I simply don't understand the choices she's made."

Now Julie was really confused. "With her career?"

"That's part of it, but also with Nick."

"What?"

"Don't get me wrong. He's a nice enough man."

Fury exploded. Julie hung on to her temper and told herself to stay calm. Gwen wasn't the most tactful person on the planet. Julie should give her the benefit of the doubt. No way the bitch was dissing her son, even if that was what it sounded like.

"Blair has a master's degree, and Nick never went to college," Gwen went on as if unaware of how she'd offended her host. "And there's no real advancement at his job."

"He's going to run the company."

"It's a towing service." Gwen wrinkled her nose. "I was hoping Blair would find an investment banker or maybe a dentist. Someone who doesn't have to carry a gun on the job. I'm sure you understand."

"No, I don't understand. I don't understand at all. Nick is a warm, caring man who would give his life for your daughter. He's honest, he would never cheat on her or disrespect her in any way. He's strong, determined and loyal. I would think that as Blair's mother, those are the qualities that would matter the most in your son-in-law, but I guess I would be wrong."

Gwen stared at her, obviously baffled. "You're upset. I don't understand."

"Then let me be clear. You have the emotional intelligence of a snail. Now, if you'll excuse me, I'm going to go hang out with my non-suit-wearing, uneducated son and be proud of everything about him."

With that, she walked out of the kitchen. She passed Dana, who was standing on the stairs.

"Did I just hear what I thought I heard?" her daughter asked in a whisper.

"Every single word."

"Now I have to hate her."

"Join the club. It seems we're all members."

8

Julie spent most of Wednesday morning watching for Heath to arrive. So far the family holiday adventure was one big cluster you-know-what, she thought, willing him to pull into the driveway. At this point, she was desperate for a supportive hug and a diversion. She and Gwen weren't speaking, Blair and Gwen weren't speaking, and Dana was avoiding Blair's mother on principle. Worse, Nick had figured out something was wrong and was hounding Julie to tell him, only she couldn't repeat what Gwen had said or the situation would get worse. It was one thing for her to resent Gwen, but it was another for Nick to resent the woman. She was his mother-in-law and therefore tied to him for life.

The second she saw Heath's SUV pull in behind her truck, she shot out the door and down the stairs, not bothering with a coat.

"You're here! You're here!" she shouted, waving at the vehicle, aware she was probably frightening the children and possibly her very young boyfriend. "I've been waiting."

Heath shut off the engine and opened his door. She raced around to greet him.

He pulled her close. "Tough time with the family?"

"You have no idea."

"I'm happy to rescue you."

"I don't need rescuing, but I would like you and the kids to be a friendly distraction, if that's okay."

"Done." He opened the back door. "Come on, you two. You're gonna love the house."

While Madeline and Wyatt climbed out, Heath let Rufus out of the back. Julie reintroduced herself to the dog.

"Hey, you. I cleared a nice square of lawn for you to do your business."

Rufus wagged his tail in appreciation. She turned to the kids. "How was the drive?"

"Okay." Madeline looked from her to the house. "I thought you had a cabin. This is really big."

"I know. Isn't that fun?"

Nick, Blair and Dana came out of the house. Julie made introductions. Neither Nick nor Blair reacted to Heath's age, but Dana smiled broadly and moved close to her mom.

"You go, girl."

"Shh."

"He's handsome."

Julie felt both happy and faintly defensive. "And young," she whispered.

Dana shook her head. "You need to let that go."

Everyone helped unload the car.

"We can help carry luggage inside," Nick said. He grinned when he saw Rufus. "Great dog. Hey, big guy."

Madeline and Wyatt stuck close to each other while Heath handed over the suitcases and bags of presents.

"We'll be going to get a really big tree this afternoon," Julie said brightly. "The ceiling in the upstairs family room is about fifteen feet, so the tree can be tall."

They all went inside. Julie had Dana take the presents to the downstairs closet, where she'd moved the others, once the decorations had been cleared out. The locked door meant no prying eyes could see them before it was time. Once the tree was decorated, the presents from friends and family could be put out, while the Santa presents stayed safely behind the locked door.

Heath showed his kids around the main level, pointing out the TV and the big fireplace. They seemed a little uneasy with the size of the house. Once that portion of the tour was complete, everyone but Julie took Rufus outside to get to know the yard and do his business.

Gwen appeared seemingly out of nowhere. "We should talk."

"This isn't a good time." Julie glanced toward the back door as she spoke, hoping for Heath and the kids to return, giving her an excuse to ignore Gwen.

"I offended you."

Julie surrendered to the fact that God didn't appear to be on her side. "Yes, you did. You said horrible things about Nick. Not only are you wrong, but he's my son and your daughter's husband. He's part of your family."

"My comments weren't really about him. I was talking about Blair."

"That's weird because Nick's name came up a bunch of times." Julie resisted the urge to poke the other woman in the ribs. "What's wrong with you? If you're sorry Blair didn't marry some guy with an MBA, fine, but don't talk to me about it. He's my kid. Of course I'm going to defend him and think you're a total bitch. You don't have many fans here, Gwen. Why are you trying to make the situation more difficult?"

"I'm not." Tears filled her eyes. "I'm getting everything wrong."

"Yes, you are. Does that always happen?"

"No. Normally I'm a very nice person. People like me."

"Huh. I wouldn't have guessed. In fact, last night you told me that your daughter hates you. Maybe you're not the person you think." She saw everyone collecting on the back porch and knew they only had a few seconds. "You need to try harder to fit in or it's going to be a really long holiday."

The other woman stiffened. "That seems unnecessarily harsh. Regardless, I'm sorry I offended you. That wasn't my intention."

The door opened and Rufus raced into the house, then shook, sending bits of snow flying. Gwen shrieked and jumped back. Julie tried not to roll her eyes.

"He's just wet. You're fine."

"He startled me."

Julie introduced Gwen, expecting the other woman to offer a tight greeting, then bolt. She surprised Julie and possibly everyone else by smiling at Madeline and Wyatt.

"Merry Christmas," she said, her voice cheerful. "Isn't the house wonderful? It's big enough for lots of adventures. Have you seen your room? It's amazing. You practically have the whole floor to yourself. But not to worry. Uncle Paul is downstairs with you and he's very good at playing games and keeping people safe."

What? Where was icky Gwen who didn't even like Mexican food? Blair moved next to her and lowered her voice.

"Remember? Mom was a schoolteacher for thirty years."

"I was," Gwen said brightly. "I taught fourth and fifth grade." She pointed at Madeline. "Let me guess. I would have had you last year or this year."

Madeline smiled shyly. "That's right. I'm in fifth grade now."

"Ah, so middle school next year. You're going to like that." She turned to Wyatt. "Are you in third grade?"

"How did you know?"

"I'm a good guesser."

Julie looked at Dana, who seemed as stunned as she was. Gwen was good with kids. Who knew?

They all went downstairs, with Heath and Nick carrying the

kids' luggage. Madeline and Wyatt met Paul, who promised to play remote cars with them. Julie pointed to their room.

"I hope you like it."

They ran inside. Julie followed, Rufus at her heels. All four beds were covered with cheery holiday comforters. There was a Christmas tree in the corner decorated with an assortment of Disney and Harry Potter ornaments.

"They really are bunk beds," Madeline said with a grin. "Wyatt, we can both have a top bunk, just like Julie told us."

Her brother climbed up to one of the beds and threw himself on the mattress. "This is great."

Julie showed them the bathroom, dresser and closet. Heath grinned at his kids.

"What do you think?" He winked at Julie. "Madeline was worried there wasn't enough room."

His ten-year-old held out her arms and spun in a circle. "It's the best house ever!"

Wyatt joined her and they spun until they were dizzy, then collapsed onto the lower bunks. Rufus barked before joining them. He draped himself across Wyatt, tail wagging.

"It gets better," their dad said, crossing to the dresser and pulling out the walkie-talkie. Wyatt immediately scrambled to his feet.

"I know what that is. We use 'em when we play army."

"Here you'll use this one if you need to get me. It connects to my room upstairs, so if something happens in the night, or you get scared, you can talk to me directly."

"I'm also right next door," Paul added from the doorway. "Or possibly on the sofa, watching TV."

Wyatt's eyes widened. "You stay up at night and watch TV?"

"Only when I eat all my vegetables."

"That is so cool."

Heath ruffled his son's hair. "Don't get any ideas. I don't want your mom hearing you stayed up past your bedtime every night."

Madeline sat up on the bed and offered an innocent smile. "Maybe she doesn't have to hear anything at all."

Julie raised her eyebrows. "You're going to be trouble, aren't you?"

Madeline giggled. "Maybe a little."

"You should come out here," Gwen said from the family room. "Look what I found."

Madeline and Wyatt glanced at each other, then went out to join Gwen. She showed them the big cupboards at the far end of the room. Inside were stacks of old-fashioned board games, along with jigsaw puzzles, coloring books and new boxes of crayons.

"I also happen to know there's a craft room upstairs," she continued. "With plenty of paper and glue, along with the fancy pens and pencils. We could make some really nice greeting cards for everyone. I have lots of ideas if you'd like some help."

She offered the children a warm, genuine smile that Julie knew she'd never seen before. They both responded in kind.

"I'd like that," Madeline said. "We have presents but we didn't get cards. Mom says personalized cards are best."

Dana looked at her brother. "Remember when we used to make cards for the family?"

"Join us," Gwen said graciously. "That way everyone gets a nice card."

Dana looked confused, as if pleasant Gwen was someone she didn't know.

"I will," she said slowly. "Thanks."

Gwen waved toward the stairs. "I'll stay with these two and help them unpack. Julie, I'm sure you want to start lunch. Heath, you can unpack. We'll meet in the kitchen at noon. How's that?"

Julie bristled as the other woman took charge, even though her ideas were good ones. Then she told herself to let it go. Gwen was obviously in schoolteacher mode, and if it kept things pleasant, then why not?

She glanced at Heath, who was introducing himself to Paul.

The two men laughed about something. Julie felt her tension ease. Maybe this was going to be okay. No one had shrieked when they saw how much younger Heath was than her, and his kids seemed happy with the house. In a couple of days they would settle into a routine. It was going to be a nice, quiet holiday and weren't those the best kind?

Heath joined her, putting his arm around her waist. "Let's go get me unpacked," he said as they started up the stairs.

"You only brought an overnight bag. How much unpacking could there be?"

His look was pointed, and she immediately felt desire spring to life. That man—she'd been very lucky the day he'd walked into her life.

"Yes," she said with a smile. "We should get you settled before I start lunch."

At the main level, Julie glanced at her kids, then looked away. "I'll be down to start lunch in half an hour."

Blair and Nick exchanged a look. "We should get settled, too," Blair murmured. "There was that, um, one suitcase that didn't get unpacked."

Julie thought that sounded weird, but she wasn't going to waste time asking what her daughter-in-law meant. Not when Heath was not-so-subtly pushing her toward the stairs.

Dana watched them for a second, then turned away. Julie thought she might have seen pain in her daughter's eyes, but couldn't tell for sure and didn't know if she should ask.

At the top of the landing, Blair moved close to Julie.

"Lock your door," she whispered. "I mean it. My mother is everywhere. Lock your door."

Dana busied herself prepping for lunch. Per the menu posted in the large pantry, they were having chicken salad sandwiches on rosemary bread, with coleslaw and cut-up fruit.

She washed her hands and started collecting ingredients, all the while telling herself she wasn't bitter. She should be happy that the people she loved had someone in their lives. So what if her mom and her brother were each locked in their rooms having great sex and she had no one? So what if she was single and tragically in love with a man who only seemed to want to repeatedly break her heart? She would be fine. She was strong, and while not self-actualized, she thought maybe one day she might be. Surely that was enough.

She chopped up the ingredients for the chicken salad, stirred everything together so the flavors could meld, then got going on the dressing for the coleslaw.

Gwen joined her about ten minutes later, Madeline and Wyatt trailing behind her.

"We're hungry," Wyatt said with a tentative smile.

Dana grinned at him. "That's perfect! I'm fixing lunch. It's going to be delicious."

"We can set the table," Gwen said, showing the kids where the main-floor bathroom was. She rejoined Dana in the kitchen. "I thought your mom did most of the cooking."

"She does, but she and Heath are upstairs, um, getting him settled."

"Them, too?" Gwen asked, her tone outraged. "What is it with you people?"

"I don't know what you're talking about." Which wasn't true, but no way Dana was trash-talking anyone's love life with Blair's mother.

"Heath's children are nice," she said by way of distraction.

Gwen's expression softened. "They are. They're much younger than I would have expected, but then so is he."

"If they make each other happy, that's all that matters."

Before Gwen could rain on that parade, the children rejoined them. Dana showed them where the flatware and napkins were kept. Together they started setting the table. Paul wandered in and Dana put him to work on the fruit salad. Julie and Heath joined them, looking flushed and satisfied. Dana tried not to wish she and Axel had come here together, reminding herself it never ended well with him. Better to focus on wanting what they had for herself with a much better guy.

Only when they were together, Axel *was* the better guy. He always stepped in where he was needed—sometimes reading her emotional state before she understood it herself. He was gentle when he was funny, looked at her with so much love and affection in his eyes. When it was good...it was perfect.

One day, she thought. She would meet a nice man and fall in love and it would be great. Until then, she just had to be strong and tell herself she would feel better with time. Getting over Axel was a multistep process.

By the time Blair and Nick joined them, lunch was ready. Julie turned on the built-in sound system and found a channel playing upbeat holiday music. They carried the food to the large kitchen table by the window, then joined hands while Paul said grace.

"This afternoon is a big deal," Julie said, passing the coleslaw. "We're getting a tree for the family room."

"A really big one," Nick added with a grin.

"Is there a lot somewhere?" Madeline asked.

"A lot?" Julie sounded scandalized. "We hike out into the wilderness, like old-timey people."

The kids exchanged a doubtful glance.

"For real?" Madeline asked.

Julie laughed. "All right, maybe it's not the wilderness. Technically, we'll be in a Christmas tree farm, but we will hike around until we can agree on the perfect tree and then we cut it down."

Heath smiled at his kids. "That will be an adventure."

"Can I swing the axe?" Wyatt asked.

"No." Julie, Gwen and Heath spoke as one.

"You're too little," Madeline told her brother. "And I don't want to." She picked up her sandwich. "It'll be cold outside. Maybe Wyatt and I should stay home."

"I don't want to stay home," Wyatt grumbled.

"We'll bundle up." Heath's tone was cajoling. "We never get to cut down a live tree at home."

She didn't look convinced. "How do we get it to the car?"

"Your dad, Paul and I will carry it," Nick said. "We tie it on the back of my mom's truck, with the top sticking over the cab. Then we drive back. It's pretty fun."

"I'm staying here," Gwen offered, frowning at her sandwich. "If either of you don't want to go, you can stay with me. We'll play games or get started on the cards."

The kids exchanged a look of silent communication. Dana told herself not to get resentful—Gwen was simply offering an alternative, not trying to keep Heath's children from an adventure.

"We'll go with Dad," Madeline said. Wyatt nodded, then took a big bite of his sandwich.

"No arguing," Julie said, looking at Dana and Nick. "I mean it, you two."

Wyatt's eyes got big. "You and Nick fight?"

"Sure," Nick said easily. "We're brother and sister. She thinks she knows everything, but I'm always right."

"Oh, please. You know nothing."

"It never changes," Julie told the kids. "It's better now than when they were your age, but picking out the right tree can be stressful."

"Dana has unrealistic expectations," Nick said, adding fruit salad to his plate. "She wants perfection."

"I want a tree that makes me happy."

Okay, maybe she was a little picky, but it was worth it to have the right tree in the family room.

"I'm building memories," she added.

"And flirting with crazy," Nick grumbled.

Julie stared at him. He ducked his head and added a quick, "Sorry."

"My children," she said. "I'm so proud."

Everyone but Gwen laughed.

Dana looked around the table, allowing herself to—once again—wish Axel was here. He'd joined them last Christmas, and while she'd been nervous about bringing him to meet everyone, he'd been a perfect fit. She wasn't sure he and her dad would get along—they couldn't be more different—but Axel had charmed them all. He'd been attentive, affectionate and had known when to step in and when to let the family have their time to connect. He'd gone skiing with her, Nick and Blair and bird-watching with her father.

She remembered the feel of Axel sitting next to her. How if she and her mom ever got into a quarrel, or Nick said something that hurt her feelings, he would reach under the table and take her hand in his. He'd been there for her, had told her he loved her. Then they'd gotten home and he'd dumped her, shattering her heart.

Not anything she needed to think about right now, she told herself.

"Mom, don't you like the sandwiches?" Blair asked, glancing at her mother's untouched plate. "They're a special recipe Julie modified so that it fit all my requirements, so maybe not to your taste. I'm sure there's some plain chicken in the refrigerator."

Gwen offered a tight smile. "This is fine for me. Thank you." As if to prove her point, she took a big bite and chewed. "Yummy," she said when she'd swallowed.

Dana looked at Madeline. "We're supposed to get more snow soon. Not a lot, but enough to give us a dusting so everything looks new and clean. In the morning we can make snow angels, if you'd like. I used to love to do that when I was your age. I think they come out the best when there's already a couple of feet of snow to fall in with that light, fresh coating to make them perfect."

Madeline's eyes brightened. "Can we take pictures and send them to Mom?"

"We can."

"Then I want to."

"Me, too," Wyatt added. "She'll really like that."

Blair found herself gasping from the exertion of walking through a couple of feet of snow. Her breath—visible in the cold air—came out in pants. Okay, maybe she'd been slightly less faithful with her morning workouts, but shouldn't she still be able to keep up?

"You're killing us, Nick," Dana called. "Can't we at least walk on the established path?"

"The best trees are the ones in the back." Nick sounded confident as he forged the way through the snow. Heath and Julie followed, doing their best to create a trail for the kids to follow. Being young, Madeline and Wyatt hopped from footprint to footprint, showing no signs of effort. Next to her, Dana groaned.

"I'm going to kill my brother. I'm sorry to make you a young widow, but he needs to die."

There was a definite wheeze between each word. Blair peered at her sister-in-law. "You okay?"

"Sure," she gasped. "Never better."

Blair glanced over her shoulder and saw her own mother was keeping up easily, although her familiar pinched expression made it clear she wasn't having much fun. Why hadn't she stayed at the cabin like she'd said she would? Familiar annoyance rose, but Blair tamped it down. She wasn't going to let anything get in the way of the fun of picking out a Christmas tree.

The promised "dusting" of snow had arrived, turning the mountain into a winter fairyland. The clouds had moved through quickly, leaving beautiful blue skies. Except for starting to sweat inside her layers, Blair felt as if she was in a scene from a holiday movie.

There were Christmas trees for as far as the eye could see. Tall ones, short ones, little baby ones that wouldn't be cut down for a couple more seasons. The beautiful scent of pine filled the air. All the good trees close to the parking lot had already been cut down—forcing them deeper into the farm. Nick wanted to go all the way to the back and then have them work their way forward. It had seemed like a good idea at the time, Blair thought, finally yelling, "I need a break."

"Thank God," Dana muttered, coming to a stop beside her.

They grinned at each other, then did their best to catch their breath.

Julie joined them, slapping her hands together in the cold. "We should be close to the end of the farm," she said, looking around, as if assessing their situation. "We haven't seen any other families for a while, and there aren't any tracks out here. Let's start the tree search. Unless someone saw the perfect tree on the way in."

"I saw a couple," Dana began, only to have Nick walk over.

"I know the one we should get. We passed it about ten minutes ago."

Gwen sniffed. "You didn't want to say something at the time?"

"I thought we might see a better one."

Julie shook her head. "And so it begins. All right, people, pair up and start picking out trees." She pulled strips of bright yellow fabric from her pocket and handed them out. "If you see a tree you like, tie this on a branch. It'll help us find it later. We meet back here in five minutes."

"Five minutes?" Nick looked offended. "I can't get back to my perfect tree in five minutes."

"Gwen's right. You should have said something at the time." His mother's gaze was pointed. "I have no sympathy for you."

"Ha ha." Dana grinned. "The two I saw are right over here."

The kids split up—Madeline going with Dana, and Wyatt trailing behind Nick and Heath. Julie stood with Blair and Gwen.

"Don't waver," she said, when everyone else was out of earshot. "Pick a favorite and stick with it. We'll have a quick vote and go get the guy to cut down the one we've picked."

"We could have just gone to a lot," Gwen grumbled. "This is a lot of work for one tree."

Blair saw a muscle tighten in her mother-in-law's jaw before Julie said, "You're right. We could have. But this tradition is nice, isn't it?" There was just enough chirp in her tone to make her sound sincere. Blair tried not to sigh at her mother. Gwen was going to do what she was going to do.

Ten minutes later, there were three trees in contention. The smallest one was quickly eliminated in a single round of voting, leaving Nick's tree and Dana's. His was perfect on three sides, and while Dana's wasn't as full, it was like something out of a greeting card.

Unfortunately, their numbers were even, which allowed for a tie on the voting—for three full rounds.

"Someone has to change their vote," Gwen said, slapping her hands against her arms. "Or we'll freeze to death."

"I agree." Blair looked at her husband and laughed. "Nick, it's a Christmas tree. Let Dana have the one she wants."

"Mine is better," he said, his tone stubborn.

"They're both nice," Julie offered, then sighed. "It was easier last year when Nick didn't want you to see this side of him."

"There's no side. What side?" Nick looked at his mom. "You know I'm right. My tree is the right size for the room and it's full. The tree Dana wants is too skinny."

"It's balanced," Dana corrected. *"Balanced."* She drew out the word. "Your tree has a bald spot."

"Which can be the back in the corner where no one will see it."

"I'll know it's there."

"You're not royalty, so why does that matter?"

Julie put her arms around Madeline and Wyatt. "Please, please tell me you never argue like this."

Both kids giggled. Heath grinned. "They can get into it." He looked at Nick and Dana, who were still glaring at each other. "We could flip a coin."

Julie looked startled. "Does anyone have a coin? Who pays cash for anything?"

"Dad does!" Wyatt pointed gleefully. "He keeps a quarter in his wallet so he can flip a coin anytime he wants."

Heath looked a little embarrassed by the revelation. "It's just a thing with the kids."

Nick slapped him on the back. "Does it feel like we're judging you? Because we are."

Blair hugged her husband. "I'm not judging you. I love you, flaws and all."

Nick grinned. "What flaws?"

"Your inability to give in to your sister."

"Is this a female thing? Are you feeling solidarity?"

"I have the Christmas spirit." And an inner glow that came from spending time with her family. She smiled to herself, thinking the great sex from that morning hadn't hurt, either.

Unfortunately, just then her mother spoke, pretty much bursting Blair's contentment bubble.

"Why don't the rest of us pick a third tree?" Gwen offered. "Then we can have one more vote." Blair would guess her tone implied it wasn't appropriate for Nick and Dana to be the only tree deciders.

Heath gave an easy smile. "It took nearly an hour to find these two. I say settle it by a coin toss." He looked at Dana. "Call it."

He tossed the coin into the air. It flipped over and over at a dizzying speed.

"Heads," Dana called. "It has to be heads."

Heath caught the coin in his gloved hand and showed it to Julie, who pointed to Madeline and Wyatt.

"Heads," they said together.

Dana's expression immediately turned smug. "The Fates have spoken."

"The Fates are wrong," Nick grumbled.

Blair slipped her arms around him. "Your tree will live to see another Christmas. Maybe it will be chosen next year."

"It'll be too big," Wyatt announced. "It's growing tall, like me. I'm going to be as tall as my dad!"

"You are," Julie said with a smile. "We'll have to get you new socks, otherwise they'll only cover your big toe. I don't know how that would work."

Wyatt giggled.

Madeline tied their bright yellow marker onto the tree and they all trooped back to the stand by the road. Heath and Nick tussled over who would pay for the tree. Julie settled the argument by pulling out her wallet and telling the guys to stand down. Blair loved how they both immediately listened. Ah, to have that much power, she thought humorously. But as much as she admired her mother-in-law, she didn't have anywhere near her confidence.

One of the workers collected a chain saw and went with Nick and Heath to collect the tree. Gwen ushered the children into their father's SUV and climbed in with them.

Julie immediately looked at Blair and lowered her voice, careful to keep her back to the car. "You doing okay?"

"What do you mean?"

Julie nodded toward the SUV. "Your mom."

Blair sighed. "I'm sorry. Is she bugging you, too?"

Julie's concerned expression never changed. "She knows how to push buttons."

"She does that with everyone. It's a skill. She manages to find the one thing that will make you crazy, then talks about it." She turned toward the SUV, where all three of them were laughing at something. "She's good with kids."

"I noticed that. Years of being a teacher. So why is she so bad with you?"

An unexpected and blunt question, Blair thought, not sure how to answer.

"Mom, don't attack," Dana said mildly.

"I'm not attacking. Blair, did I attack you? I didn't mean to. I find your mom confusing." Julie touched her arm. "This is an attack-free zone."

Blair impulsively hugged her. "You're the best."

Julie held on tight. "But I didn't do anything."

"You're worried about me. Thank you."

Julie's support was everything, she thought. Dealing with her difficult mother would be a worse nightmare if she didn't have such a great mother-in-law. She stepped back and smiled at Dana.

"You don't suck, either."

Dana grinned. "Neither do you."

Blair happened to glance toward the SUV and saw her mother glaring at her. She immediately turned away, not sure what she'd done wrong, but confident she would hear about it later.

Fortunately, the guys returned, carrying the massive tree. The man from the lot helped them drag it into place on Julie's truck and tie it down. The kids jumped out of the SUV and stared.

"That's so big." Madeline sounded both excited and nervous. "How will we get it into the house?"

Julie put her hand on the girl's shoulder. "Fortunately, today we only have to get it into the garage. It will sit there overnight. Tomorrow we'll take it outside and around to the front of the house. Paul stayed home with Rufus, but he'll help with the tree, which is a good thing. It's going to take all of us, and there might be swearing."

Wyatt grinned. "I want to swear."

"You'd better not or I'll tell Mom." Madeline looked from the tree to Julie. "Why does it spend the night in the garage?"

"Bugs," she said cheerfully. "And possibly birds. We don't know what's been living in the tree. We'll shake it out before putting it in the garage, but stuff crawls out and I don't want any of it in my house."

Madeline immediately took a step back while Wyatt peered into the branches. Gwen joined them and frowned at the tree.

"What's that smell?" she asked.

Julie looked at her. "What smell?"

"I don't know. Something."

Julie glanced at Blair, who shrugged. "I don't smell anything."

No one else did, either. Gwen huffed. "Never mind. I'm sure it's nothing."

Blair had to press her lips together to keep from repeating "I'm sure it's nothing" in a high-pitched, mocking voice. She had to get a grip. Yes, her mother was difficult, but it was the holidays and she didn't want to fight or make the time uncomfortable for anyone.

"All right, people," Julie said, opening the door to her truck. "Let's head home."

"Head count," Gwen said. "Are we all here?"

"I'm here," Madeline said with a grin.

Wyatt jumped up and down. "Me, too."

They piled into the two vehicles and made the short drive home. Once there, the guys and the kids untied the tree and wrestled it into the garage. Paul came out to help.

"Well, that's a beautiful tree," he said, admiring the even branches and deep color.

"Dana picked it," Wyatt told him. "Nick's tree was bigger around but it had a bald spot. So they flipped a coin and Dana won."

"You had quite the adventure," Paul said, grinning at the boy. "Good for you."

Blair watched the exchange, thinking that in a few years Paul would be having a conversation with their child. She and Nick wanted to start a family. As soon as the whole issue with the towing business was settled, they would start trying. She wanted children—she always had—and Nick was excited to be a father. The next logical step, she told herself happily.

Her gaze slid to her mother and her good mood faded. No matter what, she would be there for her children, she promised herself for possibly the hundredth time. No matter what pain she suffered or how bad things got, she would show up with love and a giving heart. She would be a solid presence, thinking of them rather than herself. Because she knew the cost of choosing otherwise.

9

"Crap and double crap," Julie muttered, poking around in the refrigerator freezer, even as she knew it wasn't there.

Heath, her assigned kitchen helper for dinner prep, grinned. "You did promise there might be swearing. Should I get the kids?"

She laughed. "No. 'Double crap' isn't very exciting. I forgot to get the garlic bread this morning when I pulled all the ingredients for dinner."

They were having a spaghetti-based casserole with lots of vegetables buried in the meaty, cheesy goodness. With the side salad and plenty of garlic bread, everyone should be happy. Well, probably not Gwen, but everyone else.

"How many loaves?" Heath asked as he started out of the kitchen.

"Let me get them. I know where I put them. You can start cutting up the zucchini into small, even pieces."

He chuckled. "Will you be measuring them later?"

"That depends on how good a job you do."

She went down the stairs and out through the mudroom, only

to find Rufus by the garage door. He was sniffing and whining as he paced back and forth.

"What on earth? Rufus?"

The dog glanced up at her, then scratched at the door. He barked twice.

She didn't know Rufus well, but he seemed fairly low-key. So what was so interesting about the garage?

She thought about the fresh tree they'd brought in an hour before. While they always had it sit overnight to let the spiders and other bugs run out, she'd never had to deal with any kind of actual wildlife. Maybe there had been a bird or something in the branches.

Julie opened the people door to the garage, prepared to immediately open the big main doors and let out whatever it was, all the while keeping Rufus contained. But the second she cracked the door, he was out like a shot. She followed, fumbling for the wall button that would open the main doors.

Two things happened at once. First, Rufus lunged for the tree and started barking like crazy. Second, a horrible smell smacked into her, nearly making her gag. It was musky and thick with ammonia.

Julie immediately backed out of the garage, coughing and calling for the dog. She heard footsteps on the stairs behind her. Heath got there first. Nick and the kids were on his heels.

"What's wrong?" Heath asked. "Where's Rufus?"

She wiped her eyes. "In the garage. I opened the main doors, but I don't think that's going to help."

"Help what?"

She waved toward the garage. Heath went out, along with Nick and the kids. Dana, Blair, Paul and Gwen crowded into the mudroom.

"What's happening?"

"Is there a problem?"

"Mom, are you okay?"

"There's something in the garage," Julie said, forcing herself to open the door and step out into the stink.

Rufus had quieted. He circled the tree a couple of times, sniffing madly. Finally he lifted his leg and peed on the tree.

"No!" Dana shrieked. "That's our tree. What's he doing? Make him stop."

Heath looked at her. "Sorry. Too late. Besides, what he did is the least of it."

With the big doors open, the smell had dissipated a little but was still too strong.

Gwen wrinkled her nose. "Oh, no. There's that smell again. What is it?"

Nick looked at Heath, then back at Gwen. "Cougar pee."

"What?"

He tried not to smile. "I think a cougar peed on our tree." He glanced at his sister. "Sorry, Dana, but there's no way that's going in the house."

Julie waved her hand in front of her face. "No, it's not. Nick, you and Heath drag that outside, far away from here. We need to air out the garage."

"And go get another tree," Paul said cheerfully. He put his hands on the kids' shoulders. "There's time before it gets dark. Do you remember where the second choice was?"

"Maybe." Wyatt sounded doubtful.

"My tree," Dana moaned, watching her brother and Heath drag it around the side of the house.

Julie grabbed Rufus when he started to follow them. "No, you don't. Blair, take him inside, please."

She didn't wait to see if Blair did as she asked. Instead, she went over to the bags of kitty litter they kept around in case one of the cars leaked oil. She spread that over the area where Rufus had marked the tree. Once the liquid had been absorbed, it could be swept up and disposed of. The garage was already smelling better. She would leave the doors open a half hour or so. Hopefully that would be long enough.

"I knew there was something," Gwen murmured.

Julie looked at her. "You were right. I couldn't smell it outside, but you could. That means you get to go with Nick to buy the second tree. I want you to sniff it thoroughly. I refuse to have another cougar pee tree in my Christmas."

That statement sent the kids into giggles. Paul's mouth twitched.

"That's one way to describe it," he murmured.

"Cougar pee tree," Wyatt repeated, nearly doubling over in laughter. "Wait till we tell Mom."

Nick, Blair, Paul and Gwen headed out in Julie's truck. The kids and Dana returned to their movie, taking Rufus with them, while Julie and Heath went back into the kitchen, garlic bread in hand.

"Wyatt's going to talk about the cougar pee tree for the rest of his life," Heath said with a chuckle. "The story will grow over the years, but it's going to be a happy memory."

"I didn't know that could happen." Julie shuddered. "I'm so grateful we left it in the garage. I wouldn't want that stink in the house."

She put the frozen garlic bread into the refrigerator freezer, then pulled out the defrosted ground turkey.

"Why did we have to pick that tree?" she asked, still in shock from the smell. "We've been coming up here and cutting down trees for decades. Nothing like that has ever happened."

"Nature always wins," he teased.

"I'm not sure this is a victory worth celebrating." She glanced at him. "You think the kids are doing all right? I know it's just the first day, but I want them to have fun."

"They're fine. Everyone is paying attention to them, which they like." His grin broadened. "They can't say it's boring here."

"I could do with a little boring." She put a large frying pan on a burner. "At least they're not fighting, unlike my two."

"Nick and Dana weren't fighting. It was traditional banter. Plus, Madeline and Wyatt are still settling in. Give them a couple of days and they'll be bickering."

"You're an only child, right?"

"I am. My parents weren't sure about having kids. By the time they decided they wanted one, my mom was nearly forty. That happens now, but when I was little, it was uncommon. A lot of people thought my parents were my grandparents."

She dumped the two pounds of ground turkey into the pan and used a spatula to break it into smaller pieces.

"I know you lost them both a few years ago," she said. "Any other family?"

"Aunts, uncles and cousins, all back in Virginia. We stay in touch, online mostly. I try to get back there every couple of years." He finished with the zucchini and started chopping an onion. "I thought the kids and I might go in the spring. You could come with us."

"What? No. I couldn't travel with your children."

"Why not? You're spending Christmas with them. Besides, I want you to meet my family."

She wanted to ask why but wasn't sure how to phrase the question without making her sound freakish.

"The last family I met was Eldon's, and that was a long time ago."

"You'll do fine. Besides, it's important for partners to see where we come from. Family often explains a lot."

Partners? Had he just said that? They weren't partners—they were dating. Newly dating.

Julie had never considered herself a runner, yet she had a brief but powerful need to bolt. Not that she had a clue where she would go. Once the casserole was ready, she had to prep the garlic bread, check the chore list to see who was supposed to set the table, and decide what cookies she wanted to make in the morning. Leaving was out of the question. Besides, she was the one always able to handle anything.

"Dad! Dad!"

Wyatt's shouts came from downstairs. Nick, sitting with his arm around Blair, paused the movie. Julie glanced at Heath, who shrugged as he got up from the sofa.

"I have no idea," he admitted, "but he sounds frantic."

"Dad!"

"I'm coming."

But before he got to the stairs, Wyatt raced up to the main floor, his face flushed, his eyes filled with tears, Madeline at his heels.

"Dad, my pillow. I didn't bring it." He flung himself at his father, his body shaking with sobs.

Madeline turned to the adults. "Wyatt has a special pillow. He can't sleep without it. I told him to bring it, and he said he wasn't a baby and he'd remember. But he didn't." Her tone was that of the long-suffering older sister.

"What makes the pillow special?" Gwen asked. She and Dana were seated on the oversize love seat, a bowl of popcorn between them.

Wyatt looked at her. "It just is. It's my special pillow and I don't have it." He returned his attention to his father. "I want to go home. I want to go home now!"

"I don't," Madeline said loudly. "You should have remembered the stupid pillow."

Wyatt started crying again. Heath looked at his daughter. "Maddy, you're not helping." He pulled his phone out of his pocket and took Wyatt's hand. "Come on. We'll go into the kitchen and call your mom to make sure the pillow is there. I'll drive back and get it in the morning. Or maybe she can meet me somewhere."

"Not tonight?" Wyatt's voice trembled. "I can't sleep without my pillow."

"Then let's all stay up all night," Gwen said cheerfully. "We'll have a sleepover."

Everyone turned to look at her. Gwen smiled brightly.

"Why not? The sectional sofa is huge. At least two, maybe three people can sleep there. I'm sure there are air mattresses. We'll have the fire going, watch movies and stay up all night."

Julie had trouble reconciling the accommodating, kid-centric, great-idea Gwen with the woman who had dissed Nick and seemed to always get it wrong when it came to her own daughter. But she had to admit, the idea had merit. If Wyatt didn't feel alone, he wouldn't be so upset. She would guess even without his special pillow, he would fall asleep fairly quickly.

"The love seat pulls out," Julie said. "Madeline and Wyatt can sleep there. We have a couple of cots in one of the storage closets, along with air mattresses."

"I can sleep on a cot," Heath said.

Julie wasn't thrilled with the idea but smiled as she murmured, "Me, too."

"You should take the sofa." Blair leaned her head against Nick's shoulder. "We'll take cots. Are there enough? Mom, which would you prefer? A cot or an air mattress?"

"A cot, please."

It didn't take long to make arrangements. Heath left a message when Tiffany didn't answer, then helped with the setup. Paul demurred on the sleepover and said he would keep his bed downstairs. By nine everyone had brushed their teeth and collected blankets and nonspecial pillows. Wyatt was still claiming he wouldn't sleep at all.

They agreed on a *The Santa Clause* movie marathon. Heath once again tried to get Tiffany on the phone, but she didn't answer, so he left a second message about the pillow situation. By the time Tim Allen was reading *'Twas the Night Before Christmas* to his son, both kids were sound asleep.

"Good call, Gwen," Heath said quietly. "Thank you."

"Anytime."

Julie and Heath were up a little after six. They headed upstairs to their room.

"I slept better than I thought I would," Julie admitted, putting the blanket back on their bed as he put the pillows in place.

He pulled her close. "I missed having you next to me."

"I was right there on the sofa."

His hands drifted to her butt. "We were limited in what we could do."

She smiled and pushed him away. "We still are. I have to get the breakfast casserole ready." She smiled. "But I believe I'm free in about three hours."

"I'll be counting the minutes."

"Did you hear from Tiffany?"

He frowned at his phone. "I didn't. She wasn't supposed to leave until tomorrow. I'll try her again around seven."

Julie showered first. Once she was dressed, she blew out her hair. Heath was busy undressing. She paused to admire the view—the man was very easy on the eyes, she thought happily, looking forward to their rendezvous later that morning.

She left him in the shower and walked into the bedroom. Just then, his phone rang.

She glanced at the screen and saw the call was from Tiffany. After a second of indecision, she answered the call.

"Hi, Tiffany. It's Julie. Heath's in the shower and I knew he wouldn't want to miss your call. You got the message about Wyatt's special pillow?"

There was a brief pause, then what sounded a lot like a sob, followed by, "I d-did. It's right here. He can come get it or I can meet him somewhere. I'm off work for my v-vacation."

Her voice was thick with tears. Julie clutched the phone tightly as dread filled her.

"What's wrong? You're upset, so something bad happened. Tell me."

"It's n-nothing. I'm fine."

"You're not. Tiffany, I'm worried. What is it? Did someone die?"

"What? No. Nothing like that. I'm okay."

"Don't make me use my mom voice on you. What's going on?"

Tiffany sniffed. "Ryan broke up with me."

Who was Ryan? Oh, wait. "The boyfriend?"

"Uh-huh. Last night. We were supposed to go to the Bahamas and now he's taking someone else."

The sobs returned, more urgently this time. Julie stood there, not sure what to say.

"I'm sorry. This is a sucky time to deal with a breakup. Can I, um, do anything to help?"

"I'm okay."

She didn't sound okay. She sounded heartbroken.

"It's just I thought he was special, you know. That we had a future. I was falling in love with him. But he didn't feel the same." She blew her nose. "Like you said, it's a sucky time for a breakup."

Julie sat on the bed. "He's a jerk and it's his loss."

"You're kind to say that. I want it to be true, but I don't know."

"Do you have family in the area?"

"What? No. Why would you…?" Tiffany cleared her throat. "Oh, you mean for Christmas? I'll be fine. It's all good. I shouldn't have said anything." She gave a false laugh. "It was the threat of the mom voice. So have Heath call me. I can meet him. It's no problem."

Julie told herself not to get involved, that Heath's ex-wife's breakup wasn't her problem. But she couldn't stand the thought of the other woman being home by herself with only a broken heart for company.

"You should join us for Christmas."

"What? No, I couldn't. You're sweet to offer, but no."

"I mean it, Tiffany." Julie's voice was firm. "The house is plenty big. The kids are in a room with double bunk beds. You could sleep in there with them. There's already a crowd here. Trust me, one more isn't going to be a problem. Have Christmas with us. The last thing you want is to be alone. Besides, don't you want to spend the holidays with your children?"

"Julie, that's nice, but—"

"No buts. If you're worried everyone is part of a couple, they aren't. My daughter, who's about your age—" painful to say, but true "—is single, as is Blair's mom and Blair's uncle. Plus, come on. You know you want to spend Christmas with your children. And no one should be alone this time of year. Say yes. I'll have Heath text you the address. Drive up today and don't forget the pillow."

"You mean it?"

"Yes, and I'm insisting. I'll expect you by lunchtime. Pack for snow."

"You're a lovely person. Thank you." There was another sob. "You're right. I don't want to be alone, so I'll be there."

"We'll see you in a few hours."

"Thank you so much."

They hung up. Julie sat there a second, trying to take in what she'd done. Oh, she'd made the right decision, but explaining it to everyone was going to be…complicated.

She tossed the phone onto the bed and walked into the bathroom. Heath had finished with his shower and was drying off. When he saw her, he smiled.

"I thought you were going downstairs."

"I am, in a second. Tiffany called and I answered because I didn't think you'd want to wait to hear about the pillow."

His expression was quizzical. "Are you all right? Did she say something to upset you?"

"Not at all." She paused, not sure how to explain. "Ryan broke up with her. Ryan, the boyfriend," she clarified.

She explained about the crying and how she couldn't possibly leave her home alone for Christmas.

Heath started to laugh. "Let me get this straight. You invited my ex-wife to join us for the week?"

"Her jerk boyfriend dumped her, so she's not going to the Bahamas. She shouldn't be by herself."

He hung up the towel and walked toward her. Naked. When he reached her, he pulled her close.

"That's a very Julie thing to do," he murmured between kisses. "You have to take care of everyone, and no one gets to take care of you."

"That's not true."

But there wasn't much energy in her voice, not when his hands were roaming over her body and she was returning the favor. The difference being she was touching bare skin and he wasn't.

As if reading her mind, he tugged at her sweater.

"I have to make breakfast," she protested, even as she toed out of her shoes.

"They can wait."

Blair walked into the kitchen a little before seven and was surprised to find it empty and dark. Usually Julie was up before everyone else. She flipped on lights, then turned on the oven, knowing the breakfast casserole would need at least forty-five minutes to heat up.

Unlike the kids and everyone else who had bunked in the living room, she hadn't slept well. Her stomach had bothered her, forcing her to head for the bathroom twice, after which she'd felt a little nauseous. She hoped she wasn't coming down with anything.

She set the casserole on the counter while the oven heated, then started coffee. A quick read of the posted menus told her Julie had planned sausages to go with the casserole. She was planning on serving sliced fruit, as well.

Nick strolled in and walked over to her. "How are you feeling?"

"I'm good."

"You got up last night."

"I didn't think I woke you." She offered a quick smile. "I'm fine. It's your mom who's the problem. She's not here."

He looked around. "You're right. She always starts breakfast before anyone is up. You think she's okay?"

Blair had a very good idea about what had kept her mother-in-law upstairs. "I think she's fine." She lowered her voice. "So's Heath. I like him. What about you?"

"He's a good guy. I'm not surprised. Mom has only introduced Dana and me to a couple of the men she's dated since the divorce, but they've all been decent. She wouldn't tolerate anything else."

"You don't mind that he's younger?"

Nick considered the question. "No. It seems like something she'd do. Wyatt and Madeline are great. Last night was pretty funny. Wyatt was so convinced he wouldn't sleep at all."

"But he did. The sleepover was a good idea."

Nick grinned. "Say it like you mean it."

Blair groaned. "I do mean it." Sort of. "My mom's great with Heath's kids. I'm trying not to be bitter. She gets them but doesn't get me. What's up with that?"

"I don't know. You're very gettable."

She laughed. "What does that even mean?"

The oven dinged just then, and both kids wandered into the kitchen.

"Morning," Wyatt said, rubbing his eyes. "I slept."

"You did." Blair slid the casserole into the oven. "We have time before we eat, so why don't you two go downstairs and get dressed? We've got a busy morning. We'll be bringing in the tree and decorating it."

"What about the cougar pee?" Wyatt asked with a laugh.

"My mom checked it out and said it was fine, so it must be so."

Nick ushered the kids downstairs. Paul, Gwen and Dana showed up to help with breakfast. A few minutes later, Julie walked in.

"Oh, you got everything started," she said, not meeting anyone's gaze. "Sorry, I got distracted."

Gwen made a tsking noise but didn't say anything. Blair ignored her mother and smiled at Julie.

"I put the casserole in about ten minutes ago. I saw we were having sausage with it, but I wasn't sure about the fruit."

Julie took charge and started assigning tasks. Gwen went downstairs to check on the kids while Dana set the table and Paul squeezed oranges for fresh juice. Blair started to cook the sausages, only to find the smell was bothering her, which was strange. It never had before.

Fortunately, Julie swooped in and took the spatula from her. "I'll deal with this. Do you think we should have bacon, too?"

"This seems like plenty." Blair thought of the giant casserole warming in the oven. "You don't need to worry about anyone going hungry."

"I can't help it. Feeding my family is my responsibility."

And Julie took her responsibilities very seriously, Blair thought. Even though her children were grown, she worried about them. Blair thought about the secret she and Nick were keeping and felt a moment of guilt. She understood that he didn't want to ruin his mom's holiday, but thought maybe they should have told her as soon as Nick started thinking he might like to buy Uncle Paul's business. Julie had a right to know the truth.

But it wasn't her decision to make, she reminded herself. Come the first of the year, she would insist Nick tell his mom what was happening, just like he'd promised.

Nick, Gwen and the kids appeared in the kitchen. Everyone was bumping into everyone else until Julie shooed them all to the table. Only Gwen stayed in the kitchen to help serve.

Breakfast was a noisy affair, Blair thought happily. So different from how it had been when she'd grown up. She couldn't remember much before her mother had "gone away," as she thought of it, no doubt in part because of only being four and in part because of the sadness that surrounded that time.

Little Robby had been only three weeks old. Blair had been so curious about her baby brother, often sitting in his room while he slept. She'd wanted to learn how to do everything and remembered being disappointed when her mother had explained she was breastfeeding for the first few weeks, so there were no bottles to give him.

The morning he died was a blur. Blair remembered her mother screaming. The sound went on and on, as if it would never stop. She'd tried to get her father's attention so he could explain what was wrong, but he'd told her to go to her room in a tone she'd never heard before.

Later, one of the neighbors had taken her, and a few hours after that, Uncle Paul had arrived to stay with her. She knew there must have been a funeral and that she'd probably attended, but she had no memory of it. Her next clear recollection was her father walking her to kindergarten, telling her she was going to enjoy school. Blair had hoped that was true because sometimes being in her house scared her. Not the house itself, but with the ghost that was her mother.

Gwen moved from room to room without speaking or interacting with anyone. She'd grown so thin, so pale. Sometimes Blair heard her crying, but she never heard her speak. Not for months and months. Eventually her mother had gone back to work, but she'd never become part of the family again.

"You all right?" Nick asked quietly, drawing her back to the present.

"Sorry. I was thinking about something else." She glanced at the plate of sausages she held and shook her head. "I'll pass." The smell was still a problem. She would make do with the French toast–inspired casserole and some fruit.

"This is a big table," Wyatt said. "We could fit more people around it."

"Which is good." Julie smiled at him. "We have more people coming for Christmas. There are two leaves that fit in, not that we'll need both of them."

Dana looked at her mom. "More people. I thought the only other person we were expecting was Huxley."

"Yes, well…" Julie cleared her throat. "There's been a minor change of plans."

The table went silent. Everyone stared at Julie, waiting. Well, not Heath, Blair thought, glancing at him. He looked relaxed and amused, so whatever the news—it wasn't bad.

"I invited Tiffany to spend the holidays with us." Julie picked up her coffee, then set it down. "She was supposed to go away, but that didn't work out and she's alone."

"The kids' mom?" Dana asked, sounding surprised.

Blair's breath caught in her throat. Had Julie really done that?

Madeline's eyes widened, and Wyatt jumped out of his chair.

"Mom's coming here?" he asked loudly.

"She is and she's bringing your pillow." Julie smiled at Madeline. "You get to spend Christmas with both your parents."

"You invited your current boyfriend's ex-wife to spend Christmas with you and your family?" Gwen asked, no doubt voicing the question they were all thinking.

She sounded more stunned than outraged.

Julie offered a faint smile. "Yes, well, it wasn't planned. She was upset and I felt bad for her. No one should be alone on Christmas. There's plenty of room for her."

"It's a very generous offer," Paul said. "Heath, any apprehension?"

"Not at all. Tiffany isn't difficult and Julie can handle anything. The kids will be happy."

Madeline ran around the table and hugged her dad. "Mommy's going to be here!"

"Yes, she is."

"And you. On Christmas."

Nick leaned close to Blair. "You gotta admire the self-confidence," he said quietly. "She's a hell of a woman."

"Yes, she is."

10

"Nick made this one when he was about your age," Dana told Madeline, holding up a heavily decorated star made from Popsicle sticks and rhinestones.

Madeline eyed the gaudy decoration doubtfully. "It's really purple and gold."

"For the University of Washington," Wyatt told her. "Those are Husky colors."

Dana lowered her voice. "We can put it toward the back."

"Hey, I heard that," Nick called from his place on a ladder on the right side of the tree. Heath was up just as high on the left. They were stringing the lights while Dana, Blair and the kids sorted through the ornaments.

There were the usual handmade treasures—clay palm prints, plain ornaments that had been painted, oddly shaped creatures made out of pipe cleaners, along with dated ornaments and a few dozen small Patience Brewster ornaments that her mother had always loved. The rest were a hodgepodge of store-bought and souvenir decorations. Dana had already teared up twice, handling ancient ornaments that had been so meaningful to her father. She was enjoying the tree decorating, but couldn't help noticing her dad's absence. Normally he sat right there on the sofa, telling Nick and her mom if the lights were even or not.

"Heath, we're going to need to borrow your quarter again," Nick said, passing him the string of lights.

Heath draped it along the branches, covering each one on that level, then passed it back. "Sure. Why?"

"Tinsel," Dana said, with a smile she hoped looked genuine. "We're going to fight over tinsel. He loves it and I don't." She pointed at her brother. "We alternate every year, and last year there was tinsel."

"But we have a lot more people with us," Nick said with a chuckle. "Let them decide."

"I love tinsel," Madeline whispered.

Dana gave her a quick hug. "It's okay. You can love tinsel as much as you want."

The kids were great. Dana enjoyed having them for the holidays. Right now they were a nice distraction from missing her father. She knew her mom had been worried about them fitting in, but they'd settled in quickly.

The doorbell rang. Rufus immediately sprang to his feet and started barking. Dana glanced toward the front of the house, wondering who would be... Oh, right. Tiffany.

She stayed where she was while her mom yelled from the kitchen, where she was making cookies. "I'll get it."

Heath climbed down the ladder. "Me, too."

Wyatt looked at Dana. "Is that our mom?"

"Probably."

He and his sister took off like a shot, Rufus at their heels. Paul, who was untangling strings of lights to hand to the other guys to put on the tree, tried to hold in a grin.

"I have to say, it's never boring around here."

"No, it's not."

Dana wasn't sure how she felt about "Tiffany" joining them.

Obviously she didn't care if there was one more person for the holidays. The entire celebration was about connecting. But Heath's ex-wife? Was she the only one who thought that was a little strange?

Still, it was very typical of her mother to impulsively invite someone to join them. Julie had always been about making sure no one was left behind. But Dana couldn't help wondering if her mother had really thought it all through. Heath and Tiffany were divorced. Did they get along now or were they still fighting? What if Tiffany was a bitch? They were already dealing with the apparently socially awkward Gwen. How would one more person affect the dynamics?

Not her issue, she told herself.

She got up and walked toward the entryway. Wyatt burst into the room, pulling a pretty redhead along with him.

"This is my mom. Mom, this is everybody."

Dana started to hold out her hand to offer a greeting, then stopped. She frowned slightly as she took in the familiar features. Yes, the woman was twelve or fourteen years older, but she still looked as she had.

"Tiffany?"

Wyatt's mom glanced at her with a friendly smile that suddenly froze and her eyes widened. "Oh, wow. Dana? Is that you?"

"It is."

They rushed toward each other and hugged.

Julie walked in, a pillow under one arm and a suitcase in her hand. "You two know each other?"

Dana stepped back and laughed. "We do. Tiffany and I went to high school together. She was a junior when I was a freshman."

Tiffany smiled and nodded. "We were in orchestra. Junior and senior members are assigned a freshman to mentor for the year. I was Dana's mentor."

Dana wasn't sure, but she thought maybe her mother went pale.

"You were in high school together," Julie repeated. "That's amazing. Wyatt, here's your pillow. Madeline, why don't you and your brother show your mom where she'll be sleeping?" She offered Tiffany a tight smile. "You'll have to talk to Rufus about which bunk he's been using. I'm not saying you won't win the fight, but there might be one to be had."

Tiffany took a step toward her. "I can't thank you enough. You've been so gracious." Tears filled her eyes. "You didn't have to do this."

Julie waved away the comment. "It's Christmas. You should be with family. And look! They're all here. Now go get settled. Heath, carry her suitcase down, then come back and help with the lights. We want the tree decorated today for sure."

Everyone jumped to do her bidding. While they were reacting, Julie returned to the kitchen, no doubt to continue baking cookies. Dana followed her.

"Mom, are you okay?"

"I'm fine. Wyatt has his special pillow, so tonight should be easier." She lowered her voice. "I looked it over, and honestly, I can't tell what makes it special."

"You know how kids are." Dana moved closer. "Are you sorry you invited Tiffany?"

"Of course not. I couldn't stand to think of her all alone in her house." She motioned for Dana to step closer, then whispered, "Her boyfriend dumped her. He was supposed to take her to the Bahamas, but ended things instead."

"Bastard."

"Exactly. Breakups are tough enough, but over the holidays? No way. She'll stay here with us and be distracted. It'll be great."

Dana stared at her mother. "I don't know how you do it, Mom. You're amazing. Your boyfriend's ex-wife? I couldn't be that generous."

"Of course you could. It'll be fine. You'll see."

★ ★ ★

Julie got through the cookie making and the tree trimming, then lunch, but finally, a little after two, when everyone else wanted to go ride inner tubes down the hill, she was able to beg off and retreat to her room. She closed the door behind her, walked to the bed and sat down. Seconds later, she was on her feet, pacing the length of the room, telling herself to breathe, that everything would be fine. It had to be. Christmas was still days away.

The door opened and Heath stepped inside. She instantly retreated, putting the bed between them and wishing it were a whole lot more space.

"Why aren't you out with everyone else?" she asked with faux cheer. "You love going down a mountain on an inner tube."

"Actually, I don't, and I wanted to talk." His expression was concerned. "Something's bothering you."

"Me? Don't be silly. I'm fine. Perfectly fine. There's nothing wrong."

Heath stayed by the door, watching her. He didn't say anything, and something about the way he was standing told her he was willing to wait forever.

"You're being ridiculous," she muttered, taking a step back, then another, until she was plastered against the wall. Why wasn't this room bigger?

"You're freaked out about something. Is it Tiffany? I thought you were all right with her being here."

"I am. Totally. Completely." She paused. "All right, maybe I wasn't *that* accepting, but asking her here was the right thing to do."

"You're very kind." His gaze was steady. "What changed?"

"She went to high school with my daughter!"

Heath's lack of reaction made her want to shake him.

"She's what? Two years older than Dana? Do you know what that means?"

"No."

"I'm old! I'm a crone. Why are you dating me? It's ridiculous. I'm laughable. This is a total nightmare. I can only imagine what Gwen's thinking."

"Why do you care about Gwen's opinion on anyone?"

"I don't, but she's representative of a worldview that makes me uncomfortable." She pressed a hand to her chest, worrying her heart was pounding too fast. "Why does she have to be so young?"

"Why does it matter?"

She glared at him. "Oh, sure. Be rational. You're the good-looking younger guy. There's no bad in here for you. I'm the one who gets judged. I'm the one who gets mocked."

He took a step toward her. She would have retreated, but there wasn't anywhere to go.

"Why do you care what anyone thinks?" he asked again. "You've never been that person."

"I don't," she said slowly, then huffed out a breath. "Except this time." She moved to the bed and sank down. "She's so young. And what's with the boobs? They're huge. My breasts are raisins compared to hers." Okay, not raisins, but they were substantially smaller. "How does she stay upright?"

Heath sat next to her—not touching but close enough to be a presence. She wasn't sure how she felt about that.

"They're implants, remember."

Julie glared at him. "You know that and I know that, but no one else does and it's not as if we can make an announcement. And while we're on the subject, and I don't mean that harshly, but really? You wanted your wife to get implants?"

"Hey, wait. It wasn't me." He stood and pulled her to her feet. "She did it after the divorce. We talked about it when we were married and I wasn't interested. You need to stop assuming the worst about me."

"You need to stop having a wife who's twenty-two years younger than me. And you should be older, too."

He pulled her close. She struggled to get away, but he didn't release her, and after a couple of seconds she realized she still liked being held by him.

"Why the freak-out?" he asked gently.

"I don't know, but it happened, so we have to deal."

"I agree. Julie, you're the one I want to be with. You're important to me. Tiffany and I are divorced. Whatever we had died a long time ago."

She looked up at him and saw the sincerity in his eyes. "But the age thing."

"Only exists in your mind."

"And the wrinkles on my face."

"What wrinkles?"

"They're there. Plus, I think my butt's starting to sag."

"It's not." He kissed her. "This is your Christmas, too. I want you to enjoy it."

"I will."

"Even with Tiffany here?"

She thought about how the other woman had sounded so heartbroken on the phone. Being dumped just before Christmas had to be the worst.

"She seems very nice." She tilted her head. "So you've never touched them?"

"What?"

"The implants. You can't say if they feel different or not?"

"No, I can't, but talk to Tiffany. Maybe she'll let you feel her up."

"It wouldn't be sexual," Julie murmured. "I *am* curious, but it might be too weird to ask."

Heath chuckled. "You think?" He kissed her again. "Better?"

"Yes. The age thing still bugs me, but I'm going to try to not think about it."

"Or maybe spend more time staring in the mirror. You're a beautiful woman."

Staring in the mirror? Not her style. "You're a good man. Thank you."

"Anytime."

Blair carefully folded the sweater to fit the box. Once she'd adjusted the tissue paper, she set the box in the center of the wrapping paper she'd already cut and started taping it in place.

As she did every holiday season, Julie had set up the craft room as a wrapping paper station, with plenty of supplies and a big table to work on. There was even a cardboard sign to put on the door proclaiming Keep Out! I'm Wrapping Presents in a fun, colorful font.

She'd meant to get her wrapping done before they'd left Seattle but life interfered, she thought as she reached for the next gift. No doubt Julie had finished her shopping long before Thanksgiving. She was just that kind of person. Dana was fairly organized, as well. Like mother, like daughter. Thankfully she couldn't say the same about herself and Gwen.

Everything about her mother irritated her. She paused as she mentally amended that statement to *almost* everything. Her mom was great with Madeline and Wyatt, which Blair could appreciate. She told herself that once she and Nick had kids, Gwen would probably be a decent grandmother. At least Blair hoped so. Having her do a disappearing act on her grandkids would define unforgivable.

The door to the craft room opened and her mother stepped in. "There you are. I thought we should talk."

Blair glared at her. "What's with refusing to knock? Does a closed door mean anything to you? There's even a sign. I'm wrapping presents."

Her mother closed the door and took a seat at the table.

"You're not wrapping anything for me. We haven't exchanged gifts in years. As I said, we need to talk."

Blair told herself not to get mad—her temper wouldn't help the situation. Only everything her mother said bugged her. Yes, they didn't exchange presents because her mother had bluntly told her there was no point. They bought themselves what they wanted, and everything else was just a waste of time and money. Which might have been true, but had still hurt her nineteen-year-old self.

That remembered wound, still a little tender to the touch, overtook common sense.

"You needing to talk, while interesting, doesn't define my life," she snapped. "What are you doing here, Mother? Why did you move to Seattle and why did you bother coming to the cabin for Christmas? With the exception of Heath's kids, you don't seem very fond of the people staying here. I'm wondering what you hope to get out of this, because unless your goal is to ruin everyone else's holiday, I don't get it."

She half expected her mother to stomp out of the room, but she didn't. Instead, Gwen turned away for a few seconds before looking back and saying, "I want to be involved in your life."

Blair stared at her blankly, unable to process the words. "Why? You never did before."

"That's not true. You're my daughter. I wanted to be involved, but there were complications."

"They weren't complications. You went away. One second you were my mom and the next you weren't. Do you have any idea what it was like for me?"

"I lost my son!" her mother shouted.

"I lost my brother, which was bad, but then I lost my mother." Blair put her hands on the table and leaned forward. "You had grief. I get that, but you turned your back on me for the rest of my childhood. You abandoned me when I was four years old. Four. Sure, you were dealing with the loss, but so was I. You're the mom. You're supposed to take care of your children, but you didn't. It was like the grief mattered more than anything. Certainly more than me."

She thought about how great her mom was with Wyatt and Madeline. "When Wyatt forgot his special pillow, you jumped into action and came up with the idea of us having a sleepover—all of us together—so he wouldn't feel scared."

She paused to get control. No way she was giving in to tears now. "Imagine being a small child who has lost her brother, not that I knew what that meant. Imagine how scary it was to have lots of adults in the house and not knowing what was going on. Imagine that child hearing her mother screaming and screaming, like she was never going to stop. Imagine having a neighbor come and take you away."

Her mother looked at her without speaking, her pain obvious. Blair ignored the inevitable guilt and plunged on.

"Imagine coming back home, terrified of what you'll find. And in case you can't, let me tell you what it was like. The house was so dark and quiet. I was scared to the point of shaking, but no one paid attention to me. I didn't know what had happened and I didn't know where you were. Dad was there, but it wasn't the same. Because until we lost Robby, you'd been my mom in every sense of the word. But suddenly you wouldn't see me. No matter how I begged, you wouldn't see me or hold me, and you certainly wouldn't tell me that everything would be all right." She swallowed against the thickness in her throat. "You never held me again, Mom. Not once in my life. Not once. For the rest of my childhood, only my father hugged me."

"I'm sorry." Gwen's voice broke on the words. "I couldn't. I just couldn't. Holding you was too much of a reminder that I would never hold him again."

"And now we circle around to the obvious and repetitive question. Why does your dead child matter so much more than the living one? Why was your grief bigger than your love for me? I'm assuming here. Maybe you never cared about me at all."

She thought about her teenage years when she'd been bullied in school to the point where her father had decided to move her to Seattle so she could start over.

"You didn't visit me when I went to live with Uncle Paul. I was fifteen and in a strange city, starting over. You never came. Only Dad showed up."

Her mother started to cry. "I couldn't. I hurt too much because of what had happened to you. I couldn't stand to think of it."

"Or look at me." Blair's tone was accusing. "Do you think I didn't notice?"

"It wasn't that." Her mother stared at her. "It wasn't that. Those teens were so awful to you. I was angry but also afraid of spiraling back into the grief. I was terrified of getting so lost, I'd never find my way back. I got help and got better, but by then, it was too late. The past was repeating itself. First with your father and then with Paul. You were a team and didn't need me."

The unfairness of that made Blair want to scream.

"Don't," she shouted. "Don't you dare accuse me of being the problem. It's all on you. Dad and I were a team because we were the only ones left in the family. The same with me and Paul. It was just us. You could have belonged but you couldn't be bothered."

"You don't understand."

"I understand just fine. You had enough in you to give to your kids at school, but nothing left for me. You never worried about me or how I was doing. I grew up without a mother. Not a unique situation. The only difference between me and those other kids is my mother was alive and in the same house."

Blair glared at her. "I stopped crying for you around the time I turned ten or eleven. I finally figured out you would never be there for me, never care about me. And you know why? Because that's what you taught me."

She wanted to add that she would never forgive her mother for what she'd done, but couldn't say the words. Not because she cared about her mother, but because she knew her father would be disappointed if she did.

"You chose to be okay for your students," she whispered. "You never chose to be okay for me. That's why I don't give a damn if you want to be a part of my life."

Her mother covered her face with her hands. "You don't know what it was like for me. The depression ate me alive. I did the best I could. Back when your brother was born, no one paid attention to postpartum depression—not like they do now. I was expected to simply power through. Then he died, and it was like I'd died, too. I didn't have anything left for you. I was barely alive."

Gwen brushed her tears. "I didn't want to leave you."

"But you did! Fine, you were depressed. That explains what? The first three or four years. What about after that? I get there's no timeline for grief, but from my perspective, you never even tried to let it go. What about when Dad died?"

"What does your father have to do with anything?"

"I flew out to Boise to be with you and you shut me out."

"I'd just lost the love of my life. Did you expect me to entertain you?"

Blair ignored the outrage in her mother's voice. "No, Mom. I expected you to consider the fact that I was your daughter and that I'd lost my father. We could have helped each other deal, but you don't ever want that. It's like your pain is so much worse than anyone else's and we all need to live in service of that. I had pain, too."

She still did. The missing wasn't so sharp now, but it didn't go away. Her father had been there for her, always. He'd done what was best for her, even when that meant letting her go live five hundred miles away.

"You've taught me not to trust you," she said bluntly. "When the bad stuff happens, you won't be there. Actually, you won't be there for the good stuff, either. Until I was four, you were a great mom, but after that, you left and you've never come back."

Her mother's lower lip quivered. "What are you saying?"

"We don't have a relationship. We haven't for most of my life. I don't know why you want to start over now, but I don't know if I can. More important, I don't think I want to."

Her mother began to cry. "I'm your mother."

Blair ignored the guilt and the need to say that all would be well. "Sure, you get the title, but you're not like a mother to me. You're all over Heath's kids, but you only ever criticize me, telling me what I'm doing wrong. You don't know me. You should have been there for me, and while I know we can't change the past, you're still not there for me."

"Not like Julie," Gwen said bitterly. "I know you think she's perfect."

Blair wondered if her mother was jealous of the other woman. What was there to be jealous of?

"No, I don't think she's perfect. But she's a great mom who takes care of everyone. She thinks about other people rather than herself. Even when it's hard, she does the right thing. The woman invited her boyfriend's ex-wife for Christmas. I admire her willingness to jump in and just do it, even when it's hard. She made me feel welcome."

"You're a catch for Nick and this family. Of course she welcomed you."

"You're wrong. Nick isn't the lucky one, Mom. I am. Because with him and his family, I feel loved and like I belong. No matter what, they'll be here for me."

"You're saying I won't?" Her mother started crying again.

Blair nodded slowly. "You never have been." She couldn't

help giving a bitter laugh. "Seriously, tell me one time when you were there for me. Or even showed up in a way that was supportive. Give me one example of you thinking of me and doing something for me. Something thoughtful and kind. Something a mother would do for one of her kids."

Her mother stared at her without speaking.

"Yeah, that's what I thought. At the risk of repeating myself, you taught me not to trust you. Why are you surprised that I don't?"

Her mother's harsh sobs filled the room. Blair's stomach immediately clenched, and she fought against the need to call back the words. But she knew she couldn't. They'd both been avoiding the truth for too long.

Her mother raced to the door, flung it open and disappeared. Silence filled the room. Blair felt a familiar clutching low in her belly and wondered how bad the attack would be. She always had a reaction to fighting, or any powerful emotional stressor. Which wasn't going to be pleasant, but the real problem was what was going to happen now with her mom.

She probed her heart, checking for feelings. There was guilt, of course, and a little shame. She wasn't the kind of person who deliberately hurt another person. But there was also relief for finally saying exactly what she needed to.

Julie knocked on the open door. "Hey, you okay?"

Blair held in a groan. "You heard?"

"Just the parts where you two were shouting."

"So most of it?"

Julie moved into the room and sat next to her, then hugged her. "I'm sorry. I wish I could make things better."

"Not possible." Blair looked at the doorway, then back at Julie. She lowered her voice. "I hate her."

"No, you don't."

"I do. She's awful. I wish she'd stayed in Boise."

Julie took her hand and squeezed it. "Why did you go live with Paul?"

Blair told herself the past was done and she was strong enough to handle it.

"My IBS comes in cycles. I was going through a bad time and couldn't get to the bathroom in time." She felt herself flush. "I had diarrhea in the hallway at school. I was fifteen. It wasn't the kind of thing the other kids would forget."

Julie hugged her again. "That would have been a nightmare."

Blair hung on. "It was. I was humiliated and ashamed. Most of my friends abandoned me. Nothing helped make the situation better, so we agreed I'd go live with Uncle Paul. I got a new doctor, who got me on meds that helped control things, and you know the rest."

Julie drew back enough to touch her face. "I wish I could make all this better."

"Me, too." Her stomach gurgled ominously. She pressed a hand to her belly. "Stress is not my friend."

"I'm here for you."

Blair managed a smile. "I know. Thank you."

Dana walked into the room. "You okay?"

Blair hung her head. "You heard, too?"

"Just, you know, parts of it."

"Maybe she'll leave," Blair murmured, knowing her luck wasn't that good.

"She's your mom." Julie's voice was gentle. "You need to make peace with her."

"Or not."

Dana sat at the table and touched the plaid shirt Blair had been about to wrap. "Is this for Nick?"

Blair nodded. "You know the man loves a plaid shirt." And they were practical, given how much work he did outside, in the cold Seattle winter.

"I bought him the same one."

"What?" Blair smiled. "You did?"

Julie touched the soft cotton. "I might have, too. Do you think he'll notice?"

Blair started to laugh. "Probably not, and if he does, he'll be perfectly fine with it."

11

By three, Dana was feeling restless. The snow had stopped that morning, and the sun was making a weak appearance before setting for the night. She headed downstairs, thinking a walk might do her good, what with all the weight she had to lose. She found Tiffany sitting by herself in the living room.

"Hey," Dana said, offering a smile.

Tiffany looked up. Her face was blotchy and her eyes swollen. She'd obviously been crying.

"Hi." She managed a wobbly smile.

"You okay?"

"Sure." The tone was false, but bright.

Dana pointed to the window. "We've got about an hour before it gets dark. Want to take a walk?"

Tiffany only hesitated for a second before standing. "That's a good idea. I could use the exercise."

They went into the mudroom and stepped into snow boots before piling on layers. Once outside, Dana sucked in the cold air. The temperature was in the midtwenties, she thought, and would drop to close to zero that night.

"It's freezing," Tiffany said with a laugh.

"Think of it as bracing."

They walked along the shoveled sidewalks. In the distance, kids pulled sleds and toboggans up a low hill, their parents keeping watch. The trees were still frosted with the night's snow.

"It's pretty here," Dana said, thinking how lucky she was to be able to come here every Christmas. She had so many memories and would continue to make more. Yes, she was missing her dad, but she was glad she'd come. "It's like we're in a snow globe."

"I guess." Tiffany sighed. "Sorry. It is pretty."

"But it's not the Bahamas. He's a jerk."

"He is, but you don't know him, so you're guessing."

"He dumped you a week before Christmas. He has to be a jerk. You deserve better."

"Thanks. I know you're right, but it still hurts." She shook her head. "I'm such a fool. I shouldn't have given my heart so easily."

Something Dana could relate to. If only she'd been able to resist Axel, she thought. She might have met someone else—someone who wouldn't leave her every time things got good.

"I know about loving the jerky guy," she said, then added, "Not that he's a jerk, exactly. He's more…confusing."

"Did he dump you before Christmas?"

"No. A few days after. Then he stayed with me after my dad died, only to disappear again."

Tiffany groaned. "And you can't forget him?"

"Not really. I guess it's a chemistry thing. He works for my mom. She owns a towing company. A few weeks after she hired him, I went over there to have lunch with her. Our eyes met and I was a goner."

"That sounds romantic."

"Excluding the broken heart, it is. The worst part for me is he tells me he loves me, but that he's not good enough. Then he dumps me."

"Does he cheat?" Tiffany asked.

"Not that I know of. I have no sense of him being with someone else." She blinked back tears. "I guess he just doesn't want to be with me."

"I know how that feels."

Dana looked at her. "Sorry. I was trying to bond, not make you feel bad."

"I felt bad before. You didn't do anything wrong." Tiffany looked around at the houses with their snowy roofs. "You're right. It *is* pretty here, and I do appreciate not being alone. Your family is very generous." She paused.

Dana grinned. "You're thinking 'except for Gwen.'"

"I heard part of the fight. Did she really ignore her own daughter for years?"

"I guess. She lost a baby at three weeks, which would break anyone, but Blair was only four. She needed her mom." Dana sighed. "I can't see Gwen's side in this. I can't."

"Me, either. I mean, I never had the postpartum depression thing, but come on. After a few weeks, you have to get back to taking care of your living kid." Tiffany looked at Dana. "I'm being judgy and the depression thing is real, so I shouldn't be. But at some point, don't you have to think about someone other than yourself and here I am being judgy again. Grief is complicated, and we don't get to say when it should be over. Only it seemed like with Gwen it was never over."

"I guess without experiencing what she went through, we can't understand. But she doesn't help the situation by being so difficult. The only ones she's nice to are your kids."

"She's great with them."

They turned around and started back toward the house.

"I really appreciate your mom inviting me for Christmas," Tiffany said. "I hope it's not too awkward for everyone."

Dana laughed. "If she can deal with her boyfriend's ex-wife, then who are the rest of us to be bothered?" She deliberately softened her voice. "I'm glad you came. You'll be more distracted here and less in your head. That always helps me."

"You're right. Plus, I'm with my kids for Christmas. I'm not complaining about any of it."

"And with a little luck, Ryan will get a killer sunburn and maybe a rash."

"I'd like him to get a rash," Tiffany admitted. "A really big one."

"Here's hoping."

Dinner was an awkward affair with everyone trying too hard to act normal. Gwen and Blair sat at opposite ends of the large table, avoiding looking at each other. Julie had to admit she was surprised that Gwen hadn't insisted on being taken back to Seattle, but she'd stuck it out, even helping with dinner prep without complaining about the meal.

Fortunately, the two bottles of wine passed among the adults helped ease the tension, and the kids, who knew nothing of the fight, acted as an additional distraction. By the time the plates were cleared and dessert was served, conversation was pretty much back to normal.

After kitchen cleanup, Gwen and Tiffany stayed upstairs with the kids for an evening of board games while the other adults went downstairs to watch a college bowl game on the big TV. When it was time for Madeline and Wyatt to go to bed, Julie expected the adults to scatter, but Paul walked up to the main level, two decks of cards in his hands.

"We should play poker," he announced. "Five-card draw."

"I've never played poker," Tiffany admitted. "But I'd like to learn."

"This is the easiest version of it." Paul was moving toward the dining room table. "Blair, grab that jar of pennies from the bookcase over there."

Julie looked at Heath, who grinned.

"I'm in," he said.

"Me, too." Dana walked to the table and took a seat. "Are we buying in with our own money?"

"We'll just share from the jar," Paul said. "Winner gets to pick what we're having for dessert tomorrow night."

"Only if they're willing to help me fix it," Julie said with a laugh. "If Nick wins, he's going to want German chocolate cake, and that's a lot of work."

"Then it's time to let out your inner card shark," Heath teased.

Blair sat next to Nick. Tiffany settled by Dana. Soon, only Gwen was left standing.

"I don't really gamble," she said, avoiding everyone's gaze.

"No one's surprised to hear that." Paul looked at her. "Gwen, have a seat."

"But I—"

He pointed to a chair. "Have a seat."

There was something in his voice, something determined. For once Gwen didn't argue or run away. She sat down and primly folded her hands together on the table.

"Five-card draw," he said. "You get five cards. You can exchange up to three of them when it's your turn. Jokers are wild."

"What about twos?" Tiffany asked with a grin. "Can twos be wild, as well?"

Paul winked at her. "Next time."

He grabbed a handful of pennies from the big jar. "Count out forty. That's your stake. When you're out of money, you're out of the game."

While everyone counted out their pennies, he explained the rules. Julie listened attentively, thinking the second deck was going to make play interesting.

The first round went quickly, with Heath and Nick the final two players and Heath's full house beating Nick's three queens.

"You've played before," Julie said, watching him stack his pennies.

"Some."

"Heath used to play poker with his friends. It was an every-Friday-night thing when we met," Tiffany explained.

Julie smiled. "Really? What happened to the regular games?"

Heath shrugged. "Life got in the way. Kids and family take priority." His gaze met hers. "Now if I have a free Friday night, I have other plans."

Julie felt a little flicker of heat at his comment but did her best not to react. Tiffany laughed at something Dana said and Paul started to deal again.

"How long have you two been divorced?" Gwen asked unexpectedly.

Tiffany glanced at Heath, who shrugged.

"Two years," she said. "Give or take."

He nodded in agreement. "We were separated for nearly six months before we filed."

"You get along very well for a divorced couple," Gwen observed. "It's surprising."

"There's no reason to fight." Tiffany took two cards and studied her hand. "We have the kids, and it's not like we hated each other."

"What happened?" Dana asked. "Or is that too personal?"

"I wasn't ready." Tiffany looked at Heath, who watched her without speaking. "For marriage. I wanted to be a mom, but the whole marriage thing was just too much for me. Too confining, I guess. It's better now."

"But you're a single mother." Gwen sounded outraged. "You don't have anyone to help. Isn't that worse?"

"Not for me. The kids are great, and Heath and I have worked out a parenting plan that makes sense. I thought I was finally ready to be with someone." She swallowed and looked at her cards. "Anyway, that's me."

Her voice broke a little, but they all pretended not to notice. Play continued. After a few seconds, Tiffany cleared her throat.

"Blair, how did you and Nick meet?"

"On a blind date," Nick said with a grin.

"We didn't have a blind date." Blair smiled at him. "We were a quirk of fate."

"Yes, we were."

Blair turned to Tiffany. "I work at a retirement community. One of my residents set me up with his grandson. I don't usually believe in blind dates, but he sounded great and we met for drinks. Ten minutes in, we both knew it wasn't going to work out. He suggested I meet his friend Nick, who would be a much better match. He texted him, and thirty minutes later, Nick showed up."

Nick took her hand and lightly kissed her knuckles. "From the first second I saw you, I was lost."

Tiffany sighed. "That's so sweet. So what happened?"

"We talked for hours." Blair sighed heavily. "Then my IBS kicked in, and I had to race to the bathroom, where I spent the next twenty minutes."

Julie winced in sympathy. "Poor you."

"Thanks." Blair smiled at her husband. "Nick waited. Most guys would have run into the night, but he waited."

"That's both weird and romantic," Dana admitted.

Blair and Nick laughed, then gazed at each other.

"When you find the one, you wait," he said.

Julie felt the love between them. It warmed her heart to see her son so happy. Part of her wanted to snap at Gwen, pointing out they were an obvious love match, but to do so would mean explaining what Gwen had said about Nick, and why go there?

Tiffany turned to Julie. "How did you meet Heath?"

"He was my roofer."

Heath took one of her hands in his. "Gary was out sick, so I took the sales call to give her an estimate." He glanced at Nick. "It was one of those 'you know in an instant' moments for me, too."

"What?" Julie stared at him. "You never told me that." He couldn't be telling the truth. How silly.

"What did you think was happening? I was flirting like crazy the whole time."

"I thought you were being friendly."

"No one's *that* friendly." He chuckled at the memory. "She was all business and didn't find me charming at all."

"That's not true. I just didn't know what was happening." He'd been attractive, of course, but so young. It had never occurred to her he was interested.

"Once they started the work, he kept coming to the tow yard to give me updates, which I didn't understand. I told him I could see what they'd done every day when I got home."

Dana shook her head. "Mom, I'm shocked. You're usually better than that."

"I know." Julie laughed. "I have no excuse."

"I finally had to tell her I wanted to go out with her," Heath told them. "She said no."

"What?" Tiffany's voice was a shriek.

Dana stared wide-eyed. "Mom, seriously?"

Even Gwen seemed confused. "But you liked him."

"I did, but the age difference bothered me. I wasn't sure what to do."

"Say yes," Dana muttered.

Heath winked at her. "She did."

"I'm glad," Tiffany said, pushing three pennies into the center of the table. "You guys are a good couple."

Julie looked at her. "That's very strange to hear from you and thank you."

Tiffany laughed. "You're welcome."

Julie's cell phone rang at 5:03 in the morning. She was out of bed and on her feet before the second ring, clicking on the table lamp even as she pressed the talk button without bothering to look at the screen.

"Julie Parker."

"It's me."

"Huxley? What's wrong? Why are you calling so early? Are you all right? Do you need help?"

A thousand horrible possibilities passed through her mind, each worse than the one before. Heath sat up but didn't speak.

"I'm fine. A little too old for these predawn calls, but fine." He hesitated. "It's Axel. He's been shot."

Julie collapsed back on the bed, her chest tight, her mind blank.

"Axel's been shot," she whispered to Heath before returning her attention to the call. "When? Last night? Is he all right?"

"I got the call a couple of hours ago. I'm at the hospital. He's going to have surgery around seven. It's a through and through in his thigh. He'll limp for a while, but he'll be fine."

As Dana's mother, Julie had no problem with Axel being shot twenty times over, but as his boss, she was heartsick.

"I'm on my way."

"There you go, acting all impulsive. I got this covered. He's already talked to the cops, and they've filed their reports. He'll have surgery shortly, and they'll throw him out in a couple of days. I'll be here to take him home, then I'll join you up at the cabin. There's nothing for you to do here except get in the way."

"I could get things organized."

"What things? You want to tell the surgeon what order to do his work? I called because I knew you'd want to know what was what. It's the business. Bad things happen. Axel's been lucky for a long time, and he still is. He could have been hurt a whole lot worse."

"I swear, when this contract is up, we're done with repos," she said. "I should be there. He's my responsibility." And maybe because she was worried about him.

"Because he's so comfortable around you after what happened with Dana?"

"I never wanted him to get shot."

Huxley gave a little chuckle. "That's true, unless you were doing it yourself. He'll be fine. Once he goes into surgery, I'll head into the office. I'll check on him tonight and report in. Once I get him settled at his place, I'll head up the mountain to join you for Christmas."

"I feel like I should be there."

"There's nothing to do here. Stay up there with your family. I've got this."

She wasn't comfortable just leaving Axel to his fate, but knew Huxley was right. She would only be in the way.

"Tell him I'm thinking of him." She paused. "I mean that in a good way."

"I'm sure that'll make him feel all warm inside."

She ignored the sarcasm. "If something bad happens, I want to know. No, wait. Call me after the surgery, no matter what."

"I will. I'm hanging up now, boss."

She tossed her phone on the bed. "I think I'm going to be sick."

Heath put his arm around her. "What happened?"

"I don't have any details yet. Huxley said he was shot doing a repo. It's his leg, but he should be fine. The surgery is in a few hours. Huxley will let me know what happens."

She pressed a hand to her belly. "This is on me."

"How do you figure?"

"It's my company. Axel works for me."

"He knew what he was doing when he took the work."

"No one expects to die on the job."

Heath touched her chin so she was looking at him. "Axel didn't die."

"This time."

"You said you were done with repos."

"I am. It's just..."

She flung herself at him, not sure what she wanted to say. There were too many feelings and nowhere to put them. Guilt, for sure, and worry. Also confusion.

"I should go back to Seattle."

"And do what?"

"You sound like Huxley. I could sit with Axel this afternoon."

"That would be comfortable. Do you think he wants you there?"

She thought about her uneasy relationship with the other man. "Not really. He knows I'm pissed."

"Then let him heal in peace. Are you going to tell Dana?"

Something else Julie didn't have an answer for.

"I don't know. Part of me says she has the right to know. But if I do, then he's not just the guy who dumped her fifty times, he's the *injured* guy who dumped her fifty times. The man was shot. Hearing that would do something to her. She'd rush to his side, and then who knows what would happen. But if I don't tell her, then I'm keeping secrets, and I feel that's already happening too much in this house." She looked at him. "What do you think?"

"That she's an adult and deserves to know the truth."

Sensible, she thought. "I'm not going to tell her."

Heath laughed. "You never disappoint."

"I'm ignoring that. It's Christmas and he's hurt. If she finds out, she'll get sucked back into his world and he'll break her heart again."

"Not your decision to make."

"But it is because I know what happened and she doesn't. She never has to know."

"You don't think at some point she's going to find out he was shot and you didn't tell her? And you don't think that's going to be a problem?"

He had a point. "I'll tell her after the holidays."

"I can't tell you what to do, but I think you need to come clean with Dana and let her figure it out on her own."

"She'll go running to him."

"She's an adult. That's her decision to make."

"It's easy to be rational when it's not your kids."

He lightly kissed her. "That I know to be true. I'll do whatever you decide."

"I'm not going to say anything. Later, if it turns out I'm wrong, you get to say you told me so."

12

Julie got through most of the day without having to spend much time with Dana. The house was big, and there were lots of people around. It was easy to always be in the other room or doing something. Unfortunately, avoiding her daughter didn't make her feel any less guilty, which totally sucked.

Huxley called about ten to say Axel was out of surgery and doing well. The plan was still for him to be cut loose in a couple of days.

Once Julie knew Axel was going to be fine, she tried to forget what she knew and how Dana might or might not feel about the information. But ten minutes later, she was questioning her decision to keep the secret. Maybe Heath had been telling the truth—maybe Dana *did* have a right to know what had happened to Axel. Maybe she would be okay and simply nod a few times before going off to play with the kids. Or maybe she would race down to Seattle and play visiting nurse, handing over her heart yet again.

Indecision made Julie uncomfortable, so she retreated to the kitchen, where she could focus her mind on baking. She'd barely pulled out the ingredients for her favorite sugar cookie recipe when Gwen walked in.

"I'd like to talk."

Oh, do we have to? But Julie only thought the words, instead smiling brightly. "Of course."

She took a seat at the island and patted the stool next to her. Trying not to think about the fight Gwen had had with Blair, she said, "What's up?"

"I'm leaving."

Julie stared at the other woman. "I don't understand."

"I'm not welcome here. I'd like you to drive me home. Everyone will be happier with me gone."

While that was absolutely, 100 percent true, Julie felt obligated to protest.

"Gwen, no. It's Christmas. You should be with family."

Gwen's mouth thinned. "My only daughter has made it painfully clear that she prefers your company to mine. You're the mother she wants, not me."

Tears filled Gwen's eyes, but she blinked them away. "Things have happened that can't be undone. Words said. I'm not blaming you, exactly."

"Hey, what does that mean?" The question came out a little more sharply than she'd intended. "How is this about me?"

"She told me that you were an example of how to be a mother."

Julie held in a groan. Not the smartest thing for Blair to say. "She didn't mean it in a harsh way. It's just the two of you have been physically apart for so long and I'm right here." She offered a fake smile. "You know me, getting in everyone's business."

"That's exactly what you did," Gwen said, her voice shaking. "You stole my daughter from me."

Julie told herself not to overreact to the outrageous statement. "Blair isn't an apple sitting on someone's desk. She's her own person and there's no stealing."

Gwen glared at her. "You were the mother of the bride."

"What?"

"At the wedding. It was you, right there, doing everything. You're the one she talked to, you're the one she went to for advice. I was barely a guest at my own daughter's wedding, and it's all your fault."

The unfair accusation had Julie wanting to throw something. Or possibly choke the other woman. She gathered her mad and prepared to give as good as she'd taken.

"Maybe the reason I was there was because you weren't. You're the one who walked out on your kid—maybe not physically, but in every other way that matters." Julie threw up her hands. "Fine, you lost your son and I'm sorry. I can't begin to understand what that would have felt like. But you still had a living child. Blair is your daughter, your only child. Where were you?"

"It's very easy to judge me when you have no idea what I went through."

"It's not about you," Julie shouted. "We're not talking about you. That's what you can't seem to grasp. You're not the center of the universe. Your grief doesn't matter more than everything else happening. I'm sorry you were unhappy at Blair's wedding, but whatever problems you have with her are on you. Those were your choices and now you're living with the consequences."

Blair heard shouting, but couldn't make out the words. She moved into the hallway and recognized her mother's voice, followed by Julie's.

"Dammit, Mom," she said as she raced downstairs to the main floor, only to find Tiffany, Dana and Paul hovering just out of sight of the two women.

"This is you helping?" Blair snapped as she pushed past them and hurried into the kitchen. She walked up to her mother.

"Stop it," she demanded. "Just stop it. If you have a problem, you come to me. This isn't about her or anyone else in this house. It's between you and me. Stop dragging other people into this mess."

She spun to face Julie. "Stop engaging. I know you're trying to help, but getting in the middle doesn't solve anything."

Julie immediately relaxed her posture and nodded. "You're right. I'm sorry. I'm adding to your problems. I can't promise not to react, but I'll do my best not to."

She reached out and touched Blair's arm, then left. Seconds later, Blair heard her say, "Don't stand around listening. We're all going downstairs and shutting the door so they can have some privacy. Is Nick still out with the kids? We should check on them."

Blair returned her attention to her mother, who was wiping away tears.

"What do you want?" Blair asked sharply, her voice rising as she spoke. "I don't get it. You're not communicating with me. We're going over and over the same material. I know there's something, but you won't tell me what. If you're waiting for me to guess, then nothing will ever be fixed, because I won't ever get it right. Just tell me!"

They stared at each other. Blair was breathing hard and wishing she was anywhere but here. She knew it was wrong, but honest to God, she really hated her mother. Why did she have to be here, ruining what otherwise would be a great holiday?

"I want you back."

The softly spoken words were so at odds with what Blair was thinking that she couldn't process them at first.

Gwen drew in a ragged breath. "I want my daughter back."

"What back? There's no back. That implies we had a relationship and we didn't. We never did anything together or hung out. We spoke maybe twice a year."

Blair retreated a few steps, putting space between them. "Do you know how I longed for you to notice me? How many times

I came to your room and asked if you wanted to play a game or have me read to you? Do you know how many nights I cried myself to sleep, missing my mother, who couldn't get past what she was feeling to notice one of her children was still alive? There's no back."

Tears poured down Gwen's cheeks. "I'm sorry," she said through her sobs. "I'm so sorry. I wanted to be there for you."

"No, you didn't."

Gwen stared at her. "That's not true."

"It is. You didn't care. I wasn't important to you in any way. So why now? Is it because Dad's gone and you've finally realized you don't have any other family?"

"It was the wedding." Gwen twisted her hands together. "I saw you with Julie and the rest of her family, and I finally recognized what I'd lost. You're supposed to be my daughter, and you're not anymore. I wasn't your mother. I was an unwelcome guest."

Blair ignored the guilt that immediately made her want to apologize. She wasn't going to take responsibility for something she hadn't done.

"That moment made me see the truth," her mother continued. "I'd been so wrong. I wanted things to be different." She wiped her face. "I *want* things to be different, but I don't know how to make that happen."

Blair had no idea if her mother was telling the truth or not. Maybe more significant, she wasn't sure if the truth mattered. It had been too many years, too much pain and rejection. She couldn't escape her sense of duty to the woman, but wasn't sure anything else was possible.

"Why would I bother?" she asked. "Why would I ever trust you with another chance?"

She walked out of the kitchen and went upstairs. Once she was in her room, she closed and locked the door, then sat on the bed and gave in to tears. She wasn't sure what she was crying for or about, but knew the pain inside wasn't close to being healed. Until that process started, she simply didn't have any forgiveness in her.

Julie sat on the sofa in the living room, trying to get enthused about starting lunch. Christmas was still a few days away, but she was already tired of cooking for the large group. Or maybe the real problem was she'd never been a fan of drama and there was simply too much happening around her.

Some of it was self-inflicted. The whole Dana-Axel getting shot thing was bugging her. The problem was she'd waited too long to tell (or not tell) her daughter what had happened, and saying something now was going to be a problem. Plus, she was getting less and less brave by the second, which was, again, her issue.

The ongoing conflict between Gwen and Blair was also weighing on her. Gwen had stayed in her room the previous evening, not joining them for dinner, but she'd shown up at breakfast, acting as if nothing had happened. Blair, on the other hand, had spent much of the night in the bathroom—her IBS reacting to the situation. This morning she'd been pale and shaky, with Nick hovering protectively and Julie wishing she knew more about electrolytes and how to get Blair hydrated.

Paul, seated on the love seat, put down his book. "I can hear you thinking from here. Why are you worried? Everything will be fine."

Julie sighed. "Do you actually know that or are you assuming?"

"Most things work out."

Julie raised her eyebrows. "Really? The Gwen-Blair problem has been going on for decades." She smiled as Heath joined her.

"That one stumps me." Paul paused. "Actually, I've never understood Gwen, but my brother loved her, so there we are."

Nick and Blair joined them, taking the club chairs opposite the sofa. Julie studied her daughter-in-law.

"You look like you feel better."

"I do." She glanced around. "So where's everyone else?"

Julie assumed she meant Gwen most of all. "Your mother, Dana and Tiffany took the kids for a walk. They'll be back in time for lunch. I'm really not in the mood to cook. Maybe we should go get burgers or something."

"Or I can make lunch," Blair offered. "I'm sorry—I should be helping more. You're doing all the work."

Julie waved away the comment. "You know I get bossy in the kitchen. I'm not comfortable letting other people do things."

Paul chuckled. "I've noticed that. It's an unfortunate trait because you're always busy. I'm very comfortable letting others do their thing."

"I can delegate at work," Julie told him. "But in the kitchen, I just can't let it go."

"It's not just in the kitchen, Mom," Nick said, his voice teasing.

She grinned. "I have no idea what you're talking about." She turned to Paul. "Your business is retail, right? That's got to be tough but satisfying."

"I like it. I enjoy meeting the customers and talking about how I can help."

"It's not like the towing business," Nick added. "Paul only stocks parts for muscle cars built before 1972."

Julie was about to point out she got that from the name Nothing After '72, but Nick kept talking.

"The customers all love their cars and they mostly know about them, so it's a real meeting of the minds, you know? And even the ones just starting on restoration want to learn as much as they can. It's the only place where you can have an hour-long conversation about dual quads and no one thinks you're strange."

His enthusiasm was a little surprising, she thought. And unsettling.

"You've spent time with Paul at the store?" she asked, careful to keep her tone neutral.

"Sure. Once Blair told me what he did, I wanted to meet him. I've hung out there on my days off a few times." He leaned forward. "There are suppliers who basically go through junkyards, looking for old parts that can be reused. Some have to be repaired, but others are just fine as they are. Some companies are starting to reproduce the parts. The market's growing for sure, especially as the cars get harder and harder to find. Paul has a couple of lifts out back he rents out so guys can work on their cars right there. It's a community."

Julie had always prided herself on knowing her children. When they'd been little, she'd been the one who could tell when they wanted something but couldn't bring themselves to ask for it. She'd also had radar for when they were lying. Now all her mom-senses were tingling and not in a happy way. Nick had never talked about Parker Towing with the same energy he was displaying now.

Which meant what? He was interested in the company? She swung her attention to Paul. He was a few years older—maybe close to sixty. Was he looking to sell the business?

She stood and stared at her son. Did Nick want to buy it?

"Mom? You okay?"

She thought about all the times she'd tried to talk about Nick's future and how over the last year he'd become less and less willing to have the conversation. He never wanted to spend time in the office and learn about the logistics of handling a tow yard with fifty trucks and nearly double that number of drivers. He kept putting off committing to becoming her partner.

She took a step back, telling herself she was making something of nothing. There had to be—

"Mom!"

She looked at Nick. "What?"

"What just happened? You look like you're going to be sick or pass out."

"I'm fine." The words were automatic as her brain continued to process. "You want to buy his business."

"What? No. I mean, we've talked about it and—"

"You've talked about it? You've *talked* about it?" She took another step back. "You won't talk to me about your future at the tow yard, which I've been after you to do for months now, but you're talking to Paul about what? Buying him out? When were you going to tell me? When you got new business cards?"

She was processing as she spoke, finally understanding things that hadn't made sense in a while.

Nick seemed to shrink in his seat. "Nothing's decided."

Blair shot Nick a glare while Paul only shook his head.

"Not fully," Nick added. "Mom, you have to understand."

"Why? You won't tell me about any of this. How long have you known you didn't want to join me in the business?" She struggled to keep the hurt out of her voice. It was always supposed to be Nick. Dana had never been interested in Parker Towing, but Nick had.

"From the time you knew what I did, you wanted a part of it. You said it would be the two of us, that we'd make an empire."

"I was five."

"You said it three years ago!" she shouted. "You should have come to me and told me you were having second thoughts."

He rose. "Why? So you could tell me I was wrong?"

"I wouldn't do that."

"Since when? You always know what's right."

"Maybe," she admitted. "At first, but then I listen."

Blair stood up. "I'm sorry, Julie. You have every right to be pissed. We should have said something sooner."

"You're not the one I'm mad at." She stared at her son. "You lied to me."

"Mom, don't." He sounded more resigned than angry. "Just don't. I don't want the business and I didn't know how to tell you. I'm excited about what Paul does. Plus, I don't want to have to carry a gun for the rest of my life. Blair and I want to start a family. I want regular hours and a business that closes on holidays."

She knew he was making sense, but it was hard to get past how hurt and betrayed she felt. "You could always talk to me. I don't know when that changed."

"It didn't."

"All evidence to the contrary." She half turned away, took another step back, then faced him. "If you want to go, then go. I get what you're saying, but I don't understand why you couldn't have told me the truth when this all started."

"I'm sorry."

"I'm not ready to hear that. I'm too hurt."

She shifted her weight, ready to walk away, but something wasn't right. The top step wasn't there anymore. Even as she realized there was no more floor beneath her, Blair screamed for her to stop. Julie tried, but it was too late because she was falling and falling. There was just enough time for her to realize the landing was going to be bad. Then she hit the stairs and pain shot through her body. Her last thought before the world went dark was she'd just screwed up everyone's Christmas.

Dana rushed inside when she heard a scream. She saw her brother and Heath huddled around her mother, who was lying awkwardly on the stairs. Panic seized her, making it hard to breathe or move.

"What happened?" she demanded, her voice shrill. "Mom? Mom!"

"She fell." Paul was pulling out his phone. "I'm calling 911."

Nick stood there, ashen. "Mom," he whispered, sounding as if he were going to cry.

Julie stirred slightly. "I'm fine," she said, trying to sit up. She groaned and collapsed back on the stairs.

Heath put a hand on her shoulder to stop her. "Don't move. You might have hurt your back."

"My back doesn't hurt. It's my side and hip." She shifted, then winced. "And my arm. Oh, my head!" Her eyes fluttered but didn't close.

Dana hovered awkwardly, not sure what to do. She couldn't seem to catch her breath. Tears filled her eyes. "Mom? You need to be okay."

"It's nothing." The words were great, but Julie's voice was weak.

Heath pointed at Paul. "Call."

"Is she okay?" Wyatt asked, sounding scared.

"She'll be all right." Gwen's tone was firm. "She's banged up, and we're going to get her to the hospital. Let's go to my room so we won't be in the way."

Gwen ushered the kids upstairs. Dana told herself to stay calm, that throwing up wouldn't help anyone. She pushed Nick away, knelt down and took her mother's hand, ignoring her terror.

"Mom, be honest. How are you?"

"You're making a fuss over nothing," she said, but her voice was laced with pain and she didn't try to move again.

"You were unconscious for almost thirty seconds."

Heath sounded worried. Dana told herself to be calm. The ambulance would be here soon. She looked at her brother, hoping for reassurance, but Nick was staring at their mom, his expression worried, his skin gray.

Julie's eyes sank closed and her skin got even more pale.

"Mom?" Dana tried to keep the fear out of her voice.

"I'm fine." Julie's voice was breathy. "If it would just stop hurting so much."

Nick shook his head. "Mom, I'm sorry."

There was no response. Dana ignored the fear bubbling up

inside. She reached for her mother's wrist and felt for a pulse. The beat was strong and steady.

"She's okay," she said, then swallowed a sob. "I mean, she's not..."

From outside they heard a siren. Thank God! Blair raced to the front door.

"I'll wave them in," she said, darting outside.

The next few minutes passed in a blur. Everyone got out of the way while the EMT team stabilized Julie's neck and back. She came to and told them she didn't need to go anywhere. They didn't listen, instead carrying her out to the ambulance.

Dana watched, feeling helpless and scared. Her mother was the force that kept the world turning. If something had happened to her...

"I'm going with her," Heath said.

"Me, too." Dana started to get her bag.

"I want to go." Nick looked at Blair. "I have to."

Heath shook his head. "No. I'll go and be in touch. You two stay here and take care of things. If it's bad, you can come to the hospital, but there's no point in being there until we have more information."

"I'm going." Nick's voice was firm.

"Me, too," Dana repeated, thinking there was nothing that would keep her from being at her mother's side.

"Fine. I'll take my truck. You two can take another. That way we can easily go back and forth."

There wasn't much traffic, and it didn't take long to get to the small hospital. By the time they'd parked and gone in through the emergency entrance, Julie had been whisked away. Dana and Nick identified themselves.

"We need to know about my mom. Julie Parker," Nick said.

The woman at the desk sighed. "You know she was brought in ten minutes ago. We won't know anything for a while."

"What happened?" Dana asked. "How did she fall?"

Heath looked at Nick. "It's your story to tell."

The words were fine, but he sounded pissed. Dana turned to her brother. "Nick?"

"She found out about me wanting to buy Paul's business. She was backing out of the room, didn't look where she was going and fell down the stairs."

Dana's breath caught as she tried to take it all in. Nick hung his head. She reached over and took his hand, squeezing tightly.

The three of them sat together in silence. After maybe twenty or thirty minutes, Nick said, "If something happens to her, it's on me."

Heath gave him a look that was more dismissive than annoyed. "Save the drama until we know what's wrong."

"Drama?" Nick came to his feet. "My mother's in the emergency room because of me. I'm worried about her."

"You should have thought of that before you decided not to bother telling her the truth. This was a hell of a way for her to find out. How long have you known you weren't going into the family business? Six months? A year?" Heath rose and faced Nick. "She's not one of those crazy women with unrealistic expectations. She can be reasoned with. If you'd gone to her and told her you'd found an opportunity that made more sense for you and Blair, she would have listened. Yeah, she would have been hurt and possibly pissed, but in the end, she would have understood because she always understands the people she cares about."

Nick looked away. "I didn't want to break her heart."

"Too late for that. Next time, grow a pair and tell her what's going on. After all she's done for you, she deserves that."

Dana watched carefully, prepared to throw herself between the two men if necessary. But Nick didn't seem to be getting mad.

"How do you know what she's done for me?" he asked.

"I know her and she's your mom. Julie never backs down.

She's determined, she's strong and she has an unwavering sense of right and wrong. She would walk through fire for either of you."

Nick unexpectedly collapsed back in his chair and covered his face. "What did I do?"

Dana put her arm around him. "She's going to be okay."

"We don't know that."

"We have to believe it," she told him, then looked at Heath. "You're right about Mom. She was always there for us. No matter what we'd done, she showed up. She might be furious, but we knew we could count on her."

She rested her head on her brother's shoulder. "It's on me, too. I knew what you and Blair wanted. I should have pushed you to tell Mom."

Nick dropped his hands to his lap. "No, it's not. I created the problem. It's my responsibility. If anything happens to her, I did it."

Heath took his seat. "Like I said, let's not assume the worst. Julie's tough. She'll get through this."

"You're right," Dana said. "We should think positive."

Heath stared straight ahead. "I'm not being positive. I can't deal with the idea of her not being okay. Telling myself she'll be fine is the only way to keep breathing."

That revelation made Dana's chest tight. There was something in Heath's voice that was as powerful as his words.

"I didn't know," she whispered.

"That I'm in love with her? She doesn't know, either."

"I won't say anything."

Heath closed his eyes. "Keep the secret or not. Right now she's all that matters."

They sat in the waiting area for nearly two hours. Finally one of the nurses came out and found them.

"You can go back and see your mom. She's doing okay, considering. The doctor will be by to explain what's going on."

She paused and glanced between the three of them. "It's family only," she began.

Dana smiled at her as she pointed at Nick. "We're her kids. This is our stepdad."

"Oh, okay. Then follow me."

As they were led down a long hallway with rooms on either side, Heath stepped close.

"Thanks."

"She'll want you with her."

They found Julie in a hospital bed, her upper body elevated, her left arm in a sling. She was awake and smiled when she saw them.

"I told you I was all right."

They all rushed to her. Heath ducked around to the other side of the bed.

"We weren't worried," he told her with an easy smile.

"You're lying."

"Naw. You're tough." He lightly kissed her. "Want to tell us what's going on?"

Just then, the doctor walked in. She was a petite brunette with a confident air.

"I can probably do that." She smiled at all of them. "I'm Dr. LaTour."

"Tell them I'm fine," Julie said. "They've been worried."

"Your mother..." Dr. LaTour paused, her gaze lingering on Heath as if trying to place his relationship. "And, um—"

"He's our stepfather, so she's his wife," Dana said easily.

Julie's eyes widened, but she didn't say anything.

"Ah, yes. Well, your mother and wife is going to recover from the fall. Julie was very lucky. She has a fractured left arm and—"

"You broke your arm?" Nick's voice was loud and disbelieving. "Mom, I'm sorry. I should have said something before."

"Not now," Dana told him. "Let the doctor talk."

Nick nodded. "You're right. Sorry."

Dr. LaTour smiled. "Not a problem. As I said, she has a fractured left arm. We're going to wait a few days for the swelling to go down. Then we'll put on a cast. Until then, she has to be careful with her arm. She has some bumps and bruises that are going to hurt for a few days, but they'll heal. As long as she takes it easy."

"You need to tell her that last part more than once," Heath said, his hand tightly clasped with her right one. "She likes to do everything herself."

"That's not true," her mom said. "It's no big deal."

"What about her head?" Dana asked. "She hit it when she fell."

"I didn't!"

"Mom, you had to. You passed out a couple of times."

Dr. LaTour glanced at Julie, then looked at Dana. "We don't think she has a concussion, but we want to keep her overnight for observation. Just as a precaution."

Nick swore under his breath. "Mom," he began.

"No." Julie's voice was firm. "This isn't your fault and nothing bad happened. Like the doctor said, I have a few bumps and bruises, so I'm going to be sore, but that's all."

"And a broken arm," Dana muttered.

"Fractured," her mom corrected. "That sounds better. No one should worry. Dr. LaTour has given me some lovely drugs to deal with the pain. I feel great. Just ask me."

Nick looked at Dana. "Mom was always a lightweight when it came to prescription pain medication. Remember when that guy rear-ended us?" He looked at the doctor. "She had some whiplash, so she had some pain meds. The first night she took them, we couldn't get her to stop singing all the songs from *Mulan*. It kind of freaked us out."

Dr. LaTour smiled. "I'll warn the staff." She glanced at her tablet. "That's my report. Julie will be released in the morning. You can visit with her for a few minutes. Then she needs to get some rest. Once she's in her room, regular visiting hours apply." Her tone softened. "She was lucky. It was a bad fall, but she should have a full recovery. She's healthy and strong. I don't expect there to be any problems."

She excused herself. When it was just the four of them, Julie pulled her hand free of Heath's and pointed at Dana and Nick.

"See? I'm good. There's nothing to worry about. I want you to go home and tell everyone to get on with their lives. I'll be back in the morning."

Dana looked at Nick, who didn't seem convinced.

"I should stay."

"The doctor made it clear she didn't want us hanging around," Dana said. "We'll go to the house, but we'll come see you later."

"Don't." Julie's voice was firm. "Have a nice afternoon and evening. Don't worry about me."

"I'm not going anywhere," Heath said quietly. "I'll wait here until she's in her room, then stay until they throw me out at the end of visiting hours."

Julie sighed, but her gaze was warm as she looked at him. "I knew you'd be difficult."

He leaned over and lightly kissed her. "Then none of this is a surprise." He straightened. "I'll report in every couple of hours."

Dana glanced at her watch. It was nearly three. "You've been checking in with Blair, haven't you?" she asked her brother.

"We've been texting. She's kept everyone updated."

Not that there'd been much to tell, Dana thought. "Let her know Mom's okay and we're on our way back."

She leaned in and kissed Julie's cheek. "I'm glad you're going to be all right. We'll come see you tonight. I love you, Mom."

"I love you, too, baby girl."

"I was so scared."

"I'm not ready to leave you." Julie smiled. "Want me to sing?"

"Not really."

Her mom laughed. "Then take your brother and get out of here."

13

Blair watched for Nick's truck. When it pulled into the driveway, she went running outside. Rufus, always up for an outdoor adventure, came with her. As Nick and Dana got out of the cab, he raced back and forth, wanting to give each of them a solid greeting.

"Hey, big guy," Dana said, patting him. "We weren't gone that long."

Rufus didn't seem to be reassured by that.

Blair hurried up to Nick. "You okay?"

"You mean is my mom okay."

She smiled at him. "I know she's fine. You told me when you texted, and I believe you. You're the one I'm worried about." Her smile faded. "It's not your fault. It was an accident."

"If I'd told her before, she'd be fine now."

Dana walked toward them. "Forget it, Blair. He's going to be like this until Mom gets home and he can see for himself that she's going to be all right." She punched Nick in the arm.

"Hey, what was that for?"

"Being a coward. You should have told her when you first

knew about wanting to buy Paul's business. You put it off, and while the fall isn't your fault, you're going to think it is, all because you couldn't man up."

He glared at his sister. "I could take you."

"Technically, but you'd never try."

"All right, you two," Blair said, doing her best to emulate her mother-in-law's way of getting people to listen. "Stop. Everyone's on edge inside. We're going to go in and be cheerful so we don't scare the kids. It's Christmastime. Try to remember that. We're one big happy family."

"Is that your stern voice?" Nick asked, his voice a little lighter than it had been.

"Not even close. I can be a lot more stern."

"You're right," Dana said, leading the way inside. "She really is going to be okay."

They went inside. Everyone was waiting on the main level. Dana began unwrapping her scarf from around her neck.

"She's good," she said firmly. "We saw her. She's a little loopy because of the pain meds, but otherwise healing. She had a lot of bumps and bruises and her left arm is fractured, but that's it. They'll keep her overnight for observation and Heath will bring her back in the morning."

"Where's Dad?" Madeline asked, her voice trembling. "Why didn't he come home, too?"

Tiffany squeezed her hand. "Your dad is fine."

"He's staying with Julie," Dana told her. "To keep her company."

Blair hadn't known that. "Nice of him," she murmured, wondering whether Nick and Dana were as okay with that as they seemed, but knowing she couldn't ask. Not in front of everyone.

As if reading her mind, Dana glanced at her. "He's been a rock. He just kind of took charge. I always knew my mom wouldn't tolerate anyone who was a jerk, but he was amazing. He wouldn't let us fall apart."

Wyatt glanced between them. "Are you really telling us the truth about Julie? Because sometimes grown-ups don't."

Nick crouched until he was on the same level as the boy. "Look at me, Wyatt. Look into my eyes so you know I'm being honest with you. Julie's my mom, so you know how much I love her and need her."

The boy nodded.

"She's going to be all right. She'll be home tomorrow and you'll see for yourself. Until then, I want you to trust me. Can you do that?"

"I can try."

"Good. That's all I can ask."

Blair watched the interaction, feeling her heart swell a little with Nick's words. When the time came for them to start their family, he was going to be a good dad. Soon, she thought happily. They would buy Paul's business, then work on getting her pregnant the following year. It was going to be great.

Tiffany ruffled Wyatt's hair. "See, I told you that was what Dad said. Julie's important to him. He'd never not tell the truth about what was going on."

Dana hung up her coat. "The hardest part is going to be dealing with her while she's in the sling. Once she gets the cast, her arm will be protected, but while it's in the sling, she's got to take it easy. That is not my mom's natural state of being."

"We'll help," Tiffany said with a grin. "Between all of us, I think we can get her to do the right thing."

"I'm sure we can," Gwen said, joining the conversation. "I'm glad Julie is doing well, and I happen to know she would want us to get on with our lives. Let's talk about what we want to do this evening. We'll have dinner, and then maybe we'll play some games. I think we should do more than watch a movie. We want to be busy."

Blair told herself to be grateful her mom was so good with the kids. They were worried, and Gwen would figure out a way to distract them. She'd been doing it since the accident. Better for them to be okay than to be scared. Which sounded good, but didn't dislodge the tiny knot of resentment she still felt when she thought about how careful and sweet her mother was to Madeline and Wyatt.

At some point, she was going to have to let go of the past, she thought. Carrying it around was only going to hurt her. But she wasn't sure where the line was between doing what was best for herself and forgiving her mother for something that Gwen had never truly apologized for.

But that was for another time, she told herself. In the postholiday world, she would figure out the right thing to do. For now, getting through the next week or so without any drama was the best thing for all.

"What's for dinner?" Paul asked.

"I'll go look!" Wyatt ran into the kitchen, Madeline and Rufus at his heels. There was a long pause.

"Meat loaf," Madeline said, her voice unenthused.

"Do we have to?"

Wyatt's voice was a stage whisper. Blair felt her lips twitch. Tiffany groaned.

"We're guests here," she said loudly. "And appreciative of all the meals."

There was another pause. Then Wyatt said, "Yum, meat loaf. My favorite," in a very unconvincing tone.

Nick grinned, as did Dana. Paul chuckled. Even Gwen seemed to be holding in a smile.

"Why don't we get pizza instead?" Dana said. "That way no one has to cook."

"I'm up for pizza." Nick looked at Paul. "You okay with that?"

"I love pizza."

Dana looked at Blair. "Can you eat it?"

"Sure. We just need one without meat." The spices in sausage and pepperoni could be a problem for her tummy.

Wyatt and Madeline joined them. "It's meat loaf," Wyatt said without much enthusiasm. "With carrots and mashed potatoes."

"We were thinking pizza," Gwen told him. "Would that be okay?"

"Pizza?" Madeline grinned. "That would be the best."

Nick looked at his watch. "Let's meet back in the kitchen in a couple of hours, and we'll figure out what we want to order and how much. Heath will be at the hospital until visiting hours are over, so he won't be here for dinner."

"He might want leftovers," Blair said, thinking Heath was unlikely to leave Julie's side long enough to get something to eat. "We should order enough so he can have some when he gets home."

"Good idea."

Dana started to do a head count, then stopped. "Where's Huxley?" She looked at her brother. "He was supposed to get here today."

"I haven't heard from him." Nick looked at Blair. "But he was going to arrive sometime after lunch. Technically, he's not late, but doesn't he usually text to say he's on his way?"

Blair knew the older man always joined the family for Christmas. "Maybe there's traffic."

Dana took her cell phone out of her pocket and scrolled through her contacts, then pushed a button.

"Huxley, it's Dana. Are you all right? I thought you'd be here by now."

She listened for a few seconds, then hung up, her expression puzzled.

"That was weird. He said he got unexpectedly delayed but that he'd be here in a few minutes."

"He must have gotten a late start," Blair said. "Or there was something at work."

She knew that Huxley's assistant handled the office over the holidays, but that Huxley was always available if there was a problem. The two weeks around Christmas were jammed with tows, jump starts and lockouts. Come New Year's Eve, it was all hands on deck, so to speak. People were stupid and drove drunk, then got into accidents. Everyone would be busy with that, which was why the holiday celebration at the cabin always ended well before the first. Both Huxley and Julie had to be back in the office and Nick had to work his tow shifts.

Only one more New Year's Eve by herself, she thought happily. Next year Nick would be home with her. She wouldn't have to worry about some drunk hitting him while he was hooking up a tow or changing a tire. They would be together. Maybe she would even be pregnant.

She smiled at the thought.

Gwen looked at Tiffany. "We never finished making those holiday cards. Let's go do that until it's time to order the pizza. I think we left our supplies downstairs."

"We have to make a card for Huxley." Madeline looked at Dana. "Do we like him?"

"We do. He's great. Sometimes what he says sounds a little grumpy, but when you think about it, he's really being funny."

"I like that." Madeline grabbed her mom's hand. "Let's go make cards."

The four of them headed for the basement. Dana reached for her coat. "I'm going outside to wait for Huxley. He sounded funny. I want a chance to ask him if he's all right before we get inside."

Everyone else drifted away. Blair lingered until they were gone, then pulled Nick into the kitchen. She stood in front of him.

"Stop feeling guilty," she said, her voice low so they wouldn't be overheard.

He dropped his head. "I can't stop seeing her fall. I could have killed her."

"It was an accident. You didn't push her. She was upset and it just happened."

He looked at her. "She was upset because of me. You kept telling me to come clean and I wouldn't listen. I was wrong to keep secrets."

"Your mom didn't fall so you'd be punished, Nick. You don't have that much power."

"That's what it feels like."

"Then your feelings are wrong." She put her hands on his chest. "You're a good man and you love your family. You'd never do anything to hurt your mom."

"Except leave the business."

"She wouldn't want you to stay if it made you unhappy. You know that." She stared at him. "Don't let what happened change your mind. If you don't want to go into business with Paul, that's fine, but don't make an emotional choice and then regret it for the rest of your life."

"I won't."

She was less sure. "You're someone who takes responsibilities seriously."

He pulled her close and wrapped his arms around her. "I know what you're saying and you're right. I need to separate what happened from what I want for our future." He stared into her eyes. "I'm not going to walk away from the opportunity with Paul over this. I feel like crap, but that's on me. Next time I'll listen to you."

"If only that were true," she said, her voice teasing.

"I mean it." He kissed her. "You're the best thing to ever happen to me, Blair. I love you."

She leaned against him and closed her eyes. "I love you, too. More than you know." And wasn't that the best feeling of all?

Dana hovered by the front door until she saw Huxley's truck pull into the driveway. She ran toward him, waving frantically.

The setting sun reflected on his windshield, so she couldn't see inside. When he got out, she rushed over and hugged him.

"You missed all the drama," she told him. "Mom fell down the stairs. She's going to be fine, but she fractured her arm and she's all bruised up and I thought she'd hit her head and was going to die. She's in the hospital and won't be home until tomorrow. And Nick wants to leave the business."

Huxley drew back and stared at her. "What are you talking about?"

She explained about the fight and the fall and the ambulance. "There's even more, beyond the whole Mom-Nick thing. Blair's mom, Gwen, is here and they're fighting a lot. Plus, Heath's ex joined us for the holidays. It's a crowd."

Huxley frowned. "Your mother's boyfriend's ex-wife is here? With their kids?"

"Uh-huh. It's a lot."

"Sounds like it. But Julie's going to be all right?"

Dana nodded. "I heard the doctor myself. She'll be home in the morning. Until then, someone has to be the grown-up in the room. I was hoping it could be you."

"I don't know about that." Huxley glanced toward the truck, then back at her. "Did she say anything to you?"

"About what?"

Before he could answer, the passenger door opened. Dana hadn't been able to see into the cab, so hadn't known there was someone else inside. Had Huxley brought a friend? Was he dating? Did he—

"Hello, Dana."

She stared at the familiar man who half stepped, half fell out of the truck. While her mind registered that Axel was pale, wearing sweatpants—which he never did—and the last person she'd expected to see, her heart fainted in shock and her chest got all tight and uncomfortable.

He was here? Why? How?

Her gaze swung back to Huxley. "What were you thinking?" she asked, her voice nearly a screech.

"At the time or now? Now I'm thinking your mother should have told you. Back then I didn't think I should leave him alone for the holidays."

Betrayal, shock and a desire to bolt inside and lock the door battled for dominance. "How could you do this? Why do these holidays matter? He's been alone before."

"He's never been shot in the leg before."

Shot? As in shot? She shook off the questions, the worry, the instinct to go to him. Wait, what? She felt the blood drain and the world spun for a second before righting itself.

She swung her gaze between the two men. "Shot? I didn't know." Shot? She couldn't grasp the concept.

"I went to the hospital this morning to pick him up and take him home," Huxley said. "I thought he would be fine, but he was in worse shape than I'd anticipated. I knew I couldn't leave him by himself."

Which all sounded logical and sensible and even kind, but created a really big problem for her. She turned to the man in question. The man who had messed with her mind and broken her heart.

"You can't be here."

Axel flinched while Huxley stared at her in disapproval. "Dana!"

Axel nodded. "She's right. I told you, old man. Just leave me at home. I'll get a cab or something to take me back down the mountain."

Dana was trying to take it all in. Huxley's earlier question about her mom saying something to her now made sense. Julie had known about Axel being shot and hadn't said anything. An outrage to deal with later, she told herself, returning her attention to her ex.

She looked at him more carefully. She saw his skin wasn't

pale, it was gray, and she could see signs of pain in the way he held himself. The sweatpants (so unlike him—Axel wore jeans and only jeans) concealed what she would guess was a thick bandage around his thigh.

Oh, God. Axel had been shot! Now what? She honest to God didn't know what to do.

After another second of indecision, she decided to channel her mother. And she knew exactly what her mom would say and do.

"It's cold," she said. "Let's get you inside."

Huxley didn't move. "And then?"

If her mom could invite her boyfriend's ex-wife for Christmas, then who was Dana to turn away an ex-boyfriend who'd been injured? "Of course you're staying," she told Axel, trying for gracious but probably landing short. "I'm sorry for what I said before. It was a knee-jerk reaction."

"I don't want to be here."

She met his gaze and braced herself for all the emotions that would flood her. As much as she'd wanted to forget him, she'd never been able to get over him. Her biggest fear was that she never would.

"What you want isn't the issue, is it?" she said bluntly. "You're obviously in a lot of pain and you look terrible. You need help and it's Christmas. Believe me, if you had somewhere else to go, I'd drive you there myself. But you don't. So you'll stay." She stepped closer and pointed a finger at him. "We have kids in the house. They're excited about Christmas. Don't you dare say anything to upset them, you hear me? This isn't about you."

She waited for him to respond. Instead, his eyes rolled back in his head and he sank to the ground. Huxley swore as he bent down to catch the other man.

But Axel was a big guy—lean but tall, with plenty of muscle. Dana screamed as Huxley went down with him. Fortunately, just then the front door opened and Nick came running.

"What happened?"

"Axel's been shot," she said, pointing to the two men in the snow. "Can you help?"

"Shot?" Nick's obvious surprise meant their mom hadn't told him, either. Secrets, Dana thought. This family had to stop keeping them.

Together Nick and Huxley got Axel to his feet. He'd come to, although he was even more pale and gray than he had been.

"I'm okay," he managed as the two other men got on either side of him.

"You just fainted," Nick told him. "That's no one's definition of *okay*. What the hell happened? How'd you get shot?"

"A repo went bad."

"Sometimes they do."

They headed for the house. Dana went to the truck and grabbed the luggage, along with a big shopping bag filled with wrapped presents. Despite everything, she smiled. Huxley never came empty-handed.

She followed the three men inside, telling herself once Axel was settled, she would take a few minutes for herself to figure out how she was going to handle the next few days. She was going to have to fake normal for sure—find a way to convince everyone she didn't care that the man she loved and who wouldn't love her was here for Christmas.

Paul and Blair were waiting in the foyer. Blair frowned.

"Axel? What happened?"

"He was shot," Nick said. "Mom knew and didn't tell us."

Blair immediately looked at Dana, as if she could guess the reason for the secret keeping. Dana understood that her mother hadn't wanted to upset her, but some kind of heads-up would have been good. Not that anyone had expected Huxley to simply show up with him.

"He just got out of the hospital," Huxley added, as if he could read Dana's mind. "No way I was going to dump him at his place. Not when he's recovering and it's Christmas."

Once again, Blair stared at Dana, probably assessing her reaction. Dana waved her hand as if none of this mattered.

"It's fine," she said with a confidence she didn't feel. "He's welcome, just like Tiffany was. The more the merrier. Christmas is about connecting."

Blair's expression turned sympathetic. "You're right," she said, her tone brisk. "It's a big house. There'll be plenty of room."

"There is," Dana said brightly. "The problem isn't going to be where so much as the stairs."

Nick and Huxley got him to the sofa, where he collapsed in a heap. Rufus came tearing up the stairs and made a beeline for Axel. He sniffed his face, then gave him a quick lick on the cheek. Axel slowly sat up, then smiled when he saw the dog.

"Hey. Who are you?"

"That's Rufus," Dana said. "He belongs to Heath's kids."

"The boyfriend has kids?"

"Two. Madeline and Wyatt. I mentioned them before you fainted. They're ten and eight."

His dark gaze met hers. "I like kids."

She knew the statement wasn't meant to be anything more than his way of saying he wouldn't hurt them. He was responding to her statement from before. But hearing him say it was still a kick in the gut because it implied he was a regular guy who was just like everyone else. That he could have a normal relationship and be a dad and live happily ever after.

Maybe he could, she thought bitterly. Just not with her. He'd made it clear the first time he dumped her that she wasn't for him. And now he was here—for the duration—and there was nothing she could do about it.

Why oh why hadn't she figured out how not to be in love with him? Why couldn't she have fallen for someone else? She didn't care who—anyone would do as long as he was here, standing between her and Axel. But she hadn't and here they were.

"We'll make this work," she said briskly. "You'll have to sleep on the sofa until you can deal with stairs."

He looked at her. "I'm sorry."

"Stop saying that. It's Christmas. That's what matters. You and Mom can hang out and discuss your injuries together."

He looked around. "She really fell down the stairs?"

"It's Nick's fault."

Nick groaned. "Thanks. Because I don't feel bad enough already?"

"Just trying to keep things honest."

Huxley picked up his bag. "I'm heading downstairs to tell Paul he has a roommate."

"Tiffany is down there, with the kids."

Huxley frowned. "Tiffany's the ex-wife?"

"Yes, and Gwen is Blair's mother. She's downstairs, too."

Huxley shook his head. "So the boyfriend, his ex-wife, his kids, Nick's mother-in-law and uncle-in-law, your ex-boyfriend."

"And a dog," Blair offered. "A big, friendly dog."

Huxley grinned at her. "Now we know for sure it's Christmas."

He made his way downstairs. Nick grabbed Blair's hand and pulled her toward the second floor, leaving Dana alone with Axel. He'd managed to sit up, but he was still the color of concrete and she thought maybe he was shaking.

Concern battled with the need to protect herself by running away. Only there was no one else to take care of him and she was too much her mother's daughter to simply walk away.

"What I said before, about not wanting to be here. I was trying to do the right thing. I didn't want to ruin your holiday."

She looked at him, telling herself she didn't care that this was the most vulnerable she'd ever seen him. No way she was going to be sucked in by those dark eyes or the way the three days' growth of beard made him look even more sexy and dangerous.

"I know what you meant," she told him. "Look, this is awkward for both of us." More her than him, but why mention that? "Let's just get through it." She glanced at his bag, then around at the furniture. Where to put his stuff?

There were a couple of drawers in the entry table. She crossed to them and checked to make sure they were empty. One had a few tattered take-out menus. She grabbed those and put them on the top, then looked in the baskets below. There were a couple of blankets. She put them into one basket, leaving the other for him, then returned to the sofa and opened his battered duffel.

"I can unpack," he said, his voice low, possibly with annoyance, possibly with pain. She wasn't sure which and didn't care.

Ignoring him, she took out socks and underwear and carried them to the entry table, filling both drawers, all the while ignoring the intimacy of touching his things.

"You can barely walk," she said, returning to the bag and pulling out two sweatshirts. She took those to the hall closet and hung them up with the coats. "You're lucky that there's a three-quarter bath on this floor. I'll put your shaving kit in there."

She did as she said, made sure there were fresh towels, then walked back to the living room. Axel's color was a little better, but she could see he was in pain and trying to hide it.

"They had to have given you medication at the hospital. So what is it? An antibiotic and something for the pain?"

He nodded.

"Can you manage those on your own or do you want me to put together a schedule?"

He scowled. "I'm not five."

"No one said you are, but you've been injured and you're foggy, so this might not be the time to manage prescription drugs. You're just stupid enough to want to be macho and not take something for the pain."

"I'm fine."

"Saying that makes me think you're an idiot."

"Is that such a bad thing?"

She wanted to tell him not to help her get over him—that she was perfectly capable of doing it on her own. Only she hadn't so far, so maybe help was called for.

Why? she thought for the thousandth time. Why did it have to be him? Why couldn't she have fallen for someone else? Someone who wouldn't leave her time after time.

She pointed at him. "Take off your jacket."

He managed to get his arms out. She braced herself, then leaned forward to pull it free of his back. For one brief second they were close enough to kiss. Then she was able to draw back to a safer distance. She felt in the pockets and found two prescription bottles. They'd both been filled that day, no doubt another reason Huxley had been so late to get up the mountain. She read the instructions.

"The antibiotic is twice a day and should be taken with food. The pain meds are as needed."

She went into the kitchen and got a glass of water, then handed it to him along with one of the pain pills. She thought he might protest, but he took it without saying anything.

She shook the bottles. "I'll leave these in the bathroom medicine cabinet." She paused. "Take the antibiotic with breakfast and dinner."

"I got that."

She had more to say, like he didn't get to have attitude and that he wasn't to mention their previous relationship, but before she could get started, Wyatt came up the stairs.

"Hey, Dana. Did you want to come make cards with us?" He saw Axel and his eyes widened. "Who are you?"

"I'm Axel."

"You look like you're sick."

Dana froze, not sure what to say. Axel offered the boy a faint smile. "I cut my leg real bad, so I have stitches and they kind of hurt, but I'm okay."

"You cut your leg? Julie fell down the stairs. She's at the hospital for the night." Wyatt looked at Dana. "You said she's going to be okay."

"She is. She'll be home in the morning. It's kind of strange that two people we know were in the hospital, huh?"

"It is." Wyatt smiled at Axel. "Are you staying through Christmas? Do you like the big tree? It's our second one. The first one smelled like cougar pee."

"That's a bad smell," Axel said. "Did the whole house stink?"

"Naw, it was in the garage." He grinned at her. "It was Dana's tree."

"By that, he means my pick. It was really stinky, so we had to go back and get Nick's choice instead."

Axel looked at the tree. "So where's the flaw?"

"In the corner. We can't see it."

"But you know it's there."

With Wyatt right there, she couldn't tell him to stop pretending he knew her... Except he did know her, which was almost worse.

"We're having pizza for dinner," Wyatt said. "The menu said meat loaf, but pizza's better."

"It is," Axel agreed. "What's your favorite kind?"

"Anything with meat. And no vegetables." He sat on the sofa. "How'd you cut your leg?"

"At work on a sharp piece of metal."

"Did it hurt?"

"It did."

"Did you swear?"

Axel managed a smile. "A little."

Dana knew she should probably take the higher ground and tell Wyatt to leave him alone, but she didn't. She figured it was petty of her and made her the lesser person—a fact she could live with.

"I'll leave you two to manage things," she said, heading for the stairs so she could tell everyone else about their new guest.

14

Blair and Tiffany cornered Dana after dinner.

"Are you all right?" Blair asked. "With Axel being here?"

"I don't know." Dana sank down on her bed. "I was so unprepared to see him."

Tiffany sat next to her. "I can't imagine what you're dealing with. If Ryan showed up here, I couldn't be calm about it like you are. I'd want to beat him with something, or leave him out in the cold to freeze to death."

Blair had a feeling Tiffany wasn't as bloodthirsty as she sounded.

"Your pain is fresh," Dana told her. "Axel and I have been apart for months."

And this last time hadn't been the first time he'd dumped her, Blair thought.

She simply didn't understand Axel's problem. Why was he so determined not to be with Dana? She'd seen them together. Even knowing he left her again and again, Blair would still swear they were in love. She'd seen how Axel looked at Dana, and it was with the total adoration of someone who cared. So what was up with his actions?

"He's not a bad guy," Blair said without thinking. "He just doesn't stay."

Both women stared at her as if she was crazy. She replayed her words in her head.

"Sorry. That came out wrong. I meant when you're together, he treats you well. He's kind and supportive. He makes you laugh."

"He sucks me in," Dana said bluntly. "Then he dumps my ass."

"Men." Tiffany sighed.

"You got that right."

She and Dana touched fists. Blair stayed where she was, thinking she had no complaints about Nick. Oh, he wasn't perfect, but she loved him and trusted him, and she knew he was all in when it came to their marriage.

"He really got shot?" Tiffany asked.

"That's what I was told," Dana said.

"That has to hurt. Will he be okay on the sofa?"

"There's nowhere else to put him," Blair said. "Huxley is taking the second bed in Paul's room. There's the other lower bunk with you and the kids, but Rufus has claimed that. Plus, it would be weird to put Axel there."

Tiffany grinned. "Yes, it would. No way I'm sleeping with a girlfriend's ex."

"You wouldn't be sleeping with him, exactly," Dana murmured.

"Yeah, it's still too intimate for me."

"The sofa it is," Blair said, thinking he should be all right there, what with the bathroom on the same level.

"Mom knew." Dana's voice was flat. "Huxley called to tell her Axel had been shot and she didn't tell me."

"Oh, no!" Tiffany sounded upset. "So you weren't prepared. How could she do that?"

"I'm going to ask her about it." Dana looked at Blair. "Nick didn't know, either."

"That's what he told me." Blair was pretty sure Julie hadn't said anything to Nick so he didn't have to withhold information from his sister.

"You think she was right," Dana accused.

"No, but I can argue both sides. It's a tough call. Does she tell you so you worry and maybe leave to go see him? Does she not say anything, risking you getting mad? If you didn't care about him, she could have told you and not been concerned about your reaction, but you do still have feelings."

Blair could see the struggle on Dana's face. She wanted to say that wasn't true, but couldn't without lying. The heart was a funny organ—often taking its own path when it came to who to love.

"I'm team Dana," Blair said. "You know that."

"I do."

"This situation totally sucks."

"That it does."

The next morning Blair set her alarm so she would be up early enough to start breakfast for everyone. She wasn't sure what time Heath had come home and he was gone before she went downstairs, but there were still nine people to feed.

She and Tiffany had prepared another breakfast casserole the night before. That would take nearly an hour in the oven. There were breakfast meats to cook and the table to set. But when she walked into the kitchen she found that her mother was already there. The oven was on and the casserole sat on the counter, warming up a little.

So far she'd managed to avoid being alone with Gwen. They stared at each other for a second before Blair managed an almost cheerful, "Good morning."

Her mother nodded. "You're up early."

"I thought I'd take care of breakfast. Obviously you had the same idea."

"Julie usually does it, but with her not here, I knew there was work to be done."

"There is."

They both glanced away.

"I'm sorry about Nick's friend," Gwen said. "Was he really shot?"

"Yes. He does the repossessions for the tow company. Sometimes they go bad."

Her mother shook her head. "The whole business is dangerous. I'm glad Nick's getting out of it. At least when he's working retail, he should be more safe."

That was exactly what Blair thought, too, but hearing her mother say it was so annoying. Not fair, but still true. Which meant the problem wasn't the words, but the woman speaking them. No, she thought sadly. The real problem was her reaction to her mother.

"It'll take him a while to learn the retail business, but I know he's excited about it." She glanced at the clock. "I wonder how Julie's feeling this morning. She's got to be sore after that fall, plus her arm."

The words were out before she remembered her mother's feelings about the other woman.

But Gwen surprised her by saying, "I'm sorry."

"For Julie?"

"I suppose, but mostly for what happened with you. When you were little." She shifted awkwardly. "You're right—I made the choices I did and that's on me. I wasn't there for you, and your point is a good one. I can't blame everything on being depressed. I guess I'm trying to explain that what I went through was harder than most people realize. I wanted to be there for you, but I couldn't find my way out of the darkness to find you."

Blair forced herself not to respond. She kept her annoyance inside. They'd been over this before.

"Do you think grief became a habit?" she asked instead, knowing her mother would freak at the question, but figuring it was the best she could do.

But Gwen surprised her by nodding slightly. "I think maybe that's true. It was the emotion I knew and was comfortable with. Happiness, laughter, feeling good were so foreign to me, I couldn't imagine experiencing any of them again. Maybe if I'd been able to have another baby, I could have moved on more quickly."

Blair stiffened. "I didn't know you couldn't have more children." She couldn't imagine that kind of pain. How awful.

"No," her mother said quickly. "I didn't mean it like that. There wasn't a physical problem. I meant I couldn't do it emotionally. I couldn't take the chance on losing another child. It would have destroyed me."

Blair couldn't understand that, either. Worse, she'd been right there—a living, breathing child her mother hadn't bothered to notice. Only they'd talked about that, too. Endlessly.

"Once I was a little better, you and your dad had become so close, I didn't know how to fit in."

"That's not on me," Blair snapped, unable to stop herself. "I was the child. I needed you and you weren't there. Dad was. He took care of me. If you didn't like how things were between us, then that's your fault. You could have done something. Anything. But instead you didn't even try."

She braced herself for the fight, but Gwen only sighed. "I have so many regrets. You *were* always there. You're my only daughter, and I couldn't find my way to be what you needed."

She looked at Blair. "I'm not here because I lost your father. I'm here because I want to be in your life. I want us to have a relationship. I meant what I said before. The wedding was my wake-up call. I saw what I'd lost and it was painful and awful to know it's my fault. Just mine. I know we can't go back, but I'm hoping we can find something together for the future."

"Just like that?" Blair asked. "You're sorry and you want us to be close again and I'm supposed to say yes? Do you know what you did to me? Do you understand how many years I spent reaching out to you and you didn't care? I know you were hurt at the wedding, but everything that happened there was the result of your choices. You pushed me away over and over again. I barely know you."

She had more she wanted to say, but Gwen's silent tears stopped her. She could see her mother's pain, feel her regret and disappointment as if they were her own. She hated that she couldn't simply say what she meant and not care about the consequences.

"You're right," Gwen whispered. "I'm so sorry."

"Stop saying that. Yes, you're sorry, but it's been over twenty-five years, Mom. Whatever we had before is long gone and we can't get it back."

"But we could start over."

Blair wanted to ask why they should even bother. To what end? She wanted to walk away and never see her mother again. But for some reason, she couldn't. And maybe that was the most honest answer of all.

"I don't know," she admitted. "About any of this. You've made your point and I get it, but I don't know how I feel about it. I need you to back off and let me think. I don't want to talk about this anymore on this trip. Can you respect that?"

"Absolutely."

Blair had her doubts. Her mother couldn't be bothered to respect a closed door.

"We'll talk when we get home," she said.

Gwen nodded. "That's perfect."

They stared at each other. Her mother pointed to the casserole. "Want to finish breakfast together?"

She didn't—not really. But saying that would make her sound petty and small. So she did her best to smile, then said, "Of course. Let's do that."

"When did we get married?"

Julie was proud of herself for getting out the question without giggling. They were in Heath's truck, driving back to the house. She'd gotten through all her tests and had passed her night of observation. On the twenty-sixth, she would return to get her cast. Then she would head home, where her primary care doctor would pick up her care.

Right before she'd left, one of the nurses had given her a shot of something wonderful. She wasn't in pain, she felt good and the world looked all Christmassy and bright.

"We're not married," Heath said without looking at her. Still, she heard the smile in his voice.

"Hmm, because Dana said you were her stepdad. That implies something."

"Only family was allowed in the ER. It was your daughter's idea, and I appreciated the assist."

"Dana's a good girl. I love her so much." She eyed the radio, wondering if he would mind if she turned it on and sang along with a Christmas carol.

"I'm glad you're feeling better."

She glanced at him. "I feel great! You know there was no reason to take me to the hospital. Everything worked out."

"If we ignore the fractured arm and possible concussion. Plus the bruises and what could have happened to your back."

She flicked away his words. Unfortunately, she used her left arm out of instinct and felt a jolt of pain that went all the way to her bones. Even with the pain meds from the hospital, she had to catch her breath.

"I can't believe I fell down the stairs. I'm not usually klutzy."

"You were dealing with something unexpected."

Oh, he was right. "Nick." She looked at Heath again. "He doesn't want to go into business with me. I don't get it. I always wanted to join my dad. It's a family thing. I grew up in the tow yard. I didn't have a mom, so the guys there really looked out for me. Dad had his girlfriends and they taught me girl stuff. How could he not want the business?"

"People want different things."

"I guess." She turned the concept over in her mind. "It's not like I feel it was an empire that had to continue, but I just didn't know. I'm his mom. I should have known."

"You're not a mind reader. And maybe you should let this go for a while. Until you're off your pain meds."

She grinned. "Are you saying I'm impaired?"

"Yes. No heavy equipment operating for you."

"But I'm so good at it." Her humor faded. "I was thinking last night that there were signs. He was never interested in learning about the business. He only wanted to do his job and go home. I wanted to know everything, even when I was a kid. There was a message there and I should have listened."

"He should have told you the truth a long time ago," Heath said flatly. "This isn't on you, Julie. You didn't do anything wrong."

"Maybe, but they always blame the mother."

He chuckled. "Yes, they do."

"I just wish he'd said something. Am I too scary?"

"No."

"You don't want to think about your answer?"

"I don't have to. Like I said, this is on Nick."

He sounded so confident, she thought. Yet something else she liked about Heath. She glanced at him. He was so young and handsome. Strong. Steady. He'd stayed with her last night until the nurses had kicked him out, and he'd been waiting the second he was allowed back into her room.

"You were really good to me yesterday," she said. "I feel bad about keeping you from your kids."

"They had their mom and everyone else at the house. They'll be fine."

"Did you see them last night?"

"I got home late. Everyone was in bed and they were still sleeping when I left."

"You must be tired."

He glanced at her. "I'm fine. You're the one I'm worried about."

"Don't be." She remembered not to wave her arm. "This is nothing. But I appreciate how you took care of me. You're a good boyfriend."

"Thank you."

They turned onto their street. Heath slowed.

"Julie, don't take on Nick while you're on pain meds. You don't know what you're saying, and if things get heated, they could go south really fast. He was wrong to act how he did, but he's your kid and you want what's best for him."

"You don't know that. Maybe I'll never forgive him."

He smiled. "Not your style."

He pulled into the driveway. It was a cold, sunny day and the house looked welcoming. Smoke drifted from one of the chimneys and the walkway was freshly shoveled.

"Stay there," Heath told her. "I'll come around."

"I can get out of the truck on my own."

He pointed at her. "Stay there."

"You're very bossy," she murmured but did as he asked.

As he helped her find her balance in the new snow, the front door opened and Rufus burst out, followed by her kids and, well, nearly everyone.

Rufus darted forward, leaping off the porch and racing toward her. She bent down to pet him, careful to keep her left arm still.

"You're excited," she said with a laugh as he circled her, then leaned in so she could pet him. "Did you miss me?"

Nick got to her first. "I'm sorry," he began.

She shook her head. "Let's not get into that. I'm fine. Good as new."

He eyed her sling. "You broke your arm."

She was also bruised all over and knew once the pain meds wore off, everything was going to hurt.

"It's fractured. No big deal. I'm getting a cast after Christmas. It's all good." She turned and smiled at Dana. "How are you?"

Her daughter didn't smile back. Julie noticed Huxley, hanging back a little but looking at her pointedly, as if trying to send a message. Only she had no idea what.

"Axel was shot," Dana told her.

The guilt was instant. "Oh, no. He was and I didn't say anything. I wasn't sure if I should or not, and then there was the whole Nick thing and I fell and you know the rest, but still. I'm sorry."

"How could you? He was shot, Mom. I had the right to know."

Julie felt her eyes burning. "You did. I was wrong. I'm so sorry."

Heath stepped between them, facing Dana. "Hey, she's on pain meds and she suffered a traumatic injury. Maybe let the interrogation go for a day or two."

Dana tried to stare him down, but Heath wasn't budging. She nodded grudgingly before stepping back.

"You're right," she muttered. "Sorry." She started for the house, then glanced over her shoulder. "He's here, by the way. In the house. Huxley brought him."

What? "What?" Julie stared at her office manager, who was actually shuffling his feet in the snow. "You brought Dana's ex-boyfriend to the house for Christmas?"

"He was in bad shape. I couldn't leave him on his own. It's Christmas. You would have done the same."

Julie was less sure about that, but she suddenly realized she didn't have on a coat and it was freezing outside. Worse, she'd hurt her daughter. The burning turned into actual tears.

"Dana," she called before her daughter could slip into the house. "I should have told you right away. I'm so sorry. I'm a horrible mother."

Dana rushed to her side. "No, Mom. I get it. Things were happening and there was no right answer."

Once again, Heath got between them.

"Enough," he said sternly. "I'm taking her inside. Whatever else you have to say can wait. Did any of you notice the woman isn't even wearing a coat?"

He took his off and put it around Julie's shoulders, then carefully led her inside. Dana hurried after them.

"Mom, I'm sorry."

Heath kept Julie moving. "Back off, all of you."

Julie wanted to protest that she was fine, only she wasn't. She felt lightheaded and more than a little sick. Whatever else anyone wanted to say was going to have to wait while she decided if she was going to throw up or faint.

15

Dana paced in the downstairs family room. She had to avoid the main level because Axel was there. Fortunately, Tiffany and Gwen had taken the kids out with the sleds, so they weren't there to ask questions. Paul was in the kitchen, tending to his rum cake, so she was all alone with her guilt. Or at least she was until Nick joined her.

"You okay?" he asked.

"No. I feel awful. I yelled at Mom. She's barely out of the hospital and is obviously drugged, and I yelled at her. In the snow!"

"I'm the reason she fell down the stairs in the first place, so I'm worse than you."

"That's not very comforting."

"It's all I have."

They looked at each other. Dana sighed. "You're really not going into the business?"

"I'd rather not." He shrugged. "I was never excited about learning the front-office stuff of the tow business. Even as a kid, all I wanted was to drive a truck. That's the part I like. Mom's been after me for years to learn more, but I kept putting it off. Then I met Blair and through her Paul. The more I learned about his business, the more it seemed like a great opportunity. It's exciting in a way Mom's company never was."

His eyes brightened with enthusiasm. "I could talk about cars all day. I helped Paul with his annual inventory and everything was fascinating. Retail makes sense to me in a way the tow yard never did."

Dana hadn't realized he'd never been interested in Parker Towing. She'd known he wanted to buy Paul's company but had thought it was more about getting out of the tow business.

"She'll understand that. Once she's better, you need to talk to her."

"Only if she stays seated," he muttered.

"It's not your fault she fell."

"It's going to take a long time for me to believe that." He jerked his head toward the main level. "How's it going with you-know-who?"

"I'm avoiding him."

"The house isn't that big. At some point you have to deal."

"I know. I just can't believe he's here. I'm upset, I feel stupid. There are no good emotions here. Worse, I have to apologize to Mom."

"You need to wait on that. You'll never get past Heath until she feels better."

"He can't stop me from seeing my own mom."

Nick raised his eyebrows. "You sure about that?"

She wasn't but she was going to have to try.

She waited an hour to give her mom time to settle, then went upstairs and knocked on her bedroom door. Heath answered, stepping out into the hallway rather than inviting her in.

"She's resting."

"I need to talk to her. It'll only take a minute."

"No."

His gaze was steady, his stance determined, but Dana refused to be intimidated or put off.

"I want to apologize. That's all. You're welcome to listen to make sure I don't upset her."

"This isn't a good time."

Dana squared her shoulders. "I'm the reason you got to be with her in the ER. You owe me."

He hesitated a second before stepping back and letting her into the room. Her mom was propped up on the bed, her sling resting on her stomach. She smiled when she saw Dana.

"It's you. Rescue me. Heath says I have to take it easy, but what about everything that has to be done around the house? And there are the cookies for the cookie exchange. I'm tired of being one-upped by Jackie from across the street. Plus, it'll be lunchtime soon."

Dana sat on the mattress on her mom's right side. "You're not making lunch. We'll take care of it."

"No one else will do it right."

That made her smile. "Maybe not, but we'll still get a meal on the table." She paused. "I'm sorry I snapped at you."

Julie grabbed her hand. "No, I'm sorry. I really didn't know what to do about the whole Axel thing. I wanted to tell you and I didn't. If I'd known Huxley was going to bring him here, of course I would have said something. It was just so confusing."

"I get that. I was really surprised, but I know you'd never deliberately do anything to hurt me."

Her mother's gaze was direct. "I wouldn't. I love you. You're my baby girl." She squeezed her fingers. "How are you doing around him?"

Dana pulled her hand free. "Not great. I'm not like you, Mom. I'm not tough and I don't compartmentalize. I spent last night avoiding even looking at him. But I can't do that indefinitely. At some point I'm going to have to admit he's in the room, but I don't know what to say. If I was seeing someone, it would be better. He'd know I was totally over him and maybe feel bad rather than pitying me."

"Then have someone."

Dana stared at her mom. "What does that mean?"

"Have a boyfriend. Fake one. You told that nurse that Heath and I were married and we weren't. No one questioned you."

She was right, Dana thought. Everyone had accepted her statement.

"That was a different scenario," she said.

"Not that different. Say you have a great guy in your life. Axel won't know it's a lie. It's not like he and I ever discuss you. The closest we come is when I give him the stink eye, which is probably wrong of me. After all, I'm his boss. But I can't help it. Shame on him for what he did to you. You're my daughter and he needs to deal with that, the jerk."

"Mom." Dana touched her good arm. "You don't have to get upset on my account."

"If not for you, then who?"

Dana gently hugged her. "Thank you."

"I love you. I hope you know that."

"I do, and I think you're brilliant."

A fake boyfriend would solve a lot of problems. All she had to do was figure out who and what he was, then get all the adults on board. Her mom and Heath weren't a problem, and she knew Nick and Blair would be on her side. So would Tiffany. Huxley was feeling guilty, so he wasn't an issue. Paul seemed like he would enjoy the game, which only left Gwen to worry about.

"You're going to do it?" Julie asked. "Create a fake boyfriend."

"Absolutely. I'll stop by later and tell you the details."

"I can't wait. Oh, give him money, please. Every mother wants her daughter to marry money."

Dana laughed. "It will be first on the list."

★ ★ ★

Dana waited by the house's only printer—an ancient and slow machine—as the pages spit out one at a time. When they were all printed, she went through the house and collected the adults, telling them to meet her in the kids' room. Axel was busy watching a movie with Madeline and Wyatt, so that took care of them. She went upstairs last and asked Heath to join her.

Once they'd all crammed into the bedroom, she shut the door and handed out the printed sheets of paper.

"We need to talk about my boyfriend."

Blair and Nick exchanged a look while Tiffany's shoulders slumped.

"You and Axel got back together? When? Oh, Dana, are you sure you can trust him?"

Blair nodded in agreement. "You're a grown-up and you know what's right for you, but you've never been able to see clearly when it comes to him."

Huxley sighed. "Dana, I'm sorry. I never meant to hurt you by bringing him here. I didn't know what else to do."

"You didn't hurt me," Dana assured him, giving the older man a quick hug. "You absolutely did the right thing. I'm fine."

No one looked like they believed her.

"Who's Jared?" Gwen asked, scanning the notes.

"Jared is my new boyfriend."

They all stared at her.

"My fake boyfriend." She explained about how she'd gotten Heath into the ER.

Heath groaned. "I thought you were humoring her. Dana, this isn't a good time to take your mom's advice. You know she's drugged, right?"

"It's a great idea. I've come up with the perfect guy. You all have the information. Read it over, and then tonight at dinner someone can casually mention Jared and I'll take it from there."

"You're on crack," Nick told her. "This is never going to work."

Blair elbowed him. "We're here to support your sister. This is important. We like Jared. He's a good guy."

"There's something wrong with both of you," Nick grumbled, but dutifully began to read.

Dana felt a quiver of doubt. Was she making a mistake in asking everyone to help her with this? Was it a dumb idea? She wasn't sure, but maybe it didn't matter. One way or the other, she had to deal with Axel, and so far she hadn't been doing a very good job of it.

Tiffany smiled at her. "I think it's a great plan. You're being proactive. That's got to make you feel strong. Fake boyfriend it is!"

"An investment banker?" Paul asked. "Isn't that a little stuffy?"

"He's very successful and rich," Dana told them.

"But you don't care about money." Blair pressed her lips together. "That would never sway you."

"No, but it's nice to have."

"An investment banker is perfect." Gwen waved the sheet. "Dana's an accountant. They both work with finance. Their careers are different enough that they won't be competing with each other, but close enough that they can have a conversation and understand what the other is saying. They could have met at a conference or through a client. It really makes sense."

The unexpected support was gratifying. "Thank you, Gwen."

She smiled. "You're welcome. And for what it's worth, I think you're smart to do this. Axel is obviously bad for you. Better to let him think you're involved with someone else so he leaves you alone."

"'He's an only child,'" Tiffany read aloud. "That helps so you don't have to worry about too much family. 'He calls his mom every week.'" She sighed. "That's so sweet. You can tell a lot about a guy by how he treats his mom."

Huxley looked at her. "You remember that he's not real. Do I have to worry about you hitting your head, too?"

"Still, he sounds like a good guy."

Gwen frowned. "Wait a minute. If he's so wonderful and you're so in love, why isn't he with you for Christmas?"

Dana's stomach dropped. It was the obvious question—why hadn't she thought of it herself?

Paul shook the paper. "If he really loved you, he'd be here for Christmas. I don't know, Dana. I think you can do better."

"I agree," Nick said, earning himself a swat with the paper from his wife.

"Cooperate," Blair told him. "Why isn't he here for Christmas? I know he would be if he could."

"His grandmother," Tiffany blurted, then smiled. "His favorite grandmother." The smile faded. "She's in hospice and he needs to be with her."

Blair, Dana and Gwen all sighed together.

"That's good," Blair breathed. "Wow, Jason is a great boyfriend."

"Jared," Dana corrected.

"Right. Jared. What a sweetie."

"It's not very Christmassy," Heath said. "You sure you want to go with a soon-to-be-dead grandmother?"

"Yes." Dana's voice was firm. "That's why he's not here. He's with her. It's sad, but also very understandable." She looked at everyone. "Tonight at dinner, look for an opportunity to mention him. Be casual, but let's get the details right."

"This isn't going to go well," Nick told her. "But I'm in."

"Just follow the script and we'll be fine."

"Famous last words," Nick muttered as he walked out of the bedroom.

Julie woke up to her body complaining. It seemed as if every inch of her hurt—her arm most of all. She'd rested it on her belly, with a pillow to her left to support her elbow, but that wasn't comfortable anymore. Her back was stiff, and the bruises on her hip and shoulder were throbbing. She hadn't slept much the night before, despite the pain meds, and wondered if tonight would be any better.

She tried to distract herself with happier thoughts, but not thinking about how she was feeling made her remember what had happened. How she and Nick had been, well, not fighting, but having a heated discussion about him wanting to leave Parker Towing. Then she'd fallen and what happened after that was blurry. He had to feel horrible about her injuries. He was tough on the outside, but such a sweetie on the inside.

And Dana, she thought, feeling the guilt race through her. How upset she'd been. Julie knew she should have told her about Axel, but at the time, she just hadn't been sure.

"Hey, how are you feeling?"

She opened her eyes to see Heath getting up from the overstuffed chair in the corner and crossing to the bed.

"What time is it?" she asked, her voice scratchy.

"Nearly five."

"You let me sleep that long?"

He sat next to her on the bed and smiled. "I would have let you sleep until morning, if you could have. You need to heal." He touched her forehead. "You didn't answer the question. How are you feeling?"

"Sore." She looked from the chair to him. "Were you here the whole time?"

"Yes."

She couldn't comprehend that. People didn't take care of her—she took care of them. "You don't have to do that."

The smile returned. "I want to. Plus, I've been worried. That was a hell of a fall."

"But I'm fine. You heard what the doctor said. They did all the tests, and it was actually kind of nothing."

"Except for the fractured arm, the bruises and the fact that you're in pain."

"Well, yes, there's that."

"In fifteen minutes you can have a pain pill. After you take it, we'll get you up and see if you can manage the stairs to get to dinner. If not, I'll bring the food to you."

"I don't want to take anything now. I'll be drugged for dinner. You've seen me on pain meds. I'm totally out of it."

"I want you on a schedule. Being in pain doesn't help the healing process. Let the body focus on getting you better, not on managing how everything hurts."

She smiled at him. "You think you're in charge. I'm not sure how I feel about that."

He lightly kissed her. "Get used to it, kid. Until you're back to normal, I *am* in charge."

"You're not, but it's sweet that you think you are."

He took her right hand in his. "How are you doing with all the other stuff with Nick and Dana?"

"I feel awful about Dana. She was so mad. No, not mad, hurt, which is worse."

"You made a judgment call."

"A bad one. Like you kept saying, I should have told her."

"If Huxley hadn't brought him up here, it wouldn't have mattered."

"But he did."

"Does that bother you?"

"What Huxley did? No. He was looking out for a friend and fellow employee. What happened to Axel is my responsibility. I give out the assignments. I guess I should have thought through the whole Huxley-taking-him-home thing. I knew Axel lived alone, so who was going to take care of him? It's just how this all upsets Dana. She's still in love with him, so being around him hurts her. I know she's mad at me."

"She's not. You made up."

"She accepted my apology, but she's still hurt I wasn't honest with her."

He squeezed her fingers. "I think she's probably feeling a little better. She's taken your advice and come up with a fake boyfriend."

It took Julie a second to figure out what he was talking about. "To prove to Axel he doesn't matter? That could work."

Heath chuckled as he got up. "It's a recipe for disaster, but I said I'd tell you and that we'd both be supportive."

He returned with a piece of paper. "Jared's an investment banker."

"Really? That's so stuffy. Why couldn't she find someone with a fun profession?"

"Like a skier? This is where I remind you, he's not real and you're the one who said he should have money."

He continued to read the information. Julie wasn't sure how much she could commit to memory, but she would try.

"It's sad about his grandmother."

Heath looked at her. She smiled.

"I know, I know. The grandmother isn't real, either. Okay, this is good. She'll feel safer around Axel, and that's what matters. I just wish I hadn't hurt her. I haven't been much of a parent lately."

"Hey, you're the best parent I know. If I could do half as good as you, I'd be feeling pretty great about myself."

"You're sweet and trying to make me cry."

"I never want to make you cry."

There was something in the way he said the words. Something she couldn't fully understand, but before she could ask, he said, "Nick not telling you what was happening isn't about you—it's about him."

"Maybe. But if he'd been more comfortable talking to me, he wouldn't have kept the secret."

"He didn't want what you were offering. That made him uncomfortable. Are you mad at him?"

"No. It's his life and he has to do what makes him happy. But it's going to take me a while to internalize the changes. And now I have to think seriously about letting someone buy in or maybe even selling the business. I love it, but I'd always assumed Nick would start taking over by now."

She shifted a little, wincing at the pain.

"At the risk of repeating myself, I wish he'd told me sooner."

"He didn't want to disappoint you."

"You said I wasn't that intimidating."

He smiled. "You're not. You only think you are."

That made her laugh. "You're trying to take away all my power."

He kissed her. "No one can do that. Ready to try to sit up?"

She wasn't but nodded anyway. He put his free arm around her shoulders.

"One, two, three."

Together they got her into a sitting position. Her body screamed in protest, and she had to press her lips together to keep from crying out. Once he'd stabilized her with several pillows, Heath got a glass of water and a pain pill and held out both to her. She swallowed the pill and handed him the glass.

"It should kick in pretty quick," he told her. "We'll give it a few minutes, then see about the stairs."

"I got up them. I can get down them."

"I'll be here to help."

He sat next to her again. She took in the dark eyes, the clean lines of his face. He was nice to look at, but she had to say, in the past couple of days his actions had been even more appealing.

"Thank you for taking care of me."

"Anytime."

"I'm sorry about the sex thing."

One corner of his mouth turned up. "The sex thing? What does that mean?"

"That we can't for a little while. I know it's a big part of our relationship and you'll want to—"

He stopped her with a kiss. "Don't go there. I'm not in this to get laid."

"That's disappointing."

He laughed. "I'm not in this *just* to get laid. You matter to me, Julie. We matter. You'll heal and we'll get back to that, but until then, I'm still here."

"That's so nice," she whispered, her eyes burning a little. "I'd understand if you were mad."

"But I'm not."

The edges of her pain softened a little and she felt the strangest urge to giggle, which was odd because he hadn't said anything funny.

"I can feel the pill starting to work. You'll stop me if I start to say anything weird at dinner?"

"You'll be fine, whatever you say. Everyone loves you."

She thought about Gwen. "Maybe not everyone, but close enough."

"What does it say that no one wants meat loaf?" Tiffany asked. "This is the second night it's been a hard no. Julie put a lot of effort into the menus."

Dana was less concerned about disappointing her mom than getting dinner on the table. And avoiding Axel. Actually, of the two, the latter was a bigger concern.

She knew her plan about the faux boyfriend was a good one—with the two of them stuck in the house together, she had to find a way to make sure he didn't think she was still pining over him. Because she wasn't. Okay, she was, but he didn't need to know. He already had enough power over her, given he was the one she wanted to be with for the rest of her life, and he didn't need any more.

"Is this going to be enough?" Gwen asked, staring at the ingredients for their odds-and-ends dinner.

Dana considered their options. "A cheese plate, a veggie plate and a fruit plate. Mini pigs in a blanket, mini egg rolls, and isn't there something else?"

"I'm making chicken salad with the leftover chicken from the other night," Gwen said. "We have rolls and crackers."

"I think it's more than enough." Tiffany reached for a couple of the cheeses. "Not traditional, but still good. And we're clearing out room in the refrigerator. We're doing our last shopping before Christmas tomorrow, and I know we're going to overbuy."

The three of them started prepping the meal. Dana turned on both ovens and got the frozen things on cookie sheets. Tiffany handled the cheese plate while Gwen made her chicken salad. Blair joined them a few minutes later.

"I want to help," she said as she crossed to the sink and washed her hands.

"You can start on the fruit plate," her mother said. "Or maybe set the table."

Dana watched them to see if there was the usual tension, but they were both pleasant and relaxed. Maybe they'd come to terms, she thought, hoping they had. She couldn't imagine not being close to her mom, and given all Blair had been through as a kid, she deserved her mom to be there for her now. Not that forgiving Gwen would be easy.

"I'll set the table," Blair said, not looking at the food piled onto the counter.

Dana slid cookie sheets into the oven. "You okay?"

"My tummy's a little uneasy. Not my usual upset, but I'm sure it's related. I'll be fine."

Her mother glanced at her. "You don't have to eat anything if you're not feeling up to it. Do you want some soup? Or maybe plain crackers?"

Blair looked surprised at Gwen's concern. "It'll pass. It always does. I'm sure by the time we sit down to eat, I'll be better."

Fifteen minutes later, Tiffany yelled for everyone to wash their hands and come to the table. She turned to Dana.

"Should I go upstairs and let Heath know it's time? Julie has to be hungry."

"We're on our way down," Heath called from the second level.

Tiffany grinned. "Man, sound really travels in this house."

"Yes, it does. Remember that. Fight with the door closed."

"So far I'm getting along with everyone, but I'll try to remember your advice."

Dana watched the other woman carry the cheese and veggie plates into the dining room. Tiffany was much better than she had been when she'd arrived. She was crying less and interacting more. Being around people and with her kids had been good for her.

Her mom really was a marvel, she thought. Inviting her boyfriend's ex-wife to Christmas so she wouldn't be alone? Sure, it was the right thing to do, but Dana didn't think she was anywhere near that strong. No way she would invite one of Axel's exes to hang out, no matter the circumstances. Yet another reason to admire her mother and want to be like her.

Dana pulled the cookie sheets out of the oven and set them on hot plates. She'd just reached for a spatula to move the hot appetizers onto a platter when her mother walked into the kitchen.

"I have to help," Julie announced, swaying slightly as she spoke. "It's my job."

Heath quickly joined her. "All right, you. I turned my back for less than five seconds. Let's go sit at the table."

"But I have to cook dinner. It's what I do."

"All done," Dana told her. "Mom, are you okay?"

"She just took a pain pill on an empty stomach," Heath said, guiding her mother back toward the dining room. "She's going to be a little loopy. Don't expect rational conversation."

"I excel at rational conversation," Julie complained. "And what about dinner?"

"Look at all the food on the table. I think the meal is taken care of."

"Oh, that looks good. I want wine."

Dana looked at Heath, who grinned as he pushed in Julie's chair. "You can want as much as you want. It's not happening."

"You're not the boss of me."

Dana glanced at Tiffany, who grinned.

"I love her," the other woman said quietly. "I mean it. She's my hero."

"Mine, too."

The kids, Paul and Huxley, followed by Rufus, walked into the dining room.

"We're here," Wyatt said, coming to a stop when he saw Julie. "You okay?"

"I'm perfect," she told the boy. "Never better. How are you?"

"Good. Dad says there's going to be more snow tonight, so maybe we can all have a snowball fight tomorrow." Wyatt frowned. "Except I don't think you can, Julie. You broke your arm."

"Next time," she told him.

Nick pulled out chairs for the kids. Rufus, who'd been fed earlier, settled in the dog bed in the corner, prepared to wait for anything that might fall to the floor. Paul opened the two wine bottles that were set out on the sideboard. He was starting to pour when Axel limped into the room.

Dana did her best not to look at him. Seeing him obviously injured did things to her heart she didn't want to think about. Better to keep her distance and think pure thoughts—like how one day she would get her life back and move on and meet someone great who loved her.

Julie stared at him, her eyes widening. "Oh, no! I forgot. Axel, you've been shot!"

The room went silent. Both kids looked between Axel and Julie. Madeline took a step back while Wyatt moved closer.

Huxley sighed heavily. "Julie, what are we going to do with you?"

"Me? I'm fine."

"You were shot?" Wyatt stared at Axel, sounding more intrigued than afraid. "You said you were cut."

"I thought it was a better story."

"But you've got a real bullet hole in your leg? Can I see it?"

Julie covered her face with her right hand for a second, then dropped her arm. "Oh, no. What did I say? I didn't know it was a secret. It's just the shock. Wyatt, no, you can't see the bullet wound. It will give you nightmares. Axel, I'm so sorry. It's my fault. I should never have taken the contract with the bank for the repos."

Axel's expression was, as always, unreadable. "I'm the one who asked you to do it. I wasn't paying attention like I should."

"But you're shot."

Heath put his hands on her shoulders. "Maybe you can stop saying that."

"What?"

"'You're shot.' We were keeping it from the kids."

"What kids?"

Heath's mouth twitched like he was trying not to laugh. "My two."

"Oh, Wyatt and Madeline." Julie smiled. "I love you two so much. Are you having fun? It's almost Christmas."

His children looked at each other, then back at Julie.

"Are you all right?" Madeline asked nervously.

"She's on pain medication," Tiffany told them. "She's a little out of it. No offense, Julie, but no one is going to pay attention to anything you say tonight."

She motioned for the kids to take a seat. Wyatt muttered something about wanting to see the bullet hole, but did as his mom asked.

Paul circled the table, pouring wine for the adults, excluding Julie. He paused by Axel.

"You on anything?"

"I am."

Paul bypassed his glass. Heath got a bottle of regular apple cider from the refrigerator. Once he served his kids, he poured some into Axel's wineglass, then Julie's, causing her to beam at him.

"White wine. That's nice."

He kissed the top of her head. "You're welcome."

Dana watched the exchange with more than a little envy. Heath was so good to her mom. He was there for her, his concern and affection clear. He was great with his kids and nice to his ex-wife. If she had to bet, she would say he was also the kind of man who stayed.

Her gaze involuntarily slid to Axel, only to find that he was watching her. She had no idea what he was thinking and told herself it didn't matter. He'd had his chance, times three. There wasn't going to be a fourth.

The rest of the adults took their seats. Dana was careful to sit on the same side as Axel, a couple of seats down. That way she wouldn't have to look at him all through the meal, and she might even be able to forget he was here. Plates and platters were passed around.

"There are even more presents under the tree," Madeline said, taking two mini pigs in a blanket. "There are two more for Wyatt than for me."

"There aren't," Wyatt said. "I counted after lunch."

"You're missing the two in back," his sister said, then looked at her mom. "It's supposed to be fair."

"Is it Christmas?" Tiffany asked.

"No."

"Then let's wait to panic."

"Maybe I'll get all the presents and you'll get none," Wyatt crowed.

Heath raised his eyebrows. "Is that really where you want to go, son?"

Wyatt thought for a second, then shook his head. "No. Sorry. I take it back. It should be even."

Across from her, Nick and Paul were talking about a car. Gwen asked Julie about the tests she'd had in the hospital. Huxley and Blair were in deep discussion about something. All the conversation flowing around her was so normal. But despite being unable to see him, Dana was aware of the man two seats away. It was as if no one else was there and it was just the two of them.

She missed him, she admitted. She missed *them*. Like her mom and Heath, she and Axel were easy when they were together. They had a good rhythm, whether it was what to have for dinner or how often to make love. She could trust him to do the right thing, to be there for her, right up until he left. Having him so close was a form of torture she hadn't expected. She wanted—

"Blair? What's wrong?"

Julie's loud voice silenced the room.

Blair looked at her mother-in-law. "I'm sorry—what?"

"You didn't take any cheese. You love cheese, and it's one of the foods you can eat. Are you all right?"

Heath put his hand over Julie's. "Hey, let Blair eat what she wants."

"I will. It's just she loves Brie. I got her favorite." She looked at Blair. "It's your favorite," she repeated stubbornly.

"Mom, it's okay." Nick pointed at her. "I say this with love. Let go of the cheese obsession."

Julie ignored him. "How are you feeling?"

Blair glanced around, as if realizing everyone was staring at her. She flushed slightly. "I'm all right. I wasn't in the mood for cheese tonight."

"It's soft cheese." Julie's mouth dropped open. "You're not eating soft cheese! Oh my God! You're pregnant!"

"What?" Blair's eyes widened. "No!"

Dana stared at her sister-in-law, feeling her discomfort. Blair looked shocked, not guilty. Obviously she wasn't secretly pregnant. "Mom, stop, please."

Nick stared at Blair. "Sweetie, are you okay?"

"I'm not pregnant. I'm not." She waved at the table. "Someone change the subject, I beg you."

Julie beamed at her. "I'm so happy. I can't wait to have grandchildren. How are your symptoms? I was constipated for the first three months. It was the worst. But maybe you'd like that—what with your IBS. It would be a change over the constant diarrhea."

"Mom!" Nick stared at her. "Stop talking."

"What did I say? It's not like I asked if her breasts hurt. That's a whole pregnancy thing and I didn't say a word."

The room went silent. Blair's flush deepened. Dana desperately tried to think of something to say, but her mind was blank. Her mom had officially gone off the rails. Yes, she was drugged, but jeez, didn't she have some small connection to reality? Not only was Blair embarrassed, Julie was going to feel horrible when she realized what she'd said.

Huxley picked up his wine. "So, Dana, did you hear from Jared today?"

She felt everyone turn to look at her. Blair was obviously grateful for the question, and Tiffany was nodding encouragingly. Julie looked confused, and Dana had to admit, on this one, she was with her mom. Who on earth was Jared?

The seconds ticked by. Finally Tiffany said, "Yes, I was wondering the same thing. Have you heard from your handsome boyfriend?"

Crap. Crap, crap and double crap. Jared!

"Yes," she said, her voice too loud. "He called...um, earlier. His grandmother is rallying a little. The family is hoping she'll make it through Christmas."

"Who's Jared?" Julie asked, looking from Dana to Heath.

"Your daughter's boyfriend." Heath reached for his wine. "Remember?"

"No."

"He's not here because of his grandmother." Tiffany smiled at Julie. "We talked about how she's in hospice, and she's his favorite, so he needs to be with her. Otherwise, he would have been here with all of us."

"He's an investment banker," Gwen added. "It's a perfect match. They speak each other's language without competing. That's good for a marriage."

"He's a family man." Nick stared at Dana as if telling her she would so owe him later. "Not that he has a family of his own, but he wants one. With Dana."

"And he's handsome." Tiffany smiled at Dana. "Very, very handsome."

Dana was so grateful she couldn't see Axel. As it was, she wanted to crawl under the table. Or maybe just teleport to another century. What had sounded so great in theory wasn't playing out the way she'd hoped. Actually, it was a total disaster.

Julie still looked confused. She leaned toward Heath. "Have I met him?"

"You've seen his picture," Gwen said. "We all have."

"I don't remember."

Dana hoped her mom wouldn't ask to see it now, because, of course, there wasn't a picture. Or a man.

"Jason's a good guy," she said. "We're happy."

"Jared," Paul said quietly.

"Jared," she repeated, her cheeks flushing, knowing there was no way Axel was going to believe any of this. She'd just made a colossal fool out of herself. Worse, she was trapped in the house with him for the next few days. Avoiding him was going to be her only option.

16

Blair escaped as soon as dinner was finished. She probably should have stayed to help with the cleanup, but she'd needed time by herself to deal with what Julie had said at dinner. It was a living, breathing nightmare, and she didn't know what to do about it. Talking about her being or not being pregnant was bad enough, but the rest of it had been so humiliating. Diarrhea and breasts? Why had Julie gone there?

Nick walked in and crossed to where she sat on the bed.

"I'm sorry," he said, sitting next to her. "I don't know why she said all that."

"I don't, either." Blair shifted so she was facing him and ignored the ominous gurgling and pain in her gut. "It was horrible. Yes, I didn't want cheese. My IBS is unhappy and the cheese wasn't appealing, but it's a huge leap from me not eating Brie to being pregnant."

His gaze was steady. "You're not, right?"

"No!" She stood and walked to the far end of the room. "Nick, I'm not. Believe me, you'd be the first to know. There's absolutely no reason for her to think I am. It was just cheese!"

He walked over to stand in front of her. "Because it would be kind of great if you were."

"I'm not."

He pulled her close. "This has been a sucky vacation. We should have gone to Hawaii."

She hung on to him. "You don't mean that."

He drew back. "Yeah, I do. You've had to hang out with your mom and that hasn't been easy. I nearly killed mine. The whole point of this was to spend time with family and deal with my dad, but with everything going on, I've barely thought about him, which makes me a bad son."

"You're not."

He touched her face. "You don't get to say."

"I know things. You're a good, good man and he'd be proud of you."

"He'd be happy I was leaving the tow business. My point is this isn't the good time we were hoping for. Like I said, we should have gone to Hawaii like we planned."

"But we didn't." She put her hands on his solid chest. "We should learn from these lessons so we don't have to repeat them. No more keeping secrets from the people in our lives."

"I agree. It was a dumb move on my part. If I'd told my mom like you wanted me to, she wouldn't have a broken arm."

"She's going to make a full recovery. I hope you can let the guilt go."

"I will, but not for a while." He kissed her, then groaned. "Jeez, poor Dana. That whole thing about Jared went badly."

Blair held in a wince. "It did. Axel knows it was all a lie, and now she has to deal with that." It almost put the pregnancy/constipation/diarrhea/breast comments in perspective.

"You all right?" he asked.

"Like you, I will be."

"For what it's worth, my mom is going to feel really bad when she figures out what she did."

"Julie feeling bad isn't anything I want. She said it, I was uncomfortable and I'll get over it." She looked at him. "I know she didn't mean to embarrass me. That's not who she is."

"We need to keep her away from drugs."

"Apparently!"

He kissed her again. "We're going to watch an action movie downstairs. Want to come?"

"No. I'll stay here." She pressed a hand to her stomach. "I want to stay near a bathroom for the next hour or so. You know how I react to stress."

"Okay. I'll be up when the movie's over."

After he left she tried to get comfortable on the bed, but she couldn't escape her swirling thoughts. Telling herself her mother-in-law had been the painkiller form of drunk didn't make her comment go away. Pregnant! Why had Julie gone there? It was a pretty big leap and had come out of nowhere. Now everyone was going to be watching her and speculating—if not about her being pregnant, then about whether or not she was constipated. The last thing she wanted was to talk about her IBS more than necessary.

There was a soft knock on the door. Blair briefly hoped it wasn't Julie coming to apologize.

"Yes?"

The door opened and her mother stepped in. Gwen gave her a tentative smile. "Nick's downstairs, so I knew I wouldn't be interrupting the two of you. I wanted to see how you were feeling."

Under normal circumstances, Gwen was the last person Blair wanted to see, but oddly enough, she didn't mind having her mother here.

"I'm okay," she said, sitting up. "As much as I can be."

Gwen carefully closed the door behind her, then sat in the chair by the window. "That was quite the announcement at dinner."

"I'm not pregnant."

Her mother surprised her by smiling. "I think we all know that. The look on your face was about being shocked, not being discovered. I can't imagine what she was thinking. You often have to change what you eat because of the IBS. Julie should be used to that. It must be the painkillers. She doesn't seem to have any tolerance at all."

"I guess not." Blair picked at the comforter. "Plus, my stomach's been off lately and she knows that. I'm guessing somehow the thoughts got a little twisted in her brain."

"Not to get too personal, but what are you doing for birth control? I know you can't be on the Pill."

Gwen was right—it interfered with her other medications. Or rather they interfered with it.

"Right now we're mostly using condoms. We tried an IUD, but it made me bleed too much."

Her mother's expression was carefully neutral. "Blair, I'm not interfering, I'm just asking. What does the word *mostly* mean in the context of using condoms?"

Blair felt uncomfortable with the conversation. Yes, they were both adults, but this was her mother and they were talking about sex.

"I, um, know we have to use them consistently, and we do. I know they're not foolproof, but they've been successful for us."

"I'm glad they're working out."

"Me, too. And, well, the week after my period, we get a break from them."

Her mother stared at her. "Excuse me? What kind of break?"

"You can't get pregnant right after your period, so we take advantage of that."

Gwen's eyes widened as her mouth dropped open. "You don't use birth control for a week?"

"Just after my period. I keep track."

"Your body doesn't work that way. You can ovulate during

your period and drop an egg right after. Darling, your father and I wanted children very much, but we were going to wait another year. I went off the Pill and we used an almost identical method. And you're the result. There's no week off. Besides, you were never very regular with your periods. Has that changed?"

"What? No." Her head spun with the information. Was her mother right? Could she ovulate during her period or right after? She thought it was two weeks later. Were they really taking a chance?

"I'm not pregnant," she said, more to herself than her mother. "I can't be."

"I'm sure you're not. You didn't eat cheese, Blair. That's hardly a sign." She paused. "Although you have been tired. Julie's comments aside, are you noticing any changes in your body? Do some smells bother you?"

Blair thought about how she'd had to leave the kitchen a few times because whatever was cooking made her nauseous.

"Nothing comes to mind," she lied. Pregnant? No. She couldn't be. It wasn't the right time. There was too much going on.

Her mother surprised her by smiling.

"What?" Blair demanded.

"I'm just thinking of the future. I look forward to saying my baby is having a baby. I love the idea of grandchildren." Her smile faded. "I know I don't deserve that. But it would be nice. A chance to start over and begin to earn your trust again."

Not anything Blair wanted to think about. This nicer version of her mother was almost more difficult to deal with than the one she was used to. At least old Gwen was predictable. "We should change the subject. I'm not pregnant."

"When was your last period?"

"I have no idea."

Which also wasn't true. Blair had an app on her phone. Without looking at it, she would say her best guess was about six weeks ago. But that was often the case with her.

Her mother leaned toward her. "I'm not pushing. I'm offering. I could go into town tomorrow and get a pregnancy test. It would be easy for me to go by myself. I doubt anyone would offer to go with me. You'd have a bit more of a problem getting away."

Blair knew that was true. Nick would want to drive her and most likely Dana or Tiffany would join her. Maybe even Paul. There was no way for her to sneak off and buy the test.

"I'm not pregnant," she said, for what felt like the eightieth time.

"But you'd like to be sure."

"You can't know that."

Her mother watched her without speaking. Blair squirmed on the bed.

"All right, yes, I'd like to know, but not now. Not here with everyone around. It's only a few more days until we head back to Seattle. I'll get a test when we're home."

"That sounds like a good plan."

Blair waited to see if her mother would say something to make her feel bad, but Gwen only smiled at her.

"If you change your mind, let me know. I'll go out and get the test. Otherwise, I won't say anything. I'm sure you're right. It's just your IBS acting up. Oh, what about your medications? Would you have to go off them if you were pregnant?"

"No. My doctor is really careful. It's why my symptoms aren't as well managed as they could be. Once we have our family, Nick will get a vasectomy so there's no accidental pregnancy and I'll switch to more powerful drugs that will help a lot more."

"You have it all planned out."

Blair touched her belly. "I hope so."

"You do. You're going to be a great mom." Gwen raised a

hand. "In the future, when you're ready." She rose and started for the door.

"I'm not like you," Blair blurted.

Gwen turned back to face her.

"I don't know how to be around kids. I'm not really good with them, like you are. I work with old people all day."

Her mother smiled. "It's not hard. You'll figure it out. And when the time comes, you'll have lots of support. I hope..." She pressed her lips together. "I hope by then, you and I will have started to be more connected and you'll let me help, too."

Yesterday, Blair would have blanched at the thought, but tonight it was a little less scary.

"Thanks, Mom. For everything."

"Anytime."

Dana loved the family cabin. It had always meant good times and happy memories. When she'd been old enough for sleepovers, she'd often brought friends with her in the summer. She'd learned to ski and snowboard up here, she'd had her first real kiss the summer she'd turned fifteen. Then her dad had caught her and eighteen-year-old Thomas and he'd banished the kid from sight and threatened to go to his parents if he ever came back.

She loved the traditions, the quirks, such as sound carrying from floor to floor if you forgot to close a door. She loved the wood accents, the big kitchen, the way it felt cozy in a winter storm. But tonight of all nights she really, really wished there was a way to get from the bottom floor to the top without using the big staircase that went directly by the living room. The living room that had been turned into Axel's space. Because going past it meant the possibility of running into him, and based on what had happened at dinner...well, if she never saw him again, it would be too soon.

Why had she thought the whole Jared/Jason fake-boyfriend

thing was a good idea? Why hadn't someone tried harder to stop her? Okay, sure, Heath had said something, but he hadn't been talking loudly enough, and now she was stuck with the specter of the lie sitting out there for Axel to mock her.

She briefly debated hiding downstairs until she was sure he was asleep, but knew that was the coward's way out. Better to gather what was left of her dignity and march upstairs as if she had every right to be wherever she wanted in the house. Which she did, so there!

She went up the stairs as quietly, yet confidently, as she could—an uneasy combination that nearly caused her to slip. Once she reached the main level, she quickly glanced around, then relaxed. Axel was nowhere to be seen. She took the three steps to the staircase leading up and turned, only to practically run into the man.

"Dana."

That was it. One word, just one. Every part of her began melting. Her heart said to linger, her hormones danced. Even her brain, which should know better, pointed out he was one good-looking man and that mouth of his knew how to do magical things.

"Axel."

She kept her voice as crisp and disinterested as she could, reminding herself to keep her chin up and her shoulders square. She was powerful and in charge. She didn't care about this man at all.

"We need to talk."

Her first response was to point out they, in fact, did not need to do anything together. He was here by chance, not invitation. He was nothing to her. Nada. Zip. So what conversation was there to be had?

"Please."

Oh, if only he hadn't said *please*, she thought as the last of her pathetic defenses crumbled. She thought about running for her bedroom—she doubted he was well enough to take the stairs just yet—but that wasn't the mature response. Better to let him say what he wanted to say, pretend to listen and then run.

"Fine. We'll talk."

She turned and led the way to the small craft room behind the kitchen. Once they were inside, she deliberately closed the door, then faced him.

"So talk."

He carefully lowered himself to a chair. The faint tightness in his body told her that he was in pain. No doubt he was playing the tough guy and not bothering with enough pain medication. Because that was so like him.

She found herself wanting to ask about his condition or even offer to get him something to make him more comfortable, like a pillow.

Ack! No. She wasn't going to take care of him. He was just some guy she barely knew—at least that was the ultimate goal, because in truth, he seemed to be the man she couldn't stop thinking about, most likely because she was still desperately in love with him. Which was probably a topic she should address first.

"I'm not in love with you," she blurted. "I'm totally over you. Whatever we had is gone, mostly because you killed it. I'm sorry you were hurt and I hope you make a full recovery, but other than that, you have no place in my life."

"What about Jared? Or was it Jason."

She'd never been a particularly physical or violent person, but at that second, she found herself wanting to slap him across the face. She didn't—it wasn't who she was—but for a second, she imagined the sting on her palm and knew it would feel good.

"It's unlike you to make fun of me," she said stiffly. "But maybe I didn't know you at all. After all, you kept telling me you loved me and wanted to be with me. That usually happened a couple of days before you ended things."

He dropped his smile and his gaze. "I'm sorry."

She pressed her lips together, determined not to speak.

He looked at her. "I hope you're telling the truth. About being over me. I hope you've moved on. I was never the right guy for you. I kept waiting for you to figure that out, but you were determined to see the best in me."

"So you led me on," she snapped. "You lied about loving me?"

"That was never a lie."

"So you meant it but you left anyway?"

She walked to the other side of the small room and turned to glare at him. "What is it? Just tell me once and for all. You've totally screwed up my Christmas, so let's say you owe me. What is it? Why do you say all those things and then leave? You don't cheat, so I don't think you're compelled to be with multiple women at the same time. Am I not interesting enough? Is the sex not what you want? Should I lose weight? Get a different job? When we're together, it's so good and you seem happy, but then you tell me it won't work and you dump me and I just want to know why."

Her voice rose with every word until she was shrieking at him. She consciously lowered her voice.

"Axel, if I ever mattered to you, tell me why. I deserve that."

"You do." His face tightened with pain. "You deserve everything good. I'm sorry. If you knew how sorry..." He turned away. "I never wanted to hurt you. I didn't."

"Too bad, because you're really good at it."

"I've told you the truth and you won't believe me. I'm not good enough."

She sank into one of the chairs in the corner. "That crap again. I was hoping for a little honesty."

"I *am* being honest. It's the truth. I'm not in your league. Not even close. You think you know what would happen between us, but you're wrong. One day you'd realize you made a mistake and that I was dragging you down. You hang out with professionals and smart people. I wouldn't fit in."

She stared at him, unable to understand what he was saying. "I hang out with my mother."

"Not at work. Can you really see me at some party your accounting firm has?"

She looked at his gorgeous face, his thick hair and kissable mouth. He was tall, fit, broad-shouldered and walked with a confidence that straight women found irresistible.

"You'd fit in fine."

"I wouldn't. I'd say the wrong thing or do the wrong thing. I'd embarrass you and you'd be ashamed of me. I'm not like you. I don't have ambitions beyond what I do. I like my job and I like the business."

"This is stupid." She stood and crossed to the door. He grabbed her arm, spinning her to face him, then rose.

They were so close, she thought. Close enough that a single step would put her in his arms. How was it possible that even as he blew smoke up her butt, she still wanted him to hold her?

"I'm telling the truth," he said quietly. "One day you'd wake up and realize you didn't want to be married to a tow truck driver anymore, and you'd leave me. That's why I walk away. I can't do that, Dana. I can't survive losing you. That makes me the biggest bastard on the planet, but it's the stone-cold truth. I'm too weak to survive the inevitable. So I do it first, but because I can't get you out of my head and my heart, I keep coming back."

She blinked several times, trying to take it all in. She wasn't sure what shocked her most—that he'd said the *M* word or that he'd admitted to a weakness.

He'd seen them married? She hadn't been sure he'd ever imagined them lasting past the next full moon. This had to be some kind of play. Only except for leaving her, Axel had never been into games. Unless their entire relationship was a game and she was the one who didn't know the rules.

"Let me get this straight," she said. "You're claiming to be in love with me and unable to forget me. In fact, you see us getting married. But you're convinced that over time I would get tired of you and leave, which you couldn't handle. Rather than discuss any of that, you told me you loved me, made me believe we were in a long-term relationship, then dumped me. Three times. Is that about it?"

"Yes."

It was bullshit, she thought sadly. All of it. She didn't know what kind of twisted mind came up with that, but whatever was going on, she really didn't want to be part of it. She could believe a lot of things, but not that he was so in love with her, he couldn't handle her leaving.

"I was hoping for a better story," she said, stepping back. "I was hoping you'd tell me the truth. I should have known better. I may not be over you, Axel, but I have to say, you're helping me get there. So thank you for that."

She turned and walked out of the craft room, then up the stairs. Tonight she was going to cry and scream into a pillow, but tomorrow she would be a little bit more over him. Of that she was sure.

17

After dinner, Julie stood in the middle of the bathroom, tired, but not clear what to do next. The pain meds were fading, and she hurt all over. Not just where she'd fractured her arm, but down her hip and leg and across her back. The ache was deep and throbbed with every heartbeat. Generally she wasn't a fan of drugging herself, but maybe she should rethink that philosophy. Last evening a lovely nurse had given her a shot of something amazing. Now that she was home, no such magical creature would show up to rescue her from what she thought could be a very long night.

Adding to her general discomfort was a nagging sense of... she wasn't sure what in the back of her mind. It was as if she had to tell someone something. But somehow she couldn't quite remember what was bothering her.

"I need a shower."

Just being under the warm spray would make her feel better, she told herself. Once she was clean, she could crawl into bed and try to sleep. Everything would be better in the morning.

She stepped out of her slippers and undid her jeans one-handed, but her sweater was more complicated. Yes, technically, it buttoned up the front, but she couldn't seem to work them easily, and pain jolted through her arm when she accidentally bumped it. She wanted to rip off the thick cotton, but that wasn't going to happen when she couldn't even undo a damned button!

She tugged and spun and nearly lost her balance, which had her reaching out to grab something stable, only she ran into the vanity instead, jamming her already bruised hip into the corner.

The instant and intense agony nearly brought her to her knees. She gasped even as her stomach gave a threatening lurch, as if warning her she'd reached her pain threshold.

"I can't," she whispered, tears burning. Despite the warm floor, cold started to seep into her, making her shiver. She felt sick and exhausted and fragile—all sensations she didn't allow in her regular life. She was tougher than a few bruises and a broken arm. She had to be!

The bathroom door opened and Heath walked in. His brows drew together as he stared at her.

"What are you doing?"

"Taking a shower. Or I will be as soon as I get off this stupid sweater."

"You can't take a shower by yourself. You're still in shock from the fall and probably hurting because the pain meds are wearing off. You haven't slept, so you're exhausted. How are you supposed to wash yourself with one hand? What if you slip?"

She glared at him. "I can do it. I'm capable. I don't need help."

"Too bad, because I'm not leaving."

"I'm not interested in giving you a show. Leave me alone. I'm fine. Just let me take my shower!"

Her voice was oddly loud, and she had the feeling the tears in her eyes were more than threatening. Any second now she was going to start crying like some weak, ineffectual, useless person. She wasn't a crier, never had been. She dusted herself off and got on with whatever needed doing. Her father had taught her that years ago, and it was a lesson she used every day.

But instead of stepping back, or better yet, leaving her to deal with the situation herself, Heath only shook his head and put his hands on his hips.

"Not happening. I'm staying here and helping you, whether you want it or not."

"Then I'm going to scream."

"That'll probably bring your kids running, which will be embarrassing for them and you, but if it's what you want, go ahead. I'm not leaving and you're not showering alone."

"You can't be here," she snapped, irritated by his stubbornness. "Go away. Go!" She used her good hand to point to the door.

Heath watched her. "What is going on with you? Why are you being so difficult? It's just a damned shower. You've been injured, Julie. Why are you so pissed? I'm not the bad guy here. I just want to help."

"Well, you can't. I don't need help."

"All evidence to the contrary?" He moved toward her, stopping when he was in front of her. "You're shaking."

"I'm fine."

He gently moved her to the tub surround and had her sit. "Okay, start talking. What's this really about?"

She stared at the hem of his sweater because it was easier than looking at anything else—especially him.

"I'm independent."

"I know that. It's part of why I like you so much. You're strong."

She looked up at him. "I don't ask for help."

His gaze met hers. At first he seemed confused, but then his eyes widened. "Ever?"

She turned away. "It's not my thing. I'm the one everyone comes to when they need something. I'm in charge. I know what needs to be done, and I do it."

He crouched in front of her and lightly touched her cheek. "Hey, I get it, but come on. It's a shower."

"It represents the fact that I'm weak. I'm not weak. Not ever. I don't need anyone."

"What about when you were married to Eldon?"

She rolled her eyes. "Oh, please. I think we're all clear that I was the strong one in that relationship."

"Do you think you're stronger than me?"

Even exhausted, sore and still a tiny bit dizzy, she recognized the danger of answering that question incorrectly. But she was too out of it to come up with the politically correct response and went with the truth.

"I think we're both about the same level of strong. But I do some things better than you."

He flashed her a smile. "Like organizing Christmas for a hundred people? Yes, you do that much better than I would."

He started unfastening her sweater buttons.

She pushed his hands away. "I can do that myself."

"You can," he said easily. "But you don't have to. You said it yourself. We're partners. Right now you need a little extra, and I'm happy to give it. Sometime in the future, I'll need your help with something. It's how this works."

Partners? She'd never said that word. She wouldn't. "We're not partners. We're dating." She paused. "I might be willing to go so far as to say you're my boyfriend, but that's absolutely all."

He surprised her by chuckling. "Admit it or not, it's true. We're good together. And right now I'm going to take care of you because I can, and helping you makes me happy."

He carefully removed her sling, then eased her sweater down her arm. She did her best not to react but couldn't help the gasp of pain when the fabric slid off her swollen forearm.

She hadn't bothered with her bra in the hospital, so all that was left were her panties. But before helping her to her feet,

Heath stripped down to nothing, which was a very nice distraction from how awful she was feeling.

"The spirit is willing," she murmured. "But I'm just not sure I can do much more than lie there."

"We're not having sex," he told her. "Not until you're feeling better."

"Then what...?"

He drew her to her feet and pulled off her panties, then got the water going in the shower. Once the temperature was right, he guided her inside, then joined her.

"I'm going to do all the work," he told her. "You just stand there."

"I can do it myself," she said stubbornly.

"I'm sure you can, but now you don't have to."

Heath bathed her, even carefully washing her hair and using the good conditioner. When he was done, he turned off the water and wrapped her in a thick, fluffy towel. He quickly dried off and pulled on pj bottoms, then got her into yoga pants and a loose T-shirt. Once the sling was back in place, he wrapped her in a blanket while he carefully blew out her hair.

After pulling back the covers, he got her a painkiller and a glass of water.

"Don't argue," he said, holding out both.

"You're so bossy."

"Yes, I am."

After she took her meds, he helped her into bed. He got extra pillows so she could lie on her back and rest her arm on her chest, without it sliding off. Only then did he carefully get in beside her.

"But it's early," she protested, feeling her eyes start to close. "You can't be tired."

"I didn't get much sleep last night."

"Oh, right. You stayed until visiting hours ended, then were back early this morning. But what about your kids?"

"They're fine. We talked earlier. They get you need my help right now."

He *had* been a help, she thought, even as her mind started to drift.

"Thank you."

"You're welcome." He kissed her forehead. "Go to sleep."

"I didn't expect you to be so good to me. It's nice. Weird, but nice."

He chuckled. "I'm happy to defy expectations."

"Even in bed. I knew you'd be good, but you're even better than I imagined."

"You are, too."

She waved away the comment with her good fingers. "I don't think I'm the one bringing the spark. Okay, sure, I'm up for nearly anything, but you're the one with the magic." She thought about what he'd said before.

"I'm not sure about the partner thing, though."

"You don't have to be. I'm sure enough for both of us. Go to sleep, Julie. I'll be right here."

Dana didn't sleep much. Every time she tried to relax in bed, she started replaying the conversation she'd had with Axel in her head. She wasn't sure which surprised her most—his casual assumption that they would get married or his belief that she would leave him because he didn't fit in. Regardless, his actions proved he'd been making the decision for her—which had propelled her to the top of the stairs more than once in the night. Each time she'd talked herself down, knowing it wasn't smart to try to have it out with her ex-boyfriend at two in the morning. Better to tell herself he didn't matter and try to convince herself that he was just a fool who'd lost the best thing that had ever happened to him.

Which should have made her feel better, only it didn't. Mostly because she had no idea if he'd been telling the truth or just playing her. Stupid man!

By five she'd given up on sleep, so got dressed and crept downstairs. It had been Blair's turn to assemble the breakfast casserole, something she'd forgotten to do, Dana realized as she checked the contents of the refrigerator. No doubt her sister-in-law had been freaked out by Julie blurting out "You're pregnant—are you constipated?" at the dinner table.

"Oh, Mom. You're such a lightweight."

And poor Blair, Dana thought, locating the recipe and then collecting ingredients. Her friend wasn't the type of person who enjoyed being the center of attention. She was much happier sitting back and letting someone else be the star. Her low-key nature and steadfast loyalty made her perfect for Nick. When they were ready to have kids, they would both be great parents.

While she cut up day-old French bread, she allowed herself to think about having children of her own. Not with anyone in particular, because honestly, who would that be? Just generically. She imagined feeling happy and loved, touching her rapidly swelling belly.

In her mind's eye she felt more than saw the man she loved coming up behind her and pulling her close. But the second he touched her, the vague image became incredibly specific and she had to shake off the longing. Axel was incapable of sticking around long enough for milk to expire. No way he would ever stay long enough to be a father.

She wanted kids, she thought sadly. She wanted a good guy in her life and all the normal trappings. A house, maybe a dog. Rufus was great—so one like him. She wanted a strong marriage, but how was she supposed to make any of her dreams come true when she couldn't even figure out how to fall out of love with a man who kept breaking her heart?

She whisked together eggs and milk, then added seasonings. All that was left was the bacon.

Tiffany strolled into the kitchen. "Hi. You're up early."

"I could say the same about you."

"I'm an early riser." Tiffany looked at the various bowls and the big frying pan on the stove. "This is for the breakfast casserole?"

"It was Blair's turn. I think she forgot."

Tiffany winced. "I can't say that I blame her. Poor Blair. She was so upset. And Julie was on a tear. I know it was the drugs, but still."

"Mom doesn't do anything by half." Dana shook her head. "At some point she's going to remember what she said to Blair and feel awful."

"You gotta love how Julie never holds back. I respect that." Tiffany glanced at the clock. "Weren't you going out with Nick this morning? Isn't it time? I'll finish up here."

"Thanks. You're right. We're supposed to leave now."

As if he knew they were talking about him, Nick walked into the kitchen.

"There you are," he said, unscrewing the top on a thermos and pouring in coffee. "You ready to go?"

Dana looked at Tiffany, who smiled. "Scoot," she said cheerfully. "I'll finish this and get it in the oven. We'll be sure to save you some to heat up when you get back."

"Thanks."

Dana followed her brother to the front of the house. They put on coats and hats, then stepped into snow boots. Once in Nick's truck, she took charge of the thermos.

"I'm glad we're doing this," she said.

"Me, too." He glanced at her as he started the engine. "The whole point of coming up here was to honor Dad. With everything happening, I feel that kind of got lost."

"He knows we're thinking of him. Plus, he would have loved that the cabin is jam-packed with people. Dad enjoyed a party and a crowd."

Nick drove toward the main road. "I'm not sure what he would have made of Axel being here."

Dana glanced at her brother, but he was staring out the front window. "Maybe we shouldn't talk about Axel."

"But you're okay?"

No! How could she be with Axel around? But she didn't want to have that conversation with her brother at any time, and certainly not this morning.

"I'm doing great."

It was still dark out, but there was a hint of light on the eastern horizon. Light snow fell from the sky. Nick turned on the radio, pushing buttons until he found one playing Christmas carols.

"Remember that Christmas Dad wanted to get you a bike?" her brother asked.

Dana smiled at the memory. "Mom said they should wait until it was my birthday, in the spring, when I could ride it. They fought about it so much, I found out." She remembered not liking that her parents were arguing, but she'd been excited about the bike.

"Mom refused to have anything to do with the purchase," Nick reminded her. "She said it was totally on Dad, who forgot to pay the extra money to get it put together for him. So there he was, three days before Christmas, trying to figure out how to assemble a bike."

"I hadn't known that part," Dana admitted, thinking that as much as she loved her dad, she knew there was no way he could put together something as complicated as a bicycle.

"I tried to help, but I could only get so far."

"You were what? Eleven?"

"About that." He grinned at her. "I called Grandpa, who came over and got it together in a couple of hours."

"How didn't I know that?"

"I guess it never came up. Mom came out at the end and Dad admitted he'd been wrong. It was kind of sweet."

"Dad always went for the gusto when it came to the two of us," Dana said with a sigh. "Remember how he learned how to fly-fish because you wanted to learn?"

"He did the same with your horseback riding."

She thought about their long trail rides, up in the mountains. Her father hadn't enjoyed the outdoors, but he'd shown up, enduring what had to feel like endless afternoons.

"Fortunately, my horse phase only lasted that summer. You still go fly-fishing."

"Blair finds it relaxing."

"She's a good woman."

They talked about the traditions they remembered. How their father would take each of them out to breakfast every other week, making sure there was plenty of time to talk and just hang out. Her dad had been the one to encourage her to go into accounting. Julie had initially pushed for Dana to join the family business, but her dad had known she couldn't be less interested. Her mom had come around pretty quickly as well, but her dad had been the one to tell her to explore different options.

He'd been the one she'd sat and read with on snowy afternoons up at the cabin. Her mom and Nick had been the adventurers. When she'd been a kid, her dad had been the one to stand in line with her at midnight to get the latest Harry Potter book.

They pulled into an empty parking lot by the park on the meadow. Their dad's favorite of all the places they liked to go in the warmer months.

How many picnics had they shared up here? she wondered sadly. How many times had they laughed and talked over store-bought fried chicken and sandwiches from that shop by the lodge? Her mom and Nick would eventually pull out a Frisbee or a baseball and start throwing it back and forth, but Dana had sat with her dad and talked.

They got out of the truck. Dana had to take a couple of bracing breaths to let her body get used to the cold. The snow was letting up, and the sky was lighter now as night slowly turned into day.

She and Nick walked to the edge of the meadow and looked out over the expanse of snow.

"For a city guy, he loved it up here," Nick said.

"He loved the family time more than the nature part. But he was always there for us. Remember how he used to get up so early to take you to hockey practice?"

Ice time was limited and a team took what it could get. Sometimes that meant meeting at four in the morning.

"He was never crabby," Nick said quietly. "He would come and wake me up without once complaining. He and Mom didn't have a great marriage, but they were both good parents."

"They were. Dad loved us right to the end."

Nick unscrewed the top of the thermos and poured coffee into the cup. He passed it to her.

"He was a good man. When Blair and I have kids, I want to be just as focused, just as present for mine."

"You will be." She took a sip and nearly choked at the flavor. "What did you put in here?"

"Whiskey."

"It's not even eight in the morning."

He looked at her. "It's for Dad."

She took another drink and shuddered, then handed the cup to her brother. Nick took a long swallow.

They stood facing east, watching the sky brighten. The snow stopped, and the clouds shifted just enough for them to see a sliver of blue sky. Dana's eyes began to burn.

"I miss him," she whispered.

Nick put his arm around her. "Me, too. I wanted him to live a whole lot longer. We need him with us."

They did, she thought sadly. Her dad would have known what to say when Axel showed up.

"He really was a good man," she said.

"And he was proud of us, no matter what."

She leaned against Nick. "We miss you, Dad. And love you."

Nick cleared his throat. "You'll always be a part of us. Love you, Dad."

They stood there for a few more minutes, then turned and went back to the truck. Dana thought about turning around for one last look, but she knew her father wasn't there anymore. He'd moved on—hopefully to a happier place. But he would always be in her heart.

18

Julie stood in the entryway to the kitchen feeling crabby and out of sorts. She hurt all over, she hadn't slept well, and as far as she could tell, Tiffany and Gwen were doing their best to mess up breakfast.

It was a casserole, along with scrambled eggs and sausage, and cut-up fruit. How hard could that be? But even as she watched, Gwen was slicing the pineapple too thick while Tiffany seemed intent on doing a thousand things that weren't keeping an eye on the sausage.

"You might want to turn those," she said as calmly as she could, when what she really wanted to do was shriek loudly, then grab the spatula from Tiffany and flip the meat herself.

Tiffany looked at her and smiled. "I just did. They need to brown on this side now."

The fingers in Julie's good hand twitched a little. "Are you sure? Did you want to check?"

Gwen looked up. "I'm sure I'm prepping the pineapple all wrong. Come tell me how to make it better."

"You're doing fine." Julie managed to speak the lie without

clenching her teeth. Everything about this was so annoying. She should have stayed upstairs, in her room, only Heath had been sleeping after a night of what she was sure was her being restless. The man needed his rest.

"Who made the casserole?" she asked. "Are you sure you remembered to put everything in it?"

"I don't know." Tiffany smiled at her, while still ignoring the damned sausage. It was sausage. It needed to be turned.

"Dana had it mostly done when I got upstairs. She said she'd done it all right, but maybe she forgot something. I guess we'll find out."

Gwen glanced at Tiffany. The two shared a secret smile that really bugged Julie, although she couldn't say why. Something was going on for sure. She'd never felt so out of place in her own house.

She started to step into the kitchen, only to stop herself. First of all, a third cook always made things crowded. Second, she had a broken arm and really couldn't do much. Third, they were handling the meal, even if they were doing it wrong.

"Oh my God, I can't stand it," she said loudly. "Turn the sausage. Turn it. Turn it now!"

Tiffany picked up the tongs. "Do you need to take a pain pill? You're kind of on edge this morning."

"Bitchy," Gwen said calmly. "The word you're looking for is *bitchy*."

"I'm not a bitch," Julie snapped, only to realize the force of her reply might mean she kind of was. Not that she would admit that to either of them. Oh, saying she was sorry to Tiffany was easy enough, but to Gwen? No way.

"But you *are* in pain," Gwen told her. "You need to stay ahead of it. If nothing else, aren't you supposed to be taking an anti-inflammatory?"

"Now you sound like Heath."

Gwen smiled. "That's a lovely thing to say. Thank you. But you didn't answer my question about the anti-inflammatory."

The woman was so annoying, she thought, eyeing the giant chunks of pineapple she was shoving into a bowl. The pieces were huge. Why bother cutting it at all? Why not just toss the fruit on the table and they could rip it apart like dogs?

Julie glared at her. "I have pills to take with breakfast."

"Good. They'll make you feel better."

"I feel fine now. You don't get to say how I feel."

Tiffany and Gwen exchanged another look. What? Were they getting friendly? Julie didn't want that, but didn't know how to stop it.

"Madeline gets cranky when she doesn't feel well," Tiffany said as she once again began to ignore the sausage. "And unreasonable. Don't take this wrong, Julie, but you're the most together person I know. It's kind of nice to know you're just as flawed as the rest of us."

"I'm so happy my broken arm brings you pleasure."

The second the words were out of her mouth, Julie felt a wave of shame. "I'm sorry. That was horrible. I don't know what's wrong with me this morning."

"You didn't sleep, you hurt all over and you're too stubborn to take your medication." Gwen smiled at her. "Did I miss anything?"

Julie's instinct was to repeat "Did I miss anything?" in a mocking voice, but something told her that doing that wouldn't give her the high ground in this discussion.

"I need to be doing something. I'm in charge here."

Tiffany waved the tongs. "And yet you're not. Now take your crabby self to the living room and wait until breakfast is ready."

"I can't go in there. Axel might be sleeping."

"I'm not," came the call from that direction of the house. "It would be tough to sleep through all the talking."

Julie immediately started toward the living room. She could

fight with Axel. He was fair game. Okay, sure, shot, but he was feeling better and he kept breaking Dana's heart, so there was that.

Unfortunately, the second she saw him, she knew that he, too, was in pain. Worse, he'd been injured on the job, so whatever happened to him was her fault.

"No," he said sharply as she sat in one of the chairs, careful not to bump her arm. "No sympathy. I'm tired of it."

Something in his gaze warned her not to go anywhere mushy, but whether he meant that for his protection or hers, she couldn't say.

"Who's being sympathetic? You're the fool who got shot."

"Damned straight."

She eyed his leg, but couldn't see anything through his sweatpants. "Is it infected?"

"No."

"Are you sure? Because it's not like you have any medical training."

He surprised her by grinning. "That's more like the boss I know. As for my bullet wound, the last time I looked, it was healing well."

"But it hurts."

"Yes."

"Good." She shrugged. "I say that in defense of my daughter."

"I accept it in the way you meant it." He nodded at her arm. "Still bad?"

"You have no idea." She remembered the bullet. "Okay, maybe you do. I can't believe I fell. I'm normally so aware of my surroundings."

"Everyone slows down as they get older."

She glared at him. "Excuse me?"

One corner of his mouth twitched. "You're over fifty. It was bound to happen."

"I was feeling bad for you. Thankfully that's over."

"Good. You're not responsible for what happened."

"I'm the one who sent you out there."

His dark gaze settled on her face. "I volunteered. This kind of shit happens. I'm fine. Let's move on."

"I know I said this before, but I mean it. When this contract is up, we're done doing repos. They're too dangerous and not worth the money."

She gently shifted her arm, trying not to wince as pain shot through her. "You heard about Nick not wanting to go into the business?"

Axel's expression was unreadable. "Someone mentioned it. You thought he was going to take over or at least start to learn the business side of things. What happens now?"

"I don't know. I'm not ready to sell. That would be too drastic." But she didn't like the idea of going it alone for the next twenty-plus years.

"You should take on a business partner."

She snapped up her head. "Work with someone?" She thought about what had just happened in the kitchen. "I don't seem to play well with others. Parker Towing's been my responsibility for a long time now. Giving half of it to someone else… I can't see how that would work."

"You wouldn't be giving it, you'd be selling a piece of it. Maybe you'd like not having to deal with everything that goes on in a day."

"Maybe, but I don't see anyone handing me an envelope full of money." She struggled to her feet. "I have to go talk to Blair."

Amusement darkened his eyes. "What time did you realize what you said last night?"

"Shut up," she muttered as she made her way to the stairs. Three, she added silently. She'd awakened suddenly, filled with horror and guilt for embarrassing her daughter-in-law.

She walked down the hall and tapped on the still-closed door. Blair opened it and frowned slightly.

"Are you all right? Do you need something?"

Julie told herself to just say it. Apologizing wasn't anything she enjoyed, but she'd been totally in the wrong. More important, she loved Blair.

"I'm sorry," she said quickly. "I was drugged, which I mean as an explanation, not an excuse. I was so awful. Even if I really did wonder if you were pregnant, I shouldn't have blurted it out like that. Plus the other things I said. I embarrassed you and made you feel bad. I would never do that on purpose. I swear."

Blair reached for her and gently hugged her. "It's okay. I know you weren't yourself."

"Whoever I was, I don't want to be her again. Ever!"

Blair pulled her into the bedroom and shut the door. "I'm okay. I was a little stunned last night, but I'm over it."

Julie searched her face, wanting to be sure. "You shouldn't forgive me so easily. I deserve to be punished. Plus, I've been so crabby this morning. I'm snapping at everyone. I think it's the guilt."

"Or the pain. Are you taking your meds?"

Julie sank into the chair by the dresser. "Why is everyone on me about what I am or am not taking?"

"So that's a no. Julie, come on. You need to let your body heal."

"I know. I'm taking some at breakfast, even though I don't like taking pills. I mean, look at what happened last night." She leaned forward. "I really do feel awful."

"I'm fine."

The words sounded normal enough, but there was something in Blair's eyes.

"What aren't you telling me?" Julie asked. "Is there something? Are you sick?"

"No, I'm fine." Blair settled on the edge of the bed. "It's just after dinner last night, I was kind of freaked."

"I'm sorry," Julie began, but Blair stopped her.

"No, that's not my point. My mom came to check on me."

Julie didn't know what to say to that. "Okay. Did she make it worse?"

"No, she was supportive and nice."

Julie was careful not to say anything flippant or mean about Gwen. "Supportive is good. She's your mom. She *should* be on your side. So things are better."

Blair shook her head. "To tell the truth, I don't know if they are. She says she regrets not having a relationship with me and I want to believe her, but there's a voice in my head that says I should never trust her. She turned her back on me for years. I was right there, begging her to be my mom, and she didn't listen. So what's different now?"

Julie was torn. Part of her agreed with everything Blair was saying. Of course she should be cautious—Gwen wasn't to be trusted. But she also knew what it was like to find out that she'd screwed up as a parent. Nick should have been able to come to her and tell her he was having second thoughts about taking over Parker Towing. But he hadn't. Whatever the reason, he hadn't been comfortable being honest. She was his mom—he should know he could tell her anything.

"Do you believe she has regrets?"

Blair shifted uneasily. "Sort of. She said when she came to the wedding, she felt like a guest rather than the mother of the bride." Her gaze dropped. "She said a lot of things."

Julie could imagine. "She was upset because you and I are tight and I was the one you turned to."

Blair's eyes widened. "How do you know everything?"

"I don't, but it's not a big leap. I was happy to help you with the wedding. You and I get along, and we don't have the dramatic history of most mother-daughter relationships, so it was easy. If I suggested something you didn't like, you had no trouble telling me you wanted to go in another direction." She thought about the day and how wonderful it had been.

"You were such a beautiful bride, and everything worked out perfectly. Your mom would have noticed that, as well. Now that I think about the day from her point of view, I'm not surprised she realized what she'd been missing."

"You're not weirded out?"

Julie frowned. "About what?"

"My mom suddenly wanting to be in my life. You don't see that as taking away from our relationship?"

"No. Am I supposed to?" Julie smiled at her. "Blair, you're my daughter-in-law and nothing will ever change that. Plus, we're friends and I trust that relationship will withstand you reconciling with your mom, assuming that's what you want. I'll support you either way."

"I can't go back, and I don't know if I can forgive her for abandoning me all those years ago."

"There's no back. There's only forward. You're not that little girl anymore. You're an adult who has created a wonderful life. The forgiveness is your choice. Forgiving someone is about you, not them. It doesn't mean excusing what they did. It means letting go of the anger and need to punish—for your own sake. Do you want her in your life?"

"No." Blair looked at her. "Is that awful?"

"You feel what you feel, but I wonder if you really mean it."

"How can you say that?"

"If you weren't willing to let her in a little, you wouldn't have anything to do with her. But you brought her to Christmas."

"She's my mom. I couldn't leave her by herself."

"So she matters."

Blair groaned. "I don't know. Maybe. I wish I just hated her completely. Then this would be easier."

"Yes, but you'd be a smaller person. The real problem is she's your mom. However badly she's treated you in the past, she'll always be your mom. One day you'll be a mother yourself and understand all the complications that come with that. You need to think about what message you want to pass along to your own children. What lesson are you going to teach them and even yourself if you lock her out of your life?"

"But what about what she did?"

"She was a hundred percent wrong in that, and the two of you need to talk about it. If you really are unable to forgive her, then you probably need to talk to a psychologist about how to deal with the emotional trauma. Maybe you need to take her with you and process what happened in a safe space. If she's not willing to own her part in what she did, then I say the hell with her. But if she gets it and wants to make amends, then maybe you two could find your way to have something like a relationship."

"That sounds so mature. I'm not sure I'm ready."

"Take your time. You know I'm on your side in this, right?"

"I do, but what if I don't want to give her another chance?"

"Then don't." Julie paused, wondering how blunt to be.

"Just say it," Blair told her. "I can handle it."

"I love you. I think you're amazing, and I also know how softhearted you are. I'm afraid if you don't give your mom another chance, the guilt is going to eat you up. How sad would it be to suffer even more because of her?"

"That would totally suck." Blair sighed. "I'll think about what you said. I don't like what you're telling me, but it's possible you're right. I have my future to think about."

"And my grandchildren, because in the end, this is all about me."

The cold air hurt her chest, but getting out of the house felt good. The sky was blue, the houses and trees covered in snow. Blair glanced over at her husband.

"I'm glad you suggested we take a walk," she said. "I've been inside for too long. How was your time with Dana this morning?"

He took her hand in his. She was wearing lined gloves and of course he wasn't.

"Good. Sad. We talked about Dad and how much we miss him." He looked at her. "There was always going to be a last Christmas—I just didn't know when it was. I should have paid more attention."

She stopped and stepped in front of him so they were facing each other. "You didn't know he was going to pass away in January. No one knew. I know we're supposed to live like every day is our last, but while that sounds like a really great way to do things, it's not practical or realistic. Your dad knew you loved him and enjoyed being with him. He was proud of you and excited for your future. You don't have any behavior to regret."

"I miss him."

"I know. I do, too."

Eldon had always been kind to her. Thoughtful, in his quiet way.

Nick touched her cheek. "How are you doing? Have you talked to my mom?"

They started walking again. "She came to see me this morning and apologized for the whole 'you're pregnant' thing."

He grinned. "It was a showstopper."

Blair tried not to think about the shock and embarrassment of the moment. "I know it was the drugs talking and we're fine. I mean, seriously, who can stay mad at your mom?"

"If she's not the one you're upset with, then who is?"

"How did you know—" She bumped her shoulder against his arm. "You know me too well."

"That's not possible. Besides, I love you."

"I love you, too. And I'm not upset, exactly."

He exhaled. "That means it's your mom. What did she do this time?"

"Nothing bad. I've just been thinking about what she said before. About wanting a second chance. And she was really sweet about the not-being-pregnant thing."

"Your mother is never sweet."

"Maybe that wasn't the right word."

"It wasn't."

She understood that Nick was protecting her—that was his way—and while she appreciated the gesture, she couldn't help remembering how good Gwen had been offering to get a pregnancy test. Something she didn't want to discuss with Nick until she knew more. Getting his hopes up seemed mean. She wasn't pregnant. She was sure. Sort of.

"I talked to your mom about my mom," she said.

"I don't think I like that."

Blair looked at him and smiled. "You mean because she was rational, fair and might have said some hard-to-hear truths?"

"That's what she does best." He looked at her. "I know she was reasonable, and I'm not sure Gwen deserves that. She's hurt you over and over." He put his arm around her. "I don't want to make you feel defensive, but in this discussion, you're the only one I care about. I've held you while you've cried, Blair. I've seen what she can do to you and that was from a distance. Imagine how bad things could get with her here and you making an effort."

"I love that you worry about me." He'd always been that way—totally there for her, no matter what.

"But?"

"Your mom pointed out that I have to think about myself. If I cut her off for real, will I feel guilty for the rest of my life? She's not wrong to ask that."

"My mom's rarely wrong. It's pretty damned annoying."

She laughed. "Not for me."

"Just wait. It'll happen."

"Maybe. In the meantime, what about when we have kids of our own? How do I explain to them I don't talk to their grandmother? How do I tell them they have to work out their problems with their friends when I'm not willing to do that myself, with my own mother?"

"I don't have an answer for that."

"Me, either."

She shifted so she could take his hand again. They continued walking, their feet crunching in the snow. Blair thought about all she'd been through since they'd arrived at the cabin. Her emotions were a roller coaster—at least when it came to her mother.

"I know Julie's right about how the guilt will affect me," she said slowly. "I'm just not sure how to deal with it."

"You don't have to decide today."

"You're right."

Maybe that was the best solution. To take her time. If she was to allow her mom back in her life, if she wanted to let go of her resentment and anger, there was a lot of work to be done. On both sides.

19

Dana eyed the half-full bottle of wine. The responsible thing to do was to put the cork back in so the bottle would be there for tomorrow's dinner, but in her heart of hearts, she wanted another glass. Or twenty.

"I'm in for whatever you want to do," Tiffany said lightly.

"Getting drunk won't make me feel better."

Sad, but true, Dana thought as she pushed the bottle away. She put her arms on the table and rested her head on them.

"Why does it have to be like this?"

"You're still in love with Axel. Until you can get over him, or figure out a way to make the relationship work, you're going to feel awful. It just is."

Dana sat up and looked at her. "Really? That's your answer?"

"It's the truth."

"You sound like my mother."

Tiffany smiled as she pushed the cork back into the bottle. "That's so nice. Thank you. Julie's the strongest person I know. I'd love to be more like her."

They were sitting in the dining room, in the farthest seats

from the doorway. It was the only place Dana had thought where they could hang out and talk without being overheard by everyone in the house.

"I should be more like her, too," she grumbled. "She would never let any guy treat her the way he's treated me. She keeps a baseball bat in her office. The woman knows how to take a swing. I wish she'd taught me."

"So you could go after Axel?"

"Maybe." Dana thought about it for a second. "No, I couldn't deliberately attack him or anyone. I just don't know how to stop hurting so much. You're right—I've got to figure out a way to get over him. I've been living with my life on hold. I'm either with Axel and all is well, or I'm not and it's like the world is one big gray cloud. I've given him too much power."

"Or yourself not enough."

Dana nodded. "You're right. I'm defining myself by him. It's just everything is so much better when we're together, you know? He's so…there. He does the dishes without being asked. He buys those ridiculously expensive bodywashes I love and puts them in the shower. Then he uses them, swearing he doesn't care if he smells like a vanilla coconut cupcake."

She thought about the other things he did—the private things, when they were alone in bed. With Axel, Dana never worried her forty extra pounds were an issue. He told her she was beautiful and that sex with her was incredible. He locked eyes with her when he came, letting her see what her body did to his.

A shiver rippled through her—two parts longing, one part regret. The longing was easy, but the regret was more complex. She wasn't sure whether it was about what she'd lost or what she couldn't have. Maybe the answer was both.

"Wow," Tiffany breathed. "The look on your face. You have it bad, girlfriend. You sure there's no way to make it work?"

"He doesn't stay. He tells me he loves me and then he leaves." That was the essential pain of their relationship.

"And he told you it was because he didn't think he was good enough?"

"Yeah." Dana looked at Tiffany. "I don't understand. He's not a game player. He says what he thinks. He shows up when he says. When he makes a promise, he keeps it. To the best of my knowledge, he's never lied to me. All the times we were together, he went out of his way to make sure I knew where he was and who he was with. I could depend on him for anything."

"What if he's telling the truth?"

Dana had just enough wine in her to be comfortable rolling her eyes like a twelve-year-old. "Is that the best you have? He's terrified I'll marry him, figure out it was all a mistake and then dump him?"

"Occam's razor."

"Armadillo jewelry."

Tiffany blinked at her. "What?"

"I thought we were saying random words."

Tiffany started laughing. "No, it's a thing. Occam's razor."

"You can keep repeating it all you want, but I still don't get it."

Tiffany did her best to stifle her giggles. "It's a theory—the simplest solution or answer is probably the right one. We don't have to overanalyze or complicate things." She locked her gaze with Dana's. "What if Axel is telling the truth?"

Dana still didn't know what her friend was talking about. "You're saying accept what he's saying and deal with it as reality?"

"Yes."

"But it's ridiculous."

"Is it? Why?"

"Because there's no reason for Axel to feel uncomfortable in any situation."

"No one feels comfortable all the time."

Dana wanted to say that wasn't true—what about her mom?

Only Julie had been afraid to say she was dating Heath because of the age difference. Dana wouldn't have guessed it was possible for her mom to be anything but totally secure and in charge.

"Besides," Tiffany continued, "guys are weird. They get ideas in their head and then they react."

"But if you're right, then Axel's been breaking my heart over and over again because he's afraid of something I haven't done and may never do in the future."

"I think it's possible."

"I'm back to thinking I should go talk to my mom about borrowing her baseball bat."

"Or you could talk to him."

Dana glanced longingly at the wine bottle. Why had she thought she was done?

"You mean have a rational conversation about our feelings and his fears and try to find a solution?"

"Yes."

"No." Dana sighed. "Sorry. Knee-jerk reaction. It is the mature thing to do. And I will. When I'm feeling brave."

"Or you could do it now."

Dana's eyes widened. "It's after midnight. I'm sure he's asleep."

"He'll want to wake up for this."

"Talking to me about our relationship and why he keeps leaving me? I don't think so. I'll talk to him tomorrow."

"On Christmas Eve?"

"It's already past midnight, so technically it's already Christmas Eve day."

"You're right. And speaking of which, I have to get to bed. The kids are going to be crazy in the morning. Madeline really gets shrill when she's excited, so brace yourself."

"I will."

They both rose and hugged.

"Thanks for the advice," Dana said.

"Anytime."

Tiffany headed downstairs while Dana went through the main floor to the staircase she would take. She'd just put her hand on the railing when she came to a stop.

How long was she going to put off talking to Axel? Shouldn't she get things resolved so that she could get some closure and start to have a happy life? Okay, a case could be made that he'd already told her what he thought about their future, or lack thereof. He was scared.

"Of a bunch of accountants?" she murmured to herself. "Sure, they're good guys, but they're not scary. Besides, we don't wear suits anymore. And half the people I work with are women."

She thought maybe she wasn't making sense and possibly she'd gotten off the point of whatever this was. Still, she turned on her heel and marched toward the big sofa in the family room. The soft glow of the Christmas lights from the tree allowed her to see where she was going. She clicked on one of the lamps, prepared to shake Axel awake, only to find him already sitting up.

"Oh. You're awake."

He looked at her. "I have been for a while."

There was something in his tone. Something pointed, as if he were...

"You could hear us talking?"

She was proud that she asked the question without as much of a shriek as it deserved.

"You know what the acoustics are like in this place."

Humiliation flooded her, making her cheeks burn and her feet start moving. But before she could take more than a step, Axel was up and had grabbed her wrist.

"Dana, wait. Tiffany's right. We should talk."

She tried desperately to remember what she'd said. She was fine with the baseball-bat threat, but the rest of it was so embarrassing.

"Please," he said, tugging gently.

She pulled her wrist free of his touch and glared at him. "You want to talk? Fine. Here's what I have to say. You don't get to decide. You don't get to tell me you love me and then walk away. It's cowardly and wrong."

"I know. I'm sorry."

"You're just saying that because you want me to stop telling you you're wrong."

"You can say that as many times as you want and every time I'll agree. I *am* wrong. I should stay."

The unexpected words knocked all the mad right out of her. She sank onto the sofa. He sat down, as well.

"You terrify me," he said, his voice low. "You have no idea what it's like loving you. I've met your friends. They're all smart and successful. Your best friend Shelley's married to a nurse practitioner. How many years of college does that take? Blair has a degree. Your mom's with a guy who owns a successful business. You could have anyone. Why would you stay with me?"

"Why do you think my love is dependent on what you do for a living? I've always known what you did, and I was fine with it. For the record, my grandfather drove tow trucks, as did my mom, as does my brother."

"But they all moved on. Your grandfather started the business, your mom runs it and Nick's leaving to buy into a retail place. You have a four-year degree, Dana. Hell, a couple of years ago you were talking about getting your MBA."

"For like a week. I wasn't sure I wanted to put in the effort." She'd been restless, looking for something more fulfilling. Then she and Axel had started dating and she'd realized the thing she wanted was him, and them and a family.

"I don't believe you," she said flatly. "That's what this comes down to. I don't believe you really want to stay. I don't know what this game is, and I wonder if that's why I can't let go. You've never played games with me except about this. I don't know if it's a power play or some emotional sickness you won't own up to, but one way or the other, I'm going to get over you."

She was watching him as she spoke and saw the pain flash through his eyes. It was gone in a second, but she'd seen it.

"I'm glad," he said hoarsely. "You deserve someone better."

Impulsively she grabbed him by the front of his T-shirt and tried to shake him.

"Why?" she demanded. "Why do you want me with someone else? Why won't you fight for me?" Tears filled her eyes. "Why are you so willing to let me be with someone else? If you loved me, you wouldn't let me go."

And there it was, she thought, releasing him and covering her face with her hands. The truth of it all. Even if he was telling the truth about why he kept leaving, he wouldn't fight for her or stop her from falling in love with someone else. He could say the words, but he wouldn't take the chance.

"You're not going to change," she whispered, wiping her cheeks. "You're never going to change."

"What if I could? What if I wanted to, but didn't know how?"

She shook her head. "You're just saying that to keep me hoping. To get one more heartbreak out of me."

"When I was lying on the street, shot and wondering if I was going to die, you're who I thought of, Dana. You're who I regretted. I thought of all we could have been together, the life we could have had, and I knew I'd regret losing you forever. I wanted..." He looked away. "I wanted to be the right man for you—someone you could be proud of."

She wanted to shake him again, although she'd been unsuccessful in her first attempt. "I don't care about your regrets. I want you to look me in the eye and tell me you're desperately in love with me, and no matter what, you're never leaving again. I want you to swear it, and then I want you to live it. Every day prove to me that you're staying."

"I don't understand."

"What's not to understand? Regrets are stupid. If you're telling the truth, then everything you want is sitting right here, telling you she loves you. How dumb do you have to be to let me go again?"

"Pretty dumb." He touched her cheek. "I can't be like them, Dana. Those fancy guys."

"The accountants? Trust me, they're not all that, and you could take any of them in a fight."

That earned her a half smile that quickly faded. "You're everything. If I could be just half the man you need, I'd take a chance. But if you knew what you were asking..."

She wanted to scream or hit him or throw a piece of furniture, but mostly she wanted to know why he couldn't see what she saw. He was defining himself by his lack of what he saw as education and refinement.

"I don't agree with the premise of your concern," she told him. "You don't need to be like them."

"I don't think you need to lose any weight, let alone the forty pounds you're always talking about."

She drew back. All righty then—that was a twist in the conversation. She ignored her instinctive need to fold her arms across her midsection to hide the bulges there.

"My being fat has nothing to do with you being able to handle yourself at a stupid Christmas party with my work associates. What you wear doesn't matter to me, but you seem obsessed with the suit thing, so we'll get you a suit." She paused, thinking of Axel all dressed up. "Or not. A few of the women in my office are going to be all over you, regardless of how you're dressed, but in a suit, you'll be irresistible."

"I still won't have an education."

"Not everything is about going to college. You're good at what you do. You're kind and you treat me like a princess—except now when you make me want to throw you out a window."

"You're amazing, Dana, but you don't have the upper body strength."

"Gee, thanks." She looked at him. "I can't tell if we're making progress or if we're talking in circles. Just tell me what's going to happen. Claim me or let me go forever. If you ever loved me, do that for me."

She thought he might make a joke or turn away. Instead, he stared into her eyes.

"I meant what I said about lying in the street and thinking about you. It was cold and raining, and while I knew it was just a flesh wound, I figured there was a better than even chance the guy was going to come back and finish the job."

He cupped her cheek. "You're all I could think about. You and us and what we could have had. I'll never be one of them, Dana. I'll never know which fork goes where or what kind of wine to serve with dinner. But I would face the devil himself for you. I wouldn't need a fair fight to win, either. I'd take him, I'd die, so you'd be okay. I love you. I've always loved you."

The words warmed her heart, but she knew better than to accept them as the answer. Because loving her wasn't the problem.

"And?"

"I want to be worthy of you. I've been working on some things and I'm hoping..." He shook his head. "No, that's not it, is it? This isn't about me being worthy. It's about me growing a pair and saying I'm willing to face my greatest fear."

He took her hands in his. "Dana, you're right. I've been running because I couldn't face what I knew was going to happen. If you leave me, you leave me. But until that day, I'm going to show up. I swear to you, I'll be here, no matter what. If this thing ends, it's going to be you calling it quits. Not me. I'm in this to the end. You talk about how you never stopped loving me, well, I felt exactly the same. I've loved you from the first moment we met. You're the most beautiful, exciting, smart, funny and sexy woman I've ever known. I don't know why you want to be with me, but I'll be grateful for the rest of my life for that."

Then he shocked the crap out of her by sliding off the sofa, onto one knee. He flinched slightly, no doubt from the pain in his bad leg, but he stayed in place.

"Dana Parker, will you marry me?"

"Get up," she said, trying to drag him back to the sofa. "You'll bleed out or something."

He got to his feet and pulled her into his arms. "Why are you crying?"

"I'm not." She realized she was. Seconds later, the meaning of his words sank into both her brain and her heart. Wait, what? Had Axel really just proposed? "Did that just happen? You said you wanted to marry me?"

"Yes. I love you and I want us to be married. I want babies with you and a good life. You're the one for me, and I'm hoping you think the same about me."

When the man went in, he went all in. Joy filled her. Joy and hope and a sense of sureness that made her want to fly. She flung her arms around him. "Yes! Yes, of course."

He kissed her. "I don't deserve you."

"Probably not, but you're stuck now. The second we tell my mom, there's no going back."

"I don't have a problem with accountability." He kissed her again, then drew back. "I meant what I said about being worthy of you, Dana. I want to make that happen."

She waved his comment away. "I don't even know what that means. You love me and you're staying. That's enough."

"You've always been too easy on me."

He kissed her again, lingering this time. Wanting exploded. She'd been without Axel in her bed for far too long. And they were getting married. Sex was absolutely required.

She took his hand and started for the stairs, only to come to a stop.

"Oh, no. Can you make the climb?"

He chuckled. "Yes. I'm motivated, Dana. I could get to the top of Everest, if you were the reward."

They started up the stairs.

"We're going to have to be quiet," she said, her voice low. "Gwen's room is right next to mine, and the walls are kind of thin."

He slipped his hand down to cup her butt. "I don't think I'm the one who has to be reminded to be quiet. If I remember correctly, you're the one who likes to scream."

Another shiver rippled through her. "Then you'll have to make it less incredible."

"That's not going to happen, babe. You deserve the best, and I'm the man for the job."

20

Julie woke up feeling pretty good. Her arm was still sore and swollen, but she'd been able to sleep and she felt more herself. She managed to brush her teeth and use a washcloth on her face, all one-handed, but still needed Heath's help to dress. He stared at the sweater she'd laid out on the bed and shook his head.

"I know it's Christmas Eve, but there's no way," he began. "Not with your arm…"

She pointed to the bright red pullover sweater with a giant Santa face on the front. "This is what I wear today. I've been wearing it since the kids were little. It's my Christmas Eve sweater. I have to put it on or the holiday will be ruined."

"Isn't that a little extreme? You're giving your sweater a lot more power than it deserves."

She smiled. "The power doesn't live in the sweater—it's in the tradition. My kids expect me to wear this."

He moved close and kissed her. "They know about your broken arm. They'll understand."

"It's their first Christmas without their dad. Nick and Dana need me to be wearing my sweater."

"You're the most stubborn woman I know."

"That's very possible."

He eyed the sweater, then her arm in its sling. "I haven't got a clue how to make this happen. Put your arm in first, then pull it over your head somehow? I don't want to hurt you."

"I'll be fine. I can't get it on by myself, Heath. We have to do this."

She slipped off the sling and tossed it onto the bed. Heath gathered up the sweater. She slipped her injured arm into the sleeve, trying not to wince as pain shot through her. Once the sleeve was in place, she held her arm tightly against her body, then shifted while Heath pulled the sweater over her head and helped her wrestle her good arm into place.

She only groaned once and ignored the fact that she was starting to sweat from the effort. Once the sling was back in place, she would be fine. A little coffee, a bit of Tylenol and she would be good as new.

"You're gray," he said, staring at her. "Are you going to pass out?"

"Me? Never. I need coffee. Go shower. I'll meet you downstairs."

"Julie, wait. I won't be long. Wait for me."

"I'll be fine." She did a little spin in place to prove her point, then wished she hadn't when the room took a full two seconds longer than her to settle back in place.

"See," she lied. "I'm perfect."

Before he could say anything else, she slipped from the room, pausing only a second in the hallway to make sure she wouldn't tumble down the stairs. She'd just gained her equilibrium when Dana's door opened and Axel stepped out. They stared at each other.

It didn't take a rocket scientist to figure out what had happened. Disappointment blended with anger. Why did her daughter keep giving in to this man? He'd proved he wasn't good for her over and over again, but did she listen?

She opened her mouth, then closed it. What was there to say? Dana was a grown woman, capable of making her own very bad decisions. Julie wasn't going to get into it with her or with Axel. Tomorrow was Christmas. She would pretend she hadn't seen anything—at least until she and Axel were back at work. Then she would tell him exactly what she thought about him in a loud, scary voice.

She brushed past him without speaking and went down to the main floor. When she was in the kitchen, she started the oven, followed by the coffee maker, then pulled out the menus for the day, just to refresh her memory. She heard footsteps on the hardwood floor, but as she had a good idea of who had followed her, she didn't bother turning around.

"We need to talk."

"No, we don't. I'm busy. Go away."

"Julie, please."

She exhaled sharply, then looked up at the man watching her.

Intellectually, she understood the appeal. Axel was every woman's definition of the irresistible bad boy. He had that faint air of danger, a bit of a swagger and a knowing smile that promised he was good in bed. Add to that an oddly gentle sense of humor, and very few women could walk away. The thing was she didn't care about other women. She only cared about her daughter.

"You're going to shatter her heart again, just like you always do. You don't know what it's like when you're gone. You're not there to see the pain and questions in her eyes. You're not the one who holds her while she tries to understand what she did wrong. And no matter how many times I tell her that it's not her fault, she still blames herself. You break her, Axel, and

I help her put the pieces back together. And every time it happens, she's just a little less herself."

He hung his head. "I know. I'm sorry."

"I don't give a shit about your apologies. You're nothing to me."

He looked up. "I'm sorry to hear that, Julie. Because I asked Dana to marry me and she said yes."

Julie eyed him warily. "Is that for real?"

"We're talking spring. Neither of us want a long engagement." He took a step closer. "I know you think I'm an asshole and I deserve that. I won't excuse what I've done to her, but I want you to know I had my reasons. They were stupid, but still real. I'm putting it all on the line for her. I think we both know one day she's going to wake up and realize she's made a mistake, but until then, I'm all in."

Was that what he thought? "You're wrong," she said. "Dana won't leave you. You're everything to her. That's always been the problem. She's a one-man woman, and you're the man she picked."

His expression was unreadable. "You must hate that."

And me.

He didn't say the words, but she heard them all the same. "I don't hate you, Axel. I hate what you did to her. If you're serious about committing to her and she wants to marry you, then you're going to be part of this family."

"Are you okay with that?"

She thought about all he had done and all the tears her daughter had cried. "She's my little girl. If you're the one, then yes, I'm okay with it."

He didn't look like he believed her, which was fine with her. She'd meant what she said, but if it took him a while to accept the words, that was good, too. Engagement or not, Axel deserved a little suffering in his life.

"I'm going to do everything in my power to make her happy." He flashed her a smile. "Everything legal, of course."

"Good. She deserves that." She looked at him. "I want to say working with my son-in-law could be awkward, only I've been working with Nick for years and it's been fine. Excluding what happened with Dana, you and I have always gotten along."

Axel had always been who she'd turned to when she had a difficult situation to deal with. She could trust him to do the hard stuff.

"About my job," he said, only to stop talking when Dana hurried into the room.

"I woke up and you were..." Her voice trailed off as she glanced between them. "You two okay?"

Julie held open her good arm. "Hey, baby girl. I hear congratulations are in order."

Dana looked at Axel. "You told her."

"We needed to talk about some things."

She swung her attention back to Julie, her expression tentative. "I know you don't especially trust Axel, but it's different this time."

Julie hoped that was true. As a mother, she had her doubts and a burning need to punish, but this wasn't the time. Honestly, there'd never been a good time and didn't that suck.

"I love you," Julie said, moving close and hugging her as best she could with her arm in a sling. "I want you and Axel to be happy together. Have a great marriage, and on your one-year anniversary, expect me to start bugging you about having kids."

Dana held herself apart for about a second. Then she sagged against Julie, putting way too much pressure on the fracture, but she took it knowing the connection was more important than her pain.

"You're really okay with this?" she asked hopefully as she took a step back. "You're not mad?"

Julie smiled. "I could never be mad at you."

Dana laughed. "We all know that's not true, but I hope you'll see this is different."

Axel put his arm around Dana. "I'll take care of her. You have my word."

"My head accepts what you said. My heart is going to take a little longer to trust." She smiled to take the sting out of the words. "Of course, if you give me grandchildren, then you'll be my favorite."

"Mom! Don't you think it's a little too soon?"

"Oh, please. As if you didn't have sex at least twice last night."

Dana flushed slightly. "We're going to wait on the kid thing, but we're thinking about getting married in April or May."

"Pick a date and tell me how I can help. You know I'll want to give you more advice than you want to hear, but we'll get through it." She smiled at her daughter. "I'm happy for you." She slid her gaze to Axel. "For both of you."

A generous, not-quite-true statement, but with a little time and a whole lot of work on Axel's part, in a few months she might actually mean it. And for now, that was enough.

"I can feel you monitoring me," Julie said, but there wasn't much energy in her voice.

"I want to make sure you're all right."

She and Heath were in the dining room with dozens of shortbread cookies in need of yet more decorating. Tiffany, Dana, Nick and Blair had taken the kids out for sleigh rides down the hills to burn off post-breakfast energy. Gwen had gone into town for a little last-minute shopping, and Axel, Huxley and Paul were downstairs with Rufus, watching basketball.

"I'm a little overwhelmed," she said, motioning to the cookies on the table. "The first couple of days everyone wants to help, but it gets old fast."

He smiled at her. "Maybe if you didn't pick a design that requires three different colors of icing, you'd get more help."

"You're right. I was too ambitious for the cookie exchange. It's just Jackie across the street always has those damned multilayer cookies that look so fancy." She sighed. "It's not a competition, but sometimes it feels like one and I really hate not to win."

"Jesus would be so proud."

"Jesus would want me to kick Jackie's butt in the cookie exchange."

Heath laughed. "I'm sure He would." His humor faded. "You okay otherwise?"

Julie tested the black frosting on a sheet of white paper. The first two tries had been too light, but this iteration was dark enough.

She'd cut out and baked basic five-pointed star shortbread cookies, using the shape to create her Santas. One point was his head, the other four were his feet and hands. The red had been applied a couple of days ago, along with the white for the trim and his beard. All that was left was a couple of tiny lines for eyes, mitten shapes for hands, a blob for feet and the belt across the middle. Julie figured she and Heath could knock out the decorations in about an hour.

"My arm's fine," she said absently, handing him one of the piping bags. "As long as I remember to hold it still." And the sling helped with that.

"I wasn't talking about your arm. Are you okay with Axel and Dana getting married?"

"Oh, that." She took one of the cookies and carefully squeezed on the black icing. When she was done, she studied her work before nodding. "I like it. So use this one as your template." She reached for another cookie.

"I don't know how I feel," she admitted, returning to his question. "Surprised, I guess. Maybe resigned. He's the guy Dana couldn't get over, so if he's now willing to stop leaving, there's no way she wouldn't take him back."

"He's going to be your son-in-law. You'll be seeing a lot more of him."

"You forget I see him nearly every day at work." She put down the piping bag. "Except for how he hurt my daughter, I actually like him. He doesn't take a lot of crap from other people. When we hire someone new, I nearly always put them with Axel to learn how we do things. He shows up on time, doesn't take unnecessary risks." She grinned. "He laughs at my jokes, so we know he's not a fool."

"Just checking. It's an unexpected development."

"It is. Like I said, my concern is Dana. But he's who she wants, and that makes it okay for me. I'll enjoy helping with another wedding."

He held up the Santa he'd finished. "Victory worthy?"

She smiled. "Jackie will have to up her game to beat us."

"The Christmas spirit is alive and well in the cookie competition."

"You know it."

Blair helped Madeline and Wyatt take off all the layers going outside required. They were cold but happy, and hopefully a little of the Christmas Eve day energy had burned off.

"That was fun!" Wyatt tugged off his snow boots. "I'm hungry. Can I have a cookie?"

"It's only an hour until lunch," Blair pointed out. "Let's wait on the cookies."

"But I'm hungry now!"

Tiffany shook her head. "Remember what we talked about this morning? I know you're excited, but you're still expected to behave. Let's rein in those impulses."

"I'm fine, Mom," Madeline said, her tone superior.

"Let's get out the racetrack and race cars," Nick suggested. "Madeline, you should play with us, too."

"I did win last time."

Madeline and Wyatt ran downstairs, yelling for Paul and Huxley as they went.

Tiffany smiled at Nick. "I owe you."

"Happy to help." He paused to glance at Blair. "You okay?"

It was the question he always asked. She knew she'd been distracted while they'd been sledding, and had let him assume it was because her stomach was bugging her. She didn't want to tell him otherwise until she had information to share.

"I'm good. I'm going upstairs for a little bit. Julie and Heath are probably still working on the cookies. Tiffany, want to join me in the kitchen in half an hour so we can take care of lunch?"

"Sure. Sounds good."

Blair walked through the main level and up the stairs as calmly as she could. While she wanted to race, she didn't want anyone wondering what she was up to.

For the past couple of days, she'd told herself and told herself there was no way she was pregnant. Her period was erratic—it always had been. But Julie's words had unnerved her, and hearing her mother point out the fallacies of their birth control system had made her nervous to the point where all she could think about was the possibility of being pregnant. Which she wasn't.

Blair reached the landing and crossed to her mother's closed door. She knocked.

Gwen opened it almost immediately. "I got the test."

"No one saw you?"

Gwen smiled. "No. When I got back, Paul said he would have taken me into town, but that was it." She handed over a small shopping bag. "For whenever you want."

Blair took it. "I don't know if I want to take it."

"That's up to you. It's here. You can do it now or when you get home."

She'd thought her mother might pressure her more, but Gwen didn't say anything else.

"I appreciate you getting it, Mom. Thank you."

"Of course." Gwen sat on the edge of her bed. "I think I'll read for a little while. I need to finish my book, or I'll be up all night."

Blair smiled. "Page-turner?"

"Hard to put down."

Blair went into her bedroom, where she carefully closed and locked the door. She got out the pregnancy test and stared at the box. She wasn't. She shouldn't be. The timing was all off. Nick was going to buy Paul's business, so they would be busy with that. In a year was better for them. Of course her scheduling concerns didn't really affect reality. Either she was or she wasn't, and there was only one way to find out.

One pee and several agonizing minutes later, Blair stared at the lines on the pregnancy stick. The message was very clear. She was going to have a baby.

She stood there, her heart pounding, her breathing shallow. She and Nick were pregnant. It was real.

Almost real, she amended. Because she didn't feel any different than she had ten minutes ago. With her stomach issues, it would be difficult to know what was feeling off and what was her normal why-doesn't-my-stomach-behave?

A bubbly sensation started inside of her. She felt herself smiling. Pregnant! She was pregnant!

She touched her belly. "Hi, little one. It's me. Your mom."

Oh, wow. She was going to be a mother.

A thousand emotions flooded her. Happiness, mild concern, a determination not to act like *her* mother had. She thought briefly of the medications she took to control her IBS. Her first instinct was to dump them all, for the sake of the baby. Only she knew her GI doctor had coordinated with her ob-gyn to find her the right combination that helped control her symptoms without putting any pregnancy at risk.

"I'm going to do this right," she whispered. "I'm going to

take care of you before you're born. Your dad will be just as attentive, I promise."

Nick! She had to tell him.

She started for the door, then stopped. No way she could go grab him from whatever he was doing. There were too many people around to ask questions. She pulled out her phone and sent a quick text.

Can you come to our room for a second? I'm fine. I just need your help with something.

Seconds later, she saw the thumbs-up emoji. She unlocked the door and waited.

Less than a minute later, Nick walked in. His brows were pulled together as he hurried to her side.

"What's up? You all right?"

"I'm fine." She took his hands in hers. "I couldn't stop thinking about what your mom blurted out a couple days ago. About me being pregnant. I asked my mom to get me a pregnancy test and I just took it. I'm pregnant!"

He stared at her, his expression blank. She waited, knowing the meaning of her words would sink in eventually. Then his eyes widened, and he grinned and grabbed her, pulling her close.

"You sure?" he asked, then whooped as he spun her around. "For real?"

"Yes. We're having a baby."

He set her down and reverently touched her belly. "How do you feel? How far along? Holy crap! We're going to be parents!"

"We are." She put her hands on his upper arms and stared into his eyes. "I know this wasn't the plan, but—"

"I don't care about the plan! We're having a baby." He hugged her. "I love you so much, Blair. This is what we wanted. As for the timing, we'll make it work." He released her and smiled. "Now I'm even more motivated to go into business with Paul.

I can have regular hours and be home every night with you and the baby."

"Plus holidays off," she said, watching him. "Nick, I need you to be sure about leaving your mom's business."

"I'm sure. I never had her enthusiasm. Your uncle is giving us a once-in-a-lifetime opportunity. I want to jump on it. I want us to be happy."

His happiness, his plans for their future, only added to her joy. This was right, she thought. Them together, the baby.

"When do you want to tell everyone?" he asked.

"I don't know. Not right now. I need a minute to let it all sink in." She paused. "I need to say something to my mom. She was really good about getting the pregnancy test and leaving me alone to take it. Not letting her know the outcome seems mean-spirited."

He kissed her. "I'll do whatever you want. You're in charge."

She grinned. "If only that were true."

"It is." He looked at her. "Are you feeling all right? Is your stomach…?"

"I'm fine. I feel good." She thought about the queasiness and the way smells affected her. "I'll always have issues, but the chance of me getting pregnant is why I've never taken the superstrong drugs. I can stay on what I'm on now and the baby will be safe. Once we've had our family, I'll try some of the others available."

"Then we have a plan. And a baby."

She touched her still-flat belly. "Well, right now we have a rice grain, but in about seven or eight months, we'll have something a little more tangible." Although she knew for her, the baby had already crept into her heart, where it would be forever.

She pointed to the door. "You need to get downstairs before people start wondering about us, and I need to go talk to my mom."

He kissed her once more before heading for the hallway. She

followed him onto the landing, then knocked on her mom's closed door. Gwen opened it and immediately stepped back.

Blair thought she might ask about the test, but her mother stayed quiet, only watching her.

"We're not telling anyone just yet," Blair began. "I need to catch my breath." She smiled. "But I'm pregnant."

Her mother pressed a hand to her chest, then reached for her. Blair was so surprised, she didn't have time to move forward, step back or react at all. As Gwen held her tightly, Blair tried to remember the last time they'd been this close or she'd felt her mother's embrace. It had been years. Possibly decades.

The contact felt strange. Not exactly unwelcome but certainly unfamiliar. Yet a part of her remembered what it had been like to get mommy hugs. Sense memories filled her mind. Of being on her mother's lap, of being told she was a sweet, sweet girl who would be loved forever.

"I'm so happy," her mother murmured. "Thank you for telling me."

Blair started to speak, only to find she couldn't. Everything hurt and her throat was tight. From nowhere came a loud, unexpected sob.

"Blair?"

She tried to say she was fine, that she wasn't crying, only she was and she couldn't seem to stop. Instead of letting go, her mother held on more tightly.

"I'm sorry," she whispered. "Oh, Blair, I'm so sorry. I hurt you so much. I was selfish and wrong. Worse, once I was able to see what I'd done, I was too ashamed to be around you, let alone talk to you about it. All these years wasted. All the memories lost. I hurt you. My only daughter. I hurt you so much."

Blair continued to sob. Gwen guided her to a chair and had her sit, then collected a box of tissues. Blair struggled to get control, but it was several minutes until she could catch her breath and the tears began to slow. Her mother stayed next to her, lightly stroking her back.

Finally she was able to take a breath without crying. She felt drained and yet oddly light.

"I don't know what that was," she said, then blew her nose. "Pregnancy hormones, I guess."

Her mother sat on the bench at the foot of the bed. "Maybe it was a little more than that."

Blair thought about the hug. "Maybe it was."

Gwen drew in a breath. "I meant what I said. I've been awful and I know that. I want to change. I want to be in your life and not because you feel duty bound to look out for me. I want to be there because you actually like me. You're having a baby. My first grandchild. I want to be there for you, however you need me."

"You want us to be family," Blair whispered.

Her mother's eyes filled with tears. "Is that even possible?"

A week ago Blair would have said absolutely not. Just being around Gwen was depressing and a burden, but now she was less sure of her feelings. Some of the anger had faded. There was still resentment and wariness, but also hope.

"I don't think we're ready for family," she said. "But maybe we could start by trying to be friends."

Gwen nodded. "I'd like that. It's less fraught."

"I think we need to see a therapist to help us navigate our past. A lot happened and we have to work through it. Otherwise, we'll just keep reacting, rather than figuring out how to move forward."

She braced herself for outrage or rejection, but her mother only smiled.

"I was thinking the same thing. I know therapy helped me in the past. I'm grateful you're open to that. When we get back to Seattle, I'll start looking for someone. Once I have a few names, you can vet them and pick the one you'd like best." She paused. "If that works for you."

Tears burned again, but this time they were the happy kind. "Thanks, Mom. I think that would be great."

Her mother got up and pulled a small bag out of her nightstand drawer. "Not to be presumptuous, but I got these at the drugstore. When I was buying the pregnancy test." She handed the bag to Blair. "In case you want to tell everyone tomorrow at dinner or something."

Blair opened the small bag and saw a pair of tiny, yellow booties. She touched the soft knit, then stood and hugged her mom.

"Thank you. They're perfect. I wasn't sure what to say and these are exactly right."

Her mother held her tightly, hugging her back. This time was less unfamiliar and more right. They still had a long way to go, but they'd started down the path to finding each other again. It was going to take a lot of work on both their parts, but Blair found herself looking forward to the journey. And to having a mother again.

21

After lunch Julie sat at the kitchen table going over her notes. The menus were set for tonight and tomorrow. They would eat Christmas dinner about two—a ridiculous time but a tradition. On the bright side, it meant only cooking two meals instead of three. She was going to need help with the turkey. Given her fractured arm, there was no way she could prep it herself, let alone get it in the oven.

But for today, she needed someone to take the turkey out of the wrapper, pull out the weird bits from inside, rinse the inside and outside of the bird, dry it and set it in the roasting pan. Once that was done, the uncovered turkey would go back in the refrigerator overnight so the skin would dry out. It was the secret to crispy skin out of the oven.

A loud shriek came from downstairs. She knew eventually Madeline and Wyatt would run out of energy, but it hadn't happened yet. Oh, to be young and that wired about Christmas, she thought with a smile.

Once she knew she had all the ingredients she would need, she turned to her other lists. As far as she knew, all the presents were wrapped. The ones from Santa were locked in the storage closet downstairs. They would be set out after church. The funny doggy coat she'd ordered for Rufus had been delivered that morning. Heath had wrapped it for her and slipped it under the tree. There were plenty of logs for the fire, the board games they always played Christmas Eve afternoon, and the special reindeer mugs for the obligatory hot cocoa had been washed in readiness. Dana had already helped her get out all the serving pieces they would need.

"Hey, Mom."

She looked up and saw Nick walk into the kitchen. He took a seat at the table.

"How are you feeling?"

She stared at him, thinking she should ask the same thing. He wouldn't look directly at her, and he had an air of…expectancy. No, that wasn't right, but all her mom-senses were tingling.

"What?" she demanded. "There's something on your mind."

He gave her a faint smile. "I can't just be here to make sure you're all right?"

"No. Tell me."

He glanced at his hands, then back at her. "I'm sorry I made you fall down the stairs."

What? "We talked about this. It's not your fault." She raised her hand, showing him the pen. "Look, I can write and everything."

"I still feel bad."

"You shouldn't. I'm healing nicely." Sure, there was still pain and she would get her cast on in two days, but other than that, she was totally herself.

He finally met her gaze. "I'm sorry about Paul and going into business with him. I know it's not what you wanted."

Ah, so this was what he really wanted to talk about. She felt her tension ease. Kid guilt she could handle.

"It's not," she said bluntly. "I always assumed you'd do what I did—take over the business."

He flinched. "I know. I should have said something sooner."

"Yes, you should have and I still feel bad that you weren't comfortable coming to me, but I also understand that you didn't want to disappoint me."

He groaned. "Can't you talk in euphemisms and generalities? Do you always have to cut to the heart of every issue?"

She laughed. "I try to be honest, but what you're reluctant to say is that I can be too blunt. I'm sure that's true." She set down her pen and reached across the table. He grabbed her hand in his.

"I wish I could care about the business like you do."

"I know." She squeezed his fingers before releasing them. "But you don't, and while I would have loved to work with you, I want you and Blair to be happy. Paul's giving you a wonderful opportunity. He's a good man and he'll teach you what you need to know. So go and be successful."

She smiled. "I mean that, Nick. I want everything for you and your sister."

"What about Parker Towing?"

"That's a question without an answer." She honestly didn't know what to do. "I'm too young to sell the business. What would I do with myself? But I don't want all the responsibility."

"Maybe you could—"

She held up her hand. "Nope. Not your rock. You have your own future to worry about. I'll figure out this one."

He rose, circled the table, then kissed the top of her head. "You're the best, Mom."

"Thank you. So are you."

He left. Five seconds later, she remembered she hadn't asked for help with the turkey. She was about to get up and follow him when Axel walked into the kitchen.

"Hey," he said, shoving his hands into his pockets. "You have a minute?"

She eyed him. He was certainly strong enough to help, and she would be right there to talk him through turkey prep.

"I do."

He pointed to the back of the kitchen. "I thought we could step into the craft room."

"Why?"

"Because it has a door."

She laughed as she remembered the acoustics in the house. "So you heard my entire conversation with Nick."

"We all heard it."

She and Axel went into the craft room and shut the door. She assumed he wanted to talk about Dana or the wedding. Her daughter had said something about a spring wedding, which didn't give them much time to plan.

Once they were seated across from each other, Julie said, "Even May is a little early for a backyard wedding in Seattle. It's still cool and we can get a lot of rain."

Axel's mouth twitched. "I'm not here to talk about the wedding."

"Oh." She drew in a breath as another thought occurred to her. "Are you quitting? Of course you have to do what's right for you two, but I thought you liked working at the company. We've already talked about the repos. Those are going away."

But maybe he, like Nick, wanted a different life. Something easier and possibly safer.

Instead of answering her question, he asked one of his own. "Did you mean what you said to Nick? About not wanting all the responsibility of the business?"

Oh. Not what she'd expected. "Sometimes it's a lot. I've been running the place for over twenty-five years. Are you worried about me selling? I can see where that would be a problem. I'm not ready for that. I honestly don't know what I want to do."

His dark gaze was steady. "Ever thought about taking on a business partner?"

"No." The response was automatic. "Okay, I haven't really thought about it. You mean work with someone? I don't know. It would be a way to share the workload, but I'm not sure. It's never been a thing for me."

"Would you consider it?"

"Why are you asking?" She laughed. "Right, because you're sitting on a million dollars." She paused. "I have no idea what the business would be worth, let alone what a partner would have to pay to buy in."

"About one-point-three. Give or take. I had to have the evaluation done without you knowing about it, so there's some guesswork in that number."

Julie was grateful she was sitting down. Her head was spinning and she couldn't quite catch her breath.

"You're saying my business is worth two-point-six million dollars?"

Axel's gaze was steady. "That's a rough estimate."

"I had no idea." She smiled. "I'm rich." Of course, all that money was tied up in a business, but still. "Wait, why would you know that?" The obvious answer to that question slammed into her. "Are you offering to buy into the company?"

"Yes."

"Just like that?"

He shook his head. "No. It would take time. We'd do a real evaluation and then come up with a number. We'd have to discuss sharing responsibilities." He gave her a faint smile. "You can be bossy."

"That's hardly news," she murmured, still trying to take it all in. Axel was talking about being her business partner.

"We'd write up a contract."

"As business partners," she confirmed.

"If you're interested in working with me. We've had a bit of trouble in the past."

"You were stomping on my daughter's heart. I get to be protective."

"As you should."

She leaned back in her chair and studied him. Except for the Dana thing, she'd always liked Axel, but she still had a lot of questions.

"If you're so rich, why are you working for me towing cars and doing repos?"

The smile returned. "I got an unexpected inheritance a few months ago. Two million from my father."

Well, that was serious money, she thought. "You never said anything. Wait! You never mentioned your dad. I didn't know your parents were still alive." Come to think of it, she didn't know much about him at all. As he was marrying her daughter, she was going to have to change that.

"My mom's been gone for years, and my dad and I have never had a relationship." He paused. "My parents weren't married. My dad came from money and my mom was his longtime mistress. When she got pregnant, he ended things. He never wanted a kid with her. She shamed him into showing up a couple of times, but that was it. I sure as hell didn't expect him to leave me anything."

The ghost of a smile widened. "I'm sure the inheritance came as a shock to my half brothers and sisters."

Julie thought about Dana telling her that Axel never felt good enough. Maybe this was the reason.

"Dana hasn't said anything to me."

"She knows about my dad, but not the inheritance."

Julie stared at him. "Then why are you telling me?"

"You asked where the money came from." He rested his hands on the table. "I wasn't sure I was going to ever use it. It's been sitting in the bank. I had this twisted idea that touching it meant my old man won. But then I started thinking about the business and the possibility of buying in as a partner. Only

I didn't want to do that without Dana in my life, and I wasn't sure I could be with her."

"What changed your mind?"

"I got shot. Lying there on the street, in the rain, I looked at my past and how I messed up. I walked away from the only woman I've ever loved because I didn't feel worthy. I knew I had to figure something out. I was going to buy into the business first, but then I heard Dana saying she was still in love with me, so I knew I had to put myself out there. I had to take a chance."

"But you've proposed and she said yes, so why doesn't she know about the money from your dad?"

His mouth twisted. "I didn't want her pressuring you about me buying in. I wanted that to be between us. If you want to consider taking me on, I'm ready to move forward. If you don't want to, no hard feelings."

Her heart ached for all he'd been through. So much made sense now, and she found herself just a little bit less pissed at how he'd treated Dana. Oh, she wasn't over it, but she could see eventually letting her anger go.

As for him being her partner—it was an unexpected solution to a complicated problem.

"Let's talk next week," she said. "Just you and me. About the business and what you'd want to change."

"Who says I'd want to change anything?"

She grinned. "Oh, please. You're going to come in with enthusiasm and about five hundred ideas. Between now and when we get together, I suggest you rank them in order of importance. You'll be lucky to convince me to agree to ten percent of them. If I were you, I'd start with the important ones first."

Axel was never one to show emotion—at least not in front of her—but just then she saw surprise, happiness and gratitude in his eyes.

"You'd consider a partnership?"

"I would. Plus, then I get all that money. It could be a real win for me."

She stood and motioned for him to come close, then hugged him. At first he was all stiff and A-frame, but after a couple of seconds he relaxed.

When they stepped back, she pointed her finger at him. "You need to tell Dana all this. No keeping secrets. It doesn't help."

"I'll go talk to her right now."

"Actually, you won't. First you're going to help me with the turkey."

He frowned. "I thought we were eating it tomorrow."

"We are. But it has to be prepped." She smiled. "Ever touch turkey guts?"

"No."

"Good. Because you're about to."

Julie slid into bed, careful to keep her arm close to her body. It was late—nearly midnight. After evening services, they'd all come back to the house and had cocoa and cookies before prepping for Santa's visit. She had no idea how quickly the kids had gone to sleep, but knew Tiffany would do her best. Hopefully they weren't up too early in the morning.

Heath rolled over to face her. "Merry Christmas," he said, before lightly kissing her.

"Merry Christmas." She smiled at him. "This has been a good holiday."

He chuckled. "You know it's not over, right? We have about twenty-four hours to go."

"Yes, but I doubt it can get better." She shifted her pillows so she could sit up. "Nick and I made up about the whole buying-Paul's-business thing. I was already fine with it, but he had things he needed to say. Axel proposed to Dana, so it's official."

"You're all right with that? He's been a jerk for a while."

"He has, but I feel better about him."

Especially now that she knew his past. She would tell Heath, just not right now. First she had to make sure Dana knew about the inheritance. Plus, it was better to be shared privately—when they weren't in the middle of a big family Christmas. All she'd told him was that Axel had unexpectedly inherited some money.

She grinned. "It would be really awkward if I wasn't willing to welcome him into the family, what with him wanting to be my business partner."

"That came from nowhere."

"It did."

"And you're okay with sharing Parker Towing? You've been the one in charge for a while."

She considered his question. "I'd always planned for Nick to come on board. Having Axel in the business will be different because I don't know him as well and I won't be able to boss him around as much."

Heath laughed. "You were planning on bossing Nick?"

"I don't think it was a plan, but it could have happened. Nick is more of a go-along-to-get-along guy. Although he went his own way with his future and that's for the best. I want him to be happy."

She touched Heath's arm. "You're still in your early forties, so you don't feel this way, but I've been running the company for a long time. I'd like a break from getting a call at three in the morning or having to deal with a thousand different problems. I have a great staff. I'd be lost without Huxley, but he's not going to work forever. Replacing him will be difficult, if not impossible. With a partner, it's not all on me."

What she didn't say, because she was afraid it would make her sound too old, was that she was hoping in ten years or so, Axel would buy her out and take over the business completely. Yes, it would be tough to figure out how to have a life without Parker Towing, but by then she had a feeling she would be ready.

"You're amazing," Heath said.

"Why would you say that?" She laughed. "I mean, I am, but what specifically brought this on?"

"Look at you. A week ago you didn't know your only son wasn't interested in taking on the family business. Now you're fine with it and have a new business partner. You're not pissed, you're not emotionally devastated. You fell down the stairs, and yet you're fine. You've forgiven Axel for all he's done because it's what Dana needs you to do. You would have been completely in your rights to have a total meltdown after all you've been through, but that's not your style, is it? You do what needs to be done and you move on. You don't blame, you barely accept help from anyone. You show up and you do what needs doing, whether it's telling your son he's making the right choice or being happy that Dana and Axel are getting married."

She didn't think she deserved the praise, but it was nice to hear. "What else is there? They're my kids and I love them. I have to do the right thing."

"You don't have to, but you always do. You're strong, Julie, and you don't take crap. You're beautiful, you're sexy and I admire you." He met her gaze. "I'm also in love with you."

And just like that, all her warm fuzzies evaporated.

She glared at him. "Don't say that. Don't. I don't want to hear those words. It's too soon."

He loved her? He loved *her*? No. Just no. She could barely deal with him being her boyfriend, a title she wasn't completely comfortable with.

He sat up, exposing his gloriously naked chest, but what really caught her attention was the hurt in his eyes.

"I didn't think you'd say it back, but I wasn't expecting that reaction. Why are you pissed?"

"I'm not. I'm just..." She waved one hand. "Like I said, it's too soon."

"You don't get to tell me how I feel."

The need to put distance between them had her scrambling

to her feet. She glared at him, careful to keep her injured arm against her chest.

"Why are you doing this? Why are you pushing?"

"Why are you so freaked out by me saying I love you?"

If she'd had two good arms, she would have raised them to cover her ears. Why did he have to keep saying that?

"I just am." She pressed her lips together to avoid pointing out *for the third time!* that it was too soon.

He shook his head. "I don't get it. Don't you want love in your life?"

"Not like this. Not, you know, romantically."

"Where did you see this going?"

"What this? Us? I don't know. It's only been a few months. We were taking things slow and that was better for me. Suddenly we're thrown together in a family situation and it's been fine. Good, even. I like your kids, I like Tiffany. Why can't that be enough?"

As she spoke, her chest got tight, and she both wanted to run and to throw something. She was uncomfortable and uneasy—and wasn't sure why.

"You don't see a future for us?" he asked, his voice quiet. "You never saw yourself falling in love with me?"

A voice in the back of her mind whispered she'd just stepped into very dangerous territory.

"I don't think like that," she said defensively. "Why are you pushing me? You're ruining everything. We were doing great. Why does that have to change? Why do we have to label everything?"

"You're overreacting, Julie, and I can't figure out why."

"I'm not." She glared at him. "I can't do this. I can't be with you anymore."

The words came from nowhere, and the second she said them, she wanted to call them back, only she couldn't.

Heath's expression shifted from concerned and unhappy to unreadable.

He rose. "If that's what you want, I'll get the kids and Tiffany and we'll leave."

"No. Don't do that. You'll ruin everyone's Christmas."

"Mine already sucks pretty bad."

She ignored that. "Just stay and we'll have the holiday. We can deal with this after."

She grabbed a blanket from the chair in the corner and draped it over her shoulders. "You stay up here. I'm going downstairs."

She walked to the door. There was more to say, she thought. More *she* should say, only she couldn't find the words. Telling Heath she didn't want to end things made the most sense, but somehow she found herself on the landing without having said a single thing.

22

Julie made her way downstairs and was surprised to find Tiffany in the living room, her tablet in hand.

Heath's ex-wife looked up and smiled at her. "You can't sleep? Me, either. The kids are out, thank goodness, but I've never been able to sleep on Christmas Eve. So now staying awake is kind of my thing. Huxley and Paul are playing cards downstairs, so I guess they're awake, too."

She set her tablet on the coffee table. Julie joined her, not wanting to explain why she was downstairs. She couldn't believe it herself. What had just happened and how had it happened so fast? She really liked Heath. No way she was going to dignify his stupid "I love you" comment, but until then, everything had been great between them.

Tiffany angled herself so they were facing each other. "Thank you so much for inviting me to spend Christmas here at the cabin. Despite the reason I got here, it's been a great holiday. I know I cried a lot at first, but I'm feeling so much better."

Julie grabbed on to the distraction with both hands. "I'm so glad you came. You fit in perfectly, and I know the kids appreciated having both you and their dad with them for Christmas."

"How do you do it?" Tiffany stared at her. "You're so gracious and lovely. I'm the ex-wife and yet here I am. Happy and welcome. I admire you. You're strong, but kind. No wonder your kids are as amazing as they are. I hope Madeline and Wyatt turn out as well."

Julie tried to feel the praise, but so much of her brain was still processing her fight with Heath. Maybe she was as strong as Tiffany said, but she was also baffled by what had happened.

"Your two are wonderful," she said automatically. "You don't have to worry about them."

"Thanks." Tiffany smiled. "This is going to sound weird, but I'm really glad Heath picked you. When we split up, I knew he wouldn't stay single forever. As a mom, I worried about who he'd start dating. I'm glad it's you."

The kind words made Julie both happy and sad. Unexpected tears burned, but she blinked them away.

"You're sweet to say that."

"It's true." She laughed. "Okay, don't take this wrong, but in a way, I'm jealous of the two of you." She held up her hand. "Don't go to the bad place. I'm not still in love with Heath. We're friends now and that's so much better."

She paused. "It's the way he looks at you. We can all see how he feels. He never looked at me that way. You're so great together. That gives me hope and something to strive for. I want what you two have."

"We just broke up," Julie said flatly, staring at her lap. "He told me he loved me and I couldn't deal with that, so I ended things." She looked up. "We're not going to say anything. We don't want to ruin anyone's Christmas."

She waited, confident that Tiffany would be shocked or scold her. What she didn't expect was for the other woman to burst out laughing.

"No way. You ended the relationship because he's in love with you? Oh, Julie, that's both funny and very, very sad."

"It's not funny," she snapped.

"I'm sorry. I know that sounds insensitive, but come on. We were just talking about how you're the most together woman I know. I thought there wasn't anything you couldn't do, but here you are, terrified of being in a relationship with a great guy who's crazy about you."

"I'm not afraid!"

"Yes, you are. I can see it in your eyes. You're always in control, only you can't control Heath. He's just as strong as you are. You have different styles, so it's not easy to see. But I know him and he's definitely your equal." She paused, her gaze speculative.

"Oh, wait! Is that the problem? You not being able to control him? You're not in charge, so you don't get to say what happens next. It's kind of a dumb reason to end the relationship, but I can see why you did it."

Julie stared at her, wanting to say Tiffany was wrong about all of it, but somehow she couldn't. Horror crept through her as she wondered if the other woman was right. Was she afraid because Heath was his own man?

Ridiculous, she told herself. Of course not. Eldon had been... She paused as she realized her ex-husband had never truly gone toe-to-toe with her. He'd always deferred or withdrawn. She'd been the one in charge—possibly the main reason their marriage had ended.

"You're like Axel," Tiffany added. "You have exactly what you want, and you're too scared to admit it. Only he figured it out. Although that took him getting shot, and I'm not sure you want to go that far."

"Heath isn't exactly what I want." Julie's words were automatic.

Tiffany didn't say anything.

"He's fun," Julie added grudgingly. "Funny, and yes, he's strong, which I like. Kind. I don't have to take care of him. But it's not perfect."

"Nothing ever is." Tiffany drew in a breath. "I'm really sad that you're going to blow this because you're scared."

"I'm not afraid."

"But you think you could do better?"

"No. That's not what this is about. I don't want anyone else. I want..."

Understanding dawned. She wanted Heath. They were, as Tiffany had pointed out, great together. He got her and she got him. Just as important, he wasn't intimidated by her strengths.

"It's the love thing. I can't do that."

"Why not? You have no problem loving your kids."

"That's different. I'm their mom. They have to love me back."

Oh, no. Was that it? Heath didn't have to love her back? Which came from what? Why was she so afraid? She'd loved a man before. She and Eldon hadn't lasted, but when they'd married, she'd been in love with him.

But not like this. Not like Heath. She drew in a breath as she made herself face the truth. There'd never been that easy sense of connecting. She'd picked Eldon, she'd been the driver in their relationship. It hadn't been a pairing of equals, so he'd never had the power to hurt her the way Heath could.

"I don't want to deal with loving him, because if we go that far, he can hurt me," she whispered.

She raised her gaze to look at Tiffany. "I think that's it. From the outside, it looks like I have it all, but I've never had the right man. Now it's been so long, I'm afraid to take a chance on him. I'm afraid to need him. What if he's not there?"

"What if he is?"

But it wasn't Tiffany speaking. Julie turned on the sofa and saw Heath at the bottom of the stairs. Her breath caught as she remembered the acoustics in the house.

"You were listening," she accused.

He started toward her. "Yeah, I was. I started to come after you, but you were already talking to Tiffany, so I waited to hear what you'd say. This is my life, too, Julie, and I needed to know what was going on with you."

His expression softened. "Why didn't tell me you were scared?"

She held in the reflexive *I wasn't*, and forced herself to say, "I didn't know I was. I reacted. Badly, it seems."

There was a shuffling noise from the upper landing. She groaned. "Who else is up there listening?"

"Everyone."

She covered her eyes with her good hand. "This is humiliating."

"It's too late to go somewhere private now," he said, moving closer. "Come on. Be brave. I'm worth it."

She gave a strangled laugh, then looked at him. "You're asking a lot."

"I am. You put everything else on the line. Why not your heart? Because as much as you don't want to hear it, I'm in love with you."

Was this really happening? Every fiber of her being told her to run. No, wait. That wasn't true. Her heart told her to accept what the wonderful man in front of her was offering.

"I'm not asking you to marry me," he added, then smiled. "Just to admit that you love me, too, and that the sex is incredible."

"Oh, Mom, no!"

"Yuck. I didn't need to hear that."

Both comments came from the upper landing. From down below, Huxley shouted, "Stick to the point, people. I'm sitting on a straight flush and want to collect my winnings."

"This is a private moment," she said loudly. "Everyone stop listening."

"Like that's going to happen," Nick muttered.

Julie told herself to ignore them all. This was between her and Heath. She knew she had a choice to make. Either she was going to suck it up and do the scary thing, or she was going to be a coward. Worse, she knew if she walked away from him, she would regret it for the rest of her life.

She stood. "I love you, Heath."

She had more to say but everyone started cheering. Everyone but Heath, who crossed to Julie and kissed her.

"Finally," he said, pressing his forehead to hers. "You don't make it easy, do you?"

"No, but I'm worth it, too."

"I think this calls for champagne," Dana said, hurrying down the stairs. "I know there are a couple of bottles in the beverage fridge."

Gwen joined her. "Not for me. It's a little late. Or possibly early. But I wouldn't mind some sparkling apple cider. Don't we still have a few bottles of the nonalcoholic kind?"

"We do," Julie said, thinking she would rather everyone went back to their rooms so she and Heath could go to theirs. But Blair and Nick joined them, as did Paul and Huxley, so champagne and cider it was.

It took nearly an hour to have their drinks, toast the season and have the night wind down enough for everyone to retire. Julie slid into bed, then turned so she was facing Heath.

"Sorry I was so difficult."

"It's nice to know you have flaws."

She smiled. "Would you call it a flaw? I think *quirk* is a better word."

He carefully drew her close, used a pillow to support her bad arm, then kissed her. "Let's argue about that tomorrow. Right now I have plans."

"Oh, good. I like your plans. Very much."

★ ★ ★

Dana sat on the sofa, snuggled up against Axel. Around them, chaos reigned. The kids, hyped up on sugar and too many presents, chased each other through the upstairs. With each lap, their shrieks got louder and louder. Rufus was rooting through the piles of wrapping paper, looking jaunty in his new coat. Piles of presents filled the floor space, and Dana wasn't sure how they were going to get them all in their various vehicles.

But that worry was for later. Right now, with the turkey in the oven and her family and friends around her, she was happy. Later, she would help get dinner on the table and soon she and Axel would return to Seattle to start on their new life. For now, he would be moving in with her, but once tax season was over, they would start looking for a house to buy together. Oh, and she had a wedding to plan. Nothing fancy, she thought blissfully. She and Axel agreed that small was better. Something intimate and easy.

Julie and Heath were sitting together, as were Nick and Blair. Gwen was talking with Paul, and for once both of them looked relaxed with each other. Tiffany and Huxley had made a halfhearted attempt at cleanup but had gotten distracted by Wyatt's partially assembled Lego set.

This was what Christmas was supposed to be, she thought, feeling gratitude. How lucky could she be?

Nick whispered something to Blair, then stood and walked to the tree. "I think there's one present we forgot."

"Not possible," Julie told him. "We all checked. Is anyone missing a gift they wrapped?"

He reached into the tree branches, pulled out a small box and waved it. "Here we go." He handed it to their mom, but looked at her. "You might be interested in it, too."

"You bought something for the two of us?"

Dana eyed the box, wondering if it was theater tickets or

something. She wasn't sure what else she and her mom might want to share.

Julie ripped off the wrapping, then set the box on her lap so she could open it one-handed. Instantly her eyes widened. She stared at Nick and Blair.

"Are you kidding me?"

Her loud voice cut through the house. Everyone stared. Before Dana could ask what was in the box, Julie held up a pair of yellow baby bootees. Dana stared at them in confusion. What were they—

"You're pregnant!" Dana jumped to her feet and ran to her sister-in-law. "You're pregnant."

Blair hugged her tight and they both screamed. Julie joined them, holding on to them. The kids raced into the living room.

"What's up?" Wyatt asked. "Did Julie fall down the stairs again?"

"Julie's fine," Heath said.

After a few seconds, Dana pulled back. "When did you know? Are you feeling all right?"

"Is that why you've been sick?" Julie asked. "Oh! I was right. You're pregnant."

Blair grinned. "I didn't know when you blurted it out at dinner. But I began to suspect." She smiled at Gwen. "My mom got the pregnancy test for me yesterday."

Paul hugged Gwen. "So that's why you were so secretive about your trip to town. I wondered what was up."

Dana turned to Axel, needing him near her. He moved to her side and pulled her close.

"Maybe next Christmas it can be us making the announcement," he murmured in her ear.

Love filled her. "I'd like that a lot."

Julie started laughing. "That's why Gwen made such a big deal about the apple cider last night. Blair can't drink."

"When did you have apple cider?" Wyatt asked. "Did you

have fun after we went to bed? You're not supposed to stay up. What if you saw Santa?"

"But we didn't," Tiffany said, hugging him.

Madeline ran to the window and pointed. "Look! It's snowing." She spun in a circle. "This is the best Christmas ever!"

Dana hung on to Axel and knew Madeline was telling the truth. For all of them.

★ ★ ★ ★ ★

Discussion Questions

We recommend that you wait to read these questions until after you have finished the book, to avoid spoilers.

1. Julie is embarrassed that she's dating a younger man. How did you feel about the age difference between her and Heath? Do you think it affected their relationship in the story? Why or why not? What complications might they face in the future that wouldn't exist if they were closer to the same age?

2. Discuss Blair's food restrictions, how different characters reacted toward them and how their reactions revealed their personalities.

3. Did your feelings about Gwen, Blair's mom, change as you read the story? If so, how so? Did the trauma she experienced make her treatment of Blair understandable or acceptable? Why or why not? Would you have been able to forgive her, if you were Blair? Why or why not?

4. In *One Big Happy Family*, it seemed nearly everyone had a secret, and all those secrets came tumbling out during the

time at the cabin. Chat about each character's secret and how its revelation impacted the story.

5. When Julie found out that her boyfriend's ex-wife was going to be alone at Christmas, she didn't hesitate to invite Tiffany to join them at the cabin. How did you feel about that? What would you have done in Julie's shoes?

6. Which character did you relate to the most? Why?

7. What emotions did you feel about the ending of the book?

8. What is your family's holiday tradition? Do you get together as a big group? What do you eat? Do you do anything special to commemorate loved ones who have passed away?

A Treat to Eat Julie's Shortbread Cookies

A note from Susan Mallery: I am not nearly as talented as Julie in *One Big Happy Family*. Fortunately for me, I only need to make the decorations work fictionally and not in real life. However, this cookie recipe is mine and is really delicious, even if you decide to, like me, decorate them with one solid color instead of the supercute Santas that Julie makes in the book. If you do make the Santa cookies, I would love to see a picture! Post it to social media and tag me, or send it to me by direct message. I'm @susanmallery everywhere!

3 sticks (1 1/2 cups) of butter, room temperature
1 1/4 cups granulated sugar
3 1/4 cups all-purpose flour, plus some for dusting the rolling surface
1/4 cup cornstarch
1/2 tsp salt

Makes about two dozen

Cream the butter and sugar on medium speed until pale yellow and smooth, about 3–4 minutes.

Whisk together the flour, cornstarch and salt until thoroughly combined. Add to the butter mixture. Stir by hand or mix on low speed just until combined. Form the dough into two balls, then flatten into four-inch disks. Wrap in plastic and refrigerate for one hour.

Preheat the oven to 325° and line cookie sheets with parchment paper. Roll out the dough a half-inch thick and cut into desired shapes. Place the cookies about 2 inches apart and bake until the edges just begin to brown, about 15–20 minutes. Cool on wire rack. Decorate as desired.